Stormbound
by Maggie Maren

Copyright © 2022 Maggie Maren

Published 2022 Rivermoon Publishing,
Salt Lake City, UT USA

Library of Congress Control Number: 2022919723

ISBN: 979-8-218-08752-4

All rights reserved. No portion of this book may be reproduced in any form without permission from the publisher, except as permitted by U.S. copyright law. For permissions, please email at: Contact@MaggieMaren.com

This is a work of fiction. Unless otherwise indicated, all the names, characters, businesses, places, events and incidents in this book are a product of the author's imagination or used in a fictitious manner. Any resemblance to actual persons, living or dead, or actual events is purely coincidental.

Copy editing by Norma Gambini at Norma's Nook
Cover & book design by TW Designs

Note to the Reader

This novel is intended only for a mature audience and contains strong language as well as frequent and fully described sexual acts.

Other content warnings include personal injury, blood, violence, and sexual harassment. Due to the nature of Harley's job as a forest ranger, search and rescue missions are mentioned with passing descriptions of tragedies. These are brief and handled with as much sensitivity as possible.

Your mental health matters to me. If have any questions about these content warnings before reading this book, feel free to email me at contact@maggiemaren.com

Stormbound Playlist

Contents

Chapter One	1
Chapter Two	7
Chapter Three	20
Chapter Four	28
Chapter Five	35
Chapter Six	40
Chapter Seven	50
Chapter Eight	57
Chapter Nine	71
Chapter Ten	79
Chapter Eleven	92
Chapter Twelve	106
Chapter Thirteen	115
Chapter Fourteen	121
Chapter Fifteen	142
Chapter Sixteen	157
Chapter Seventeen	168
Chapter Eighteen	197
Chapter Nineteen	214
Chapter Twenty	227
Chapter Twenty-One	250
Chapter Twenty-Two	268
Chapter Twenty-Three	279
Chapter Twenty-Four	287
Chapter Twenty-Five	294
Chapter Twenty-Six	310
Chapter Twenty-Seven	324
Chapter Twenty-Eight	328
Chapter Twenty-Nine	342
Chapter Thirty	348
Chapter Thirty-One	364
Chapter Thirty-Two	370
Chapter Thirty-Three	382
Chapter Thirty-Four	385

Dedication

To Elora, for always encouraging my hopeless romantic tendencies and love for reading. Well hell…look what I've gone and done now!

To Trog and Bear, your enthusiasm, support, and humor helped me along the way. Thank you for always reminding me I can kill the beast.

And to my own mountain man, thank you for showing up and loving me fiercely. I wouldn't understand the intricacies of enduring love if it wasn't for your kindness and devotion.

Most of all, this book is for all the women who have been told they're too weird, wild, or witchy—keep making people nervous.

Chapter One

I drove away from Boston like a banshee in need of a Midol. I needed to get away. Truth be told, I had already gotten away, but this current situation wasn't freaking fantastic! I was stuck living in a town I hated, away from everything and everyone I loved. Now, on top of all of that, I'd found my boyfriend balls deep in my favorite barista.

I felt completely blindsided. It was a typical Saturday afternoon in ugly January. I'd ordered my usual iced coffee concoction and gone to use the restroom, only to swing the door open to find the illicit affair in mid-thrust. Rosie had opened her legs, scrambling down from where Tyler had pinned her against the wall. Tyler, ever the gentleman, had looked around for an excuse for having his dick out. As if she could have slipped and fallen on it.

My purse had swung off my shoulder, triggering the paper towel machine. A pained, squeaky noise had filled the air while it had robotically spit out a new section, making the situation even more awkward. I'd blinked slowly to make sure I wasn't hallucinating while they'd stood there panting, slicked with sweat.

I'd responded ever so eloquently with a bold, yet effective, "Ew! You cheating asshat!" before I'd flown out of the coffee shop like a bat out of hell.

I'd hopped in my mint-blue Mini Cooper and torn out of town. My hands now clutched the steering wheel like death talons while my back was perfectly straight with adrenaline and shock. I felt a constriction in my chest, as if I were wearing an ill-fitting corset like one of those hot tavern wenches at a Renaissance festival. My jaw clenched so tight, my teeth creaked. Realizing I was a ball of nerves, I willed myself to take a couple of deep breaths.

"It is fine, Kaylee. You're fine. He's not worth the bail money, and you're too friendly to survive prison," I said to myself.

I kept driving to sort out my thoughts, reminding myself this situation wouldn't ruin my life. Sure, messing with my coffee connection was damn near as rude as flat out cheating on me, but I would survive. I could go to Dunkin' instead. There was one on every block in New England. Yet the overall feeling of rejection and a secret twinge of loneliness flooded my body. I couldn't ignore it.

I'd moved to Boston last summer, and Tyler had been one of the few people I'd met in town. He was a junior associate at a law firm across the hall from my suite at work. He'd made small talk with me in the elevator for months before he'd worked up the guts to ask me out. He'd opened with a cheesy pickup line of, *hey, so I've seen you in an elevator, but I'd like to see you across from me at dinner.*

I'd wanted to roll my eyes at that line, but I'd said yes anyway because I was a curious person. He was handsome, but more in a Ken doll sort of way, vacant of any physical flaws or uniqueness, making him charming but eerie. He was too clean cut and a suit type. Nothing about him surprised me or enthralled me. Behind his back, I referred to him often as a beige sweater. He was boring and a safe choice . . . much like a beige sweater. He wouldn't be my first pick for a night out on the town or to make me feel my best, but I'd been glad he was hanging around.

I'd used the comparison to not get overly attached to someone like Tyler. He lacked depth. I couldn't put my finger on it, but something about him felt wishy-washy. Tyler was emotionally stunted. It wasn't my fault he was never encouraged to find something he liked more in life than hockey and pussy.

The man was a walking red flag. Sure, he was shallow, but he was always willing to entertain my crazy date night ideas, like graveyard yoga and test-driving cars with fake Minnesotan accents. Plus, he was a good kisser. I hadn't slept with him yet because I just didn't feel comfortable, and now I felt validated in that instinct.

When I'd finally let him visit my place, it had been a mistake. Instead of feeling at home in my romantic bachelorette pad, or simply intrigued, he'd scoffed at my whimsy. No one scoffs at my whimsy, dammit!

I still remembered his dull brown eyes, the same shade as cheap leather shoes, fixed on me while he'd asked in disgust why I had a flower vase in the shape of boobs. Everyone loved boobs! He also hadn't liked my plum velvet couch or artwork. I gripped the steering wheel tighter, recalling how he'd scowled at the picture of Jesus cradling a baby dinosaur on the front of my fridge, not appreciating the humor of it.

Some relationships had an expiration date, but I hadn't known things with Tyler would expire so soon. Perhaps I was an optimist, but I thought our relationship was taking its time to blossom, much like the peonies in my titty vase.

I could see why he'd picked Rosie. She was sweet, friendly, and had a cool style. Her auburn hair flowed down her back in glossy ribbons, and the rune tattoos on her fingers had always caught my eye when she'd push my drink across the counter with a smile. We'd bonded months ago over the crystal-beaded bracelets she wore—usually carnelian, bronzite, jasper, and amber.

She'd even wished my Pagan ass a happy winter solstice back in December and drawn a sun on my cup with a marker. It had made my day! I couldn't hate the girl. She hadn't known we were a thing, and he'd been the one who cheated on me. I felt rude for being so boisterous about finding them and fleetingly hoped she didn't get fired.

Never a quitter, I continued driving brazenly north with zero plan. I pushed my foot harder on the gas pedal with such vigor, a squeak escaped from the water on the bottom of my boot. I shook my head and let out a feral shriek, banging my hands on my steering wheel.

"Mother! Fucker! Dammit, you frat boy looking asshat!"

Gaining composure, I tossed my long blonde hair off my face and over my shoulder in mild annoyance. I searched blindly in my cup holders until I found my trusted piece of tumbled green aventurine. I held the small crystal in my right hand while steering with my left. Taking a couple deep breaths, I willed myself to feel the soothing energy of the stone, allowing myself to calm down and let go of my rage. After a few moments, I dropped the crystal in my left bra cup with a resolute huff.

Feeling calmer, I realized I was driving in total silence. I had already been on the road for over an hour. I was starting to feel tired and I still needed to pee, so I took the next exit to recoup and fill up my car with fuel. While getting some questionable gas station iced coffee and a muffin, I realized I wasn't ready to head back to Boston. I needed geographic and emotional space from the shitshow I'd witnessed. I wasn't even ready to call anyone to dish all about it.

A punch of emotion rolled in my chest, a new sense of humiliation and hurt. Where had it all gone wrong? To my knowledge, boyfriends in the past had never cheated on me, but I was no stranger to rejection. Being a weirdo and a witchy woman growing up in the Bible Belt of America hadn't been the tits. Guys had loved the thrill of dating me at the beginning, but had then reported I was too "out there" for them, or too headstrong. They'd wanted to find someone who they could marry and take seriously.

I tried not to take it personally. I'd chalked it up to the wrong place, wrong time, and wrong girl. I seemed to be the wrong girl for everyone.

Some women wanted to be soccer moms in the PTA, and some women wanted to do witchcraft naked in the forest every full moon. Both were valid. Women were magical, and it pissed me off that society wanted us to behave and stifle our innate urges if we didn't fit a certain mold.

The hurt morphed into indignant rage as the acceptance of Tyler cheating on me really cemented in my mind. Good hell, he'd been lucky to date me! He'd punched up. At least I had an original thought rolling around in my head! I thought that was why finding him cheating stung so much. I knew on some level I was a bit too much for him. Too wild, too guarded, too different.

I needed my own thoughts and the open road. Driving around to clear my head was a habit I'd gotten from my dad. He had a steady love for motorcycles and basically anything with wheels. He'd told me my whole life, *honey, if it has a transmission or testicles, it's bound to give you problems*. I let out a sad sigh, thinking how right he was.

With the penchant to always be on the move, my dad had taught me to be prepared for whatever adventures life threw at you. He made sure I always had a duffle bag in my trunk with a swimsuit, an extra coat, cold, hard cash, and some good whiskey. Oh, and some survival gear just in case I needed to start a fire in suburbia. He'd assured me worst-case scenario cash and booze were great tools to bribe people with, and fire was power. Apparently, he'd been a pirate in a past life.

Thinking about his kooky ways put a smile on my face. With a full tank of gas, I figured I should make the best of this. I needed an adventure or some time to wallow. Nothing was waiting for me at home. I didn't have any pets, kids, or other obligations. I could keep driving with all this coffee humming in my body. If I got too tired, I could pull up to a hotel and order takeout.

Waiting in line to pay for my coffee and muffin, I picked up my phone and saw I had missed calls and texts from Tyler. I cleared the notifications with a scowl, not wanting to deal with good 'ol fuckface.

I exited the gas station in a slow, languid walk. The cold air felt refreshing and cleansing in my lungs. I noticed the beautiful pinkish-lilac sunset with gray clouds streaking across the horizon. Toward the west, a bright crescent moon hung in the sky. I smiled, looking at her, taking in her lunar beauty. I was a complete moonchild, and the sight of her always anchored me in peace. This moment was no different.

"Here's to an adventure," I mumbled to myself and the moon. The wind picked up, and I felt a new chill in the air. Looking at the moon, I felt a distinct flutter in my body, a good omen. For the first time all day, something felt right to me. The clouds quickly covered the silvery crescent, closing the gaps of sky, making the world around me darken with the hint of dusk. I ducked into my car and, on sheer instinct, picked the path feeding farther north.

Chapter Two

Kaylee

I switched to a true-crime podcast to distract my racing mind. The episode was fittingly about Lorena Bobbitt and the infamous incident in which she cut off her man's penis in his sleep. I contemplated what I'd like to do to Tyler and his traitorous schlong. What would I even say to him if I ever saw him again? While I was deep in thought, the miles passed on and the road under my tires rocked me into a calming daze while I ate my blueberry muffin and sorted out the details.

Twilight morphed into true night, and before I knew it, road closures detoured me away from the main highway, pitching me to back roads and side streets. The pathways snaked and weaved through deep forests and around hills. Snow flurries fluttered the long stretch of a two-lane road shrouded in forest on either side. No longer on the main interstate, I could relax even more as hours passed.

The sight of a massive creature in the middle of the road shocked me out of my daydream. Recognition clicked in my brain that it was a giant fucking moose. I didn't think people realized how big moose could get, but up close they looked damn near prehistoric. I immediately, albeit dramatically, slammed on the brakes to slow my car down, all but standing on the pedal. My mind halted in pure disbelief. I felt the chunky ice and snow under my tires accompanied by the distinct crunching of brakes.

The back end of the Mini Cooper fishtailed as I tried to remember what to do in this situation. Was I supposed to turn in the direction the car was sliding or away in the other direction? More whooshing and gritty sounds paired with snow spraying up the passenger side, blocking the windows, creating a cocoon of chaos within the cabin of the car. Everything unfurled in slow motion. I felt a scream crawl up my throat, but I didn't have time to let it escape.

After drifting to the right, to the left, and back to the right, I lost complete control of my car. It spun embarrassingly, like some dizzy ballerina, only to pick up speed and careen off the side of the road. Now screaming, I watched the car burst into a snowdrift with a sickening crunch underneath, helping it lurch to a complete stop.

Whatever had just happened sounded expensive.

I flicked my wipers to clear my windshield, only to see the moose slowly chomping while staring at me a few feet away in silent judgement. I could have sworn he had a red Christmas tree ornament dangling from one of his antlers like some cursed earring. Blinking hard, I cleared my shock only to watch him lazily walk back into the forest. That bastard!

Puffing in frustration, I undid my seatbelt, turning down the podcast so I could assess the situation. I couldn't handle this wreck while listening to Lorena throw a dick out of her car window! Shaking my head to clear that image, I pressed the button to turn my hazard lights on and took a long sip of coffee that miraculously hadn't spilled thanks to the lid. I squared my shoulders to gather my thoughts, only to be blinded by lights behind me.

Checking the driver's side mirror, I saw bright headlights beam from a truck. By the looks of it, it wasn't a cop, which was good. The last thing I needed was some cop shaming me for almost hitting a moose and driving like an idiot. Grumbling in defeat, I turned off my car while waiting for whoever was coming. The true-crime podcast droned on as a quiet babble, which instantly catapulted me into a fear spiral of all the possibilities of how this situation could go bad.

I hadn't told anyone where I was or that I was driving across state lines. My stomach sank and my mouth instantly went dry. Farther back, I noticed I'd made it to Maine. Wasn't that where Stephen King lived? The last thing I needed to think about was a horror movie.

An embarrassing yelp escaped my mouth, and with panicked hands, I reached into my purse to find some pepper spray I'd gotten years ago in college. It was in a pink, bedazzled canister. I shook the bottle, wondering if expired pepper spray was even more painful.

The headlights of the truck behind me were still blaring in the rearview mirror, filling up my car with lights brighter than the gates to heaven. It made me even more annoyed with how intrusive the situation was. Why did trucks need that bright of headlights anyway? What are they trying to see into? The future?

As I squinted and tilted my mirrors, a deeper panic erupted in my body when I realized a tall man had hopped out of the truck, surely to walk toward me.

Thinking quick, I got the fixed blade in a leather holder I kept in my center console and stuffed it in the right cup of my bra. Next, I selected the option that called my best friend Maisie over Bluetooth. The call trilled on with three rings before Maisie picked up the phone with a boisterous, "Hey, beeetch!" greeting.

"Hey, girl," I prattled on quickly. "I don't have time to explain, but I almost hit a moose and now some random guy is stopping to help me. I need you to be on the call to listen so I don't get murdered. I'm somewhere in Maine. Do you still have my shared phone location?"

"Yep," Maisie said resolutely, understanding the assignment. Girl code was so real.

The man was almost to my car. I could hear he was relaying information on a walkie-talkie. That was a little more reassuring. I took another sip of coffee and took charge of the situation by rolling down the window while bashfully saying, "Heeeeey."

"You're on a tree," the man said. As if that were not the most bizarre shit you could say to someone. *I'm on a tree? Excuse me, sir?*

His voice was gruff but smooth, and he was clearly annoyed but protective. With his truck headlights piercing my eyes, I couldn't get a good look at him from where he stood several feet away and in my peripheral vision. The only thing I could tell was his shoulders set his frame wide, and his height was generously tall. He was intimidating as fuck.

Without a word, he walked back to his truck while continuing to discuss the situation with his dispatch. Was he not going to introduce himself or ask if I wanted help? *What if I have a head wound?*

When he came back with a snow shovel, he made a path starting at the back of my car. I shielded the left side of my face from his bright headlights with my hand and spat out, "Are you going to introduce yourself or something?"

With measured patience, he cleared his throat and softened his demeanor by the sound of it. I still couldn't see him because of the lights. "My name is Harley. I'm a ranger in the area. It looked like you were busy when I got here. Now I see why. You were digging for a weapon or some ancient relic from 2003," he said, looking at my pink, bedazzled pepper spray.

I scoffed in offense and clutched it tighter to my chest. Okay, I would admit that was funny, but I wasn't in the mood. He could see me all lit up, but I couldn't see jack shit.

"You can't blame me! You could be a murderer. It's always a bad idea to accept help from strangers in the middle of the woods. It's basically how every horror movie starts."

"The only thing murderous out here is your driving, sweetheart," he replied dryly.

My jaw dropped. I couldn't decide if I wanted to laugh or punch him.

"I'm going to shovel a path to get you out safely. I don't know if you realize it, but you're teetering on a tree that fell over on the side of the road. It's covered in snow from the plows. Your car could tilt to one side and roll with you in it at any moment."

I looked around the cab of my car in terror, not realizing how serious it was. My airbags hadn't deployed. How could it be that bad?

"I watched you lose control, but it didn't look like you hurt yourself. Are you feeling alright?"

"Yes, I'm okay," I said, biting my lip in shame. Why had I been so freaking rude to him? I didn't need to take out my shitty day on this guy.

"Since you're high centered on the tree, I will have to get someone out here to shovel and tow your Mini out. I bet you damaged underneath it as well, but we have a skilled mechanic in town who can help." His shoulders moved with an uneasy shrug from what I could tell from the outline of his figure.

Not wanting his pity, I swatted the air dismissively. "Oh, I will call AAA for the tow. I have a membership somewhere. You can go on ahead." I dug in my purse for my wallet with the card in it.

"Please, I insist. I'm already here."

"But I—"

"I don't like the thought of you sitting here waiting. It's cold and dark. Also, your erratic behavior is a general threat to wildlife and public safety." I scoffed, and before I could retort, he added, "Plus, that moose might come back for revenge."

"Um, Kaylee, he sounds hot. Let him help you, dammit! And what are you even doing in Maine?" Maisie's voice boomed through my car speakers. I instantly sat upright in my seat, whipping my head to the dashboard. A moment of stunned silence filled the air, then a manic cackle tore from my throat.

Busted! In all the commotion, I had completely forgotten Maisie was still listening.

I felt my cheeks blush with slight embarrassment. I collected myself and turned my attention away from the dashboard to lock eyes with Harley, who had shoveled closer to my car. Near enough I could see him leaning against his shovel in amusement. Maintaining the eye contact with the mystery man while still speaking to Maisie, I responded boldly, "You're right. He is cute."

He chuckled and looked down for a moment, only to pull his eyes back up to meet my gaze in apparent confidence. For a split second, I felt completely mesmerized by this man. Even in the depths of winter, he filled up the surrounding space with warmth. I could see now how handsome he was, even with the sharp contrast of his truck headlights shining a harsh light on his features.

He had a dark, sexy beard trimmed close to his face. It was well-groomed and filled in, perfectly framing his angular jaw. Kind, knowing, but mischievous eyes met mine. They were hazel, almost the color of rich soil, with honey suspended in their depths. His nose and cheeks were the slightest shade of pink from the cold, but his lips, a darker shade than his cheeks, parted to reveal a bright smile that crinkled lines around his eyes. A knit beanie hid his hair, but I imagined it was dark and thick, not yet grayed. He couldn't be any older than early thirties. His warmth was enamoring, his features striking.

"Hon, call me in 30 minutes. And Harley, Mr. Ranger, I have her GPS location, so if she goes missing, people will look for her. Got it?" Maisie assertively quipped.

"You got it. Like I said before, the only thing scary out here is your friend's driving." Harley fought a smirk while picking up his shovel once more.

"Oh girl! I like him! I'm not the only one who fears your driving skills! Remember when you T-boned that hearse?" Maisie giggled, loving the embarrassment she was serving.

"I mean, in my defense, they were already dead! There wasn't even damage to the coffin!" I barked out defensively.

"You hear that, Harley? They were already dead," Maisie teased.

"Good thing," he added, shoveling away.

"Okay, well, I'm going to hope the earth opens up and swallows me whole because both of you are so hateful," I said, shaking my head in shame. I knew I was a chaotic driver, but now there was evidence. "I'll be in touch. Thanks for coming in clutch."

"Sure thing. And Harley, take care of my friend. She's precious. She plays a mean game of Monopoly. Oh, and don't give her tequila unless you want a real problem on your hands. Come to think of it, maybe you should give her some—"

"Bye, Maisie." I mashed the button on my steering wheel to end the call. Sucking in a deep breath, I turned to awkwardly smile at Harley, willing him to forget what he'd heard.

"She sounds like a good friend. Okay, Kaylee, was it?"

"Yep, and you're Harley?"

"Yep, or Ranger Kouris, whichever you like." He shrugged. "I'm going to shovel a bit more. Please grab your insurance info and everything you're going to need out of your car for the night."

"All I have is whiskey and a swimsuit in the trunk, so no need to get that out." I pointed nervously to the back of my car.

Okay, now I wanted the earth to swallow me whole. Why did I have to bring my apocalypse-ready, pirate pack into this? Harley gave a confused nod and continued shoveling. His walkie-talkie occasionally bleated out static-filled dispatch while snow flurries swirled in the air. He shoveled on, completely unperturbed by both.

I'd always been good at reading people. One could say I was an excellent judge of character. My instant inclination was Harley was trustworthy, but I had listened to so many true-crime podcasts today, I was on edge. The adrenaline from the car wreck made my anxiety even worse. I was sure the giant-ass iced coffee wasn't helping either.

I didn't want to be on high alert, so I quickly rifled through practical solutions while Harley shoveled away. I needed to corroborate his identity or get someone in town to know I was with him. "How do I know I can truly trust you?" I asked through the open window, squinting in discernment.

He stood up from shoveling. "Um, well, I'm not sure, but I want you to feel safe." He shifted the knit hat he was wearing as if to scratch his head, making me notice the official logos on both his hat and coat, a shield of yellow and green with a pine tree in the middle. Around the tree stated Forest Service, U.S. Dept. of Agriculture. The benign symbol I had seen my whole life now gave me peace of mind, making Harley look more legitimate.

"I help a lot around town. You could call Sheriff Thomson's office and he could tell you that himself. There's an officer coming out for an incident report anyway," Harley mused helpfully.

"I'll Google the station's number. What city am I in?" I didn't want to call 911 since I was okay.

"You're in Pine Bluff." He shot me a polite smile and continued shoveling, his long arms hoisting masses of snow around like it was easy.

A woman answered in a friendly tone. "Pine Bluff PD, what can I help you with?"

"Hi," I said, feeling instantly foolish and paranoid.

"Yes, dear?" Her voice was matronly and sweet.

"My name is Kaylee. I was driving through town, and I almost hit a moose, and now my car is stuck in a snowdrift." I glanced at my GPS. "According to my GPS, I'm on Conifer Road?"

"Oh dear, yeah, I heard about that on dispatch from our local forest ranger. His name is Harley. He is usually in those remote areas. Do you need a medic?"

I smiled with relief. "No, no, I'm okay. Harley is with me. I wanted to make sure he was a legitimate ranger and not some serial killer."

"Oh no, dear! Harley is a complete gentleman. I've known him since he was a little boy. His family has lived here in town for a couple generations back. They own the local hardware store. It almost shut down in 2008. You know how that all went with the recession." She trailed off, trying to recollect the details mostly for herself. I darted my eyes from Harley shoveling back to the dashboard.

"But I totally get why you're being cautious, dear. So many wackos out there. It's scary for us women. You're such a smart girl to think about calling me. Oh! And he also makes an excellent elk burger. Do you like elk burgers?"

Harley stopped shoveling with his back to me and cleared his throat. He walked his shovel back to his truck while muttering under his breath and shaking his head.

"Um . . . I can't say I've had one."

"Oh, well, maybe he can make you one," she said mischievously. I could hear her smile through the phone.

"Perhaps." I blinked slowly, trying to comprehend what Hallmark movie I'd crashed my car in.

"Sorry, I'm being rude. I didn't introduce myself! My name is Sherry, Sherry Barnes!" she explained warmly.

"Well, Sherry, thank you for putting my worries at ease. I need to stop listening to true-crime podcasts," I said right when Harley returned to my window.

"No problem, dear! Call me back if you need anything else. Hope to see you around town." Sherry then ended the call.

"There you have it." His tone felt rushed, as if each minute passing made him more concerned.

"Should I just open the door and crawl out? I'm a little high off the ground, but I can jump."

"Absolutely not. I need to pull you out." His patience was now running thin, and his brow pinched in concern. He took a deep breath and collected himself. "Please let me do my job." I bit my lip, trying not to interrupt, and gave a pathetic nod. "Let's get your bag out first." He held out his hands, and with a trusting toss, I flung my giant shoulder bag toward him.

"Jeezus Christ, this is heavy! What's in here?"

"Rocks!" I said with a playful smile.

Walking it to his truck, he held it like a bomb might detonate from inside it. Returning, he explained, "I'm going to remove you from the car, which I want to remind you is unsteady. Since it might rock a little, I need to carry you out. Do you feel you can stand on your own?"

"Well, yeah, but I can probably—" Harley let out a frustrated grunt, and the next few moments were a blur. The driver's side door opened, and I felt his massive arms encircling me, pulling me from the car and pressing my body along the side of his before twisting me away from the carnage.

When my feet touched the ground, I grasped his arms to stabilize my shaky frame, swaying with a few dizzy steps. He held me close, gazing down at me while fighting a small smile. Looking up at Harley with snowflakes landing on my lashes, I realized he was quite tall compared to my five-foot-three frame.

"You're right. I needed help," I whispered into the quiet night.

His lips pulled to one side in a charming smirk. He stepped back, giving me space, and took off one of his gloves to extend his huge hand for me to shake. It was a cute, good-natured attempt of a proper introduction.

"It was a pleasure rescuing you, Miss Kaylee." His low voice was barely intelligible while puffs of white filled the air with his breath.

His hand was warm, rough, and completely engulfed mine in size. The shared reverie between us stretched on for a few extra heartbeats. We both jolted our hands away when the moment caught up to us as headlights down the road signaled the tow truck and police officer. Yet I could have sworn, for a moment in time, this man had looked hungry, and not for food.

Harley walked me to his vehicle, opened the door, and even held my hand so I could steady myself as I hopped up into the tall truck. He busied himself putting an olive-colored, wool blanket over my lap for warmth. After tucking the blanket around my legs, he looked up at me from where he stood by the open passenger side door. His eyes seemed gentle, almost concerned. "Your neck." He reached out to touch it and pulled his hand back on second thought. I pulled the visor down to look in the mirror, only to find a large welt forming on the left side of my neck from where the seatbelt had rubbed against me in the wreck.

"It's nothing. I'll be fine, I promise."

He let out a determined huff and walked to open the back door, only to shuffle through a bag on his back seat. He came back around and broke a cobalt blue pack in half and handed it to me. "This is an ice pack. It might help keep the sting away." His brow furrowed in concern. Sherry was right—he was a gentleman. He was still radioing in to his dispatch about the incident and that I didn't need medical attention. While he did that, I immediately texted Maisie.

Me: I'm safe. I called the local police department and they vouched for this guy. I fucked up my car, so I'm going to get a hotel for the night. I walked in on Tyler banging that cool barista I told you about. My suspicion was right. I hopped in my car and rage-drove all the way here. You know how I am.

Maisie: Aw, fuck, I'm sorry. Let me know when you get to your hotel, so I know you're safe. Or, you know . . . maybe stay the night with ranger daddy.

Me: Omg, please never say that again. Haha!

Harley looked down at my phone, causing me to clutch it closer to my chest. "Nosy!" I teased with what little playful energy I had left in me.

"Sorry, I wanted to make sure you weren't calling Sherry again," he said jokingly. "It looks like you've had quite the day already." I nodded in agreement, feeling more tired now that my adrenaline was crashing. He continued, "I'd be more than happy to handle this. Can I get your info and keys?"

I plopped my keys in his hand and handed him my AAA card, proof of insurance, and driver's license. "This might take a while. Hopefully, you stay warm, but call your insurance to start a claim or whatever. Honk if you need me or start getting sleepy. You might have a concussion, so you must stay awake for at least three hours." He held up three fingers to further make his point.

"Got it."

Each guy greeted Harley with a bro handshake that turned into that weird half hug with a slap on the back move guys did. Both men respected Harley, gauging how they greeted and interacted with him. I watched how incredibly sexy his body language was, the sight of it making me giddy and mesmerized.

The tow guy appeared to be nice, but the cop gave me the creeps. A disgusting prickle ran down my spine as I assessed his energy. His aura gave me the heebie-jeebies, but Harley's was bright and safe. Even from a distance, I could tell he was *good people*, as my grandma would say. All three men circled my car, mapping the plan of digging it out and towing it. It must be complex because they stood there extensively inspecting the scene that befuddled them. I sat on the phone with my auto insurance, staring at the entire debacle through Harley's truck windshield and flurries of snow.

When an agent finally got on the call, they had to fight back laughter while I explained the moose story, but overall, it was a good start to putting this whole mess behind me. The agent explained I could get a rental car with my coverage a couple towns over. I didn't want to drive anymore tonight, so I planned on picking it up tomorrow. I Googled the closest lodging and found a cute place nearby called Stonebriar Inn.

I plopped my phone in my bag and put it on the floor of the truck. My mind no longer preoccupied, the adrenaline from the wreck quickly vanished from my body, exhaustion taking its place. My limbs felt heavy, my eyes overly dry, and my head buzzed with a headache. I suspected it was a mix of stress, too much caffeine, dehydration, and slight whiplash.

I lifted the wool blanket to act as a barrier between my head and the cool window. My other hand still held the cold compress to my injured neck in a balancing act. Now more comfortable, I shut my eyes for a second to collect my thoughts while the men finished what they were doing.

I felt a deep, dreamless sleep threaten to swallow me up immediately, cruelly, against my will. My last shreds of consciousness reminded me I was in a stranger's truck, hours away from home. The last thing I remembered was a thought rolling around in my head, a mantra of sorts, echoing to me. *Harley is a rescuer.* And from there, the dreamless undertow took me.

Chapter Three

Harley

I'd seen a lot of crazy shit in my life, especially working for the United States Forest Service. The moment most people left the city and breathed in clean air, it went to their head and they did some wild things. A good rule of thumb to remember was when people visited a national park or forest, they had the best day of their lives . . . or the worst. They might camp, hike, fish, or overall enjoy nature. Or they committed crimes, took their own lives, or suffered from poison oak rash on their asses. I'd seen the whole gambit, ranging from weddings to orgies, dead bodies, and animal attacks.

Yet, this situation was even more shocking to me. It wasn't every day I found a gorgeous woman cussing like a sailor, high centered on a pine tree, half immersed in a snow bluff. And that was after almost hitting a moose. It might be helpful to mention a moose was the largest mammal in the woods, so almost taking one down was impressive or reckless. This was a new level of bizarre, even for me.

Kaylee was lucky I'd been doing rounds before going home for the night and had seen the entire debacle. She'd had zero control of her car and had completely over-corrected. She must not be from this part of the country. With how cautious her behavior was, I was a little shocked at how wild she'd been with driving. I hadn't been expecting someone like her in the driver's seat. I'd thought maybe it was a drunk driver or a senile elder.

When I'd approached her Mini Cooper, I'd found her like a rabid raccoon, clutching a pink can of pepper spray and throwing back iced coffee like a shot of liquor. I didn't feel equipped to handle this situation that was happening in my town, in *my* woods that I'd promised to keep safe and thriving. If she could do this much damage in a Mini Cooper that looked more like an Easter egg than a car, imagine what she could do with matches. Who knew someone so cute could be a general threat to wildlife and public safety?

I didn't want to admit the slight pang I felt in my chest when I looked into her beautiful eyes. They were gray like the ocean right before a storm. She felt like a storm—completely untamed, strong, and strangely captivating. Something deep within me wanted to protect her. It was like an instinctive beast rearing its head with a roar only I could hear. I couldn't ignore it. Chivalry wasn't dead, but that moose had almost been.

Despite that, Kaylee intimidated the fuck out of me. I respected her because she was wicked smart. She'd quickly vetted me for her safety. She'd called her friend when I'd first approached her car and later called the police department in town. I didn't mind her checking for her safety, but I minded Mrs. Barnes playing matchmaker within seconds of talking to her. That shit was seriously embarrassing. Sherry had unintentionally hurt my game. Now this girl was going to think I was some weirdo who joined the knitting circle with all the old ladies in town.

The moment I'd first seen her still played on repeat in my mind. Seeing her gorgeous face for the first time had sent a wave of shock through me. Her pale, golden, silky hair had shrouded her until she'd turned to look at me. It was a disarming feeling, the visceral attraction that felt like a zing and pulled at me, trapping me in desire.

I've been alone in this forest for too damn long, I chided myself.

She'd looked so out of place in such a harsh environment with no distinct destination. I'd gotten the feeling she felt lost, not only in the real world, but in her inner world as well. I could see her forcing herself to think about each move she made, her energy waning from exhaustion. It had been painful to watch. Even in her exhaustion and stress, she'd maintained banter and eye contact with me, two things I found intoxicatingly sexy in a woman.

Long eyelashes framed her expressive eyes that would flutter when she'd blink fast, thinking through the weird situation she'd found herself in. Underneath her stormy eyes, shadows showed a level of weariness. Above them, light eyebrows knitted together in concern and cocked when she'd give me shit. Her small, straight nose had a dainty hoop running through her left nostril, hugging it close. Her skin was a soft alabaster against her blonde hair. *Milk and honey.*

Everything about her was simultaneously attractive and unpredictable. She tossed me her purse, a hippie sack with coins and embroidery on it. It jingled and smelled like incense. It was heavier than most of my hiking packs, so I asked her what was in it, and she said rocks. What the literal fuck?

Once I got her out of the car, I realized her hair went to her waist, which distracted me for a second. I was a sucker for long hair. The lengthy strands shimmered over the hood of her coat, falling like golden light. I instantly wanted to touch it, to feel its softness.

I wasn't one to notice anyone's clothes, but hers were unique enough to stand out. She looked like Stevie Nicks on her way to go ice skating in Middle-earth with the elves, for fuck's sake. The hood of her gray coat tapered to a point, as well as her sleeves, making the cut look mystical. She wore soft leather boots that laced up high on her legs, giving way to dark-purple, tie-dyed leggings that clung to her soft thighs.

She was short but had long legs for her height. Her body felt limber and able as I pulled her from the car with how she quickly regained her equilibrium. She felt strong, not at all frail or skinny. She looked healthy and sane, which was a good start. Her eyes and speech were clear with reasoning.

Not drunk or senile, just a loose cannon.

I could tell she wasn't from here. She didn't look overly sleek or stuck up like a big-city type. Something about her felt old worldly, like she could sprawl out with creepy cupids in a Renaissance painting. I couldn't peg her for anything specific, simply fucking gorgeous and feminine. Distractingly so.

Her perfume smelled heavenly, like vanilla with an undercurrent of something exotic, like the spice markets I'd visited in the past. When I shook her hand, it was so smooth, it made me ache for her to touch me all over, and she had dark red nails which I immediately pictured scraping down my back.

God dammit! Who was this woman crashing into my life? Was this some sick joke? Had I completely imagined everything?

Truth be told, I wasn't used to finding people alive. The constant struggle of pulling people from the forest dead and mangled was a reality for me. To find someone so brazenly alive felt unsettling. It shouldn't be that way, but years upon years of finding people in difficult situations had hardened me. Finding someone so feisty made me feel like I was losing footing, unable to plan my next move. I liked it.

Admittedly, the past couple years, I had focused on lining up my life so my family didn't think I was a complete piece of shit because I hadn't taken over the hardware store. My brother, Carson, still hated me for it because it had caused him to step up to bat. After graduating college with my forestry degrees, I'd landed the ranger job I had now, and I'd finished building my cabin.

My life was simple. Most days, I got up, tended to my land, and went to work. I loved being a ranger and working toward conservation, search and rescue, and outreach in the community to educate people how not to set the entire fucking forest on fire with a gender reveal party. The land here was a part of me. Keeping it pristine was important, and when I wasn't working, I was usually enjoying my time here in other ways. Spending ninety percent of my life deep in the forest wasn't exactly fruitful for dating, so pulling up to a not-so-damsel stranded had derailed my night in the best way.

I was sure she wanted to get out of this small town as fast as possible. I bet she thought I was some bumpkin trying to get some. That couldn't be further from the truth, but from what little I knew about her, she was already proving to be stubborn, so I had a feeling this wouldn't be easy. For some reason, that put a smile on my face.

"Who's the dumb blonde?" Officer Boyd asked, glancing at her Maryland driver's license while signing the incident report.

I glanced at my truck. My headlights had shut off from having it parked for so long. I could see Kaylee holding the ice pack to her neck while on the phone, the snow now falling on the ground, lighting up the world in a wintery light. Barrett was chaining her Mini Cooper to the bed of his tow truck, the loud metal chains clanging in the silent night.

"She's not dumb. My guys didn't remove the tree that had fallen over before the plows got it, and a moose walked out right in front of her. I watched the whole thing myself." I shot daggers at Boyd while he stared at his papers. "It could have happened to anyone."

I stood up straighter, letting my height tower over him. If there was anything I was in life, it was tall and intimidating. I knew that. I tried to use it on asshats like Boyd with his pitiful hairline and attitude. Nothing was more insufferable than a small-town cop who thought he was actually helpful.

"Don't get all defensive, Harley. Damn, bro, you're as sensitive as all the women in town."

"Did you mean to say that out loud?" I asked. He looked up from his paperwork, and I could finally give him the death glare he deserved.

Officer Boyd dodged eye contact with me like the chickenshit he was and clicked his pen. "Cute little thing. Does she need a ride into town?"

My jaw clenched in disgust at the mere thought of Kaylee with him. Boyd was a womanizer who cheated on his wife every chance he could. Rumor had it, he'd fucked every waitress who worked at Tilly's Tavern, and most women officers quit within months of working for Pine Bluff PD because of his toxic behavior. I didn't care who had sex with whom, but it was obvious he saw women as conquests, not full-fledged humans, so every chance I got, I made him squirm. I could never let Kaylee be around him with a clear conscience.

I immediately lied to protect her. "No, she has someone coming to get her. I'll stay with her until they get here."

That wasn't an outright lie. *I think?* Honestly, I didn't know what Kaylee's plans were. Considering the situation, she was up shit creek without a paddle, or so the saying went. Hopefully, she was on her way to visit someone she knew in town because there wasn't any lodging open within 50 miles of Pine Bluff in the late winter season. Even if she could get a rental car through her insurance, the rental car place was closed for the night and wasn't open tomorrow because it was a Sunday. Plus, a giant snowstorm was about to roll through, making travel impossible.

Regardless, she was in my truck now, and all I wanted to do was protect her from the storm, Boyd, and whatever else life was throwing at her. Now I needed to find a way to not fuck it all up.

Coming back to the truck after getting the tow situated, I found Kaylee leaning against the window, fast asleep, like I told her not to. When I opened the door, the dome light turned on, waking her in a harsh jolt. Her eyes locked on mine, and I had to dodge the ice pack she hurled at me in shock.

"Jeeeezus, woman!" I said, catching it and recovering.

"Harley! I am so sorry! You scared me!" Her feminine voice rang out high and shrill. She busied herself with the wool blanket I'd given her for warmth.

"It's fine. I guess I deserved that. You need to stay awake, though, if you have a concussion. Here, I talked you out of a ticket." I handed her the ice pack and the incident report, along with her cards. Her delicate hand brushed against mine as she placed them in her purse without a glance.

"Thank you," she murmured shyly. "I'm so glad I knew you all of five minutes before I chucked an ice pack at your face." She held it back to her neck.

I bit back a chuckle. "Don't mention it." I turned over the ignition of the truck and buckled up. "I didn't have time to ask you. Where were you heading?"

She nervously bit at her lip. I hoped my question wasn't too intrusive or suspicious. I added, "Can I take you somewhere?"

"Yeah, I actually Googled lodging nearby and came across a cute place called—"

"Stonebriar?"

"Yes, can you take me there? I can pay you."

"Stonebriar is closed for the season. Eugenia, the owner, is a dingbat and forgets to close out her reservations online. She's a snowbird who travels south this time of year."

Kaylee fished out her phone from her bag, swiping on it frantically.

"Do you know someone in Pine Bluff?" I asked.

"No, I don't even know anyone in Maine. I was just passing through." Her voice was small, frustrated.

"On your way to?"

"Just a drive." She shook her head as if to clear it. "A long drive after a hard day." She looked out the window, unwilling to make eye contact. I could see her head bob while she swallowed hard in panic. Collecting herself, she looked back at her phone.

"Kaylee, do you have a plan?"

"No, I don't. I went for a drive to clear my head, and I found the moose, and wow." She gulped hard, tucking some hair behind her ears. "It takes talent to get this stranded, doesn't it?"

I bit the insides of my cheek in discomfort. She was so stressed. I felt bad for her. In all my adventures, I'd ended up stranded a few times, and it was never fun.

The white light of her phone cast shadows on her beautiful face in the darkness of the truck, her nose ring glinting. Her long eyelashes cast shadows while her lips and their beautiful shape stood out. The gentle indent of her philtrum between her lips and nose appeared in contrast to the light and shadows. She looked like a goddess, a beauty that men surely swooned over.

"Um, let me see if there's another place to stay." Her wine-colored nails clicked against her phone screen.

I interjected, "I'm sorry. It's a rough time of year to be up here. Nothing is open in January. There isn't lodging for another 50 miles."

"Maybe the rental car place is still open somehow?" She opened a new Google search. I paused, wanting to offer her time to research it on her own so I didn't look overly eager to tell her anything. Seeing they were closed, she hissed out, "Shit!"

"There's a place a couple of towns over, but they're closed since it's Saturday night. They're not open Sundays. Visitors complain about it a lot. That's the only reason I know." I fought a grimace, hating being the bearer of bad news.

"Shit, shit, shit!" she muttered then huffed and slumped more in her seat.

"Don't worry, I got you." I put the truck into drive, heading north on Conifer Road.

Chapter Four

Kaylee

Now that Harley was in the truck with me, the entire cab filled with his scent. I discreetly breathed in, loving the smell of woodsy spice that hit my nose. The broadness of his chest overfilled his seat, his left shoulder hitting the side of the truck, and the right shoulder stuck out over the middle section. Being next to his sheer mass and his calm disposition made me feel instantly protected.

As I let the feeling of safety wash over me, flashbacks of twirling around in the wreck and the affair violently flashed in my mind, as if in opposition. I blinked hard, trying not to freak out. I let the emotions of fear and embarrassment flood through my body. Opening my eyes, I caught Harley saying, "Don't worry, I got you." That was rather vague.

He pulled out on to the street I'd wrecked on and maneuvered the truck on the snowy road with ease. Now out of gloves, his hands rested on the steering wheel, causing me to glimpse at veins on the tops of them, along with no wedding ring in sight. I blinked hard to distract myself from staring.

"What do you mean?" I asked.

"For starters, you need medical attention."

"No, I don't." I held up my hand dismissively.

"You were just in a car wreck."

I wracked through my brain for a counterargument. "Don't all rangers have EMT training?" His mouth went into a fine line. I was onto something. "You do," I continued defensively. "I know you do because you help with search and rescue. So, ranger man, did you notice anything distressing?"

I could see his tongue running across his front teeth under his lips in annoyance and contemplation. "No, just your neck. Your eyes dilated fine once we got into the light of the truck. When I shook your hand, your pulse was fine. Lord knows you feel fine enough to be the most defiant person I've ever rescued." He mumbled something under his breath I didn't catch.

My eyes widened in annoyance at feeling so clocked. "Well, there you have it. I'm fine." Here I was thinking he liked me. No, he had been taking my vitals!

"You could have a broken rib or whiplash that you're not aware of because of adrenaline. We should get you checked out before the storm hits. We're almost in town. Let me run you by the urgent care."

I lifted my arms and wiggled my torso in circles. "See! No pain. My ribs are fine."

Harley chuckled and shook his head. "Are you always this stubborn?"

"Are you always this bossy?"

"I'm not bossy. I'm . . . experienced." He leaned his left arm against the door of the truck, resting his mouth in his hand and looking amused.

"Experienced. Right. I can work with that." He lifted his head up from his hand and shook it, smiling. I had to admit, I already liked the banter. Before we both could soften, I added, "I'm still not going to the doctor," causing him to roll his eyes in exasperation.

"Okay, so let me get this straight. No plans in Pine Bluff, no car . . . and no lodging."

I nodded nervously. His eyes darted around the road above the swath of darkness of his beard. The dash lights of his truck cast a blueish-green tinge to his face that shouldn't have been flattering but was. The dim light cut his cheekbones, making him look even more angular and sexy. I could see him planning something in his head.

"You should stay with me." His eyes pulled away from the road for a moment, his expression soulful and kind with an undercurrent of intensity. His gaze on me sent a buzz through my body.

My mind caught up to what he'd said. "Stay with you?"

"Yes, consider it some Maine hospitality." One eyebrow cocked as he flashed me a loaded look. His deep voice made the statement even sexier with the double entendre. I felt a flutter in my chest.

"I don't want to be a burden. Don't you have some, I don't know, ranger shit to do?" I did air quotations with my fingers for the phrase ranger shit. I had no clue what rangers did specifically, but I didn't want to interrupt his work.

"Don't worry, I already did my ranger shit. That's how I found you. I was putting out snow poles to mark the roads for the storm."

"I don't want to be a liability."

Harley gripped the steering wheel tighter, biting back an amused smile. "Oh, you're a liability, alright. But not in the way you're thinking."

A swirl of attraction formed deep in my belly, causing it to feel like it was sinking. Trying not to get swept up in it, I stared at him for a couple of seconds, wanting to make him squirm. He had most of the power, so I needed this little ounce of control. Trying to hide how flustered he was getting, he sighed and added, "I have a bed for you and everything. I insist. I need to know you're safe."

"I'm the crazy lady who almost hit a moose! Hell, I chucked an ice pack at you! Why would you want me in your home?"

"Good points, but I want you with me. By my side."

That did it. That sent the flutter in my chest and the swirl of desire all the way down . . . down . . .

"I need to know you're safe." He tried his best to position his idea while remaining casual, but I could tell this wasn't normal for him. His low voice went on. "I don't want you to take this the wrong way or sound like some brute caveman, but I want to keep you safe. Plus, you're a general threat to the forest. I've seen you driving. I don't want to know what you could do on foot. Hagrid was lucky he didn't get hit."

"Hagrid? You named the moose Hagrid?!"

He shrugged, "Of course. He's the town menace. Last summer, I caught tourists feeding him ice cream. He hasn't been the same since."

"I could have sworn I saw a Christmas tree ornament on his antler," I murmured, staring pensively ahead, slightly haunted.

"Oh yeah, he charged the Christmas tree in the town square a month ago. I've been trying to knock it off him with clear paintballs ever since."

My jaw dropped. "You're kidding?"

"No." He grinned.

I blinked hard, wondering if I had knocked my head in the wreck. "Wait, you want to keep me safe?"

He shrugged his shoulders under his heavy coat. "Like I said, I don't want you to be offended. I feel like maybe you're out of your element up here. I mean, you're hurt, and you wrecked your car. You're not from here. Plus, there's a giant storm coming and you have nowhere to stay. I can't sleep tonight wondering if you're safe."

I sighed, hearing how screwed I was on every level. "Wait, a storm is coming? Like, more than these flurries?"

"Yeah, didn't you see the storm warnings?"

"No, I must have missed them. It only said road closures." I stared out the window, watching the snowy forest pass by in a rush of indigo and icy white. Had the daydream of hacking off Tyler's dick distracted me that much? "I didn't plan on driving this far away from home. I just let the road take me."

"Well, keep letting the road take you. You're safe with me. You can stay with me until the storm passes and Dane fixes your car." He nodded, agreeing with himself.

"Do you live in some tent in the forest with other rangers and Smokey Bear?"

"No, a cabin that way." He pointed his hand that rested on top of the steering wheel.

"Do you have a person living there with you?"

"Just me."

"I thought rangers had to live in the park?"

"You're probably thinking of park rangers. I'm a forest ranger. Think less tourism, more conservation, search and rescue, and fire prevention. I have my own home on the outskirts of Pine Bluff." Before I could ask more questions, he went on. "We're almost in town. I'll run you by the urgent care, then we can be on our way."

"Absolutely not, Harley." Saying his name created a buzz in my body once more. He let out a resigned sigh. "I could use a store, though." I looked around at the beginning of civilization while we drove to the outskirts of a town.

"Oh right, for actual winter clothes?" He glanced over at me again, raking his eyes up and down my body. "It looks like you're ready for an Enya concert."

"Ohmygawsh, I love her! Did you know she lives in a castle with a bunch of cats? Talk about goals."

He fought back a smile and turned on another road, popping out on a wintery main street. From what I could see past the falling snow, trees lined the curbs with fairy lights wrapped around their branches. Storefronts squished together in historic charm on both sides. The entire road was on a slight incline, making it look like a cozy mountain town. It was mostly empty, with only a few businesses still open.

"I'm going to run by Dane's shop to let him know about your unique situation."

"You're never going to let me live that down, are you?" I asked directly, leaning forward in my seat to make eye contact with him.

"Um . . ." He rubbed at his jaw. "No. Probably not." His handsome face broke into a grin. "Have you ever driven in snow?"

"Yes, and it's not every day a forest beast makes an appearance!"

"Then explain the blue Mini Cooper. That's basically a glorified golf cart, not ideal in the snow."

I held up my finger, correcting him with sass. "First off, it's *mint*, not blue."

"My apologies, ma'am. *Mint* Mini Cooper." We both chuckled while Harley pulled up in front of a market and put his truck into park. "Everything is about to shut down and close for the storm. Including the roads into town." He glanced at the clock on his dashboard. With a disapproving look, he asked, "Have you eaten anything today?"

I opened the truck door and slid down to the pavement. "Only a muffin," I said with a small smile, knowing he was going to hate that fact.

"You're not a vegan or anything, are you?"

"Nah! I'm not a picky eater, either. It's one of the few things I can brag about." I held up my chin with fake pride while I slung my bag on my shoulder.

Harley looked me up and down slowly, not even hiding his eyes drinking me in. "The only thing you can brag about? Hard to believe. I have food covered, don't worry about that detail. I'll be back soon. Try to be quick."

To torture him, I purred, "Oh, I need more than 20 minutes. Take your time." I watched his mouth open in shock, only to close while I shut the door.

Check. Mate.

Chapter Five

Harley

Gripping my steering wheel, I tried to focus on any other sensation than all the blood rushing to the wrong part of my body. I dropped Kaylee off at the market, which bought me some time. Thankfully, she didn't think it was odd I didn't want to go in with her. I was sure she wanted to shop in peace, not feeling rushed or weird.

Truthfully, I was avoiding being seen with her so people couldn't talk. That was the only thing people did in a small town—talk.

I could hear it now, *Oh, that Harley is with some blondie! Does his mother know?* I groaned, thinking about my mom finding out. She was a hopeless romantic and sex therapist. I didn't need her opinion, at all. While most people were raised by a Karen, I'd been raised by a Maxine—a liberated woman who thought various watercolors of vaginas was appropriate wall décor. I let out a stressed sigh while turning on Walker Lane. I pulled up to the back of Dane's shop and parked my truck.

"Hey, fuckface!" I bellowed when I opened my door. I knew he could hear me.

He opened a window, yelling back immediately, "The door is open, asshat!"

He lived in an old two-story industrial space. Dane didn't have the heart to stay in the same house where he'd witnessed his parents pass away. It remained vacant still to this day. Last spring, I'd found out he was living in the space above his shop with a mini fridge, a microwave, and an air mattress. I'd stepped in and insisted we build it out, so he wasn't living like a drifter. I'd helped him run proper electric and better plumbing to the space. We'd knocked out some space in the walls for more windows to make it not so depressing. It was absolutely against code, but everyone in town turned a blind eye. Back then, I'd been helping a buddy out, and now he was returning the favor.

Opening the back door, I ran up the stairs to his unit, taking two steps at a time. I found him sitting on his couch with a beer, watching *Breaking Bad*. He paused the show and went to the fridge to grab us both a bottle. He plunked back down on one side of the couch as I sat down on the other end, preparing myself for the 20 questions I was about to get.

Dane ran a calloused hand through his hair. It was almost as dark as mine, but I had the better beard. His was always barely stubble. Mine filled in, but I never let it grow long. I didn't want to look like some *Duck Dynasty* cast member, and I wasn't old enough to look like I should join ZZ Top.

His green eyes widened in an expression of mischief as he brought the bottle of beer to his lips for a sip to stop his smile. Dane was a bit of a smartass, but deep down, he was a softie. Not enough people saw that side of him. I wished I got that side of him right now, instead of this nosy douche who reveled in my torment.

"What?" I asked in exasperation, already annoyed. Anticipation filled the air, thick with questions. I knew Barrett had told him when he'd dropped off the car to Dane's lot with his tow truck. He would have had to be buzzed in, since it'd been after hours.

"I heard you've got a girl with you," Dane said, wiggling his eyebrows and shifting in his seat, trying to contain his excitement at my torture.

"Yes, dude, she almost hit a fucking moose." I waved the hand that wasn't clutching my beer bottle. "She was driving like someone from Texas or something. Like she had never seen snow in her life."

"What's her story? Why is she here?" he questioned, now knitting his brow in confusion.

"She claims she was going for a drive to clear her mind before the accident. Her record was clean when Boyd pulled it up for the incident report, so I don't think she's on the run or anything. But she's going to stay with me since everything is closed."

Dane raised his eyebrows. "Dude, no shit?" He was eating up all this dirt.

"Yeah, I mean aside from no car or place to stay, she might be hurt. She's so stubborn, she won't even let me take her to urgent care. What the hell else should I do? I can't let her freeze! She's at Pine Mart now."

"Poor thing. Is she hot? How old is she?"

"She's better than hot. She has such a pretty face, long blonde hair. I think she's a couple of years younger than us, maybe late twenties. She's feisty, though. I'll tell you that much."

"Are you going to hook up?"

"She's stranded. I doubt she's even thinking about that. Fuck, are you only capable of thinking with your dick?" I bit out defensively, acting like I hadn't wondered that myself.

He shrugged, refusing to confirm or deny. "Listen, all I'm saying is you have some girl with you during this nasty ass storm. That doesn't suck. Things could be worse."

Now it was my turn to shrug, unable to confirm or deny.

"Does she seem cool?" he probed.

"Yes, I think so." I traced the rim of the bottle with my thumbnail. I could feel my brow furrow as I thought of the woman I'd rescued. "She's unique. I can't explain it. She feels fun. Lighthearted."

"Fun is good." His head bobbed enthusiastically, his mouth pulling down slightly in consideration.

"I mean, I feel bad she's stranded. She's a free spirit. She didn't even have a plan or know about the storm. Now she's stuck here."

"Oh, I get why you're here, you little bastard!" Dane said, putting his beer on the coffee table. "You want me to buy you time? If I delay fixing her car, she can't leave kind of thing, eh?" he said with a grin.

I bit back a smile and stared down at my bottle. I mindlessly peeled back the wrapper, unable to answer his question.

"That's it, isn't it?" he said, now chuckling. "You want time with her?"

"Yeah," I said with a disgusted sigh. "I wouldn't hate time with her. I want to know she's safe. If you order parts, what day will they arrive?"

"I haven't looked at anything since I'm off work now, jackass. Plus, you only beat the tow by like five minutes. With it being a Mini Cooper, the parts might be tricky. Since she high centered herself on the tree, I'd guess damage to the bumper, drip pan, maybe even the gas tank. I could milk it a couple of days."

"Okay, text me along the way. I don't want her to stress about the details." I tipped the bottle to finish the beer and stood up.

"Such a gentleman! Oh man, you got it bad. You let me know if we need to finish it sooner. Wait! What if she's a mom? Like a hot, single mom? And you're keeping her from her kid?" He laughed nervously at his own question.

I stood there, wide-eyed, for a couple seconds. "Well shit! I hadn't thought of that. See! This is exactly why I come talk to you! But you're the one with mommy issues, not me. Plus, she didn't mention obligations like that. She sure as hell didn't mention a husband or boyfriend coming to help her. I'm running with that."

Dane yelled at me while I bolted down the stairs. "Remember what I always tell you! Wrap it in foil before you check her oil!" He laughed at his own joke, making me chuckle too. That nosy shithead was such a good friend.

Chapter Six

Kaylee

As I walked into the marketplace, appropriately named Pine Mart, a pretty woman around my age greeted me. She had an earthy elegance about her, with shiny brown hair and a sage-colored fleece pullover. She smiled at me while sweeping by the entrance.

"Hey, hon, we're closing in about fifteen minutes. Can I help you find anything?"

"No, thanks. I promise I'll be quick." I smiled back at her good-naturedly while I picked up a basket.

I walked directly to the personal care aisle to grab some essentials, like a toothbrush, shampoo, conditioner, and other things I'd need to shower. Luckily, I had my staple makeup items in my purse. When I walked toward the end of the aisle, a section of condoms stared me straight in the face. I gulped, thinking of the possibility of needing them. I had the sneaking suspicion I annoyed the shit out of Harley, that he saw me as some rescue project, almost like a wounded deer in the forest. Yet underneath all his concern, I couldn't deny the tangible chemistry between us.

I sighed and picked up a box of condoms, considering my next move. Because, you know, casually buying condoms for a man I'd met an hour ago after a car wreck was totally typical.

Wait, wait, none of that! You can have safe, consensual sex whenever you want. Pleasure is sacred and your birthright, I mentally chided myself.

As I stared at the limited options, the idea of Harley being hung like a horse made a lump of dread rise in my throat. On the opposite end of the spectrum, what if the lumberjack wasn't swinging serious wood? The notion of staring at him from across the cabin in silent disappointment for the duration of the blizzard entered my brain. I bit back a bark of laughter while clutching the handle of my shopping basket.

Prior to moving to Boston, I'd had my routine OB/GYN appointment to tide me over. They'd done a complete panel that had come back clean as a whistle. I'd opted for that tiny bar of birth control they implanted in your arm so I wouldn't have to worry too much for the next five years. I might be a shitty driver, but it turned out I was a pro at micromanaging my vagina.

Admittedly, I hadn't had sex with anyone since that appointment, not even Tyler, so I knew I was still in the clear on all levels. But what about Harley? Was he a complete animal, nabbing tourist twat every summer?

A set of overhead lights shut off, dimming the store. I stared up at the ceiling with mild panic before I refocused. What if we ended up getting cozy? Was this too forward? Would it turn him off if I whipped out a box of Trojans right after he whipped out his own Trojan soldier? With a resolute toss, I put a regular-sized box in my basket. If nothing else, I could add it to my apocalypse-ready, pirate pack.

Searching for clothing, I realized the store was a conglomerate of things people would need in a small town. It was a bizarre mash-up of a gift shop, an outdoor retailer, and a small grocery store. They had basic clothing staples and a mix of high-end outdoorsy brands, like Patagonia, and souvenir-type items. Overall, not much to work with. Especially since I wasn't a size small, which was the only size left on most of the racks, as per usual.

What would I need to stay for a couple of days? I stared at the rack of thermal underwear and nervously bit my bottom lip. I didn't want to be caught dead in long johns. Nothing said come fuck me quite like head-to-toe thermals. A part of me chided myself for being caught up in a situation with another man so quickly and, worse, focusing on frivolous things like looking cute after the day I'd had. Another part of me, admittedly the part between my legs, said, *Eh, fuck it! Have some fun!*

Another set of lights shut off above me. I glowered at the ceiling and quickly snatched what I could find in my size, hoping everything fit. I grabbed some leggings, two sweaters, and a bundle of underwear and thick socks. Eyeing a navy-colored, oversized, touristy shirt that said Acadia National Park on it in white scrawl, I sighed and picked it up, and also a long-sleeved thermal for layering in case it got super cold.

From the corner of my eye, I saw a table filled with items made of satin and lace. I smiled, realizing it was for Valentine's Day, which was a couple weeks away. A rush of excitement flushed through my body. *Just in case*, the whorish voice in my head tempted. I grabbed a handful of satin, obeying.

Rushing on, I got what I needed to make my famous chicken parmesan. He'd said not to worry about food, but I was going to ignore that request. The least I could do was make him a nice dinner. I also got some wine to go with the meal.

Feeling like a well-thought-out, organized whore, I took my harlot self to the register, only to realize there wasn't self-checkout. I groaned internally, thinking about having to talk to a townie while buying lingerie and condoms like some vagabond hooker. Before I could abandon my mission, I saw Harley's truck headlights pull up in front of the small store.

I stepped up to the counter to see the same woman who'd greeted me. "Did you find everything okay?" she asked kindly.
"Yes, I did."
She scanned everything faster than her system could keep up with. Various beeping and dings graciously filled the air. I saw a charger for my phone and put it in the pile.
"Sorry to keep you late."
"Don't worry about it. I was mainly getting the locals out of here. They always panic buy beer when it storms." She smiled sweetly at me. "Are you just passing through?"
"Something like that, yeah." I was grateful it was her ringing me up and not some old guy. Looking her over, I noticed her name tag.
"Azalea? That's such a pretty name! It's a flower, right?"
"Thank you! Yep, my mom's favorite."
I tapped my card on the machine and glanced up at her only to notice her side-eyeing Harley's truck in front of the entrance. "You have a great time here in Pine Bluff, hon. Stay warm." Her eyes twinkled in amusement as she handed me three paper bags across the counter.
Harley hopped out and walked around the passenger side, insisting on helping put the bags on the back seat. I sighed in fake offense and smiled while he took my hand to help me up into the truck. Once we were in the cab, I took a deep sigh of relief, realizing I had shelter and necessities.
The heavenly smell of pizza filled the air. "Mmm, carbs." I hummed, suddenly happy.
"I'm glad you're okay with pizza." He put his right arm behind my headrest while he backed up the truck. The move wafted his cologne at me in an intoxicating rush. His profile shifted fleetingly and sexily closer while he stared back to reverse. His hands ran over the wheel to move the truck with assured skill. "I figured you could use some food in you."
I could use something else in me, too.

"Thanks! Plus, it's always fun to try new pizza places. I feel like every region of the United States has their own take on it. But don't get me started on the type of people who are passionate about if pineapple belongs on pizza."

Harley looked at me, trying to hold back an amused smile. "Well, does it?"

"I think that's such a lame conversation starter that people rely on! It's like everyone debating whether *Die Hard* is a Christmas movie! Like, grow the fuck up and learn a new icebreaker!" I broke off in self-amused laughter. "Sorry, I interview people for a living, so I'm all too familiar with small talk. I'm probably just sick of it."

"If it's any consolation, I don't think *Die Hard* is a Christmas movie, or even a decent movie, and as far as pizza goes, people can put whatever they want on it. I mean, it's bread and cheese. Can you mess it up?"

The night had morphed into steady snow, making it hard to see everything around me. From what I could tell, our path took us away from town, quickly leaving the valley. It ushered us into the mountains, through the thick forest. Around one bend, the truck hit an icy patch and swerved. I let out an anxious yelp, and before I knew it, Harley grabbed my hand.

"It's okay. I got you," his low voice assured me while he stared at the road.

He pulled our clasped hands up from my lap onto the center console, his thumb stroking the back of mine. At 27 years old, I shouldn't be giddy over holding hands, but something between us felt different. It was electric, sensual, and soft, with an undercurrent of primal need. After a few breaths, I felt my inner thighs clench closer together to stop the throbbing in my core.

"Hey, I like your rings, by the way. Is that opal?" He looked down at my hand, continuing to hold it on the center console. The feeling of his energy mixed with mine was heady, and I had to pull myself from the lull of attraction.

"Rainbow moonstone, actually." I blinked hard, trying to center myself. I was undoubtably feeling excited he'd noticed something important to me. We both looked at the ring on my left pointer finger. "It's my birthstone. Pretty cool, huh?"

"Very cool."

I lifted my thumb. "Oh, and this one is from my friend Maisie, the one we talked to. We got matching ones in San Francisco. They're little flowers, a nod to the hippies." I chuckled, recollecting the trip. "We hung out at the pier and gave tourists terrible directions in fake Swedish accents."

"Messing with tourists. I like that. You sound fun to hang out with."

"Why thank you!"

Harley steered the large truck along a bend before we set for a slight decline, heading into an even more remote area. Tall pine trees edged each side of the truck, reaching up into the snowy sky like silent citadels. The bright headlights illuminated the snowfall in front of us as classic 70s rock music escaped the speakers in an indistinct murmur. Between the presence of Harley's quiet strength and the familiarity of the music, I felt my nerves soothe.

Coming out of a bend in the road, the truck went over gritty snow, causing me to flinch in panic. Harley squeezed my hand again. "We're good. I got this. It's just snow."

I moved closer to him discreetly, unable to help myself. He was going well under the speed limit on the country road. The sparks were flying and something as simple as having our hands pressed together felt like holding a live wire. I caught Harley's eyes dashing down at our hands and over to me. His eyes broke contact with mine and returned to the road as he sucked in a deep breath.

His walkie-talkie interrupted our little bubble of tension, crackling with a voice saying, "Rangers, we have an incident needing service. Who is responding?" I jumped in my seat, and

Harley begrudgingly let go of my hand to spin the dial, turning the device off.

"Stupid electronic piece of—"

"Don't you need to get that?" I pointed to the walkie-talkie on his dash.

"Nah, I'm off for the night."

"Oh, I see."

Harley's now free hand lifted for a moment, shaking as if to clear any misconceptions. "I don't want you to feel guilty for staying with me. It's no problem. I'd be done with my shift anyway. You're a welcomed guest."

I frowned, thinking about real life. I needed to email my boss because I wouldn't be back by Monday. I felt uneasy thinking about work and life in Boston.

"Do you like your job?" I asked.

"Yeah, I do. I worked hard for it. What about you? What do you do for work?"

"I'm a medical recruiter."

I stared ahead while Harley took a right-hand turn. Sprinkled on either side of the main road were entrances to other cabins. Over most, a sign would show the name of the property, almost like the arching ranch signs we had back in Texas. Deciphering each one in the snow was challenging, but I read one that said *Cabin Fever* and another one that said *Retired and Tired*. I snickered under my breath, quickly pulled back to reality by Harley's surprised tone.

"A recruiter? Like a headhunter?" His eyebrows sank in uncertainty.

I smiled, amused by his reaction. "Yeah, I guess you could say that. I hire medical professionals for three large hospitals in the Boston area." I could hear how flat my voice sounded.

"That's surprising to me." Harley side-eyed me in disbelief.

"Why is that?"

"You come off like a wild card, like you'd have some unconventional job is all." He shrugged and turned down what I could only assume was his own private drive.

"You're right. Before this stage of my life, I taught nude yoga."

"Nude yo—"

"What does your sign say?" I interrupted him, wanting to leave him guessing. I pointed to the sign as we drove under it. The metal scroll framed in rich wood read something in a foreign language I didn't recognize.

"I can't tell you. It's inappropriate."

"Harley, c'mon, I need to know!"

"It basically says fuck off. It's a family joke." He shrugged as if that sufficed.

"Ah, so you're a frequent entertainer, I take it." All he provided was a nod as an answer.

The long, forest-lined road opened to a clearing with Harley's cabin lit like a jewel in the night. The lights around the exterior made it look warm and inviting, casting enough light for me to see beautiful stone halfway up, rich lumber finishing the rest of the way. Topping the cabin was a heavy-duty, dark metal roof to hold the masses of snow. A wraparound porch with a string of lights with round bulbs added a homey charm. From what I could tell, past the cabin was a modest-sized barn.

"This place is gorgeous."

"Thank you. It's been a labor of love, that's for sure."

After parking in the garage that was tucked discreetly into the side of the cabin, we took off our coats in the mudroom. When Harley shrugged out of his, his broad chest emerged with a long-sleeved flannel stretched across it. Thick muscles across his pecs and arms emerged without warning, making me flustered with how they moved underneath the fabric. He wore simple pants and a black thermal underneath the flannel. With practiced motion, he yanked his beanie off his head, revealing, as I suspected, dark hair trimmed nicely, like his beard. He ran a hand through it, making it neater.

Standing close together in the small vestibule, I noticed how much taller and bigger he was than me. His chest heaved right at eye level to me. I looked up at him, trying to fight a smile because I felt giddy as all hell. Reaching past me, he flicked on some lights and opened the mudroom door, revealing the beautiful interior.

Harley's voice echoed behind me. "Make yourself at home. I'll get the rest of the stuff from the truck."

I began walking into the open area with a peaked ceiling and sturdy beams. Most of the space was a living room with a stately stone fireplace, certainly the focal point of the entire cabin. It was massive, reaching to the ceiling like a tower. The stones were of perfect masonry, mixed with smooth and rough, ranging from all shades of hickory brown to clay and even gray in some parts. The mantle appeared to be a giant slab of some distressed wood that surely had a story behind it. I walked to it mindlessly and found my hand running along the exposed materials, feeling the cold of the stone and burls in the wood.

A dark-brown fur rug layered on top of a large, deep-red Persian rug lay right in front of the fireplace. They anchored the space and filled it with some color. Directly across was a coffee table made of the same wood as the mantle and a chocolate-brown leather couch that looked manly yet cozy. To the side of the couch, framing the seating area, was an oversized chair that matched. A small table between the two pieces had a rustic lamp. I looked up and noticed a giant chandelier made of antlers, and various busts of animals were mounted high on the walls. One wall even had stuffed ducks fake flying upwards. Yeesh. Subtle.

Windows on either side of the fireplace flowed into the space, showing the swirling snow outside. Between the sitting area and the kitchen were French doors leading to part of the wraparound porch. The kitchen itself wasn't super fancy, but it looked welcoming with its warm woods, earthy colors, and granite counters. Above the stove was a gorgeous copper range hood. Everything was neat, mostly clutter free, but it still felt lived in.

A couple of rooms filled up the other side of the cabin behind me. To my left, past the seating area, appeared to be a short hallway leading to the main suite.

It smelled woodsy and felt inviting. The size was modest and felt cozy with its natural accents. Instead of the cheesy yellowed knotty pine motif on every damn surface people used so often for cabins, this was different. It felt more intentional with its mixed woods and materials, clean and distinctly masculine. It felt safe and warm, just like Harley.

It was all one level, and it didn't appear he lived with anyone else. Thank goodness. I didn't see any signs of a woman living here, let alone kids. That made me feel better. I didn't see a TV, which made me fleetingly worried he was one of those outdoorsy type guys who only whittled or reread *Walden* at night while he lived out his *Little House on the Prairie* fantasy.

After making my short round of inspection, I noticed Harley stood by the mudroom door, watching me take it all in. Feeling his eyes on me, I smiled at him. "This place is beautiful. Thanks for having me."

An unnamable chain of emotions flashed across his face, pulling his eyebrows together. All he did was nod and walk to the kitchen with the pizza box.

Chapter Seven

Harley

Watching Kaylee walk around my cabin stirred something in me. Sure, I'd had parties here. I wasn't a total hermit, but I hadn't had a woman in here, not one I desired. Being a rather private person, I felt vulnerable having a stranger look at my man cave. Even worse, watching her gentle hands brush across the materials I'd picked out put a pain of longing in my chest I wasn't ready to feel.

As soon as we got in the cabin, we unloaded the bags Kaylee had bought from the store. From what I could tell, she was going to make an Italian meal. I'd told her not to worry about food, but she had completely ignored my request. She was headstrong, something I was quickly realizing was sexy as fuck.

She peeked inside a bag, whisking it away, asking if she could throw some clothes in the wash before wearing them. I explained the machines were in the mudroom and to help herself. Watching her walk there, I tried not to gawk at how her hips moved with each step.

"I'd offer you a beer, but I don't think you should drink if you have a concussion," I yelled out before washing my hands.

She let out what I could only describe as a feminine grunt and yelled back, "Dude! I don't have a concussion!" She emerged after a few moments, washed her hands, and shuffled to my fridge to inspect her options. "Water is fine. Oh, do you have the good ice?" With a squeal, she added, "Oh, you do!"

I handed her a glass and tried not to lose my shit at how cute she was being over something as simple as crushed ice. She was unpretentious, and I liked that about her. After grabbing us each a plate, I met her at the kitchen island. I lifted the lid of the pizza box in a swift motion, presenting the meal with pride. We each placed a few slices on our plates in unison, not wasting time. I brought one to my face and tried my best not to inhale it.

Kaylee delicately bit into her slice and wiggled slightly. It must've been good. Why were women so damn cute when they ate? I fleetingly stared at her hands holding the pizza to her mouth and imagined it was my dick instead. I gulped away my pervy musing, reminding myself she was literally eating to sustain herself after a damn car wreck.

Kaylee looked even more beautiful in my house. Her hair had a shine to it, and her skin looked soft even in the overhead pendant lights of my kitchen. Now indoors, I could finally see more of her body, which was a blessing and a curse because it was so damn tempting. She had taken off her coat and boots, only to reveal her tight leggings running up to a slouchy black sweater that covered her ass but didn't fully conceal her perfect boobs. From where I sat beside her, I could see silver earrings trailing up her ears that matched her silver nose ring. When she tossed her hair over her shoulder, it smelled sweet and clean. I had to fight from inhaling it like some creep.

"Did you build this place yourself? Do you like being so remote?"

"Yeah, it's a lot of work since it is just me up here, but I like it that way. In the summer, there is so much tourism in the area, it's nice to come home to some peace."

"How long have you been here?"

I tilted my head, considering. "I've lived in this cabin now for two-ish years, but I grew up around here. When I moved back from college, I got my ranger job and started the build."

God, had it been that long already?

"Did you mean to decorate it like the Gryffindor common room, or is that a happy accident?" Her nose crinkled in humor.

I barked out a laugh. "Oh shit! You're right!" We chuckled together for a few moments, chewing in between. "Look, I'll be honest. Luckily, my sister helped me pick some of the stuff out, like the rug and couches. I didn't know what the hell would look good. I told her I wanted it to feel like me, you know? Outdoorsy but not like a tacky cabin someone stays in twice a year. This is my home."

"Of course! I noticed you went with a safe motif of decorating your cabin with dead animals. Solid choice." She flashed her light eyes up to my antler chandelier with a playful smile that made my stomach roll with how pretty she was.

"I mean, it is a classic for a reason. Nothing says relax like twelve antlers ready to impale you while you watch TV."

We both smiled in acknowledgement of our natural chemistry, pleased with the easy banter that was forming between us now that we'd let our guards down a little. We were doing some invisible dance of not being in each other's way but also wanting to get familiar with one another.

"I wanted it to feel nice and warm in the dark winters here. The first year living here alone was brutal. Since my family owns the hardware store in town, it was a simple decision to build this place myself with some help. I worked in construction for an uncle who is a contractor throughout high school, so I had some clue what to do. It was a humble beginning while I built it out and saved up. But it has been cool to build how I like it. It gave me something to do during the long winters. I wanted it to feel like it still had elements of nature in here. Like the stones and the woods." I gestured at the fireplace and the ceilings.

"That makes sense." She nodded, nibbling on her pizza politely. "I like how it doesn't feel closed off."

"Yeah, I went with high ceilings with the beams exposed. Honestly, I'm a little claustrophobic. Oh, and I wanted to keep the view of the lake. You might see what I'm talking about if there's a break in the storm. Anyway, my family has been here for generations, so luckily, I inherited the plot of land."

"Mmm." She bobbed her head in agreement while chewing and swallowing. Her eyes on me made me suddenly self-conscious. I got the feeling she was reading me like a damn book. I wasn't used to someone listening so intently, especially not someone as gorgeous as her. It felt like I couldn't keep air in my lungs and at any moment I would need to gasp. From where we sat next to each other at the kitchen island, our legs pressed together, creating a constant warmth I had to fight from noticing.

She got up from her chair and looked at the pizza box with a giggle. "Oh, my hell! That is hilarious! Yeti's Spaghetti?!"

Yeti's Spaghetti was the best place in town for Italian food. The pizza boxes had a dorky-looking, cross-eyed Sasquatch holding a big bowl of noodles with rogue meatballs bouncing out of it. I chuckled at her amusement, loving the way it lit up her face. The cabin had often been silent, but now with her here, laughter was already echoing from the walls and beams. I felt another stirring of longing in my chest and chided myself for being such a simpleton. A woman laughing shouldn't thrill me.

"I have to take a picture of this. That's too funny!" She picked up her phone and snapped a picture before smiling at it again. While she did that, I cleaned up dinner. Staring at her phone, she turned and all but ran into my chest where I stood. I wasn't used to having someone in the cabin with me. She steadied herself by holding on to my arms with a feminine yelp.

"Here, have a seat, and I'll build you a fire." I wanted her to relax and get settled in. I glanced at the clock on my oven, calculating how much longer I had to keep her up with her concussion.

As if reading my mind, Kaylee scoffed. "Are you keeping me awake because of my alleged concussion?"

"Yes, and it's only been two hours."

"I don't have a concussion!"

"Woman!"

"Woman?!"

"Yes, woman! You are stubborn as all hell! Jeezus! Here, take some ibuprofen now that I'm thinking about it."

I pulled out two ugly terracotta pills from the bottle I stored in the cupboards by my microwave and put them in her hand. She glowered up at me and popped them in her mouth with a defeated mumble before tipping her glass of water back.

"Be glad I'm too tired to argue."

"You don't feel pain now, but it's coming."

Kaylee lifted her arms to wiggle her torso and hips. "Look! I told you. No broken ribs." I smiled at how adorable she was as she fought back her own laughter. "Would I be able to do this with a broken rib?" She flayed her arms side to side and wiggled her hips even more vigorously. I took in the view of her curves in motion, enjoying how raising her hands showed off where her soft thighs met. Something else caught my eye.

"Is that a tooth?" I gestured at her long necklace.

She ducked her head, picking up the necklace from where it rested on her solar plexus. "Oh yeah, it's from my favorite yak."

I dipped my chin in wonder. "You have a favorite yak?"

"Well, yeah. I spent some time in Montana when my dad's motorcycle broke down meandering after Sturgis. We stayed at a yak farm while it got fixed."

What?

She walked even closer to me, unfazed, and held up the necklace so I could see it better. "This is a lucky yak tooth from Lady Goldenrod. She was the prettiest girl. Oh, but this baby tooth is all mine. I had a metalsmith put it in a pendant for me with these little bells." She jiggled the pendant as a gorgeous smile spread across her face, listening to it chime.

I was even more intrigued. "What's that?" I pointed to another charm on the necklace. "Is it sea glass?"

"Good guess! It's Libyan desert glass. It's kind of like moldavite. Have you heard of moldavite?" She tipped her head in curiosity, looking up at me. I shook mine, wondering if she was even speaking English.

She patted my chest. "That's probably a good thing. Basically, this is a tektite. It formed when a meteor crashed into earth like 30 million years ago. Pretty neat, huh?"

"Let me get this straight. You have a yak tooth, your own tooth, and something from a meteor hanging around your neck?"

"Yep! They bring me good luck." She looked at me warmly. "So far, I think they're working."

An elaborate sequence of dings stopped her. She looked around the cabin in confusion.

"That's the washer. The load is done."

"Oh! I see!" She walked toward the mudroom, and I tried my hardest not to watch her ass move while she strutted but couldn't help a glance.

"I'll be right back. I need to get more firewood from outside." It felt weird yelling across my own damn cabin. I wasn't used to having to explain myself here.

I exited the French doors by my kitchen, slipping on my boots. I stored firewood inside by the hearth, outside on my covered porch, and there was a full stash in my woodshed. Considering the storm was hitting, I moved more from my shed to my porch before it was too deep to use my wheelbarrow.

Coming back into the cabin with an armful of logs, I found Kaylee curled up on my couch, leaning against the arm of it, fast asleep with her phone in her hand. I couldn't have been outside for longer than fifteen minutes. A twinge of uneasiness filled my body when I realized she must've been exhausted. I quietly put down the wood and walked over to her, expecting her to stir. Her soft frame curled in a fetal position made me want to scoop her up.

Biting back the urge to wake her, I walked into my bedroom and prepared it for her. I changed my sheets, put out some towels for her to use, and got some clothes for myself. I closed the shutters and turned on the gas fireplace in the corner. I looked around the room, hoping she wouldn't wake up in the middle of the night freaking out in confusion.

I scooped her up from the couch. Her body felt lovely and warm in my arms. Her hair was soft against my chin, and her limbs hung heavy with sleep. I eased her onto my bed, gently plucking the phone from her grasp before sitting it on the bedside table. Covering her with blankets, I stared at her sleeping face. She stirred, her brow creasing while she slept. I slowly inched out of the room, shutting the door.

No big deal. Only the most gorgeous woman I'd ever met. Sleeping in my bed.

Chapter Eight

Kaylee

I woke up with the distinct sickening feeling of being too hot. I sat up immediately, realizing everything around me smelled like Harley. Harley! How had last night even been real? Rubbing the sleep from my eyes, I assessed my surroundings. Underneath the blankets, I was still wearing all my clothes except my winter jacket and boots. He must've wrapped me up like a burrito and put me under the covers of this cushy bed, hence the reason I was so damn hot.

I sensed I was alone in the room. Double-checking, yep, I was on a bed, a nice fluffy bed that was rather high off the ground. Where the hell was I? I sat for a moment, recollecting yesterday, realizing my last memory was sitting down on Harley's couch after texting Maisie I was safe.

A surge of panic crept into my body. Had I passed out on his couch like some drunk sorority girl? I looked around for clues, but everything was dark except in the right corner of the room opposite the bed, where a fireplace blazed with a comforting flame. The wall around it had smooth river stone expertly cobbled, making the entire room feel cave-like and protected. Directly across from the foot of the bed was a large window that had shutters.

I reached to the bedside table on my right, fumbling around before managing to turn on the lamp. I instantly noticed the ceiling gently slanted up from the window, with wood beams framing the room in a way that felt rugged but not overly spartan. Hardwood floors spanned the room, and a long, simple dresser was to the left of where I'd slept. Dark, distressed wood that was thick and sturdy framed the large bed. It must've been handmade with how high quality it appeared. The linens were simple and topped with a down comforter, a soft quilt, and some blankets piled on for good measure.

I stretched, yawned, and cracked my back while assessing the beauty of the room. It was plain but cozy, a little undecorated. Unraveling myself from the layers, I got up and opened the shutters, revealing an overly bright snowy day. I winced at the light, feeling hungover from sleeping so long. After a moment, I acclimated to see a breathtaking view of a small lake. Not far off in the distance, pine trees and hills framed the view that was filled with lazy snow flurries. I stood there for several minutes, taking in the simple tranquility of the wintery morning.

Assuming past the wall the headboard was against could only be a bathroom, I rounded it to see I was correct. It was simple with no tub, only a walk-in shower across from a one sink vanity built in the wall. Rich woods and dark, masculine colors were used, along with a wide, round mirror over the sink. It was large, framed in what looked like driftwood. While washing my hands, I saw a stack of towels neatly placed on the side of the sink counter. I smiled, thinking of Harley's consideration. Next to the stack was a note scrawled in boyish handwriting:

Good morning, beautiful,
You passed out last night. I didn't want to wake you. You're safe here, make yourself at home. I have some "ranger shit" to do, but I'll be back soon. The Wi-Fi password is Kevinbaconiscreepy with a capital K.
-Harley

    Good morning, beautiful? I blushed at the passing praise and couldn't fight the smile that spread across my face.
    Would Harley even see me that way? I mean, he'd rescued me from an embarrassing wreck, and I'd passed out on his couch. Shaking my head to clear my self-doubt, I reread the note. I chuckled at the Wi-Fi password, wondering what his issue with Kevin Bacon might be.
    I found the toothbrush I'd bought at the store next to the towels and note. My eyes widened in horror when I considered if he'd found the box of condoms in my bag with my other items. Brushing my teeth in a panic, I looked in the shower to see my various bottles neatly placed beside his manly products. I violently spit out my toothpaste and walked back into the bedroom in a slight panic.
    All I could see was my phone on the bedside table, but none of the clothes I'd washed or my purse. Exiting the room, I turned back to look at where I'd come from, gaining my bearings of the cabin. As I suspected, I'd spent the night in the room off from the living room that must be Harley's.
    "Hello?" I said out loud in case he'd come home. The sound of my voice echoed from the tall ceilings as no response came. From there, I saw where I'd left my purse on the back of the chair in the kitchen. Grabbing it, I saw a glass of water, orange juice, and a slice of toast with peanut butter slathered on it. A bottle of ibuprofen was next to the plate as well. Harley must've left it out for me. My stomach sank once more in panic and now hunger.

Sticking to my plan, I made my way to the mudroom, where I, thankfully, found my clothing in the dryer. I'd taken a very calculated risk by putting everything in there, lingerie and sweater be damned. I hadn't wanted to leave my clothes drying all over the place, and in true bachelor fashion, Harley didn't have a drying rack. After plunking the bundle on the bed along with my purse, I called Maisie while I folded.

She appeared on the screen almost immediately. Her shock of neon-pink hair was short and coifed to perfection, beautifully framing her pixie face that beamed with warmth. It felt nice to see a familiar face in such a foreign situation. She was at work, which was an adult sex shop, so behind her was a wall of lube and edible panties. By this point, I was so desensitized to seeing her like this. It didn't bother me to talk to my bestie with crotchless panties hanging behind her ears. It was an acquired taste.

After our greetings, I felt like puking, crying, and rambling all at the same time. The past 24 hours had truly overwhelmed me. Being a genuine friend, Maisie could tell so she led the conversation. "Kaylee, are you safe? Are you okay?" She popped in an earbud so our conversation would be private. Bless her.

"Yes, I'm totally okay, and Harley went to work so we can talk openly."

"Good, tell me everything. Start with Tyler."

"Okay, so I went to get a coffee, as one does on a Saturday afternoon. I have this cool book that I planned on reading before Imbolc, and I thought coffee would be—" I huffed out a sigh, interrupting my tangent. "I went to use the restroom at the coffee shop, and I walked in and there he was with that cute barista. We're talking mid-hump, halfway through a moan, full on fucking her brains out!"

"No!" Maisie's mouth dropped.

"Yes!" I shrieked, clenching my fist in front of me.

"That sounds so unsanitary, too. Did he say anything?"

"No, I didn't give him a chance! Fuck, who can pop a boner in a room that smells that heavily of Pine-Sol?!" I flailed my hands around in disgust while Maisie nodded in agreement. "I left, got in my car, and drove and drove and drove some more. I ended up in Maine, and I almost hit a damn moose. You know how that ended. Harley got me in his truck while they figured out the tow, and I fell asleep waiting for him."

"Wait, how did you get into his house?"

"Get this. I woke up and chucked an ice pack at him. Oh, and because my seatbelt was a little bitch that did this—" I pulled my sweater away from my neck, showing my seat belt burn. Maisie hissed in sympathy. "He wanted to take me to the urgent care in town and I said no. Oh, and get this, the town has an urgent care but no hotel or rental car place."

"What the hell?"

"Right? Since it's January, there isn't lodging available. The nearest rental car place is over an hour away, but they're closed on Saturday nights through Sunday. I went on a Googling rampage. Turns out, I'm stranded." I grumbled while folding a pair of panties, realizing how chaotic all this must be to an outsider.

"Wait, what?"

"Harley, Mr. Brooding Lumberjack Ranger Man, insisted I stay with him since his dinky ass town only has a bed-and-breakfast run by a boomer who lives in Florida all winter." I angrily fought with a pair of leggings, trying to fold them. "I said yes, but I don't know what to do now!"

"What happened when you got to his place?"

"We ate this bomb-ass pizza, and immediately after, I fell asleep on the couch like some drunken toddler in a carb coma! Wonderful! Fucking wonderful!"

Maisie snickered at my embarrassment. "That's nothing to be ashamed of. You probably had a concussion or exhaustion from the wreck."

"He carried me to his bed! I slept *in* his bed, Maisie! By the looks of it, I was in it alone." I assessed the bed in front of me in slight worry.

"You're a very heavy sleeper. Remember spring break? You passed out on the beach and got that second-degree sunburn that put you in the ER."

"How could I forget? You called me lobster tits for weeks! But you helped rub aloe vera over my boobs the rest of the vacation. Talk about a bonding moment." We chuckled together at the memory.

"It's kind of romantic! I mean, some mountain man rescued you!" Maisie clasped her hands together, swooning, her long black nails looking shiny with the overhead lighting in her store. "Does he give you good vibes?"

"Absolutely. I trust him. He has a gorgeous aura." Remembering I had a crystal and knife in my bra, I took both out and put them on the dresser, only to put my hand back in my bra to rub the indents on my boobs. Maisie watched, completely unfazed. "And your car?"

"We towed it to a shop in town. Apparently, his buddy owns it, so I hope it's in excellent hands, but I have no clue how bad the damage is or how long it will take to fix."

"And it's still storming?" she asked.

I looked out the window behind me and back at her. "Yeah, at least a couple of inches overnight."

"It looks like you're stuck there for the foreseeable future. I mean, I can think of worse things. Poor dude is probably worried about you. Imagine some gorgeous girl wrecking her car and falling asleep in your truck and then again on your couch. It's adorable! He took care of you!" She tilted her head with a wistful smile. I felt one spread across my face as well.

"You know what? You're right. And we totally have chemistry. I felt it last night. Plus, I found nothing sketchy here in his cabin, no sex dungeon. He lives alone, zero traces of a woman or kids. I feel okay about staying here until I can get my car back and the storm blows over." I shrugged, leaning over my phone propped on the bed.

"Good, those are all green flags. His name is Harley Kouris, right? That's what pulled up when I Googled the shit out of him last night based on your pinged location and his property records." She giggled mischievously and wiggled in her seat, clearly pleased with herself.

"Indeed, it is! Tell me what else you got from your FBI-worthy search. I'm dying to know!" She was so good at this!

"He's been a ranger for several years and even has articles published in some ecology journals. Fancy-schmancy. His social media is pretty locked down and very sparse. Mostly outdoorsy stuff. You know, like sunsets and shit. No embarrassing racist tweets or awkward selfies. By the way, he's incredibly handsome. Great smile!"

I beamed, feeling validated for swooning over him.

"You should go for it if you like him. Oh, and he has some cute friends in some of his photos, other beardy boys." We both wiggled our eyebrows. "And he's a registered Democrat, so you can keep up your streak of never fucking a Republican."

"SOLD!" I bellowed, thrusting my hands in the air in victory, making Maisie giggle.

"You should totally have fun with this. I know you're very selective of who you get physical with because you're so sensitive to energy and all that, but damn! If nothing else, you can keep each other warm."

I took a deep breath, feeling swamped by how my life was unfolding. Sensing my panic, Maisie switched topics. "Is it safe to say Tyler has competition?"

"Tyler is dead to me." I gritted my teeth, thinking of his stupid face.

"He's a rat bastard. You always felt unsure of him, Kaylee. You need to remember that and trust your instincts." She pointed at me with her finger.

"Thank you for reminding me. You're a good friend and I love you to pieces."

"Aw!" She held her hand to her chest. "I love you, too. Plus, you know what they say. The easiest way to get over one guy is to get under another."

"True!"

"Okay, have fun with your lumber daddy. Tell him you have an axe wound you could show him!"

"Maisie!" I cupped my hand over my mouth to strangle my laughter. "That's so fucked up! Okay, but don't say shit to my mom about this. You know how she gets carried away with things. She's a lover, not a fighter."

"I'll try my best. I want details. Check in when you can. Happy whoring!"

Getting into the shower, I was grateful for the warm water trickling down my back that was aching with tension. I shielded myself from the pain when the spray hit my bruised neck. Snooping in the shower, I was impressed to find Harley wasn't using a 3-in-1 shampoo, conditioner, body wash situation. Toward the end, I came to my senses and realized I was basically showering in a stranger's home, far away from where I lived. It had only been yesterday that I'd walked in on Tyler having sex with another woman. Now I was snowed in with a stranger, figuring out what the hell to do with my car that I'd probably gutted on a rogue tree.

Drying off and piling my long hair on top of my head with a towel, I stared at myself in the mirror. I looked sad and tired. The bruise on the crux of my neck was angrily spreading to my collarbone. The red mark was already morphing into a purplish hue. My pale skin was clear, but I could see slight shadows under my eyes.

I exited the bathroom, clutching the second towel around my body. I pulled out a pair of underwear, wool socks, black leggings, and the thermal shirt I'd bought. The heather-purple thermal made my bruise look even more noticeable, and it hugged my body too tight, making it feel like an unintentional belly shirt. Scowling at it, I put the slouchy cream sweater I'd gotten over it to hide the injury. Regretfully, I had to wear the same bra from the day before, but it was better than nothing.

Looking at the green aventurine crystal and knife, I put those back in my bra for good measure. I grabbed an oil in a roller bottle I kept in my purse that I used for spiritual protection and perfume. It was a blend of myrrh, sandalwood, and frankincense, along with tiny chips of amethyst for some extra magic. I rolled it on my wrists, neck, and on my sternum between my breasts, tracing symbols that I'd used for years in my craft for protection.

Taking a deep breath and feeling calmer, I dug out the small stash of makeup I kept in my purse: some tinted moisturizer, concealer, liquid eyeliner, and mascara that boasted it was better than sex. I had a theory a nun had named it that because it was, indeed, not better than sex. I combed my hair until it was more manageable, hoping it would quickly dry or I would freeze all day.

Hanging the towels up on some empty hooks I found, I noticed the note again on the counter. Picking it up, I reread it then tucked it in the book I kept in my purse like some stalker souvenir bookmark. My heart raced while I glanced at the note with Harley's scrawl one last time before closing the novel.

Now that I was put together, all my real-life responsibilities flooded my mind in a worried whoosh. I clicked on my email icon and quickly composed a message to my boss explaining I'd had a personal emergency. I informed her I'd be traveling out of state for a couple of days and that I would check in later. That wasn't technically a lie, but I felt a wrench of guilt. I prided myself on being an honest person. My intuition told me I was going to be here for a few days, whether it was to resolve my stranded situation or perhaps for something more interesting, like spending time with Harley. Butterflies swirled in my stomach and a definite bout of nerves came along with it.

I should be done with men. They never seemed to want me. They liked the idea of me, but not for long.

I didn't think Harley was interested in me, or any human. He'd obviously carved out a solitary life for himself. I was sure I would annoy the shit out of him in a matter of hours. Yet here I was, lusting, swooning over something as simple as handwritten notes and bedsheets that smell like him.

I stared at the crumpled bed for a second. A distinct ache of desire appeared low in my belly as I imagined him sprawled out on it. I chided myself to get a grip while I made it, pulling the covers taut as if to erase my intrusion into this mountain man's sanctuary. Standing back to look at the result, I couldn't help feeling flattered that he'd let me sleep alone in his bed. Tyler would have left me on the couch. Come to think of it, he wouldn't have even pulled over if he'd seen me wreck. I felt dizzy, like this was too much to process.

I looked back down at my phone with the unsent email to my boss, Tamara, trying to muster up the guts to send it. I was a very diligent worker, usually putting in long hours and working through the holiday season without complaint because I didn't have children or family near me. As a healthcare recruiter, I felt like I always had to be available to take on the next request. After all, I was hiring people who saved lives in the medical field. I was good at what I did because I could read people and place them where they'd thrive. It was an extremely demanding job, and I was burning out. I'd felt pressured to outperform ever since I'd begun my newest role in Boston last summer. Here I was, well into the end of January, and I hadn't taken a single break or sick day from work.

Feeling justified, I hit the send button and waited for the confirming ding it sent thanks to Harley's Wi-Fi. Tamara was understanding and professional. I doubted there would be an issue. Plus, this was technically an emergency. I had no way out of here until the storm stopped or my car was drivable. Feeling a slight weight off my shoulders, I went to social media and posted the picture of the funny pizza box. The caption read: **some damn good pizza, and as for bigfoot #ibelieve.**

Maisie liked the post and commented the cat with heart eyes emoji. That was code for enjoy your dick appointment.

My stomach growled in hunger, and I headed back into the kitchen. I chugged the water and filled up another glass. Moving to the toast, I chomped gratefully into the bread and looked around. Being the incurably curious person I was, I picked up the cup of orange juice and explored around the house while I had time. I went through the kitchen and turned a corner to see the entryway of the cabin with a heavy pine door. On the other side of the entry, three rooms filled up the west side of the cabin. The first archway closest to the front door led to what appeared to be Harley's study or office. The south wall to the left when I entered had a slight alcove of large windows that overlooked the pathway to his front door and more of the lake.

Directly across from the entrance was a massive desk made of dark, rich wood with a couple of notebooks and journals splayed across it. I also spotted a laptop on a stand which quickly dissolved the *Little House on the Prairie* fear out of my mind. Whew!

Behind the desk, tall bookshelves made of the same dark wood lined the wall. I walked closer to judge the books on the shelves. Glaring at an actual copy of *Walden*, I continued scanning the spines to find a mix of science fiction, like *Dune*, fantasy, like Tolkien, endless field guides about nature, history books, and an entire shelf of *National Geographic* magazines. He had some titles that looked like real doozies, like environmental sociology, bushcraft medicine, and a bunch of books about guys freezing to death on Mount Everest. The only thing more depressing than dying like that was reading about someone else dying like that, yeesh.

Of course, he had some Muir, Frost, and Abbey, which was no surprise if he was into forestry and nature. I continued scanning the shelves, only to see a beat-up copy of *Twilight*, some old westerns, a copy of the *Kama Sutra*, and next to it was a book I'd never seen titled *She Comes First*. Tilting my head sideways to ensure I'd read that correctly, I pulled the copy off the shelf. The papaya on the front cover cleverly served as a metaphor for lady parts. I reread the title, *She Comes First*. Hmm, nice play on words. The subtitle, *The Thinking Man's Guide to Pleasuring a Woman*, made my eyebrows raise in curiosity. Opening the book, I saw a handwritten note on the title page.

Harley,
Happy sixteenth birthday. This book will teach you everything you need to know about keeping a woman happy. It has all the answers aside from where she wants to eat dinner on date night. That's an eternal mystery. Welcome to manhood, fucknuts.
-Carson

The note made me throw my head back with a cackle. As I put it back on the shelf, a vision of Harley gliding over my body in the bed I'd woken up in intrusively entered my mind, making me blink twice to clear it.

"Get your shit together! You probably don't even remember what he looks like!" I whispered to myself out loud. But that was a lie. I knew he was handsome. Even in my post-wreck stupor, I'd noticed how attractive he was, which made my embarrassing situation even more humbling. To be found by some old guy with a beer gut would have been easier, but no. A hunky lumberjack around my age had rescued me instead. Sweet gods, I was in over my head!

To my right, I saw diplomas from Oregon State University above the computer on the north wall. I leaned over to see the details. He had a bachelor's degree in forest management and a master's in forest ecosystems & society. I tilted my head in awe; I'd never considered how niche things like forestry and ecology could be. That he'd dedicated so much time to earn these was impressive. Gazing a moment longer, I spied that printed boldly on the diplomas was the full name of this mysterious ranger, Harley Demetrios Kouris. What a name! It was kind of growing on me already.

I smiled, staring up at the diplomas while clutching my glass of orange juice. He had other pictures of his adventures with buddies: hiking, fishing, and going to baseball games. There was a cute picture of him as a grinning kid holding up a fish with what could be his dad. He had one with what looked to be his brother, who was pointing to where he'd drawn a mustache and a dick on a teenage Harley's face while he'd been sleeping during a car ride.

A dark-blue evil eye talisman was hanging off one of the picture frames. I wondered where he'd gotten it. It was the only thing in his cabin that had the slightest connotation of spirituality or superstition. I stared up at a deer bust and whispered, "Bambi, I'm so sorry he got you," before exiting.

Moving back into the entryway, I looked in the next room to find a simple bathroom with a cool oval window on the west wall. The next room proved to me that Harley was a bachelor. What could have been a spare bedroom was a mash-up of random items, mostly weights and training equipment, and an entire wall of hooks for his gear. The man clearly had a hobby of being an outdoorsman because this looked like it belonged at REI or Cabela's with the various tents, backpacks, and canvas sacks. Seeing something so overtly practical and guy-ish made me feel a little better. He wasn't hiding anything that I could tell, and the spare room showed he was a single dude with ample hobbies. *That's a good sign*, I thought to myself.

Finalizing my loop, I glanced at the now familiar mudroom door and walked back into the open space in the middle of the cabin. The windows in each room were open, casting gray, snowy daylight into the space as the storm continued to unleash on the land. A view of pine trees along the western side of the cabin opposed the eastern windows that showed off the view of the lake and deck, with clusters of pine trees as well. From what I could tell, no other neighbors were close by, and the lake was just big enough that I couldn't see any cabins across the way. It felt secluded and peaceful, a balm to my anxious soul.

I craned my neck to peer at the pitched ceilings that gave some spaciousness yet maintained a cozy feel, with gorgeous woodwork and structured beams. Harley had a penchant for using the best materials to build and let that do the talking, rather than artwork or lots of knick-knacks. Overall, the cabin was cozy and ruggedly masculine in the best way.

I took a deep breath, soaking in where I found myself in the present moment, realizing this was my fate. I was to stay here for the foreseeable future with a man who was a bit . . . mysterious.

How could I crack his walls? How could I show him kindness in return?

It was then a sage tidbit of wisdom flickered in my head: the fastest way to a man's heart was through his stomach.

Chapter Nine

Harley

No big deal. No big deal at all. There was a gorgeous woman currently in my bed and I could barely sleep all night because of a raging boner, like a goddamn 14-year-old. I'd slept on the couch and woken up before sunrise. Terry had sent me a text, asking for my key to the supply room along with some annoying GIFs, so I'd gone to work early to save his ass. The intern, Noah, had lost Terry's copy when he'd lent it to him, and they needed supplies for the storm. I pulled up to the station and walked into the office, dreading being there when I'd rather be with Kaylee. The unanswered question on if she was okay or not lingered in my brain. Her vitals last night had been fine, even if she'd slept like the dead.

The station had fluorescent lights flickering that drove me nuts. I enjoyed being out in nature. That was why I'd gone into this line of work. I was itching to be out under the open sky, not stuck in some cubicle, dammit.

"Hey, Har!" Meghan turned her head to greet me where she sat at her desk. She was cute, but too young for me. Her thick brown hair was in two braids, making her look extra granola. She was a hard worker, and I appreciated having a woman around for diversity. I loved it even more that she could hold her own with skills. It kept the cocky new grads in line.

"Hey, Meg, apparently Noah lost the key to the supply room?"

"Yeah, he's been scrambling to find it for days. It's been funny watching Terry give him a hard time. The remote supply shed over on the north trail loop is low and we need more shovels."

"Got it." I retrieved the key from my pocket and opened the door, propping it open with a doorstop.

"I'm sorry you had to come in early and bring the key." I'd been doing that a lot lately. Terry was inching toward retirement and losing his shit. I'd been working my ass off for years, hardly taking days off to compensate for his unhelpfulness. With winter being the slowest time of year, we only needed a skeleton crew working, and even that wasn't enough to offset his shenanigans. Regardless, it was nice to hear Meg remorseful. Shared misery was sometimes a mild comfort.

"HARLEEEEEEEEY!!!!" Terry's voice boomed from the doorway.

"Hey, Terry. I heard you lost a key again." I crossed my arms to stare at him teasingly. Terry was totally a typical boomer, with white hair and a pale beard that split on either side of his face, making him look like a walrus. He loved lobster and Dan Brown novels. And, of course, his wife Karen more than anything. He was a nice guy, but fucking L-O-U-D. Noah, the poor intern, was doing his entire job. Terry was mostly harmless, and luckily, with my organizational skills, the things that needed to be delegated were.

"Ayuh, it was that fucking Noah kid! I'm telling ya, Harley, kids these days don't get how to work hard! You guys are always on your phones, watching your blogs and tweetering." He slapped my back hard after saying that, as if we were bonding. I filtered out about half of everything he said and never took his raving personally.

"Yes, tweetering is my favorite pastime." I shot a side-eye at Meg. "The closet is unlocked. It looks like Meg will hold down the fort with you. I think you guys should be good. I'll be out running rounds and checking caches."

He leaned in, whispering like we were in some locker room. "I heard you have a girly locked up in your cabin with you. Is that true?" Meg's head whipped back around, and her eyebrows raised in intrigue over her oversized, gold-rimmed, circular glasses.

"Terry, where do you come up with these things?"

"Sherry told Karen. Apparently, the little thing hit a gigantic tree last night, and you can see a Mini Cooper parked at Dane's shop."

Yeah, she hit a tree because you didn't patrol well enough to catch the giant piece of timber alongside the road before it snowed, you dipshit!

This small town was out to embarrass me. It had only been a few hours, but word had traveled. I didn't want to give them that power. They needed to get their noses out of my business. Pine Bluff was not about to cockblock me.

"I helped a lady last night, but she was passing through town." That wasn't an outright lie. I was usually a straight shooter, but I felt protective over Kaylee. She was in a vulnerable position.

"Ah, old biddies gossiping to gossip! Am I right?" Terry did an awkward, open-mouth wink at me while he grabbed a clipboard with his dry, chapped hands.

Changing the subject, I asked, "Hey, did you complete the reports on tipping season?"

Pine and fir tips were common in wreaths for Christmas, causing what we referred to as tipping season. Basically, it was a bunch of dumbasses cutting down trees and boughs, only to transport or sell them illegally. Nothing said happy holidays like the destruction of the forest. With it being late January, we needed to report our incident numbers in the area.

Terry's mouth opened in fake confusion, causing his whiskers to hang over his lips in an extra walrus-y way. "You know what, son? I forgot. What kind of report would that be?"

Oh, just the same fucking report we do every January, Terry!

I stared at him, wanting so badly to hit him upside the head with his stupid clipboard. Instead, I reminded him where to find the reporting templates on Google Drive. After, I explained for the hundredth time what Google Drive was and how to attach a report to an email. *Jeezus Christ, this man votes?*

Before leaving, I casually added I was taking some days off to eat up unused vacation hours. Meg waved at me dismissively, not even bothering to turn around while I walked out. It was Sunday and the end of my work week. Monday and Tuesday were my usual days off since the weekend was the busiest days for us rangers. I thought they all knew I'd covered their asses and deserved some time off, especially in the slow season. Plus, I was in charge, so they could eat shit.

I spent the next couple hours at work worrying about Kaylee and realizing I hadn't left my cell number on the note. I mentally chided myself for the stupid error. Best-case scenario, she was completely okay. Not hurt but bored as hell in my cabin. Worst-case scenario, she was hurt and all alone, waiting for me. I rushed through my tasks, the snowfall making everything take longer than it should.

On top of all that, I needed to get to Dane's and threaten him within an inch of his life so he wouldn't tell anyone details. I let out a stressed sigh and pulled up to the front of Dane's shop on Main Street instead of my usual way from his back lot. From here, his two-story, brick building looked well maintained, given the decades of use. It had a mural on the side exposed to Main Street traffic. Dane had commissioned my asshole of a brother, Carson, to paint it, which had resulted in a retro throwback of a bunch of muscle cars in the 1950s parked at a drive-in movie theater. It was alright, I guessed.

The bottom portion was his auto shop that consisted of three bays and a small office. I could see Kaylee's Mini Cooper jacked up and mangled in the first bay. The sight of the carnage made me instinctually angry.

"Hey, dude," I greeted him while approaching, seeing my breath in the cold air.

"Hey, man, how's it going?" Dane said, standing up and wiping his greasy hands with a red cloth. We gathered around the space heater that was whirling in the corner by his tool chest.

"I spent my morning at the station, saving Terry's ass again because lord knows that man can't do his job." I blinked in annoyance. "He knew all about Kaylee. Apparently, Sherry over at the police department told Karen already. Can you believe that shit?"

"So what?" He puffed out air from his nose dismissively. "You know how the old ladies in town will talk about damn near anything. Remember how weird they were when I moved back home all tatted up? They came up with that rumor I was in the mafia."

"Good point, but they also saw her car here." I gestured at the bay in exasperation. "Did you say anything?"

"No, I didn't say shit! You should already know that. God! What is with this girl that has your tits in a tizzy?" Dane flung his rag on his tool chest and took a sip from an insulated water bottle covered in grime from his hands.

"I don't know! It's not like I don't know I'm being an ass. Please just don't say a single fucking thing to anyone. Even if they know what's going on."

He squinted at me, "Why are you wanting to hide her? If she's cute, why does it matter? You worried the town will scare her away? Pressure her to get with one of the last eligible bachelors, besides me of course." He smiled cockily. "I'm the better looking one."

I slugged him in the shoulder, making him swing back slightly.

"Bitch!" Dane exclaimed, rubbing the navy Carhartt coveralls that covered his shoulder. "But is that it?"

"Yes. She has enough shit on her plate. Plus, I don't want to look like I'm some opportunist or something. Even though I guess I am. Fuck, I don't know! I just feel like I should help her."

"Nah, it's nice. Chivalrous even." He shrugged, convincing himself with his train of thought. "You're overthinking it. You saw a lady who needed help, so you helped her. Big whoop."

"You know what happened last time I dated a tourist. That shit was traumatizing." I groaned, looking down at my boots where I kicked snow out of the grip.

"That was beyond your control. People in this town love you, Harley, even if they talk shit. You help people. Look, do you want me to tell you what's going on with her car so you can get her out of here? I mean, it's my day off, but I'm looking at it because you're my buddy." He ladled on a layer of guilt, making me feel even more foolish.

"Thanks, yeah. Hit me." I tried to wrap my head around all the moving parts of the shitshow. I leaned against the brick wall of his shop, bracing myself.

"So far, from what I can tell, the frame is bent. There's a broken axle with possible additional drivetrain damage, and a punctured oil pan to boot." He crinkled his nose, uncomfortable at delivering such bad news.

I shifted my beanie on my head out of habit. "Well, fuck."

"Yeah, the thing is a total loss. We need to get an insurance adjuster out here so she can go on with her life."

Something about the notion of Kaylee going on with her life made my stomach sink. "Okay, I understand."

"Are you sure you even want to be with a girl who drives a Mini Cooper? And drives it badly, I might add. I found pine boughs where there shouldn't be. I mean, that tree ate her car."

I knew he was joking and trying to make me laugh, but it didn't help. Kaylee had just crashed into my life, and I wasn't ready for her to leave.

"Nah, man, her driving like a maniac is one part of her."

"Did anything happen last night?"

"No, we had a good time talking over dinner, then she fell asleep on my couch. She's easy to talk to"—I groaned miserably—"and she's so fucking hot." I looked up at his shop lights, trying not to smile or make eye contact with Dane, who was enjoying my confession. "If I didn't save her, I don't know if she would have even given me the time of day. She's like a loose cannon. I don't know if I can keep up with her."

Dane smirked. "Remember those tourists we took on a double date to Tilly's Tavern and the lake last summer?"

"Fuck, don't remind me."

"They didn't talk about anything but themselves. They kept bitching about the slow service, and that one girl had that fake laugh that sounded like a dolphin." We both chuckled at the memory. "You're telling me Kaylee isn't like that, right?"

"Right, Kaylee is the opposite. She's interesting and funny. God, she is so funny!" I mushed. "She's more than happy to chill in my cabin. Not like those two women, who wanted us to play tour guide for their boring asses." I chuckled quietly, recalling how Dane had made me pull my boat to the dock to let the two women out because they hadn't wanted to get their hair wet and we'd been sick of their shit.

"Remember that stupid boat ride?" Dane's eyes grew large. We were always on the same page; we had spent so much time together, we basically shared a brain.

"Exactly! Who fucking goes to a lake in the summer and doesn't want to get wet? Kaylee would have totally jumped in. She's not uptight."

Dane took another sip of water. "So, you're getting her wet?"

I rolled my eyes at him. "Anyway, I'll try to lighten up. Who fucking cares?"

Dane nodded his head and sat back down on his shop creeper, rolling back and forth idly. "Exactly. So, you'll tell her about the car? And that she needs to get an adjuster to look at it?"

"I might wait a couple days to break the news. Even with a rental car, I don't want her driving in the snow, especially if she's recovering from the wreck. Plus, the highway is closed in and out of town." Dane nodded in agreement.

I took the long way home, driving through the winding roads to sort out my thoughts. It took me longer than usual because snow was falling diagonally into the direction I was driving. With time to sort out my thoughts, I realized all I wanted was the opportunity to understand this puzzling woman who currently needed my help and protection.

Now, all I had to do was juggle three goals:

First, I had to keep Kaylee, the most stubborn person I'd ever met, safe in a blizzard.

Second, try not to pounce on her like the horny caveman I was turning into.

And third, keep the nosy ass townspeople of Pine Bluff out of my business.

What could go wrong?

Chapter Ten

Kaylee

When Harley walked in the door, my heart stopped for a split second. I looked over my shoulder from where I sat on the couch to see him make his way through the mudroom door. He was even better looking than I remembered. His wide chest and shoulders filled up the entire doorway, his head damn near skimming the top of the doorframe with his height. I was mesmerized taking in all his masculine glory.

His eyes gleamed for a moment, while a bashful grin spread across his face, his white teeth contrasting against his dark beard. "Hey." His voice was a deep timbre, his demeanor calm.

"Hey," I echoed back, feeling like some intruder. I was sure coming home to a stranger was, well, strange. Harley sniffed the air and looked around his cabin in confusion.

"I made some stew in your Crock-Pot, hope that was okay. I figured you'd appreciate something warm." Now, with him here, I felt self-conscious for digging through his freezer and cupboards for ingredients. He had an impressive pantry. I guessed that made sense since he was Mr. Prepared.

"No, that's great. It smells wonderful." His eyes darted toward the kitchen and back to me. A look dashed across his face I couldn't decipher.

"It won't be ready for a few hours, though. I-I didn't know when you'd be back." I glanced at the clock, noticing it was early afternoon. "Thanks for taking care of things last night. And for giving me a place to stay." I looked around the cabin, unsure of what to say next.

"Don't mention it. Are you okay if I hop in the shower quick? I'm filthy from work." He looked down at his hands in worry. Unable to get past the sound of his deep voice saying the word *filthy*, I simply nodded in answer.

His uniform was a long-sleeved tan shirt and army green pants. I was sure on the average person, it would look bland, maybe even dorky, but against Harley's olive complexion and muscles, it was way more attractive than it should be. Watching him walk to his bedroom, I picked up the book I'd been reading and waited for him to return. Ten minutes later, he emerged in a black-and-gray flannel with jeans. His dark hair was damp, and his beard looked perfect in what I could only imagine was beard oil, since it smelled fucking amazing. It stirred my feminine brain in a jostle of sensory overload, causing me to cross my legs to distract myself.

"Sorry 'bout that. How are you doing, though?" He walked closer to the couch and sat down beside me. Seeing him this close in snowy daylight made me swoon even more. His eyes were clear and full of concern. His spicy, woodsy scent filled the air between us, making a flutter run through my chest now that the smell was even closer.

"I'm totally fine." I smiled pathetically at him, not wanting to be treated like a wounded animal.

"We didn't have time to talk much last night before you fell asleep. Can I look at you?"

"Of course." Without hesitation, I uncrossed my legs and turned my body even closer to him. I didn't have a personal bubble to begin with, and I didn't mind him being close. I wanted him that way.

He scooted closer, our knees touching as he wrapped his fingers around my wrist to feel a pulse. Even the slight contact of our skin together caused a zing of warmth. He leaned in, counting the beats as his hazel gaze cast to my eyes, so he could make sure they dilated correctly. The direct eye contact this close made my stomach drop. His presence was magnetic. I had to fight myself from leaning into his warmth. His calm breathing, along with the rhythmic feeling of my pulse against his hand threatened to pull me into him. I wanted to crawl into his arms already.

"May I?" He gestured at my neck. I nodded and swept my hair out of the way, tugging at the neck of my sweater and exposing my bare shoulder. Harley swallowed heavily, his Adam's apple bobbing under his beard line. I wasn't sure if it was in response to my exposed skin or the violent-looking bruise that now splayed across the gentle slope of my neck. His hand hovered over the injury, barely a whisper of a touch.

"Just making sure it's not overly hot," he assured me. The warmth of his hand permeated my senses, causing me to focus on my breathing, so it didn't get too labored with him being so close.

"I wish I had some arnica oil," I said pensively, distracting myself.

"Yeah, or comfrey to help with the bruising," he added, squinting at my neck.

"Wait, how do you know about comfrey root?"

He shrugged. "Bush medicine. Nature is a healer."

My little witchy heart swooned at the idea of him knowing as much about herbs as I did. Before I could daydream of that, his hand brushed up my neck, making me breathless. "Not much would help with how close the bruise is to your artery."

It took my mind a second to catch up to what he'd said. All I could do was nod, feeling the absence of his energy when he pulled his hand away from my neck.

"What about your ribs? Any pain when you lift your arms? The second wave of the storm is rolling in, but if you need to get to a clinic, I can get you there." His eyes darted to the windows, noting the streaming snow that had been falling all afternoon.

"No, I didn't wake up to any pain. I'm fine."

"I get the sneaking suspicion you're the type to keep how much pain you're in a secret. You wouldn't tell me if you needed help, would you?"

"Nope!" I said with a smile, knowing it was going to taunt him.

He stared at me a moment longer. His fingers remained encircling my wrist for no reason other than to keep contact. The connection point between our skin felt like a warm hum. He nodded and pulled his hand away from my wrist. "Okay, well, for starters, we should get some meds in you for the inflammation in your neck." I followed him begrudgingly to the kitchen. He looked at the bottle on the counter, worried I'd refuse them.

"Thanks for the toast, by the way. And the towels. And for, you know . . . evidently carrying me to bed last night." I flung the pills in my mouth and swallowed quickly.

"Don't mention it. You must have been tired."

Thinking about how I'd gotten into his bed made fear slightly course through me. I was short, but I wouldn't consider myself a small woman. My grandma had always told me we could survive a potato famine because our ancestors had. I groaned internally thinking about it.

"I don't think I've ever been carried in my adult life. I'm kind of impressed you could pick me up."

Standing against the island across from me, he put his hands on the counter and leaned in wickedly. "Sweetheart, I've literally pulled grown ass men from freezing rapids. It was nothing." He looked me up and down with a cocked eyebrow. The moment sent a tingle down to in between my legs. He pushed off the counter and walked by me, his frame skimming mine while he passed. I bit my lower lip, trying not to notice.

"Right. Ranger rescue stuff," I said, trying not to sound flustered.

Harley sat diagonally from me at the end of the kitchen island. He grabbed an orange out of a bowl on the counter and offered me a piece of fruit. I refused since I didn't like oranges, and I didn't want to eat a banana in front of him. I was confident, but not that confident. His mannish hands hacked into the orange, expertly tearing the skin with ease.

"I have to ask . . . . What were you running from?" He looked up from his orange, a penetrating expression dancing through his eyes. He was onto me. I felt exposed and didn't want him to think I was some psychopath. I had to lie, to evade the truth. I didn't want Harley to think I was going to fly off the handle any second. Sure, I was a bit of a wild card. I mean, who drove aimlessly into the night in the depths of winter? Was I free-spirited? Sure. Unstable? No.

"Boston bores the shit out of me. I figured it was a Saturday, a nice drive would be fun. I was hoping to find a cool town to explore or maybe a fun event."

"You don't know anyone in Maine? You were driving for the hell of it?" His eyes squinted in disbelief, pulling at his dark brows. We had been through this before, but I understood I was a stranger in his home, and he had every right to be suspicious.

I met Harley's gaze and, with as much sincerity as I could muster, I offered a new slant on my journey. "Listen, I moved to Boston last year and I'm homesick. I grew up on the road a lot, and when I'm upset, that's what I do. I take to the road."

That wasn't a lie. I missed Maisie and my parents daily. It was a real struggle for me. Tyler was one of the few people I knew in Boston, so I thought that was why I'd tolerated him. I worked too much, so on my days off, I'd either vegged out or gone on a date with him. It helped he was a local who'd known fun things to do. I hadn't even set up a booth at the farmers' market to sell my boob vases, nor had I found a goddess circle or coven.

"Homesick? Where might home be for you?" Harley's head tilted in interest, his expression melting from suspicious to more curious.

"Texas." I smiled, waiting for his reaction.

A small smile tugged at Harley's lips, making me want to kiss them. "Texas? You don't say. That explains your capabilities of driving in the snow. May I ask what part?"

"Originally Lubbock, then Austin."

His brow furrowed. "You don't have much of an accent."

"That's a good thing. It usually comes out when I'm drunk or mad. I could say the same about you."

He chuckled and piled up the peel of his orange into a stack. "How did you end up on the East Coast?"

"I was born in Texas, but my dad is a bit of a vagabond, so I've been all over the place. Texas was always a home base though. Austin is where Maisie and my mom live, so I still consider it home. I graduated high school a year early and went to massage therapy school. I fell for the lie that you could work on a cruise ship and enjoy yourself. That shit is slave labor. I mean, a cruise ship is lawless. It's one of the few places you can eat lobster in the middle of the night with zero judgment. People would get so bloated and sunburnt from the beach and want me to massage them somehow. I'm not a miracle worker, Harley." I touched his forearm alongside my joke.

He smiled, clearly amused. "Sounds tricky."

"After that, I worked at an alien museum in New Mexico, as one does."

He nodded in good humor. "Naturally."

"I did yoga every day, so I was like, wait, why don't I teach this? So, I went to yoga teacher training in Rishikesh, India, for a few months."

His expression wasn't what I expected. Usually when I told a guy I was into yoga, their pervy brains immediately imagined me contorted in some sexy way, which was Western propaganda's fault. Most of the time, I could literally see the thoughts drain from their brain. But not Harley.

"What? No pervy downward dog joke?"

He shook his head. "No? I don't know a lot about yoga, but I know it's sacred to some people. Not just yoga pants. While we're on the topic, though, is this where you did nude yoga?"

"Yes, but it was all women. It was like, *Oh! Let's get naked under the full moon in sisterhood.* You know?"

"I don't, but I wish I did." He bit into an orange slice to hide his amusement.

Continuing before that open compliment could marinate any longer, I delved into more memories, unable to keep eye contact for a moment. "I loved India. I wish I had spent more time there. The people I met were interesting. Oh, and I almost joined a cult. Which is actually a high risk when you're doing yoga with a bunch of white people."

"I mean, statistically, that makes sense." He chuckled, his demeanor softening with every passing moment.

"To avoid joining a cult eating nothing but fruit in the jungle of Costa Rica, I got my ass in gear. Maisie had graduated by then, so to shock everyone, we went to college in Florida, where my grandma lived. We have all these ideas for business ventures, so a good foundation with an education sounded like a place to start."

"I can barely keep up with you. This is great." Harley leaned in, his broody exterior melting with my candidness.

I picked up a banana and twirled it around in circles on the counter to do something with my hands. "Well, it wasn't super great for long because my grandma died, as grandmas do. We had some good years together." I looked out his kitchen window, squinting in consideration. "It was kind of like a bizarre version of *The Golden Girls* but with better hair. The last year together was arguably the worst because my grandma kept taking melatonin mixed with Ambien and she'd sleepwalk to CVS in only a T-shirt. Like, a full-on Pooh bear situation. Even that's weird by Florida standards."

His brow creased. "I can't tell if you're being serious."

I tucked my chin slightly. "I never joke about Florida."

His brow furrowed even deeper in unease, my deadpan humor lost on him. "I'm sorry for your loss. That's tough. Basically, you were a hospice nurse and a college student?"

"Yeah, and a yoga instructor with unpredictable hours. Thank gods Maisie was there to help me. After we graduated, we moved back to Texas, and I helped her open a sex shop. It was her big dream. It's cheeky and woman centered, almost more of a boutique."

His eyes widened, causing me to smile mischievously.

"It's called Pretty Kitty," I all but purred. Harley's cabin roared with his laughter. It was the first time I'd seen him really laugh, and it was glorious! "They get phone calls with people thinking it's a veterinarian, which is a fun conversation."

He laughed even more. "That is fantastic!" He pointed at me while holding a piece of orange. "Remind me to never let my mom and Maisie meet. It would be pure chaos."

"Why is that?"

"She's a therapist. A sex therapist. She calls herself a sexapist. Damn! How many times can I say sex in a sentence?" He bit into another piece of orange and shook his head with a chuckle.

"Wait, your mom is a sex therapist?" I fought an amused grin.

"Yep, literally traumatizing. When I lost my virginity, she somehow found out and asked if I wanted to write a poem about the experience."

I blinked several times. "Wow."

"She hosts a senior sexuality class at the community center. She calls it *Lunges and Plunges: Bringing Sexual Mobility to Senior Lovers.*"

Now it was my turn to roar with laughter.

"Whenever I see a flyer for it, I want to gouge my eyes out. I constantly dodge awkward conversations about it with this guy, Terry, at my work. Apparently, he's a big fan. She also teaches a couple nights at the community college nearby. Everyone within an hour of here has talked to my mom about their sex life. It's horrible."

He got up to throw the orange peel away and washed his hands. "How did you get to Boston if you were handling your Pretty Kitty in Texas?"

I laughed again, feeling lighter than I had in months, and noticed he sat down even closer to me than before. "Ah, excellent question. What happened is my dad got in a terrible motorcycle accident in Maryland. I went there to stay with him while he recovered. My parents split when I was fourteen and he never remarried, so he was kind of on his own."

Harley nodded in concern.

"Now, I can assure you, nothing good happens in Maryland. Unless the guys from the Naval Academy are running around the city of Annapolis without shirts. But the whole situation had a silver lining because I was at the hospital so often, I landed a job there on the administration side of things. I would hang out at the cafeteria and nurses' station to listen to gossip. I started suggesting internal positions to some workers. HR caught wind of it and hired me to recruit for them. Pretty Kitty was running smoothly, so Maisie was okay with me stepping away."

"Let me get this right. You went from working at an alien museum and teaching yoga, to opening a sex shop, to hospital administration?"

"What, like it's hard?" I giggled. "In all seriousness, I'm good at reading people and I use it to help in whatever way I can. It turns out I'm good at finding people and placing them in the right role." I shrugged, feeling braggy.

"All you do is hire people? Like doctors?"

"Exactly, but in specialized roles in a clinical setting, it's extremely stressful and high stakes. It's hard because I must find the right person for the role and meet the requirements for the hospital. I usually wine and dine the candidates to accept the position. Luckily, I'm persuasive if I need to be." I smiled at Harley playfully.

"Good to know." He leaned back in his seat and crossed his arms over his chest.

"In Boston, there's a staffing firm called Tate Staffing. I usually call it Taint Staffing because I'm petty." We both snickered at my joke. "They reached out to me and offered me a role last summer. To be recruited as a recruiter is a compliment, so I jumped on the opportunity."

"And your dad recovered?"

"Yep. It felt right to move on. If I'm being honest, it's mostly because of the salary. I mean, I want to pay off student loans because America sucks. I'm basically done, and I can't wait to be free."

What. The. Fuck.

Why did I bring up student loan debt at a time like this? Debt? The only D-word I was interested in was dick!

"No, I totally get it. It makes sense you stay there even if you hate it. Having something like that looming over you would be stressful."

"Boston is such a medical hub. There's more than enough work to keep me busy for a lifetime." I stared off into nothing, letting the miserable idea invade my mind for a moment, shrugging in defeat. "I don't love Boston, though. It's not my vibe. I work too much, and the men are assholes."

He jutted his jaw up playfully. "Oh, you'll find the men in Maine are far superior." I nodded and looked at him bashfully while putting the banana back in the wooden bowl of fruit.

The snow outside was getting more intense, the sky darkening, covering what little daylight still clung on. The stormy light mixed with the lighting above the kitchen island shouldn't make anyone look attractive, but it made Harley look handsome as hell. It cast shadows of his browbone on his smooth complexion, darkening his eyes in a sexy way.

"Maine has been a mixed bag for me so far. Good thing I don't have a pet at home. Just some needy houseplants." I looked around, realizing he didn't have any plants or a pet either. "Do you have pets? I feel like this would be the perfect place for a dog."

A fleeting look of discomfort dashed across his face. "I had a dog, but he passed away last autumn."

"Oh, how sad! Was it unexpected or . . . ?"

"He was a good old boy, a goofy lab. He helped me out at work and everything, but it was his time."

"I am so sorry. What was his name?"

"Puck." Harley smiled to himself.

"Like a hockey puck?"

"Yeah. When I got him, he was little and black. He'd race around on the floor like a hockey puck, so I figured hey, let's go with that." I felt a roll of sympathy in my stomach for him. Harley gave me a pathetically small smile and changed the subject. "What about other needy things like children, boyfriends, or husbands? Do you have any of those?" He gave me a wry smile.

"Nope! I am completely unattached. What about you?"

"Same, but you probably already know that from snooping around my house."

"Hey now! You can't blame a girl! I had to make sure you weren't a serial killer with some sex dungeon."

"Ah, that's what I forgot to include in this cabin, a tasteful sex dungeon!" He smiled. "Well, Officer Boyd ran your record on your license, so I knew you weren't a criminal. I thought you were a drunk with how you were driving. That's why I called the police to begin with."

I let out a giggle. "I wasn't that bad! Okay, so no girlfriend?"

"Nope," he said, shaking his head.

"Boyfriend or non-binary partner?" I countered, trying to cover all my bases.

Harley tilted his head at me in amusement. A patient smile formed on his face. "I'm straight and an ally to people who aren't."

"Good. Good." I nodded. He looked at me expectedly.

"Oh me? Of course! Same! I'm an ally for sure."

A moment of silence fell between us, and it left me wondering why such a handsome guy was single. As if reading my mind, Harley continued, "Did you know Maine is hella old?" His tone was light and conversational. "The dating apps up here look like a damn bingo hall."

"Ah, is that so?"

"It's unfortunate. I'm sure it doesn't help that most people my age up this way are tourists or that I'm usually deep in the forest most days." He shrugged and tried to look casual, but I didn't buy it.

"You know what's worse than tourists?" I crinkled my nose to show disdain. "Accidental tourists who crash their car and ruin your plans."

"I promise you're not ruining my plans." He stood up and stretched, his flannel shirt lifting enough to show his lower abdomen, which looked hard with natural muscles. The deep V-shape of his torso going down to his pants made me swoon against my will. "Plus, I have Mondays and Tuesdays off. Weekends are usually the busiest times for us, but it's the slow season."

"Oh, I see." The idea of having Harley around here for two days filled me with a mix of anxiety and desire. What were we going to do alone in this cabin? Bible study? Bitch, please!

"Speaking of, since you don't need me to run you into town, I'm officially considering myself off duty. I'm going to take my gun off me. Don't freak out. Okay?"

I nodded and watched as he reached around behind himself to drag out a gun. Checking the safety, he unloaded the magazine calmly. From there, he held the gun in one hand and the magazine in the other. I reached in my bra to pull out my fixed blade to place it on the counter between us with a devious look. It was only an inch longer than my hand. The wooden hilt clanked on the granite counter. The leather sheath had a crescent moon stamped on it with my initials. "If we're disarming, I guess it's only fair." I gestured to the blade and folded my hand under my chin.

Harley stared from the blade back up to me and back to the blade. He licked his kissable lips in awe. "That was the last thing I was expecting." I bit back a smug giggle. He gestured to the blade on the counter. "I've never seen a woman with a . . . boob knife." He said the term with a mixture of awe and confusion. "That's strangely hot." He looked me dead in the eyes, overtaken by his own thoughts. He blinked, considering. "Well, if we're disarming." He reached into his front pocket and put his own knife on the counter.

"Touché," I purred. I leaned forward playfully. "I have throwing knives in my purse. Should I get those?"

"No, but let me go lock this up." He shook his head in disbelief, chuckling while he left all the blades on the kitchen counter and went to lock his gun up somewhere in his study.

Chapter Eleven

Harley

Kaylee leaned in the archway to my study, looking like an absolute angel. It was beyond me how someone could pull out a boob knife one moment and look so innocent the next.

"Oh, sorry, I never showed you around," I chided myself for being a shitty host. I'd basically left her here most of the day alone. Aside from buddies from college, she was the only person who had stayed here with me, and I'd apparently forgotten all my manners.

"Can I give you a tour?"

"I'd love that." As she slowly walked closer to me, her curves moved noticeably under her clothing. Her good luck necklace was nowhere in sight today.

"So, you snooped?" I asked, looking down at her.

She smiled and tossed her hair playfully. "Snoop is such a harsh word."

"Well, did you?" I couldn't help but smile, amused at her shamelessness.

Her face broke into a mischievous smile. "I sure did! And I have some questions." She touched my beard and walked past me. The bold contact made my groin pool with warmth. "Okay, so I love the whole lumberjack living out his ranger fantasy in a cabin vibe, but I need some backstory here."

I chuckled at her assessment of me. "You're familiar with the kitchen, mudroom, living room, and my bedroom," I offered. She flirtatiously lifted her eyebrows at the mention of my bedroom. I tried to not let that distract me. "So, this is my study, lots of books and a computer. Nothing much to see."

"Why did you kill Bambi?" she asked, pointing a glossy nail up toward the deer bust hanging on the wall over the door.

I let out an anxious sigh and scratched my head. Her eyes were knowing, not entirely innocent. She was giving me a hard time and enjoying watching me squirm.

"I didn't kill Bambi. I-I, you know, put him to sleep . . . for a while." A nervous noise escaped me while I glanced down at her, hoping she gave me a pass. She stood so close to me, our arms touched. "I helped nature out. Hunting is a responsible way to maintain health in herds, especially near winter."

She stared at me in disbelief. "Listen." I put my arm around her shoulders to draw her close, loving the instant buzz of having her side pressed against mine. Her sweet scent wafted into my senses immediately. "You can't appreciate the whole lumberjack, outdoorsy guy thing and not expect a hunter. It's part of the gig." She nodded in agreement, seeing my point. Her eyes drifted to my diplomas, and I instantly felt a wave of embarrassment. She leaned forward to read them, sounding out my last name. Oh, good freaking hell. This again.

"What kind of last name is Kouris? I haven't heard it before."

"Greek, from my dad's side. My mom's side is French Canadian or something." My voice sounded bored. Explaining the whole Greek thing got exhausting.

"Wait, have you seen—"

"*Mamma Mia*? Yeah, that shit is terrible, like the world needs any more ABBA." I would admit, I sounded like a frustrated douche for a split second.

She looked up at me, fighting a grin. "What about—"

"*My Big Fat Greek Wedding?*" I nodded, considering. "Less terrible, more accurate."

She threw her head back in a cackle, shocked I knew exactly where she was going with it. I couldn't help but notice how good it felt to hold her. She fit so perfectly against me, all small, soft, and warm.

"They forgot to mention the part about having your pappou getting drunk off Tsipouro then dancing to Shakira yelling, 'My hips don't lie!'" I said, imitating my grandfather's thick accent.

She smiled and stared at the diplomas a moment more before looking back up at me. "Do you speak Greek?"

"*Fysiká*," I answered, nodding yes. "My dad speaks to me in Greek sometimes. My yaya and pappou almost always. They insisted we learn it to maintain our traditions. Mostly, I use it to swear or talk to my family when I don't want others to know what we're saying."

I chuckled to myself, thinking about all the times my brother and I had blatantly talked about what girls we were trying to pick up right in front of them, never getting caught. Carson was a shitty wingman, though.

"Ah, so your sign saying 'Fuck Off' at the entrance of your cabin is in Greek?"

God, she was sharp! "Exactly."

"Gotcha. Kouris. I like it. Do you know what it means?"

I fought back a smirk. "You're never going to believe it, but it actually means forest dweller."

"Fitting! That's super interesting." Her bright eyes fixed on mine, taking in this new side of me she hadn't expected.

"What about you?"

"My last name is Waters. It's Irish. My family has zero culture like that, so I'm jealous."

"Don't be. I do like your last name though. Waters." I nodded, taking it in and remembering it from the incident report. Yeah, that fit her. She had a watery sense to her. She was calming and flowing like a cool stream, but other times she was tempestuous like the sea.

"Oh, and my middle name is Litha. It's another word for Midsummer. My mom is kind of earthy."

That was the last thing I was expecting. I couldn't help but love that. It made so much sense.

"Wait, Midsummer like the summer solstice?"

"Yeah, I was born on the summer solstice." She beamed, looking like the sun personified. I wanted to scoop her up with how cute she was.

"That's cool! You know, I appreciate the solstices and equinoxes more than traditional holidays. I celebrate them and Arbor Day instead of Thanksgiving. It drives everyone nuts. But I mean, we are on Earth, so we should observe the cycles of nature. I think it's important to stop and take in the experience of what it's like to live a life within nature, not separate from it. You know? Even if it's something simple, like watching a sunset."

Kaylee looked up at me with a knowing smile. "Exactly."

We scanned each other, feeling the pull between us. My gaze lowered to her lips, and I caught myself leaning in to kiss her. Trying to be a gentleman, I sidestepped and released her from my embrace as I pretended to fix something on my desk. One red fingernail pointed again, but this time to a photo of Carson and me on the wall by my diplomas. "Is that your brother drawing a dick on your face?"

"Yep, you can't even imagine what I did to get back at him. It involved raw hot dogs and duct tape. He's still missing leg hair." That made her giggle.

We exited the office, and I showed her the bathroom, which was mostly white with a cool oval window I'd put in to make it feel unique. It had been a total pain in the ass, but worth it. While standing in the spare room with all my random stuff, she touched various packs hanging on the wall, inspecting everything in confusion and curiosity.

"I will be honest with you, Harley. This room gives me anxiety," she joked while staring at my weights and copious amounts of gear on hooks and in piles. "It's almost like if a junk drawer were a room. Also, proof you are indeed a bachelor." She playfully patted my chest and walked back toward the living room. She wasn't wrong. "All jokes aside, thanks for the official tour. All one level? No creepy basement?" she asked over her shoulder.

"One and done." Feeling clocked, I put my hands in my pockets.

"Humble." Sorting through her thoughts, she continued, "I like it. You have enough gear to hike Mount Everest. Have you done something like that?" she asked, tossing her hair while walking in front of me. I glanced at her ass, the recoil of the softness of it moving with each step. Hot damn! The shape of her body made my mind sputter. She was wearing black leggings that showed off her sexy legs.

"Hey now, you got to see all my stuff, but I have no clue what your place is like," I said, distracting myself from her backside.

"My place feels a bit disjointed, to be honest. I haven't settled in and made it my own. My apartment is this super swanky, modern monstrosity in downtown Boston. I hate it. It feels soulless, and there isn't much room for all my pottery stuff."

This was news to me. "Pottery?"

"Yeah, I make all sorts of ceramics." Her beautiful face broke into a spontaneous grin in recollection. "My best sellers are some mugs and vases I make for Maisie's shop. They're shaped like certain body parts, if you catch my drift."

The thought of Kaylee at a pottery wheel with her hair all up in a wild, messy bun while she leaned over, stroking clay into a dick vase crashed into my head. I felt the smile spread across my face, too. She stared at me with a knowing smirk.

"I know, it's random to have boob mugs, but everyone loves boobs!" She shrugged and giggled some more. Her airy trill of laughter filled up the space between us.

"You're right. I mean, they're a top three favorite of mine." I shot her a look that made her cross her legs from where she now sat by me on the couch.

"Before Boston, I even had a booth at a farmers' market. I make other things too, not just dirty stuff. I even make these cool incense holders. Someday I'd like to get a pottery shed so it doesn't take over my living space. Until then, I make do."

God, she was so adorable. Each moment she spent here, she appeared lighter and happier. The slight shadows under her eyes vanished more and more. It was a contrast to the bruise on her neck that darkened. I reminded myself a car wreck had hurt her just yesterday and to stop being such a guy.

"Besides pottery, what do you do for fun?"

She shrugged. "Pretty much anything. Oh, except amusement parks. I love rollercoasters but can't stand the screaming children. They're too sticky and loud." She shuddered dramatically. "I love bookstores, roller derby, drag queen bingo, concerts. I love baseball."

"Drag queen bingo?"

"Yep, it's a blast!"

"You seem so . . ."

"Weird?" she offered brightly.

"That's not the exact word. I don't know . . . free? When I met you, it was confusing because you drove like a crazy person, but your behavior was rather cautious." I squinted, unsure if I was being a dick.

"Oh, well . . . being a woman is a risk."

"I get that, I really do, and I'm not going to sit here and say 'not all men' because it's certainly enough men that harm women. But you were so careful. It's obvious you live a full life that isn't very cautious, so I'm trying to wrap my head around it." I let out a breath with my confession.

An unpleasant look floated across her face, troubling her eyes for a split second. She licked her lips in uncertainty. "Look, I had to watch my grandma pass away and rehab my dad from the motorcycle accident. I didn't know if he'd live through it. I also watched my best friend go through a horrible divorce, so I think I'm a little shell-shocked." Her voice cracked toward the end.

No. Fuck! God dammit, Harley, you pushed her there.

"I-I'm sorry if I made you feel you owed me an explanation." Feeling even more insensitive, I shook my head at my blunder. "I'm sorry you've been through all that. You're resilient. It's impressive, truly."

She nodded, looking out the window with her brows pulled together.

"Is that what you're running from?" I asked, continuing my dumbassery.

"I'm not running from anything. I was homesick." She gave me a small, uncomfortable smile. Immediately changing the subject, she asked, "Wait, have you hiked Mount Everest?"

"I haven't, but I spent half a year hiking the entire Appalachian Trail."

Her eyes widened at this juicy bit of information. "Wait, what's your trail name?"

"I mean, I could tell you, but then you'd know the most embarrassing thing about me. Plus, that's privileged information you only find out the hard way."

"The hard way being . . ." She made a rolling gesture with her hand toward me. ". . . hiking the span of almost all the United States from north to south?" Her tone was deep in sarcasm, but it impressed me how much she knew about it.

"Exactly."

"Oh, well yeah, there's nothing I want to know enough that's worth trotting on a trail like a donkey for half a year. For free."

Was she teasing me? Why did I like this so much?

We talked for the better half of the afternoon. Hours upon hours passed while we laughed and reminisced about parts of our life. No awkward pauses or touchy subjects came up, mostly funny stories and important details. The snow would come in waves, building upon itself. The sun moved, breaking past the storm clouds in intervals. Its light cast shadows in different spots across the cabin as the day progressed. Its changing position was the only signal of the world outside of our little bubble of flirtation and discovery.

The banter was flirty, and I found out a lot about her. She considered herself a fellow introvert, but explained she was often mistaken as an extrovert because she was friendly. Her parents split when she'd been in middle school but remained cordial. Apparently, they were biker hippies. She also had a penchant for medieval history and Celtic folklore, but she had yet to travel to Europe.

"You'd love Greece. It's gorgeous and the people are welcoming."

"I didn't even think of that. You've probably been there, huh?"

"Yeah, we visit every so often. We still have some family there."

A moment of silence passed. I ripped myself back to the moment, smashing down the thought of Kaylee in a sundress on the hilly islands of the Mediterranean. I fleetingly wondered if the blue waters of the sea would make her eyes appear even more blue or a darker gray.

"I want to see all those ancient ruins." She ran her hand through her hair. "Perhaps even stumble upon the Oracle of Delphi."

"Ah, yes, oracles. They're so reliable." I rolled my eyes teasingly.

She lifted a blonde eyebrow. "Do you not believe in oracles?"

I shrugged, unsure.

She tilted her head. "Have you ever had your tarot cards read?" I shook my head. She playfully leaned forward. "Want to change that?"

She beamed with the biggest smile I'd seen on her face, reaching all the way to her eyes, lighting them up in unshakable beauty. I found myself awestruck and only able to nod. The idea of this lit Kaylee up inside and it was palpable. Moments later, she emerged from my room, explaining she always kept a deck in her purse. Apparently, on top of being gorgeous, she was a damn fortune teller. Sweet lord, I couldn't keep up with her. But I wanted to.

"Okay, I know this is a long shot, but do you have any candles?"

I retrieved three from a hall closet. "These are emergency pillar candles made of beeswax. Does that work?"

She stared at my hands clutching the yellow candles. "Yes! May I suggest plates or mason jars if you don't have candleholders?"

I nodded and retrieved some from the kitchen. "You know, Kaylee, you're pretty resourceful yourself."

"Am I?" she replied while taking her nail to carve something into the side of one candle.

"Yes, you continue to surprise me. What's that?"

"Oh, sorry. Habit. I carved a sigil into the wax," she explained, looking down at it.

"What's a sigil? Like a rune?"

"Exactly, it's like a personalized symbol you use in witchy, spiritual stuff. This is for protection." She turned it so I could see it.

"Couldn't hurt." I shrugged, making her roll her lips together to hide a pleased smile.

We sat on the ground, my red rug softening where we found ourselves cross-legged with the coffee table between us. I ignited the fireplace while I was lighting the candles. They flickered with dancing flames—one on a small plate, the other in a mason jar, and the third in a shallow bowl. The candlelight made Kaylee's features even more lovely. The sun dipped behind the pine trees with dusk in the windows of the rooms behind her, making her look ethereal in the dimming cabin.

With her delicate hands, she pulled a deck of cards from a leather holder that had a crescent moon stamped on it. "That matches your knife."

"You notice little details about me. I like that about you. I made friends with a leathersmith at a Renaissance festival one summer, and she hooked me up with customized accessories in trade for tarot readings." Before I could ask her more of the story, she went on, "Do you have a specific question in mind? An area in your life you'd like some clarity?"

I shrugged, feeling uncertain and suddenly shy. I had only seen this in the movies. "Not really. I guess whatever wants to come out?"

"Do you have a mental happy place you like to visit?" she prompted.

"Yeah, I suppose so." I felt weird admitting it.

Her mouth twisted into a grin as her gaze cast down at the cards while she overhand shuffled. "Let me guess, the base of a tall tree? Your favorite tree?"

"How did you—"

She grinned again, still watching the cards move in her hands. "I know you, Harley. Sure, we just met, but I get you, probably more than you know." She looked at me, eyes twinkling. "But I doubt your soul tree isn't something as pedestrian as a pine."

"You're right. It's a giant sequoia, from my time on the West Coast."

"I love that. Okay, imagine yourself there, completely safe and relaxed." Without hesitating, I did what she'd said, feeling instantly calmer and not the least bit silly sitting there with my eyes closed. "Now imagine a force protecting you. Whatever comes to mind is okay. Some people see white light or a bubble."

I imagined sitting at the base of the sequoia, the warm sunset casting light through the forest and on my face. I could almost smell the distinct damp earth and woods from my memories. Running with the visualization, I imagined the tree's branches bending downward, far past where they usually grew, shielding me like a tent. The visual grew darker, more cocooned. I took a deep breath, feeling calmer and protected while shrouded by the sequoia.

As if reading my mind, Kaylee's voice floated through my head. "You could even imagine branches of the tree shielding you." Too calm to smile, I stayed suspended in the visual, somewhere between my mind's eye and reality. Kaylee let me stay there for a few more breaths then calmly said, "Okay, do you feel safe to start?" Unwilling to leave the feeling, I nodded and sat up straighter, my eyes remaining closed indulgently.

"Okay, take a deep breath and imagine all that good energy filling up the surrounding space." Soon after, I heard her bridge shuffling the cards expertly, like a seasoned blackjack dealer in Vegas. With each slap of the cards on one another, the scent of cinnamon, clove, or some other spice wafted in my senses. I opened my eyes slowly, watching her place several cards in a formation that probably had some meaning behind it. The backs of them were blue with large white stars. Each one had a slight swoop from years of shuffling, proving how well-loved they were.

"Okay, so this card symbolizes you." Her moonstone ring-clad pointer finger tapped a card that was face down. I nodded in understanding, and she flipped it over. "Knight of Rods, how fitting." A smile spread across her face. "In most tarot decks, this figure is called the Knight of Wands, but in this one, they call it a rod instead. Aside from that nerdy tidbit, the Knight of Wands depicts a male figure that is strong, virile, confident, lovable, and willing to help others. He is incessant about moving forward on his path, even though he is uncertain of the outcome." A delicate blonde eyebrow raised in amusement. The card depicted a man in armor with a branch of wood over his shoulder that looked awfully like an obnoxiously gigantic dick. I gulped.

"And this card represents what's crossing you, essentially what's blocking you or making things difficult." She flipped over the card and puffed air out of her nose in amusement. "Ah, yes, Knight of Cups. A man who is in touch with his emotions, if not ruled by them sometimes. Charming, of course, and chivalrous. Sometimes sullen, moody, but overall, an excellent omen that your power lies in following your heart and intuition. Your instincts."

Her gaze moved from the cards and locked with mine, piercing with their pale glimmer. The calm from my meditation evaporated. This wasn't some party trick? I felt exposed. Were these tarot cards ruining my game now, too? First Sherry at the police station, then my walkie-talkie in the truck, after that the washing machine. Who knew so many things could be a pain in the ass?

"So, I'm a charming asshat who gets emo sometimes?"

Kaylee shrugged like I wasn't totally off base. "I see someone who has complex emotions but overall great intentions."

"What about the others?" I gestured to the rest of the table.

"These three cards are what I call the truthful trio. They show what has hurt you in the past, what keeps you stuck, and what you need to resolve to move forward." My stomach lurched in anxiety. I hadn't known it was going to be this deep, dammit! She flipped over cards back-to-back, her brow scrunching in concern. "Three of Swords, Five of Cups, and Five of Wands. Heavy, heavy stuff." She tilted her head in consideration, running her pointer finger over her lips before she looked up at me with deeply sympathetic eyes. "That must've been quite the quarrel and loss. I'm so sorry."

I stared at the traitorous tarot cards and back up to her, unable to unfreeze myself from the shock. How could she possibly know this? How could she know how big of an asshole my brother was?

She picked up the Five of Wands card specifically, shaking it while gathering her thoughts. "Sometimes you need to forgive someone because they didn't know any better, even if you think they should have. Does that make sense?"

"Yeah, it does." I nodded, freaked out that her words rang true.

She thankfully moved on, gesturing to the card on her far left. "This is your more recent past." She turned it over. It read The Chariot at the top, from what I could tell.

I looked up at her in confusion. "Chariot? Like a car?"

"Sure, it could be a car." Her mouth twitched. "But what it signifies is in your recent past. You overcame challenges and maintained control over your surroundings. The Chariot is all about acting out of sheer willpower and deciding on a course of action, a sense of anticipation, and perhaps even a commitment of sorts. It also explains the urgency in the Knight of Wands and how it conflicts with the Knight of Cups, wanting to contemplate before action. I see a man torn, interrupted."

From where she leaned and pointed at the cards, she sat upright and took a long sip of her drink. The light of the candles and sunset caught the glass and refracted trace glimmers on her neck and cheek. In that moment, in the flames, she looked ancient and mystical. A seer in modern times, wedged into my mundane life.

Knowing I was gazing at her, Kaylee tilted her head calmly. "You're safe to say whatever it is you're thinking."

"How I see it? This card signifies me deciding to rescue you when your chariot crashed. It was a decision I didn't have a lot of time to make, and now I feel weird, I guess. I'm not used to having someone around. Someone . . . like you." I gulped, trying to calm myself down from how naked I felt.

She nodded in agreement and consideration, then tapped the card in the middle. "This is your present situation, at this very moment." The instant she turned the card around, her eyes widened in shock before squinting. "The Empress. She signifies a feminine presence in your life."

"You don't say?" My voice dripped with sarcasm. I stared at the card that had a lady sitting on a chair with golden hair and a crescent moon under one foot. I mean, could this be any more accurate? It was totally Kaylee.

She licked her lips and tried to maintain a poker face. "The Empress represents a deeply sensual attraction, a connection that encourages growth, a feminine aspect that is warm and nurturing, usually considered an earth goddess personified. She is creative, kind, and vibrantly alive."

"I agree." I stared at Kaylee, trying to calm the passion rising in my body.

This response made her swallow hard and clear her throat. The sexual tension building between us was once again strong and visceral. Kaylee trembled while reaching for the next card, unable to keep up the formality. "This card represents your near future." Her pale hand flipped it over resolutely. Two naked figures embraced in a field of calla lilies, a blonde woman and dark-haired man with a beard, and at the top of the card it read: The Lovers. Kaylee swallowed hard again, shaken and stunned. Her beautiful lips parted ever so slightly in tense shock while her gray eyes moved up to mine. She was speechless.

Chapter Twelve

Kaylee

"The fates are subtle, aren't they?" I picked up the cards, hoping Harley didn't notice my shaky hands. What was supposed to be flirty and fun, had turned downright eerie. I hadn't thought throwing the cards down for Harley would feel that powerful, but it did. I was realizing everything around Harley was vibrant.

From where he sat, the fireplace roared with a blaze behind him, making him look even more masculine. The flames danced beyond his wide shoulders, casting a warm glow all around him. While he'd been centering himself before the reading, I could stare at how handsome he was without the threat of being sucked into his magnetic gaze. But after a reading like that, I felt like I was right back in the thick of it. Harley was all-consuming, and I had to fight to not crawl over the coffee table to get to him.

The piece of amethyst crystal radiated heat next to my heart in my bra. I had switched out the green aventurine when I'd grabbed my tarot deck, sensing what energy I needed for the evening. Without thinking, I reached in my bra to pull it out and placed it on top of the tarot cards. Harley's jaw slacked.

"Did you . . ." He pointed in disbelief. "Did you just pull a crystal out of your bra?"

I was unable to control myself, and my cackle echoed from the beams of the cabin. "Why yes! Of course!" I reached in and pulled out a piece of labradorite stone as well. Its schiller caught the light from the fire, flashing a slight rainbow across the dark gray stone. "It brings a whole new meaning to rock tit, doesn't it?" I joked before playfully placing the labradorite in Harley's hand across the coffee table. He stared at me, dumbfounded, then at the stone, then back at me.

Everyone in my life was used to finding crystals everywhere near me, especially in my bed, car, and bra. Hell, even my messy bun sometimes housed a piece of optical calcite when I had a migraine. All the stones were less than two inches in size, so I could easily tuck them into places. I didn't realize Harley hadn't caught onto this quirk. Seeing his shocked reaction was making my day.

I added, "Listen, women's clothing rarely has pockets, so I get creative. Plus, it's nice to have them close."

He chuckled and looked down at the stone in his palm, inspecting the labradorite's magical display of rainbows. He then reverently brought it to his mouth, kissing it respectfully before handing it back to me with an intense look. My heart fluttered at the sight of it. Why was that so endearing? "You're unlike anyone I've ever met. This explains a lot. When I pulled you from your car, something felt hard."

"Oh yeah, I also had the knife in my bra yesterday." I shrugged.

"A boob knife and titty rocks. Your priorities astound me!" He looked up at the ceiling, shaking his head with a smile.

"You could have been a serial killer! We've been over this, Harley!" I jabbed playfully.

"Sweet Zeus! You're the more dangerous one! You could have bashed me over the head with a rock at any moment, woman."

I leaned forward and corrected lightheartedly, "They're stones, not rocks."

"I'm sorry, *stones*." His gaze drifted to my mouth, lingering for a moment before looking into my eyes. I smiled at him innocently, loving how the sparks were flying between us.

"What's important is I have no more blades in my bra, and you have all my titty crystals now. So, we're good. I am hungry, though." I side-eyed the kitchen to divert away from any conversation about tarot or my tits.

Dinner was mostly dancing around the reading and the rising tension between us. We were both hyperaware of each other, down to the smallest gesture. The lustful feeling rising in my body, building between my legs, was undeniable.

My attempt at winning Harley's heart through his stomach was working. I got the feeling he was trying not to devour the hot meal impolitely. Even being closed off most of the time, he gushed about how good it tasted. I wouldn't consider myself a domestic type by any stretch of the imagination, but something deep in me enjoyed seeing a man inhale my cooking. His huge hands tearing bread into pieces shouldn't be hot, but here I was, swooning over it.

Being a straight woman was a fucking trip sometimes.

Harley spent the rest of dinner trying to clarify the difference between a park and forest ranger. Honestly, I didn't get it myself, but by the gist of it was he wasn't like a tour guide. Instead, he was involved with maintaining the integrity of the biodiversity of the national forest. He also did community outreach programs to educate people on things like wildfires, bear safety, and survival skills. He assisted with search and rescue, and by the sounds of it, he was a strange mix of a professional tree hugger and lumberjack who could cite people who fucked with the forest.

After dinner, he proclaimed he was going to clean up because I'd cooked. As much as I wanted to gawk at his sexy shoulders doing dishes, I fought the urge. Not knowing what to do with myself, I sat down on the couch and pulled my phone out, only to notice I had a backlog of texts to catch up on. I looked at the conversation with Tyler and sighed at the idea of dealing with the most persistent cock thistle I'd ever had the displeasure of knowing.

Tyler: Angel, I'm an alpha. You can't hold it against me.
Tyler: Kay, answer me. It's not what you think.
Tyler: Why are you being like this?

I cleared all three texts from Tyler with a disgusted scowl. I hated being called Kay. He inevitably realized I'd seen his texts, causing him to launch new ones at me.

Tyler: Will you please answer me? Are you mad?
Tyler: Maisie commented a rat emoji on my most recent post. What the fuck?

I snickered at the rat emoji detail and typed my reply.

Me: I didn't trust you, and you proved the suspicion correct. Maybe lock the door next time.

I let out a deep sigh. I felt more annoyed than anything. My phone buzzed with a new text.

Tyler: You fucking bitch! You were always such a frosty ice queen. You're just hating on an alpha.

I let out an evil, little laugh and continued my assault on his ego.

Me: I'm not interested in continuing a conversation with you. I already lowered my standards by giving you my number. I can't lower them any further while being disrespected. I was distant because I didn't trust you. Oh,

and a true alpha doesn't need to announce they're an alpha. You're not a damn werewolf! I have a real alpha with me right now. He's literally starting a fire in a cabin he built with his own hands. That's so much hotter than your snobby life your daddy handed to you. Grow the fuck up and get some therapy. If we run into each other at work, leave me the fuck alone. You blew it.

I was so glad to be done with him. So. Fucking. Glad.
Before I could close out of the conversation, Tyler shot back a text.

Tyler: I'm not reading all of that.

I let out a sigh and swiped it away, hiding it from my inbox. I opened a text from my mom asking how I was doing and shot back a quick message that I was fine. Both exchanges made me feel gross. I didn't want to talk to Tyler, and I didn't enjoy hiding things from my mom. Sure, I was a grown ass adult, but it felt weird being here without her knowing. I didn't want to stress her out, so I planned on telling her when this was all done and over.

I sent a dorky selfie to Maisie, positioning my phone in my lap so she could see the antler chandelier directly above my head. I flared my nostrils and tilted my head to make a double chin. It was truly unflattering, which was exactly how all selfies should be if they were going to your BFF. Along with the antler selfie, I sent a text.

Me: feeling horn-y.

Harley came in and added existing wood to the flames in the fireplace. There was an air of concentration and determination about him. He kneeled in silence and began his ritual of stoking the fire to an impressive blaze just like he'd done when we'd lit the candles for the tarot reading. All his actions had measured confidence and familiarity with the process. It was quite impressive how quickly flames licked the wood, setting the materials ablaze. Warm light cast across the room, and with it, a faint smell of something sweet wafted in my senses.

From where he crouched, he turned to look back at me over his shoulder. A primal expression crept across his face, making his features sharper than I had seen them. He set his jaw hard, his lush lips parted, and his eyes looked golden with the flames reflecting in them. He stood up, his body fluid and almost predatory. Without thinking, I got up from the couch to meet him by the fire. I wanted to escape into the warmth with Harley.

"The fire should keep us warm. I'm using maple to keep it burning through the night in case the storm knocks out power." He gestured toward his room. "You can sleep in my bed, which has lots of warm covers."

He ruined a sexy moment with logic and planning. This wasn't the right time for that sort of thing. I scoffed at him in frustration. "I thought you said you had a bed for me?"

"I do. It just so happens to be mine." His tone was now husky and testing. His piercing eyes caused my body to flood with desire. I felt my mouth open in response to how attractive that was. Too stunned to banter, I stared at him for a moment longer.

"Where will you be sleeping?" I finally asked.

"I'll sleep out here again." He gestured toward the couch.

"Wait, you don't have a guest room or something?" I pointed to the rooms behind me, realizing I hadn't seen a bed in the spare room.

"No, why would I? For my dirtbag friends?"

"Well, that's kind of rude, don't you think?"

Harley shook his head. "Dirtbag is a term of endearment. It's a phrase people use if they make their whole life about their next adventure. You know, like rock climbers who stay out in the desert for weeks on end. When my friends from college come to visit, we don't stay indoors, so why would I need a bed for them?"

He had a point. It made it even more frustrating how logically he explained it. It didn't make me feel any less of a burden. He stared at me, a mixture of offended and frustrated. "I can handle a damn couch. I've slept on ice-packed snow. I've spent days sleeping on boats. Shit, I even slept in a hammock in the rain by choice. I can live without staying in my room," he said gruffly.

His large hands rested on his hips in dominant assurance, making my core ache for him before I snapped back into the moment. "Besides, we both know I won't let you sleep somewhere that isn't a bed while you're my guest." He cocked his jaw at the side of the house where his bedroom was. "I insist you sleep in there."

I scoffed, "Look, I get that I'm a pain-in-the-ass houseguest from hell and that I'm the last person you'd want to be stuck with. But if you could be a little less bossy, it might be better while we're stuck together. That's all."

His jaw set in a stern expression. "What do you mean, you're the last person I'd want to be stuck with?" He was visibly seething at this accusation, but I couldn't understand why.

"I'm not some outdoorsy girl who knows how to distinguish animal prints or what wood burns the hottest. I don't have L.L. Bean boots and four-wheel drive. To you, I'm some chick who drove her dumb, little car into a snowstorm like a banshee. Now you're forced to shelter me because your tiny-ass town doesn't have lodging. I get it. I'm a pain in the ass. You are stuck with me, and I am sorry. Okay, Harley? I'm sorry!"

Harley took a few steps closer, his wide frame instantly blotting out the world around me, encompassing my entire view with his sheer mass. His voice was low and terse, nothing more than a pained murmur. "Don't." He pursed his lips together to collect himself, his jaw muscles moving while he clenched his teeth. He began again after a deep breath. "Don't for one second think I don't want you here with me. That I don't . . . want you." His eyes simmered. The sight of him ensnared in his fervor made a rush of desire flood my body, from my chest to between my legs.

I took a deep breath to gather myself. "What do you mean?"

Without answering, he stepped even closer. My breasts dragged against his ribs with my shallow breathing. He looked down at where our chests touched, and his gaze traveled back up to mine. His large hands held my face while he lowered his mouth to mine in a searing kiss. What was slow and intense quickly turned into a dizzying sway of lust. I could feel his arms surround me, snaking around my waist, bringing me on my tippy toes, closer to him.

He was all I could sense. His taste, his smooth lips, his slightly rough beard against my soft face. Still kissing, he walked us back, pushing me against the cool stones of the wall by the fireplace. The hard planes of his body against me paired with the even harder stones on my back made me feel soft and deliciously trapped. A sudden chill ran down my spine from the cooled stones, while his warmth melted into me. The moan of my reaction echoed into our kiss, causing him to groan in response. He pulled apart from the kiss and stepped backwards, hesitant to stop touching my face.

"I'm sorry." His deep voice was barely above a whisper while he ran a thumb down my jaw before he raked his hand through his hair.

"Don't be." I felt breathy and empty in his absence. I stood still, completely stunned against the stones for a few more moments.

If he could make me feel that way with one kiss, I couldn't imagine what he'd be like in other ways. I wanted to know, though. I walked closer and reached up to touch his beard, noticing the skin above it on his cheek was smooth. One of his large hands covered mine and held it to his face. He turned his head, gently kissing my palm. The entire time, he kept eye contact, gauging me. His eyes were steady pools of intensity, measuring me in every moment. They drifted to the bruise on my neck and back to my lips.

"I'm ok. It doesn't hurt," I muttered.

Harley moved my hand off his face and held it in a courtly manner before slowly kissing the top of it. His eyes teemed with passion, never leaving mine. "Forgive me. You're hurt and far from home. I'll try to be a gentleman." He softly dropped my hand and took a step back.

I nodded, unsure of what had happened and still dizzy from the kiss.

He wanted me, but he was trying to prove something. Was he trying to gain my trust? I stepped back, looking him up and down. I could feel his yearning for me radiating off him in waves. He put his hands in his pockets. I plucked my phone off the couch, walking toward the bedroom door, feeling his gaze on my ass the entire way there.

I was ensnared by him. It felt like he was pulling back just to make me want more. Every touch, every prolonged moment of eye contact, even down to the way his words echoed in my brain begged me to reexamine their meaning. Everything felt intentional but beyond my full understanding.

It was then I realized . . . the animals in this forest weren't the only things Harley was hunting.

Chapter Thirteen

Harley

Refraining from continuing to kiss Kaylee was one of the hardest things I'd had to do in a very long time. Everything in me wanted to have her, all of her. I had to remind myself she was vulnerable here in my cabin, in my town, and without a car. She was also recovering from the wreck, even if she refused to admit it. She had to feel sore or tired from that much adrenaline. Kaylee deserved space and rest.

I wanted to build her a fire so I could show her I was a provider and protector. Something in me wanted to take care of her. Apparently, fire was the only way men could communicate we cared still to this day, which made me feel like a Neanderthal. It was an instinct I couldn't push away. I knew she could hold her own, but that didn't mean she didn't deserve to be treated well.

She was complex and an enigma: open but guarded, shy but blunt, confident but coy. I wanted to unravel her.

I wanted to get to know all about her life. Little by little, I felt I was. I'd be lying if I didn't acknowledge I wanted to make her feel good and cared for. Stress, city life, and work had drained her. She needed some respite and someone to go down on her. It was as simple as that. I wanted to help bring her back to herself by giving her some pleasure and safety. I wanted to awaken and heal her with my touch.

On some radar I possessed, I knew she hadn't felt pleasure in quite some time. I could sense it. She wasn't good at masking her emotions, and from the moment I'd seen her, her face would twist into a worried expression more often than I'd like. Her smooth forehead would crinkle with concern and her eyes would cast over like a thundercloud. I wasn't sure what was troubling her so much, aside from her wreck.

I spared her the nerdy details about how I'd expertly constructed the fire and how the wood I'd used was the perfect level of dryness to prevent smoke. I refrained from mentioning that I'd felled the trees to ensure the integrity of the specimens in the forest and had split the wood myself. There was no need to mention that I had three plans for extinguishing the fire, just in case. And I wouldn't tell her that if the storm knocked out the power, I had specifically designed this fireplace to feed heat to the entire cabin and that I had a backup generator. No, no, I got the feeling she wouldn't care about all my antics, but eventually, hopefully, she'd fully understand how truly safe she was with me.

I felt calmer after the fire was roaring once again. She was sitting on my couch, staring at me, or perhaps the fire. She had this ridiculous notion that she was a burden or unwelcome. That couldn't be further from the truth, so I'd shown her how much I wanted her. On sheer instinct, I'd kissed her. The feeling of her soft body against mine, her silky lips parting while her wild feminine sounds had escaped her . . . The whole moment had damn near sent me over the edge because it had given me a small taste of just how electric it would be to have more of her.

Kissing Kaylee had felt like a fever dream and way more intense than I could have ever imagined. All I wanted for the foreseeable future was the flames and her body. I'd realized how touch starved I was when she'd placed her hand on my face. It had been so soft, her gaze hypnotic. It had been too long since someone had touched me that way. It had sent a deep ache through me. If it were up to me, I'd be having sex with her as much as I could until she had to leave. Admittedly, the thought of her leaving put an unfamiliar pain in my chest.

Even on a practical level, it made sense for us to stay together. My cabin could be her haven of sorts. We had nothing but free time, time I hoped I could spend making her relax and heal. Selfishly, I wanted more of her cooking. Walking into my cabin only to smell that delicious meal had made me want to throw her over my shoulder like a caveman.

I needed to get over my fear of taking advantage of her or hurting her neck. I didn't know where to go from here. She was confusing, comfortable one moment and questioning everything the next. I wanted her to sort things out on her end. I wanted her to feel truly safe before I could even entertain the nasty ideas in my head.

She retreated to my room before I could get ready for bed. I, luckily, had clean clothes in a hamper that I pulled on to sleep in, and I brushed my teeth in the other bathroom. Now on the couch, I was alone with only my thoughts and the falling snow. The notion of Kaylee in my bed, in between the sheets, made my dick twitch. I groaned, frustrated with myself and the situation. I put a pillow over my face to distract myself from my raging hard-on. After a few minutes, I broke out my trusted method of listing all the state capitals.

Alabama . . . Montgomery

Alaska . . . Juneau

Arizona . . . Phoenix

Arkansas . . . Little Rock

I fell into an anxious sleep. I felt as if it split me in half. One part of me was worried about Kaylee, the other about the fire blazing in front of me while I slept. When I'd lit it, I'd thought I'd be able to sit in front of it like a civilized man and talk a bit. Instead, I'd grabbed her like an animal and pressed her against the fireplace until she'd moaned.

It hadn't gone as planned, but I didn't want to douse the fire and waste the wood, so I played the dangerous game of nodding off while the coals died. Every half hour, I'd rip into consciousness in a semi-panicked state, only to check my surroundings to find the fire burning on. I was almost too good at making a steady fire at this point.

Around 2 a.m., the fire finally went out. My sleep deepened enough that I didn't come out of it until morning. The snow had fallen at least a foot overnight, so I cleared my land the best I could, pushing the snow off my road, creating a path from the deck to the barn. I also plowed around the area because several cabins nearby were unoccupied during the winter, so I tried to maintain what I could to be helpful.

I'd come in between tasks to check to see if Kaylee was out of my bedroom. When she emerged, she wore a crimson sweater that brought the blush out of her cheeks. I had to fight the urge to hold her face to feel the flush.

"Sorry, I slept in," she said bashfully, walking toward me.

"No worries, I'm glad you're getting rest." We stared at each other for a few moments. Thoughts raced through my head. Flashes of the kiss last night, how her breasts had felt against my chest, and how I'd promised to be a gentleman. With her here, right in front of me, it was harder and harder to maintain indifference.

"Can I see your neck?" I gestured to her injury, that was once again covered by her sweater and golden tresses. Kaylee stepped even closer to me, pushed her hair to one side, and pulled the sweater down like yesterday. A thin black bra strap stared me in the face again. It stood out against the pale shoulder I wanted to kiss.

The contusion wasn't as bad as I'd thought it would be, but its purplish mark looked hard against the alabaster of Kaylee's skin. Leaning in close, I could feel her breath on me, and surely she could feel mine on her. Kaylee tipped her head to her right shoulder, exposing the left side of her neck to me vulnerably. From where she tilted her head, she looked at me with calm eyes.

"Does it look okay, Harley?"

"Yes, you're healing well." I fought the urge to kiss it gently. She pulled up her sweater but still stood close to me. I watched her gaze travel over my face, down to my hands, and back up to meet my eyes. Kaylee looked pensive for a moment before she stepped in even closer to me. She ran both of her hands up my arms slowly and pulled me in for a hug. I closed my eyes in relief and held her even closer, my forearms greedily bracing her lower back. I chanced the risk of ducking my head into the crook of her neck. Her scent and the distinct smell of *woman* filled my senses.

Her feminine voice whispered in my ear, "I've wanted to hug you since the moment I saw you." Kaylee pecked my cheek before stepping back to look at me. "Thank you for looking out for me."

"Don't mention it," I offered, unsure of what to say. I didn't need thanking.

"I want you to know I feel safe here and that I know I'm protected around you. You've proven that time and time again." Her tone was purposeful, and she grabbed both of my hands to hold them in hers at our sides.

I nodded. "Good, that's good." Before I could talk myself out of it, I brought my hand to her face and tucked a piece of blonde hair behind her ear. The flush of her cheek radiated into my palm. I wanted to know what that would feel like pressed on my chest while she lay exhausted after I had my way with her. I wanted to know if I could make them flush even deeper. Ripping myself from my debauched daydream, I stepped back while still holding one of her hands, hoping the space from her would clear my mind. It didn't.

"I'd ask for coffee, but I forgot to get creamer at the store. Let me guess, you take yours black?" Her tone was playful and sassy.

"That is correct."

Her shoulders moved with an amused huff. "Well, how does it feel to be God's favorite?"

"Pretty good most days," I shot back in good humor, unable to stop the stupid grin spreading across my face. "Truth be told, it's more practical to take it black, especially out in remote areas. Plus, the interns at work would just steal whatever creamer I left in the fridge, so I trained myself to drink it like that to be an ass."

She nodded, clearly aware of the plight of creamer thieves. Her light eyes dashed to the stove clock and back to me. "Since it's closer to noon, I think it's appropriate to skip to lunch. Pizza?"

"Yeah, sure."

I wasn't used to having a girl know what she wanted to eat. Most of my weekends spent dating resulted in hours of delay and hunger. They always claimed anything was fine, just not anything specific.

What other ways could she surprise me?

Chapter Fourteen

Kaylee

I remained at the stove, slowly heating the frying pan. My dad had taught me how to avoid soggy pizza with this trick. I could feel Harley's gaze raking up and down my body from where I stood. I could cut the sexual tension with a dull knife.

"You mentioned you have a brother and a sister. Do they live nearby?"

"Yeah, my parents live on the other side of Pine Bluff. Carson is my older brother, and I have a younger sister named Francesca. We call her Chessie for short. It drives her crazy."

"You're the middle child? How old are all of you?"

"Well, Carson is 33, I'm 31, and Chessie is 28. What about you?"

"I'm 27 and an only child." I braced myself for his response.

"Ah, that's what I should be worried about. You're an only child."

"Oh, that's my red flag? Well, you're a middle child, and I'm not sure what's worse. So, you went to college on the West Coast. What led you to that decision? It's so far away."

Harley took a deep breath, gathering his thoughts. "I've always felt a connection to nature. As cliché as it sounds, it's my church. I knew I wanted to be a ranger since I was a kid, but it was a controversial decision. My parents wanted me to take over the family business with my brother, but I knew if I ran the hardware store, I'd be miserable."

"That made you just go for it?"

"Yeah, Oregon State University has the best forestry program in the country, so it was a simple decision. I got some scholarships, my parents helped some, and my great aunt paid for the rest. Otherwise, I would have been screwed. I thought it would break my dad's heart. He dropped me off at the airport, and I still think about how devastated he looked. By the time I came back, Carson had completely taken over the store, and so far, it's going well."

"I see. It was brave of you to step out and do what you wanted with your life. Major props for that." I chanced a look over my shoulder at him. He ripped his eyes away from my body and back up to my face when he realized I was looking.

Trying my best to avoid his hungry eyes, I looked back at the pizza, failing to ignore the warmth pooling in my body and the slight rush of heat under my skin. "Plus, it sounds like it helped your brother as well. Still, breaking tradition is hard. I get it."

"Thank you for saying that."

I heard him stand up along with the rustling of paper, then a heavy clunk of glass on the granite counter. Harley went quiet behind me, so I turned around only to see him inspecting a familiar box.

That's where the condoms went! They were in the bag with the wine!

"Sorry, I, uh, wanted . . . You know . . . I don't want you to think that I'm like or that we have . . ." I turned back to the food on the stove, mindlessly moving the pizza around in the pan to push my fluster away. I couldn't think quick because my whole body was in shock. Shit, shit, shit!

I heard Harley walking toward me, then I felt him directly behind me, pressing the entire front of himself into my back, his breath moving the hair over my ear. "You assumed you needed these to stay with me?" His murmur was tauntingly sexy. Hearing it from behind made me fight for a breath.

Before I could think, I murmured, "I would certainly hope so."

Harley snaked a muscular arm around my waist and pulled me tight against his solid form. His large hand spread possessively across the bottom of my ribs and stomach. "Good," was all his velvety voice murmured into the crook of my neck. Loosening his grip on me, he lowered his hand, trailing it across my torso to rest on the opposite hip. His voice filled up my senses once more, but in the other ear. "Just so you know, I have to get a physical every year to be a ranger, and I'm in the clear." I nodded, trying to hide how flustered I felt that he could make something like sexual health sound so natural and not awkward.

"Same for me. I'm good. Very safe."

He stepped back, allowing me to turn to face him. His hand lifted my chin, tilting my head back so I'd look at him while he said, "Good," before kissing me. The way he murmured it sounded fucking sexy. Who knew a simple *good* could make someone sound so resolute and in control?

Our kiss deepened, hungry and passionate with all the pent-up tension. Harley's large hands held my face, his thumb sweetly rubbing along my jaw while he kissed me deeply. My hands roamed his muscular arms and shoulders. The broadness of him alone caused me to feel lightheaded. The solid strength of him felt like a wall of masculinity I was pushing up against. His hands moved down to my hips, rubbing the sides of me before swooping to my back, only to press me to him. The closeness caused a breathy gasp to escape my mouth between our kisses.

Breaking apart for air, Harley and I panted. He looked up to the ceiling as if to gather himself before he reached directly into the hot frying pan to pick up a piece of pizza. He bit into it, dashing a look at me only to say, "I need to get some fresh air before I break something."

And with that, I watched him walk out the door, grumbling something that sounded vaguely Greek.

The afternoon stretched on, causing the sun to fight its way to the western horizon behind a constant sheet of white winter skies. Piles of snow clung to most of the cabin windows, and Harley had lit the fireplace sometime today. Its crackles were a constant calming companion as the heavy snow subsided most of the afternoon, with occasional pockets of flurries.

Checking the weather app on my phone, I saw the forecast was grim with another bout of snow coming tonight and getting worse tomorrow. If the weather report was correct, travel wouldn't be possible until the end of the week. I didn't dare ask Harley how long he thought the storm would be because I didn't want to pressure him into letting me stay longer or, worse, him to misconstrue it and think I wanted to leave. Considering it was only Monday, I was also wary to ask about my car because his friend Dane probably wasn't working with a storm this bad.

I didn't feel stuck, but I didn't feel completely at ease. I was used to rescuing people, not the other way around.

Almost lulled into a meditative daze, I watched the snow fall while staring out at the gorgeous view of the lake. A loud cracking noise ripped me from my reverie, causing me to jump in my seat. I looked around the cabin to see if anything had fallen off the walls, only to hear the loud crash again, making me yelp. Following the sounds, I exited the French doors in the living room wearing a pair of Harley's boots that were too big.

I carefully shuffled and walked toward the end of the deck to careen my head around the side of the cabin, only to see Harley chopping wood by the side of his barn. It appeared he had cleared a spot for his task near his woodshed with the snowy forest right behind him. Looking handsome as fuck in full lumberjack mode, he'd rolled his red flannel up to his elbows, revealing his muscular arms.

A wave of attraction moved through my body. I watched as he positioned a log atop an even larger, thick stump. Balancing the sacrificial wood, he took a couple steps back in determined measures, almost scowling before gripping the axe expertly with his hands shrouded in tan leather work gloves. He took a deep breath and raised the axe, only to hack it down, splitting the wood by sheer force with a manly grunt. The wood splintered, sounding like bowling pins while toppling over. I felt my jaw slack at the mere sight of it.

Harley grimaced further and repeated the action with another stump with such skillful strength, I found myself completely hypnotized. His large shoulders shifted, and his biceps recoiled under his flannel shirt with each swing, his wide stance bracing him. His corded muscles moving with virile strength accompanied by the gruff noises escaping him made me feel lightheaded. I crossed my arms for warmth and to feel something anchoring me into my body before sheer lust could take me.

He bent over and tossed pieces of wood onto a nearby firewood sled with practiced movement. He made it look easy, but some part of my brain knew it wasn't. I watched him pick up a bigger slab than the two pieces prior. It must've been two feet tall and extra wide, barely fitting in his arms. Groaning and plopping it on the stump, he splayed his hand on the top of the slab, and thrusting his hips and groin into it, he shoved it farther on the base. My mouth opened even wider. Completely transfixed, I blinked slowly, trying to comprehend why this was so fucking hot.

Stepping back a few steps, he raised his axe and thrust it into the middle of the wood with so much strength, it almost frightened me to watch. I knew he was strong, but I didn't know he could put that much force behind something. From what I could see, the wood cracked, but not all the way through. He let out an annoyed, "Fuck!" that I could barely hear from where I stood. He turned his head to spit and took a couple of deep breaths, only to swing again, splitting it asunder.

I gasped, causing him to spot me from where I stood on the porch.

He looked me up and down, cocking one eyebrow. "Do you like what you're seeing, sweetheart?"

"Not sure. Do you like what you're seeing?" I let out a breathy giggle, lifting my sweater to flash him my tits, giving him a taste of his own medicine. His eyebrows shot up in pure shock before his expression darkened as he hacked the axe unnecessarily into the stump to get it out of his hands. With a heated look, he brought his work gloves up to his mouth, biting the cuffs to take them off as I ran back into the cabin with an errant giggle ripping through my throat.

Chasing after me, he came into the living room, shaking his head while stepping out of his boots. His gaze was a mix of hungry and playful. He grabbed me, pulling me close for a kiss while trying to fight back an amused laugh that turned into a tortured groan low in his throat. Our bodies melted together, chest to chest, breathing in and out and filling up the space between each other. He smelled like wood and crisp winter air. His touch, which had always been controlled and gentle, was now more feverish.

He pulled me to sit by him on the couch, barely watching where we were going between frantic kisses. Our tongues darted, our lips gliding, our hands grabbing. I tore off his hat to run my fingers through his hair, loving how thick it felt. From where we sat, his arms encircled me, pulling me close.

I stared at his lips while trying to catch my breath. I had been up close to him before, but he was usually towering over me. Sitting next to him, I could see his skin was clear, his hair and beard neatly groomed. Lashes framed his hazel eyes, along with dark eyebrows. I wanted to kiss every inch of his neck that was thick with columns of muscle.

"You look so beautiful in the firelight," his husky voice muttered. One of his hands touched the side of my hair, brushing it off my cheek. The other stopped tracing circles on my back and had now migrated down on my hip, damn near cupping my ass. I wasn't complaining.

"So do you." I touched his beard, resting my hand on his chest. The heat from his pec muscle burned into my palm immediately. "What happened last night?" Even I could hear the slight hurt in my voice.

"I was trying to be a gentleman, but if there's anything I've learned from being near you, that's damn near impossible." His gaze fixed on my lips before he leaned down and caught a kiss.

"Good." I used his own favorite word on him.

Harley let out what I could only describe as a growl, and with a possessive grasp, he gripped both of my hips to place me on top of him with one smooth motion. I straddled his lap, the sensation of it immediately shocking me. I'd wanted this since I'd met him. Being this close to him made me dizzy. His hard frame and muscles pressed into my soft body in an intoxicating way, showing me our differences.

We closed the distance with another long, heated kiss. The taste and feeling of him got better and better with each passing moment, drawing me deeper into lust. Against my will, my hips slowly began grinding on him. A low groan formed in the back of his throat when he felt what I was doing, causing his hands to clutch my ass. Mine instinctively grabbed his face, rubbing his beard before running my hands down his neck and up through his thick hair, simply needing to feel every part of him I could. The hardness of his jaw and muscles were so distinctly masculine to me. It was enthralling to feel all the ways he was so damn virile and hot.

Our kiss deepened, our heads tilting and weaving to explore each other. Our moans filled up each other's mouths while we eagerly clung to one another. I felt the warmth pooling at my center, the urgent need for Harley apparent not only to me.

Breaking the kiss, he looked up and down my torso hungrily. "You feel so good," I whispered. He pulled me closer, kissing the side of my neck that wasn't hurt as he slowly thrust his groin into my center. I let out a slight whimper as he thrust against me again, making me quietly gasp before pulling me into another kiss. His hands, so huge and rough, held my ass in place against his groin. I couldn't even move if I wanted. I didn't want to though. I wanted to be right there with him, feeling him swell against me.

The rest of the world blurred, leaving only yearning for this man who was lit by fire. Everything in my body was liquid and achingly alive. While kissing my neck, he ran his hands up either side of me, starting from where they were on my ass, moving to my lower back, up under my sweater, and roaming up my sides, gently grazing my breasts over my bra for a moment, causing my breath to come out ragged.

He knew his way around a woman. His touch was intentional, teasing, possessive, but never too eager. His hands made their way back down to my hips, and completely in control, he tipped me with his wrists, bringing me down closer to him, connecting us with a searing kiss.

My hair slid down all around between us. I tossed it from side to side, getting it out of the way only to lean further into him. His tongue pressed at the line of my lips, and I opened to him to deepen our kiss. Our tongues darted back and forth, swirling and tasting. His lips were deliciously soft. The shape and fullness of them complimented mine in a way I didn't know was possible, like they belonged together.

The kiss was intense, hot, and heady. Behind my closed eyes, I could see sparks of white flashing, and my core ached and longed to be filled with him. I moved my hips again, thrusting back and forth. I could feel Harley's dick against me, his erection creating a ridge that hit my clit just right. It was already too much, causing a slight cry to break in the back of my throat.

My heat scorched through the thin layer of the leggings I wore. I knew he could feel the shape of me through the flimsy barrier of fabric. The thought of my heat mixing with his made me feel even more wild. That sensation mixed with his brawny chest against my aching breasts made me hyperaware of everything firing off in my body.

Harley broke our kiss to look down at his lap, where our most intimate areas now pressed together, and he slowly looked up to gaze in my eyes. His looked hungry, injected by his urgent, awakened need for me. It made me feel seen and desired. With a ragged breath, he brought one hand to push a stray hair behind my shoulder before cupping my face gently, gliding his thumb across my lower lip. I was sure he could feel my rapid breath on his skin.

"I like feeling you," he said with a primal gravel in his voice. The sound of it caused a throb deep in me. Out of breath, Harley trailed kisses down my jaw, trying to regain composure himself. Not wanting him to be fully in control, I pulled his mouth back to mine in a passionate kiss, working my way toward his ear.

"I want to feel more of you." My hot breath on his right ear and neck made his dick swell in his pants even more. I felt the delicious throb and continued by biting his lobe softly. Harley let out a groan and leaned into my assault on his senses, dragging at my hips to push me even closer to him.

"Babe, don't tease me like this," he said in a low, husky voice I hadn't heard before.

I smiled against his neck. Feeling like I had some effect on him made it even more satisfying for me. I was in his town, in his cabin, but this was on my terms. "Don't do what? This?" I asked as my breath tickled his sensitive ear and neck before I gently licked his earlobe. He let out a groan while I kissed my way to the other side to nibble and kiss his other ear.

One of his hands moved to the waistline of my leggings. He dipped a finger between the fabric and my bare skin, sliding it back and forth. The tiniest amount of skin to skin was sizzling. He brought his mouth to my ear with a whisper. "Are you wearing a thong for me?"

I nodded, biting my lower lip to stifle a self-indulgent giggle.

"You have such a beautiful face. I bet it's even prettier when you come. Would you like me to see that?" his husky voice whispered between kisses up the column of my throat. I closed my eyes, deep in pleasure with the sensation of his lips and breath on me.

All I could manage was a throaty, "Yes." It was hot how openly he broached my consent. Feeling tended to and safe, some primal part of me dipped into even more yearning. I murmured, "Yes, more," against his hair.

He kissed me gently on the throat one more time. "Good," he said resolutely before throwing me over his shoulder while standing up from the couch. Before I could realize what was happening, I let out a little yelp with a giggle. Having him lift me was disorienting. Another giggle escaped in the pure joy of being tossed around like a rag doll. Here I was, about to have sex with a mountain man who threw me over his shoulder like a sack of flour. This was what had been missing from my life! He walked with purpose toward his bedroom with a resolute slap on my butt.

"I can walk, you know!" I let out, still laughing. He shut the door to his bedroom with a low chuckle. The room was lit only by the fireplace in the corner, shutters closed.

"Yeah, but this"—he flopped me gently on my back onto his bed before gliding over me sensually—"is more fun." His face flashed a seductive smile before he kissed me. I opened my legs, letting him work his way between them. Our bodies undulated together, trying to get as close as possible, our slow kisses deepening and lasting longer and longer.

The weight and heat of him felt glorious against me. His warm body on top of me and the cool bedding beneath me was a sharp contrast. I wanted all my clothes off so I could feel more of him. Between kisses, I undid the buttons on his flannel shirt. With a grunt, he leaned up and pulled it off his arms, throwing it across the room. With one hand, he pulled at the back of his undershirt, ripping it off him in a quick motion, tossing it across the room as well. Seeing his bare chest muscles move made my pussy throb in response. His chiseled and broad chest looked bronzed in the firelight, the sight of it making me giddy.

I undid his pants while he kneeled over me. He pulled out a condom from the pocket before kicking them off with his socks in a quick motion to reveal dark boxer briefs. Even in the dimly lit room, I could see his long legs had thick muscles lining his calves and thighs, morphing up to a round butt. I guessed hiking did the body good.

He ducked back down, kissing me and hugging me to turn us over. Sitting up and straddling him again, I had to fight the urge to go crazy and frantically have him. He ran his hands up my stomach, plucking off my sweater, tossing it on the floor. My hair fell around me like a waterfall.

"God, you're so beautiful," he whispered, tracing his fingers on the top of my breasts where they peeked out from my black bra. He continued tracing across my chest, his brow furrowing when he saw my bruise from the wreck in its full glory. It had spread where my neck met my left shoulder, erupting in washed-out red and purple. Harley hovered his large fingers over it for a moment, taking in what he saw. He looked up at me, his eyes intense and fueled with emotion. He slowly, delicately, brought his lips to the bruise and kissed it with featherlike softness. "I'm so sorry that happened to you," he murmured before kissing the unscathed parts of my neck.

I shrugged. "It doesn't hurt anymore, I promise." My words felt like they had a double meaning. Nothing hurt in this new, little pocket of bliss together.

He nodded in acknowledgement and pushed my hair behind my back. "Your hair is so soft. I love how long it is," he said, mostly to himself, letting it stream through his hands before pulling me in for a kiss. Loving the distraction away from my injury, I melted into him. Harley clutched me closer, caressing my back before moving to my chest.

I unhooked my bra, figuring he wouldn't know it clasped in the front. Realizing what I'd done, Harley groaned into our kiss and took a breast in each hand, cupping them at first and sliding the fabric off my body. Feeling exposed to the air of the room made me instantly inflamed in anticipation. Returning, he squeezed my breasts, sending shock waves through my body. His rough hands on my soft skin felt sinfully good. Exposing myself to him this way took everything up a notch. I could feel the intensity of his desire tick higher as he kneaded them hungrily while kissing me.

He stroked my nipples with his thumbs, turning the puffy tissue hard before ducking to kiss and lick them with his warm, wet mouth. I let out a small gasp at how good it felt. Unable to stop, I moaned, arching my back to shove my chest at him even more. I swayed with pleasure against him as my pussy throbbed with need. A row of his fingertips traced a line down my spine, putting me into a frenzy that made me shove him back farther on the bed, tracing kisses down his chest and abs. "You're so damn hot. These muscles, this body."

In response, Harley rolled me over on my back. He began his assault of kisses down from my mouth to my collarbone and then back to my breasts. He caressed one breast while ducking his head to the other, swirling his tongue against the nipple. I let out a desperate whimper of pleasure. He moved to the other, increasing his affection, licking around my nipple before taking it into his mouth, only to release it and graze it, tormenting it ever so gently between his teeth.

From where he leaned, one of his thighs pressed into my pussy, and I couldn't stop squirming against it, making me even more turned on. Men hardly spent time above the waist like this, but this was about to make me burst. His hot mouth and rough hands on my sensitive chest were completely tantalizing, sending shivers of pleasure all throughout my body.

"Don't stop," I moaned out.

He smiled against me and grazed his front teeth around the other nipple, slowly letting the edges drag on either side of the peak. I wiggled and bucked under him, feeling crazed. He nuzzled my cleavage before making his way, with kisses and licks, between my breasts and farther down on my tummy before he hooked my leggings on either side with his fingers and pulled them off me, kissing my legs once each segment was bare.

"You're so fucking sexy, I could come just looking at you," Harley's gravelly voice whispered as he roamed up between my legs. The flames in the fireplace raged on, casting a glow on his muscles. I clenched at the sight of it. Suddenly, his hot breath was on the fabric of my thong, adding to my desire. It became an immediate sensation that was about to tip me over the edge. He looked up at me from where he knelt. His hands were rubbing all over me, riling me up. He was teasing me, and he knew it.

"You—" Before I could finish, he kissed the fabric that barely separated his lips from my mound. His fingers hooked on either side of my thong, flirting to take it off. "Just take," I moaned, pleading.

"I only have one rule in this bedroom," he said, looking up at me sensuously, biting his lower lip to regain his composure before gently blowing on the fabric covering my wet core. "You come once before I ever get inside you."

My mouth parted in overwhelm, and before I could comprehend or answer, he shimmied my thong down and kissed my legs while he pulled it from each one. "You're so wet. I fucking love it," he said in heated admiration, feeling the fabric with a sexual groan. His voice had a tone of awe steeped in deep desire. A couple years ago, I might have felt embarrassed if a lover had pointed that out, but I had grown up a bit and realized my body wasn't anything to be ashamed of and that if anything, it showed someone's effect on me.

He crumpled up the fabric of my thong, tossing it while watching me move side to side in yearning, wanting him to touch me already. I had been in control on the couch, but here and now, in his bedroom, he was calling the shots. Some part of me was absolutely loving it. I had never had a man savor the first time like this. Usually, it was a rush of giggles and awkwardness or a nervous chain of events, but this was a whole new experience. It was intense the way he went about it with a sense of worship, like he was unraveling me before absolutely destroying me. Harley was damn near edging me at this point.

He moved up my body slowly, running his hands up my thighs before he leaned beside me, propping himself up on a bent arm. I pulled him in for a greedy kiss. His hand roamed all over my torso and breasts, down to my core. Ever so softly, he traced my inner thighs, over my hips, and back. Finally, he brushed against my core and parted my pussy with two deft fingers. We both groaned into the kiss in unison.

He ran his fingers up and down, slowly teasing me before he swirled around my clit with a gentle caress. My body had a visceral response, causing me to press into him, meeting his hand. I ached for him; I ached for relief. With each swirl of his hand, I moved my hips in the opposite direction to create maddening friction. My moans broke our kiss, and Harley whispered, "Tell me how you like it." He kissed my shoulder, my mouth. He gazed down at his hand and back up to me. His voice was so deep, I could barely hear it in my frenzy. I didn't immediately answer him. I didn't have enough brain power to think right now, let alone talk.

He dipped one finger into me. The slight pressure of being filled so slowly and gently felt amazing. I nodded, causing him to continue moving his finger slowly as he added another, curling both and finding his own rhythm. He swallowed hard, feeling me clench his two fingers. I clawed at his shoulder blades, opening my legs even wider. "Mmm, yeah, open for me." He hummed against my mouth, bringing me to a kiss to partially distract me from the overriding pleasure of his hand on me.

He continued to curl his fingers in a rhythm matching my hips, then moved them up to my clit to dampen it further. He continued swirling around it, getting me more and more turned on. "Harder," I moaned out, nuzzling his neck. With more pressure added, my breath hitched. I ran my hands all over his body where I could reach. After a couple of swirls and strokes, he looked back at me and kissed me, stopping my heavy breathing for only a moment. I was quickly casting away into a haze of pleasure, Harley undoing me. It felt uninhibited and natural.

My pussy pulsed with a building orgasm, and I could feel how wet I was. Something in me stirred, and I came back to the moment beyond what was happening to my body. "I want to make sure you feel good too, babe," I said, covering my eyes with my forearm, trying to gain some composure.

"You will." His voice was low, seeped in arousal.

He began laying feverish kisses down my throat, between my breasts, onto my sternum, over my hips before he dominantly spread my legs. His hands grazed my inner thighs while he looked up at me with a playful expression, clearly liking what he saw. Slowly and confidently, he began kissing all around my inner thighs and mound before he pressed his mouth against my center gently with a kiss. My breath hitched immediately at the sensation.

His hands traced loving paths over my legs before grasping my hips to angle me how he wanted me. Before I could even register how intimate this moment was, how my pussy was all up in this hot guy's face, his tongue brushed against my entrance. I let out a tiny gasp at how good it felt, the sensation nearly jolting me, causing my back to arch in shock before relaxing again. From there, he stroked his tongue from my entrance upwards, licking my lips but intentionally missing the tip of my clit, only to repeat the pattern. His hands remained holding my hips, clutching me possessively. I ran my hands through his hair, trying to make sure he knew I appreciated him.

"You taste amazing, Kaylee. Better than I could have imagined." His voice floated up to me, gravelly with desire. He continued devouring me with his mouth while one of his hands moved to my face, and he pushed two of his fingers into my mouth. I held his wrist and licked them while gazing at him. Moving his wet fingers to my breast, he pinched my nipple teasingly. Between that and his hot mouth on my core I writhed and moaned, saying his name repeatedly, pleading for him to keep going. I could feel his smile against me, his enjoyment of my pleasure. Taking my cues, he inserted one, then two fingers slowly and gently, rhythmically pulsing them toward the front of me while his tongue brushed against the outside.

He continued his rhythm patiently, his beard tickling my sensitive flesh, the fire lighting up his muscular shoulders and the side of his handsome face. I felt swept away in the moment that stretched on and on. He pulled back, making his tongue's absence painfully noticed by me. I tilted forward, pressing myself against his tongue greedily, allowing it to finally touch the head of my clit. A wicked hum formed in the back of his throat while he let me rock against him, showing him what I needed before he continued his strokes. What he was doing felt lovingly present, not at all rushed but simply guiding me to my pleasure.

"Yeah, just like that!" My voice rang out in the room, echoing around the high ceilings. I was crazed. I couldn't control the moans escaping me even if I wanted to.

"Are you going to come for me? Are you going to let me—" He sensed my orgasm building and continued exactly what he was doing, not speeding up or getting caught up in his own reaction.

I nodded, wordlessly moving against him. His free hand pushed my legs closer together around his head, making the sensation of the strokes stronger. I shuddered, loving what he was doing until I quivered against him, my pussy wet and clenching around his fingers. It felt like my body was on its own course, completely out of my control. Wave after wave built up inside me.

"Yeah, come for me," he whispered against me between strokes. He held his tongue flat and still against the sensitive head of my clit as my pleasure peaked, crashing down all around us. As it rolled powerfully through my body, I grabbed the bedding to steady myself, twisting the fabric. Harley grabbed my right hand and laced my fingers in his, holding it through the roll of pleasure. I squeezed his hand, trying to offset the sheer intensity of my climax. I could feel the flush move up my neck and onto my face.

Harley pulled back to gaze at me in satisfaction. He leaned forward, gently roaming his hands over my body, staring at me lustfully while I swam in an orgasmic high. Sensing I was coming down, he moved back between my legs.

"More," his velvety voice stated.

"Huh?" I breathed out in confusion, looking down at him.

"More," he said again, his eyes piercing into mine as he returned to his onslaught with gentle attentiveness, coaxing another orgasm off the back of the one I'd just had. I came again, feeling the deep jolt once more. Harley kissed my pussy one last time, wiping his face against his forearm before moving up closer to me.

He let out a satisfied hum before his deep voice said, "Good girl," and he pulled me into a kiss. My mind floundered, trying to process how fucking hot that sounded along with how my body reacted. I started sitting up, pushing us to kneel together in the center of the bed. When I leaned in close to him, my nipples touched his hard chest. The sensation made him inhale sharply and clench his jaw as he looked down at my boobs grazing his ribs. I slowly dragged them side to side to tease him even more. I ran my hands up his bare chest, over his shoulders, and back down his arms, lightly grazing his flesh with my nails. His eyes fluttered in pure pleasure at the sensation.

Placing my fingers on the inside seam of his underwear, I shimmied them down so Harley could kick the fabric away. His rigid cock sprung up between us, and it was thick and nicely shaped. He had manscaped, and overall, it was a good-looking dick. Perhaps it was because I hadn't seen one in the flesh, literally, for over a year, but my initial reaction was that it was a lot to handle. What was I going to do with all that?!

My gaze cast downwards to his groin. "That looks intimidating," I said under my breath before I could think.

Harley tilted his head, clearly humored, "You know . . . I haven't heard that one yet—"

Before he could go on, I delicately grasped his shaft, moving my hand up and down its girth. Its hardness wrapped in soft skin immediately sent shivers down my body as I imagined the potential of what it could do to me. With my other hand, I skimmed my nails along the sensitive skin of his lower stomach and upper thigh, hearing him suck in a breath in response before cupping him. I placed a couple of kisses on his lips and moved down to his neck, still pumping his heavy cock with my hand.

"It's so thick." I stroked up to the tip and rubbed my thumb around the sensitive head. He let out a pained groan, breathing heavier. "It's perfect," I whispered, gently placing a kiss on the delicate patch of his neck below his ear, hearing him bite back a grunt. Harley brought my mouth back to his and continued to kiss me. His kisses felt like he was trying to relay something, but I didn't quite understand it in my haze. I wanted him buried in me already.

He gently pushed me back on the bed. I felt his dick swing between us as he reached for the packet. I watched as he rolled the condom onto his cock while I pushed my hair off my neck. We caressed each other's faces and shoulders, looking into each other's eyes. With a whisper of a kiss, we both nodded in agreement.

The sight of him above me, with the glow of the fire behind him, made him look masculine and primal. He held his dick and ran it up and down against me, wetting it. The tip teased my clit and opened me to him. I tilted my hips to torment him further. His jaw muscles ticked while he held back in restraint. I was still throbbing from the orgasms, pulsing against him.

Setting his jaw, he plunged into me with a dominatingly slow thrust. We both gasped at the feeling. At last, we were a part of each other. I felt myself take him, filled to the brim, unable to take any more.

He looked down at where we connected, loving the view. With one more measured movement, he pulled out and, with tortuous control, slowly thrust back into me. "Fuck, you feel so good," he hissed under his breath. He hung his head and then kissed me before slowly grinding against me.

Harley braced himself over me with strong arms, his ab muscles moving with each thrust, the sight of it making me even hornier. His wide shoulders and brawny chest blocked out the world around me. I traced my hands lovingly against his chest, grasping his biceps to steady myself, feeling them move under my hands. A shiver surged through my body as I sensed his strength.

As he leaned down to kiss me more, his warm skin against mine felt euphoric. I could feel his chest hair against my nipples, his dense muscles pressed into me, his long legs stretching well past mine. We moved together at a tantalizingly slow pace, worshipping each other, hearing each other's reactions, and seeing the flames cast light and shadows on our flesh.

I rolled my hips, taking his length eagerly, causing him to let out a deep groan. I liked that he was enjoying this as much as I was. I grabbed his face, holding him to me in a French kiss while I bent my legs, opening even farther for him, allowing his plunges to deepen. His movements were perfect, his cock dragging against my clit with every thrust. The warmth pooled inside me once more. Feeling the flutter too, Harley ran kisses down to my chest and back up to my mouth, closing off one of my cries. I pushed my body to meet him, hungry for release. His breath hitched with each push, not wanting to bust while simultaneously loving what I was doing to him.

He slowed and let out a low groan. I clutched his shoulders to anchor me while I felt his release rush through him, shuddering his massive shoulders. The pulsing movement of his dick made my orgasm tip, pushed on by his deliberately shallow thrusts guiding me to ride it out. All the sensations felt positively blinding, almost scalding.

He collapsed slightly on me. Both of us were panting and flushed, completely undone. A languid smile spread across my face while Harley slowly rolled to my side. I felt absolutely sated. Our legs were shaking, our bodies trembling. My face flushed with post-fuck blush, and the slight tingling ran over my skin from his beard against my inner thighs, chest, and face. Catching my breath, I looked over at Harley.

"Holy shit," he said in amusement, panting himself. I giggled in agreement, and he rolled me on top of him. He gently kissed my forehead and wrapped his arms around me as my hair unfurled all over his arms and chest.

We stared into the darkness, regaining composure while fighting off passing out from exhaustion. Eventually, Harley smoothly untangled from me, whispering, "I'll be right back," before he made his way to the bathroom.

Moments went by, and he returned to help me up from the bed. Experiencing three orgasms back-to-back made me feel weak and deliciously exhausted. I made my way to the bathroom while he fetched us water and messed with the fire in the empty living room. When I returned, he stood by the bed, still naked, and smiled while I took in how big his dick was even when it wasn't hard.

"Hey, my eyes are up here," he joked. I smiled bashfully. "Here, drink this, take these." He handed me a glass of cool water and placed two ibuprofen pills in my hand. I looked at him defiantly. "You might be sore tomorrow. Plus, it could help your neck." His forehead crumpled in wrinkles of worry, almost like he was sorry. He shouldn't be. I'd wanted to be railed, and he had delivered. Oh boy, had he delivered!

He brushed his hand against my face, deep in thought. I shrugged and tossed them in my mouth, washing them down with the water. "I don't like being told what to do," I said while handing the glass back to him. "Be glad I like you enough not to argue."

He brought me into his arms for a hug and nuzzled the top of my head. I could feel a low chuckle in his chest. "We didn't even make it to dinner. You're dangerous."

"Oh yeah, I need to feed you more than a slice of pizza."

We ate dinner and went at it again, in that order.

As I was on the brink of another orgasm, the power went out, shuddering the cabin into a darkness lit only by the fireplace. I was on top of Harley and damn near jumped off his body in surprise. He held my hips possessively and kept lifting his groin to pitch into me with a wicked smile. The sight of his pec muscles moving along with his abs in the firelight would haunt me like some raunchy vision for the rest of my life, I was sure.

After the second round, he lifted his blankets, ushering me into his bed. I slid in naked on the cool sheets beside him, easily tucking myself against him to be the little spoon. The weight of his arms holding me and the distinctly dizzying smell of his musk made me feel safe. After that, all I remembered was complete darkness.

Chapter Fifteen

Harley

I woke in the middle of the night only to feel Kaylee's soft legs next to mine. Her breasts pressed into my mattress from where she slept on her stomach. She looked like a golden goddess, hair flowing all around while the fire cast light on her. It didn't feel real to have her beside me. It had only been Saturday we'd met. Now here I was, being an idiot, crushing on her, and hopping into bed only to have mind-meltingly hot sex.

I'd had great sex before, but this was the best sex I'd ever had. Ever. She'd moved her hips in a way I'd never experienced with another woman. She wasn't ashamed of her body, which was exciting. I appreciated how she had curves and meat on her, like she could handle our frenzied lovemaking without it crushing or hurting her. Everything about her was perfect, like the way her tits filled up my hands, her soft stomach, how there was flesh I could grab at her hips. How she tasted and spread just for me was heavenly. She was wild and feminine, receptive to me taking the lead but still engaged.

I had been getting more firewood ready while there'd been a break in the storm, and the next thing I'd known she'd been flashing me off my porch. It had felt like a siren call seeing her lift her sweater, her blonde hair whooshing in her playful run back into my cabin, beckoning me to chase her.

I would have been a fool not to go after her.

Between the flashing and finding a box of condoms she'd bought, all shreds of my control had been severed. The next thing I'd known, I'd had her on my lap. I could feel the outline of her through the leggings she'd worn. Her wet heat on my dick while we'd kissed had made me even more greedy.

I'd done that to her. She'd felt that way because of me, and some part of my brain liked that a little too much.

I realized I was holding my breath, thinking about eating her out. The memory of her wetting my beard and moaning while begging for more replayed in my mind. From between her legs, I could watch her wiggle in ecstasy. I could see her nipples get hard and a flush radiate on her face. It had been intoxicating, and I wanted to do it again. The feeling of burying my dick in her had almost sent me into oblivion. It had been too long since I'd done that with anyone, let alone a woman who knew how to fuck.

In the middle of our time together, the power had gone out, which had put a different thrill to it. I couldn't even be bothered to stop because I could tell she'd been about to come on my dick again. I'd wanted to watch her pretty face morph with the rush of it all. Watching Kaylee jump in shock at the sudden darkness only to giggle at herself while still riding me, like some devious sexy nymph, had been the hottest thing she'd done today other than flash me.

I thought about her wild ways, letting a low chuckle sneak out of me in amusement, causing Kaylee to stir next to me. I slowly rubbed her back and whispered that she was safe, hoping on some subconscious level she'd hear me.

I slumped onto my back and stared up at the ceiling with my arms folded behind my head. How was it only a few hours ago, this woman had been sending me to the edge of sanity? I felt newly addicted, consumed by the idea of more of her moans in my mouth, more of her legs on either side of my head, more of her scorching heat pulling at me while I filled her up.

I'd never slept with someone I'd recently met. I mean, there had been drunken party sex in college, but I'd known the girl prior. Not that there was anything wrong with one-night stands. Being a more serious type, that kind of thing never happened to me. I wondered if Kaylee did this sort of thing often. I got the feeling she hadn't either. On the surface, she was a free spirit, but under that veneer was a cautious, sensitive person, so I doubted it. That notion made me weirdly happy, like what we were experiencing snowed in together was something special.

A pang ran through my chest when I considered this could be a one-time thing. I didn't want that. I felt stupid admitting that, but it was the truth. We'd talked for days already, and I felt like we had something different. It wasn't through text or social media, but right up in my space, face-to-face talking. I'd missed that. It felt like a shortcut to see her face react and change while listening to me talk. Hearing her tone and how she strung words together was fascinating. It took the guesswork out of how we were hitting it off. My generation connected anxiously over text, and this little slice of time with Kaylee was helping me see how hollow technology could make dating feel. The chemistry between us, even with our clothes on, was palpable.

When she'd touched my cock, I'd kissed her selfishly to distract her and slow down the moment. It had felt like my restraint had been crumbling all around us. I'd wanted her to know I'd genuinely wanted to make her feel good, not just to get my rocks off. I could tell she'd wanted the same for me, too, which had made it even more intense.

Slowly, my eyes grew heavy, and I drifted off to sleep again with her beside me.

She came out of my bedroom the next morning wearing my flannel shirt as a dress. The dark red and charcoal colors complemented her pale skin effortlessly. The soft fabric covering her even softer curves made my mind scatter. She walked into the living room in all her bedhead glory, her golden hair in wild waves moving with each step as her bare feet delicately strutted the hardwood floors. I felt overdressed in a white, long-sleeved Henley shirt and gray sweatpants.

"Hey, handsome." Her warm voice filled the air, along with the crackle of the fireplace in front of me.

"Good morning, beautiful." I closed my book, putting it on the coffee table to give her my full attention. She stood in front of where I sat on the couch, clearly enjoying my eyes on her. My hands grasped her thighs, bringing her closer. "C'mere," I said, smiling mischievously, pulling her onto my lap. A shy smile dragged at her lips while both of her legs dangled to one side. Her back rested against the arm of the sofa in my embrace as I cradled her, greedily touching the crook of her waist and soft legs.

Her hand cupped my face, feeling my beard for a moment before bringing me in for a kiss. Her body rolled to press against mine, allowing me to feel her boobs drag along my chest. The kiss continued, maintaining a consistent need to enjoy our newfound connection. A barrier had broken last night, and it was refreshing to not hide my attraction to her. Being this close to Kaylee was something I could get used to. She was enchanting and exciting. Every moan and move made me want more.

With each kiss, she clutched me closer to her, her arms encircling my neck. Pulling away for a breath, I could feel her smile against my lips. Between kisses, I mumbled compliments. "I like your bedhead." I kissed her sweetly. "And how you look wearing my shirt."

"I hope you don't mind me borrowing it," she said playfully. All I could do was shake my head and kiss her in answer. My hands moved, pulling her up to straddle me. I instantly realized the flannel shirt of mine was all she was wearing. My gaze downward darkened as her mouth parted in arousal, enjoying the sight of my revelation.

Our lips met in a hungry kiss. I skimmed my fingertips on the tops of her thighs, roaming to her ass, floating under the flannel until I had a hand over each cheek, kneading and pressing her into my groin. Feeling her warmth against me instantly got me hard, causing breathy cries of hers to echo in my mouth in response. I wanted her to melt into me. "Mmm, I liked last night. Did you?" she finally asked between kisses. Her nails skimmed the hair above my ears on either side, making my dick twitch.

"Mm-hmm." I stared at her body, completely distracted while I unbuttoned the flannel shirt starting at the bottom, quickly revealing where she pressed into me. My knuckles dragged up the front of her, ridging against her nipples, causing her to bite her lower lip, swaying toward me. It felt good realizing how hyperaware she was to my touch. When I unbuttoned over her sternum, my eyes flashed up to hers. A storm of passion raged on in their gray depths. I could see pure need, hunger, and surrender. I placed my palm flat on her lower abdomen and slowly skimmed up her torso in the slight gap of skin now revealed. My touch traveled all the way up from her navel to between her perfect breasts, resting over her heart

"Baby, you're gorgeous," I whispered in awe, feeling her heartbeat uptick under my palm. She leaned against my hand in my praise, breathing deeper with clear hunger. Both of my hands traveled under the fabric, skimming over her breasts with the slightly calloused edges of my palms. Her smooth skin felt warm and intoxicating.

I could feel her quiver against where our bodies met. Taking that as a cue to continue, I grabbed the hem on either side of the shirt and slowly opened the fabric to reveal her bare chest. A slight groan escaped the back of Kaylee's throat when the cool cabin air touched her nipples, making them pucker and harden. The gentle slope of each breast and how it heaved with each breath put me into overdrive. Ducking my head, I slowly kissed the tops of each one. She arched her back to meet me.

"You're perfect," I said, kissing the softness, intentionally missing her nipples. Kaylee rocked her hips against me impatiently, needing release. I kissed the delicate skin underneath her nipple, softly nibbling the delectable tissue.

"Keep going," she begged, holding my neck. Fighting a smile, I gently blew on a nipple before slowly licking it and grazing it with my teeth. She swayed her hips in response, running her hands roughly through my hair, making me hungrier to have her.

When I moved my attention to the other side, she tugged at the neckline of my shirt, yanking it off my body with a feminine huff. My warm skin pressed into hers made me even hungrier for her body. I wanted to fill her up. As if reading my mind, she confidently reached down and grabbed my dick over my pants. "Remember my rule?" I murmured between her breasts, punctuating my question with a kiss. I wanted her to recall my goal of giving her an orgasm at least once before I got inside her. It was the least I could do.

Kaylee's eyelashes fluttered in a daze. "You said that was for the bedroom. We're in the living room." Her breathy voice trailed off as she kissed up the columns of my neck and over to one of my trap muscles. Before I could find humor in her plea, she continued, "Don't make me wait." She leaned back, pulling my dick from my pants. Before I knew it, she was gliding herself against it, letting it separate her lips to rub against her slick clit. I momentarily went blind at the raw sensation. Groaning, I lunged for the side table near the couch, retrieving a condom from a stash I'd put in there. We rolled the condom on my cock together. "Mmm, I need you," she murmured, staring at my dick.

"I need you, too," I said pulling her closer to me.

Holding my cock, I brushed her core, letting the head of it glide against her clit in a teasing way. I felt her spread for me, her warmth on my hand making me instinctively push against her. Kaylee slowly lowered on my dick, pausing to give us both time to adjust. Her little cries breaking in the back of her throat filled up my mouth. The sound of it made me feel weak.

After a few strokes, Kaylee sat up straighter, taking more of my length into her. I leaned her back, moving my hands to her waist to support her. Kaylee braced on my neck and shoulders while undulating against me. The sight of her riding me while the fireplace roared behind her was a moment I wanted to sear into my brain for the rest of my life. Her beautiful body peeking out of my flannel, her feminine moans mixing with the crackle of the fire, her hypnotic hips thrusting against me, taking me all in. Each buck back gave me the most dangerous glance at her slick center spreading for me. I felt crazed with how good it looked, with how fucking good it felt.

"Mmm, I love you riding me, girl," I said while holding her.

She smiled, speeding up only to slow down to take me in deeper and at a different angle. I threw my head back on the couch, unable to look anymore or else I'd be done for. Sensing my torment, Kaylee leaned into my ear and purred, "What this?" Her hips moved side to side and in circles, in a way I didn't know was possible.

I asserted dominance and hugged her close to me, kissing her hungrily while bucking up against her, matching her lead. Her chest dragged against me, the sides of her boobs spilling over onto my biceps from where I held her. I clutched her close to me, ensuring her clit dragged against the base of my cock with each thrust.

Everything all around buzzed with the distinct presence of Kaylee.

Her scent, her sounds.

Her all around me, in every way.

"H-Harley." Her voice came out in pleading breaks. She nibbled my neck to stifle herself, but I wanted to hear her cries echo from the beams in my cabin.

"Let it out for me, we're all alone," I urged, holding her still and thrusting into her deliberately.

Her cries rang out wildly while she clawed my back, moaning my name into the crook of my neck repeatedly. The sound of it almost fucking ruined me.

I damn near crushed her, feeling her lovely form tight against me. Her pussy clenched around my cock, coercing my orgasm to build. Breathing heavily, we became one, rocking and coming undone together. While I still held her tight, we collapsed back on the couch together, chest to chest. I felt my dick release while she throbbed against me. The pulses of her orgasm were strong, trailing after mine.

Still connected, Kaylee nuzzled my neck and hummed in my ear before wickedly whispering, "Good morning." Our bodies rumbled in a hazy laugh together, but I was too fuckbrained to talk. I held her for a few more minutes, stroking her soft hair, grateful the fire was keeping her warm.

With an innocent smile, she got up and sauntered off, making her way to the bathroom. Moments went by, and I could hear the shower turn on. I collected myself while giving her some privacy. She'd started morning sex, and now I was going to help clean her up. It was the least I could do. Also, I wanted to see her all slicked up in the shower.

Collecting all the clothing we'd thrown about, I put the items in my hamper and knocked on the bathroom door. "Come on in!" she said warmly. Luckily, it was super steamy, so she didn't have to see me throw the condom in the trash can.

"Can I join you?" The question felt overly formal. Even though I could see her outline through the glass wall of the shower stall, it felt polite to ask before barging in. Something about the newness of all this made me feel like I didn't know our limits yet.

"Of course," she replied, scooting to the side. "But I'm trying not to get my hair wet, so no splashing." I slid in and immediately hugged her from behind. She let out a sweet sigh and leaned her head back against my chest.

She had washed her makeup off and was still so pretty. Wet and dewy from the shower, her face was like a vision, something that would haunt me in my dreams when she left. She smelled heavenly. Whatever body wash or soap she'd used smelled amazing. She was holding a bright pink loofah that still had bubbles on it. I pointedly looked at it, and she handed it to me. I slowly traced circles with it across her shoulder blades and down her back before I pressed her against me with my other arm and slowly washed her breasts and tummy. She leaned into my chest, letting me wash her off with water.

"You're so sweet to me, Harley."

"I want you to feel cared for when you're with me," I answered simply, kissing her hair that was now piled atop her head. It was the truth. Closing her eyes, she hummed with comfort as the warm water rinsed over her breasts.

"Babe, how do we have hot water if the power is off?" she asked, reality catching up to her.

"Propane. So, the stove works, and we have hot water. The fireplace in the bedroom is gas, so that works too. The only thing we need to worry about is opening the fridge too much. I also have a generator if it gets to that point, but it's loud, so I try not to use it."

She nodded in understanding then leaned up and focused her attention back on the present moment. "I can tell this loofah is yours because it's black and oh so manly," she joked in a deeper voice that I was assuming was her impersonating a dude. It was adorable. She picked up my bottle of body wash and inspected it. "Cedar and sandalwood because you're a man. And it's so manly, heaven forbid you smell like a flower," she said again in her guy voice, breaking out in a giggle toward the end.

In my even deeper voice, I playfully added, "This is the scent of a man who has arm wrestling matches with Smokey Bear in the woods daily. And wins." She giggled and squeezed some of my body wash on the loofah, cleaning me the same way. She ran her hands down my faint abs, admiring them, not that they were anything special. I only had some muscles from working my ass off as a ranger and keeping up my land.

"You're so handsome." Her admiration made me feel bashful. I'd been told I was handsome, I knew I wasn't fugly, but having a naked girl say anything nice about you was a self-esteem boost. Judging by her actions, she enjoyed touching my muscles and the trace amount of hair on my chest. Thank goodness I didn't have a hairy back like my dad. That was the risk of being Greek. I had dodged it. Maybe it was my mom's side of the DNA that had saved me from being an absolutely hairy bastard.

"Who knew you were hiding a cute butt under all that flannel?" she said playfully, causing me to chuckle. I could feel her soft breasts tracing against my back as she made her way around me. I blinked slowly, forcing myself not to get another boner. We needed non-sexy time for food and water. After a few sudsy moments together and some gentle kisses, she read my mind and said, "I'll let you finish up in here," before she ducked out.

I brainstormed what I could do with her today. Blizzard aside, I didn't want to leave our little bubble of happiness. I wasn't used to having a woman here, but ever since I'd built this cabin, this home, I'd secretly yearned for someone to share it with me. That was why I'd built a bigger closet and spare room. I wouldn't need the space, but I'd hoped someday my future lady would fill it up.

Not that Kaylee was my future lady. I got the feeling she'd run back to her life in Boston the second the storm cleared, never to think of me again. Even though she was fun to talk to, made me laugh, and felt so damn good sleeping next to in my sheets.

Truthfully, I hadn't thought about a future lady since the shitshow that had gone down with the last person I'd dated in

Maine. My stomach lurched in disgust, and I blinked hard, trying to not see her face in my mind.

It was over.

She was gone, long gone. It had been almost three years.

Kaylee was here now.

Kaylee was here for me and no one else.

I felt myself frowning while I turned off the water. Letting the rivulets run down my body, I imagined my frustration leaving with them. I needed to take this day by day. If there was anything my time in nature had taught me, it was that each day was completely different and you needed to show up and have patience with what unfolded. It could be a deep freeze, heat wave, wildfire, or a storm front, but it was all out of my control to some extent. I got the feeling this wisdom applied to our situation as well.

Looking at myself in the mirror, I noticed red marks on my back and shoulders. Images of Kaylee clawing at me in ecstasy flashed through my mind when I realized the marks were from her nails. I smiled looking at them, feeling weirdly proud.

I put on some pants and another flannel. When I found Kaylee in the kitchen, she looked adorable, with all her hair still coifed, light wisps around her face and on the back of her neck. I wanted to touch them. She had a glow about her now that I'd my way with her. Good.

The blizzard was still raging on, with gusts of snow blowing across the cabin in streams of white, yet it was warmer with Kaylee here. She had on leggings and a slouchy sweater. She looked cute, but comfortable. If I had to guess, she'd only put mascara on, which was good because I didn't want her to feel like she had to do anything to get my attention.

She still had rings on her fingers, which were silver with various gemstones and symbols. It was rare to see cool jewelry like that on a woman. They looked well-made and with a story behind each one. The metal rings clinked on the thick water glasses she filled up for us. I noticed her red nails and tried not to think of what I'd seen in the mirror.

"Can I make you breakfast?" I asked.

"Sure! What can I do to help?" She looked around, confused where to start.

"Nothing. Sit your cute butt down and keep me company." I pointed at the kitchen island with a spatula I'd retrieved from the drawer. "Pancakes?"

"Mmm, yes. Sex and pancakes, I like where this is going. If only you had drinkable coffee." She sauntered over to the fridge, ignoring my request for her to sit down. I smacked her butt playfully, making her giggle.

"What if we add something to it? There must be a way you can drink it." I opened my cupboard and searched for something promising. "What about cinnamon?"

She looked at me incredulously and shrugged. "Let's try it. I have a headache from no caffeine."

I mumbled, "You know what they say cures a headache?" under my breath then groaned, feeling my phone buzz in my pocket. I hated my phone and hated talking on it even more. Seeing the call was from my dad, I got worried. "Sorry, I better get this." I shot her a remorseful look as she gestured with her hand that it was fine, clearly not offended.

I answered the call in Greek in case he was being nosy, hoping Kaylee didn't think I was being rude as fuck. Putting it on speakerphone to make it less awkward, I continued making pancakes while talking. I watched Kaylee sprinkle cinnamon and sugar in her coffee, stirring it frantically and taking a sip that caused her to gag in a way that was endearingly cute, like a little bunny or something. She clutched the coffee mug and shuddered violently at the bitter aftertaste. With a determined huff, she added even more sugar and a splash of almond milk, only to take another testing sip. She gagged again and considered the taste, only to shrug and tip the mug back for another drink.

I stifled a chuckle and refocused on my dad, who was going on about how someone had hacked his American Express card and bought five hundred dollars' worth of wine from a place in Canada. I fought back the urge to ask if it was my mom. He then droned on about how my brother Carson's neurotic husky had escaped in the storm for a couple of hours yesterday.

I cringed hearing about my ass of a brother, the thought of him souring my mood. Distracting myself, I asked if my dad had cleared out his driveway. My parents lived on the outskirts of Pine Bluff, whereas I lived on the other side, about another fifteen minutes past town near the lake. I could get to them, but it would take considerably longer in the snow. My dad was in his early 60s and strong as an ox, but I worried about him shoveling the heavy snow alone.

He explained he had already done it himself as there was a crackling and a slight commotion, only for me to hear my mother taking over the phone call. I fleetingly hoped she hadn't talked to Sherry or Karen lately.

"Hey, Har." Her voice was warm. I could hear her smiling.

"Hey, Mama, what's up?" Out of the corner of my eye, I saw Kaylee's head snap my way in intrigue from where she stood watching the snow out the window.

"Are the roads closed? I'd like to still host my class tonight at the community center."

"They closed the roads into town. You can't even get out on Mill feeding north. It's bad. You shouldn't risk it for a class you can teach next week or something." I stirred the pancake batter in annoyance.

"Honey, if you only knew the number of women in this valley suffering in silence with vaginal dryness, you'd understand how important my yoni steam course is."

"Mom, I can't—" I blinked, hard.

"It's a huge issue."

"It's a blizzard and you're worried about a yoni steam?"

"You know what they say, a steam makes them cream!"

Kaylee choked on her coffee as I winced in horror.

My mom heard my noise and continued, "Honey, it's perfectly natural. Ya gotta keep things running as you get older. You'll understand someday."

"Mom, I'm literally going blind talking about this."

Kaylee covered her snicker, but I still saw her shoulders move in silent laughter. My dad's laughter echoed ruefully in the call's background—he was loving my torture.

"Harley, it's almost Valentine's Day. This is my public service to anyone with a vulva."

"Okay, and I respect that. I really do," I went on, placating the woman who'd given me life. "And I realize I don't understand the full weight of this issue as a non-vulva owner, but please, for the love of God, wait until Friday or something. Promise?"

I flipped a pancake while a long pause filled the line. "Fine."

"Okay, love you, take care. Tell Carson to get his ass over to help Dad."

When I ended the call, I shot Kaylee a troubled glance. Her eyes were already on me as she erupted in a cackle and clutched my arm to steady herself from falling over. I shook my head, dying of embarrassment.

"I take it that was family?" she asked, trying to hold back a giggle.

I shrugged, not wanting to look super attached to my parents. They might be unfiltered as all hell, but they were loving people. Catching myself in how stupid that was, I finally answered. "Yep, yoni steams and all."

I locked the screen on my phone, hoping to force the worries of my family out of my head. My parents had survived winters in Maine. They were okay. I was sure Chessie was fine, and fuck Carson. I needed to stop worrying about everyone and for once worry about myself. All I wanted was Kaylee, a fire, and a damn good time. Oh, and privacy. Which was basically a luxury in Pine Bluff.

"Are they okay? I-I don't want to keep you from helping them." She nervously skimmed the handle of her coffee mug with her nails.

"Don't even worry, they'll manage. They were talking about boomer stuff. You know, getting their Amex card stolen and the weather." I flipped the last pancake and plated the food. Kaylee gave me an uneasy look while I sat down next to her.

"By the way, you sound sexy speaking Greek." She forced a small smile. "But I can't help but feel like I'm keeping you from . . . things."

I speared a square of pancake, twirling it in syrup, collecting my thoughts. "I mean, what if I want to be kept?"

She looked over my face, reading me like a damn book. "That's a good perspective I didn't think of."

Chapter Sixteen

Kaylee

I was in heaven. Harley and I cuddled on the couch most of the morning after I'd ridden him like Seabiscuit, and he fed me chocolate chip pancakes. Sure, he'd gotten a bizarre phone call from his parents this morning, but it was weirdly assuring seeing him talk to people. It solidified he was real and not some figment of my imagination. Hearing him speak Greek was captivating. I was unable to decipher a single word, and it allowed me to focus on his sexy mannerisms and the low tone of his voice.

Hearing him greet his mom with warmth and patience made me swoon because I'd always been told how a man treated his mother was how he'd treat you in the long run. Not that I was thinking of the long run or anything. I was just some tourist warming his bed.

Now that we'd crossed the hurdle of admitting attraction and acting on it, everything felt like a force pushing us together. This new, unlocked awareness made it so we couldn't keep our hands off each other. Every walk by each other provided a graze. Every stare into each other's eyes lasted longer and longer, with little shame. Silence was more welcomed, with no awkward pauses. It all felt privately indulgent.

Not only was he an excellent lay, but he was also an excellent cuddler. Cuddling was important to me because it was one of the few times people let their guard down. His arms around me felt warm and comforting. He held me in a way that I never felt crushed by him, barely registering his body weight. The faint smell of his chest made me drowsy as I lay on it. When I jolted awake after being on the verge of dozing off, Harley's chest would rumble with amusement. His beard dragged against the top of my head before he ducked to my ear to tease me in a whisper, "Getting sleepy?"

I nodded and wriggled in closer.

"Do you know why?" he asked.

I took in a deep sigh, too tired to even talk. "Co-regulation and dopamine," I slurred out. He squeezed me closer in silence. I continued, "When your nervous system senses safety, it causes you to relax. Also, all the good sex causes dopamine, which is usually called the cuddle hormone." I lifted my head from his chest. "It means I feel safe with you."

His eyes searched mine. "Good."

Wanting to lighten the mood, I added, "Not everyone was raised by a therapist, but I took intro to psych in college." I nuzzled back into his chest, hearing him fight a smile.

"I'm honored you feel safe here. With me." It sounded like he was almost admitting it to himself, letting the notion settle. His hand mindlessly stroked the back of my neck, the rough parts of his palm skimming along the nape of it and back up into my hair before moving down to hold my hip.

The room was dim with the heavy snowstorm, the comforting snap and sputter of the fireplace making it even more relaxing. After a few minutes, I found myself almost lulled back into sleep before Harley's deep timbre rumbled through his chest. "I know you're not telling me everything, Kaylee. But I trust you. And I trust you'll feel safe to tell me what you're running from eventually."

I rose, bracing myself on my elbow to look at Harley. His eyes crinkled with regret. "What do you mean?"

He began stroking my shoulder and back. "I think you're keeping some things to yourself. I'd like to know what is troubling you when you're ready to tell me."

Panic built in my body, making me feel tense. I didn't want to talk about Tyler. No way in hell did I want to divulge how I'd found him fucking my favorite barista. How did Harley sense I was keeping something from him? I'd been honest about how much I hated my life back in Boston. That should count for something.

Harley's other hand traced my brow where my eyebrows pinched together. "See, even your beautiful face looks worried by me even mentioning it." I sighed, trying to relax while getting lost in his knowing eyes. "You're running from something or else you wouldn't be so willing to stay here with me."

"I don't have to be running from something to want to stay with you."

He shrugged. "Okay."

"It's true."

He gave me a pathetic, closed-mouth smile and shrugged again, trying to play it cool.

I continued, "I didn't plan on any of this."

"I know. Your car and the storm, I get it. I hope if there is something troubling you that you know I'm here to talk about it." He leaned up and gave me a sweet kiss to diffuse the tension. "That's all." He sat up and disentangled from me. "Speaking of the storm, I'm sorry to leave you, but I better go check on some things outside. The storm created snow bluffs all along the west side of the cabin, so don't open the garage or try to use the front door. Only exit from the porch if you have to, but just stay in here so I know you're safe. Cool?" I nodded, and he stood up, holding my hand from where I still lay on the couch. He kissed the top of my hand, like some damn prince, and got all suited up for the harsh weather in the mudroom.

"Feel free to make more coffee and read any of my books. I'll try to be quick." He leaned over the back of the sofa to kiss me goodbye. Watching him exit through the French doors, I huffed back on the couch, staring up at the giant antler chandelier of death. The fire sparked, and I could hear the whirring of the snowy wind against the cabin. I took a deep breath, collecting my thoughts.

Harley... Mmm... That man was way too good. He had given me several orgasms since I'd met him. He was a giver more than a taker, thank gods. It was like he loved simply being there in the moment with me coming undone against his mouth and body.

I'd woken up this morning and immediately thought, *Oh, I want more of his dick.* So, I'd gone and found him and had the most glorious morning sex of my life. I, like most women, rarely craved morning sex. But waking up with memories of that hard, brawny body had stirred up something in me. As Maisie would say, I'd been dick hungry.

The way he'd washed me in the shower with such gentle and loving affection made me want to burst. He was so kind and unassuming. How could a man be so wholesome right after dicking me down like that?

I bit my lower lip, thinking about how he looked all naked and wet. Barefoot, he was still taller than me, and his shoulders were huge and blocked out so much of my view in the shower that it had made me feel dizzy. He filled up everything around him without even trying. I'd ducked out before I'd felt too crowded or enticed to have shower sex.

I also needed to feed him well. He was the first man I'd ever wanted to cook for, which was something I was still trying to unpack. What they said about the way to a man's heart was through his stomach was completely correct. Not that I wanted to get to his heart or anything.

My phone chimed, showing I had a new email. I opened the notification and saw it from my boss, Tamara.

Kaylee,
Thanks for letting me know you will be out of the office this week. Please keep me posted. Take care!
-Tamara

Whew! That made me feel better. I opened a text from my mom.

Mama: How are you, sweetie?

Hmm, I wasn't ready to unload everything yet. It felt so new, so I told her the closest thing to the truth, while omitting some details.

Me: Hey, Mama. I'm okay for a Tuesday in ugly ass January. I called out of work for a couple of days. I need some time to unplug and rest. Feeling pretty burnt out. I won't be by my phone much, just a heads-up.

She responded almost immediately.

Mama: Okay, check in when you can. Love you.

Me: Love you, too.

With that squared away, I checked in with Maisie, the one person who knew all my secrets. With the power being out, I didn't have Wi-Fi, but I could still slowly lurk her socials using my cell service. She'd gone to a new Vietnamese noodle house and a dive bar over the weekend. She looked happy, and I had a slight ping of sadness that I wasn't there with her. I missed how she matched my energy, always up for chaotic or calm, depending on our moods.

I liked her posts and complimented her photos, then shot her a text.

Me: Hey, lady! I'm alone for a bit. Can I call you?

A video chat popped up on my screen. I swiped the icon to answer the call with a smile.

"Heeeey!" I said warmly.

"Hey, girl, hey!" Maisie sang.

"Was that new noodle place any good?"

"Absolutely! I thought ahead and wore a dress so I could eat as much pho as I could. Then I waddled out and sat in my car for like twenty minutes, just baking in the sun like some house cat."

"Finding the will to live past your pho noodle-induced coma?"

"Exactly!" Maisie held the phone up, and all I could see were countless dildos behind her.

"You're at work already?" I asked.

"Yeah, after Christmas inventory. Who knew a sex shop would be so popular this time of year?" she said with a giggle, looking back at the wall behind her once she realized what I could see. She had an adorable swoop nose she had pierced with a tiny gold hoop. We had gotten our noses pierced together when I'd finally turned 18 the summer after her. I'd met Maisie in high school, and we'd gotten kicked out of pottery class for trying to recreate the scene from the movie *Ghost*, "Unchained Melody" song and all. It had been hysterical, and even the teacher couldn't fight back her own laughter. We'd been besties ever since.

"Nothing says Merry Christmas quite like sugar cookie flavored lube! I mean, I guess it makes sense. It's winter, so everyone is stuck indoors. Speaking of being stuck indoors.

Tell me everything! You are glowing. I can tell you got some! Did lumber daddy give you that woooooood?"

I giggled, looking at myself in the video call. She was right, I was glowing. The bags under my eyes had disappeared and my demeanor was calmer from what I could tell. My face broke into a grin as the moment caught up to me.

"You're going to love this. I was hanging out in the cabin alone yesterday and I heard this loud cracking noise. I went outside to check it out, and he was full-on Paul Bunyan-ing outside, hacking into wood with an axe like some fucking lumberjack beast of a man."

Maisie's eyes grew wider as she gasped. "Shut up!"

"No! Get this! He caught me looking and asked if I liked what I was seeing."

Maisie's jaw dropped. "And what did you say?"

"I flashed him my tits and asked if he liked what he was seeing. And he chased after me!"

"Stop!" Maisie moved the phone erratically, eating up my story with glee.

"One thing led to another and yeah, we totally went for it." My smile spread across my face even wider while Maisie squealed. "It was the best sex I've ever had! Even better than that one guy I dated in New Mexico. You know that one with the hot air balloon? We nicknamed him Vlad the Impaler."

"Better than Vladdy?!" she shrieked.

"Yes! He's a giver, not a taker. It was insanity."

"Stop! I love this! Did he—"

"Yes! Maisie, I don't even know how to explain it! The man eats pussy like it's his last meal in prison. Like, slow, skilled, totally worshipping." A shiver went through my body at the memory of his mouth on me. "You know how some guys go right for it and damn near attack it?"

"Uh, yes. If they go down there at all." She rolled her eyes in disgust.

"Right, well, not Harley. He just savors it intensely, like it's his favorite thing in the world. He knew what he was doing. I felt possessed." I bit my lip and shook my head at the thoughts running through my mind. "It's like we know how to move together in a way that's so natural. It's all I can think about now. I'm glad I'm with him to ride out the storm," I said, shifting to rest my arm on the couch to steady the phone.

"Oh, you'll be riding something else out, besides the storm," she said jokingly.

I giggled and shook my head, loving her teasing me. "Maisie, reality check me please. What's the catch with this guy? I threw down some tarot cards for him. I think he has some serious beef with someone or, like, some tragedy, making him hole up here like some hot hermit. But the present and future were all positive cards like The Empress, Knight of Wands, and The Lovers."

"Damn, Knight of Wands? Shit, I don't know! So far, he sounds like a keeper. Not every guy is a Tyler."

"Ugh, speaking of Tyler. He was texting and calling me, saying he had to cheat on me because he was an alpha." I snorted in disgust. "But he mentioned you were putting rat emojis under his posts. I fucking love that!"

"You bet I did! He's a rat bastard. I want every side chick of his to see it and get the hint. I knew you weren't super serious with him, but he could have been honest with you."

"Yeah, I agree." I pursed my lips, trying to stifle my emotions.

"Kaylee, I think it's okay if you accept maybe you were a little more into Tyler than you realized. He was cute, in a rich fuckboy kind of way. He made you a little happier in Boston by taking you on some fun dates. I mean, you're so loveable, but you've always had a wall up with guys."

I nodded, considering what she was saying.

"I get your parents were like, kooky biker hippies and they raised you in this unique way, so it makes sense you're different, and that's okay. People love you! You're intriguing and you make people laugh. It's just shit luck you dated around in Texas and Florida, where boys weren't used to free spirits like you. You know? But don't let that stop you. Maybe it's time to try a different approach and open up a little, let your guard down."

Maisie saw right through me. She'd always been there when a guy would ghost me. She'd partied with me in college when I'd get hit on by dudes who only saw me as some bubbly blonde chick. They'd liked me until I'd started talking about weird shit, like how blind people would play the harp in the medieval era just to make a living.

"Yeah, you're right. I always had a feeling he was seeing other girls, but I kept giving him the benefit of the doubt." Emotion clogged my throat. "I wanted to feel like I was his first and only choice. I know the guys in Texas and Florida thinking I'm weird gave me a complex. They wanted a preacher's wife and innumerable children. Meanwhile, I wanted to dance naked under the full moon doing witchcraft. You're right, it was just shit luck."

"That's understandable. It sounds like this Harley dude sees you as a priority. In the short time you've spent with him, away from Boston and Tyler, you already look lighter. Towing your car and giving you a place to stay *and* multiple orgasms? I mean, he might be one of those quiet types you have to watch out for. The quiet boys are the ones who make your knees buckle. Trust me!"

"Okay, okay." I rolled my eyes in exaggerated sarcasm. "Guess I'll stay in this cabin and get railed by a dude who looks like the lovechild of the hot werewolf from *True Blood* and the Brawny paper towel guy." I shrugged as we both giggled.

"Exactly! I'll live vicariously through you while I scan all my dildos alone."

I felt a pang of sympathy looking at my friend who was on the mend after heartbreak and a messy divorce. I fleetingly felt rude as fuck gushing about all this lovey-dovey stuff in front of her. Between the two of us, we had plenty of memories of how nightmarish or wonderful dating men could be. I hoped things with Harley were the latter.

"I miss you, Maze."

"I miss you, too. Maybe when all this is over, you can get your ass on a plane and come see me?"

I clapped, loving this idea. Not only did I want to see her and my mama, but escaping the harsh New England winter sounded wonderful. "I'd love to. We should find a concert or something."

"On it! Check in later, okay? Oh, and don't forget to hydrate!"

I stayed on my phone a little longer, clearing out emails and checking in on the world. The entire process took forever with spotty cell service. I typed Harley's name into Google and found his address, along with several articles and interviews pertaining to his work as a ranger. I found his lone social media profile. It was weirdly assuring to see his name with a picture of him. I stared at it, swooning. Gods, he had such a gorgeous smile.

Was this stalking? If so, I didn't care. I clicked on his name to find his profile was private. Fuck, that tracked. He was a guy who liked privacy. Maisie had skills to dig and find what she had. I fleetingly wondered if Harley had Googled me. Realizing I both loved and hated technology, I decisively walked back to Harley's room to put my phone back in my purse.

Taking off my sweater, I changed into my Jimi Hendrix shirt I'd had on under my sweater Saturday. I was using it as my only undershirt because the thermal I'd bought was too tight around my armpits and it drove me fucking nuts. I decided since Harley had been face-deep in my tits already that I could basically give up on bras at this point.

Making my way to the spare room, I found a plain black yoga mat and rolled it out to drop into a yoga flow, hoping it would center me. Holding a deep pigeon pose, I sent quiet gratitude to my body for being limber as fuck. Continuing my flow, I found myself lost in my own little world, only interrupted when Harley walked in and saw me leaning up against the wall upside down. My legs and butt pressed flat against it while my back arched into a handstand.

Harley stopped mid-stride while walking down the hallway. I pushed off the wall, flipping myself over slowly. He looked impressed and simply said, "Damn."

"Everything okay?" I asked, leaning into warrior pose. *Virabhadrasana* in Sanskrit, my inner yoga critic added.

"Not really. It looks like several pines toppled from the heavy snow and are hanging precariously. I'll need to get my chainsaw and use my winch to help get them out of the road since it's a safety hazard. That's also probably why the power went out. Stay in here and keep warm, okay?"

I nodded, loving his lingering gaze on my body as he left.

After an extra-long yin yoga flow, I lay flat in corpse pose, *shavasana*, and meditated. It honestly made me more tired, so I went back on the couch with a book of Harley's about wildflowers in the Northeast.

Chapter Seventeen

I woke up with a slight headache and the book across my chest. Sitting up, I promptly walked to the kitchen for some water. A note on the fridge said:

Open up and have a taste. I'm outside in my shop if you need me, beautiful.

I snorted at the innuendo and opened the fridge to see a turkey sandwich on a plate. Sweet guy. I liked how he left me notes. It was fun to see his handwriting, and something about it felt old-fashioned. I took the note and put it in the book of his I was reading as a bookmark, realizing since I'd been around him, I'd hardly seen his phone in his hand. That was so refreshing.

I put a log on the fire, watching sparks dance up from impact. Biting into the sandwich, I hummed with happiness and walked around the cabin to check each window to inspect what was happening outside. The day had progressed into afternoon, and the house was dark with the snowstorm and lack of electricity. Powerful gusts of wind pushed flurries of snow around the cabin, making it look almost submerged in silvery, swirling wind. At least another foot of snow had fallen, blanketing the outside world in white. The piles that lined the windowsills had stacked higher, and I could occasionally hear tinkling against the panes. The forest was quiet, still, and energetically buried with the storm, as if Harley and I were the only signs of life.

I sucked in a deep breath, closing my eyes and trying to sense him in the barn. Almost immediately, I felt I could. His presence was steady, focused, and familiar. Opening my eyes, I glanced out the French doors only to have a vivid daydream flood me.

It was Harley on a rocking chair out on his porch overlooking the lake, with a full moon reflecting on it. A sky full of dappled stars framed his handsome profile while he turned to look at me.

A pang in my heart became so apparent, I brought my hand to my chest. Realization seeped into my being—I wanted that moment so badly. It was hard to admit to myself, but it was undeniable. I knew it wasn't possible. He didn't want anyone else here in his little bubble. That was why he'd built this cabin so remote and had the job he did. He was a lone wolf.

I'm only a visitor here, I reminded myself.

Just a visitor.

Yet something about the grumpy hermit who lived alone in the woods stereotype didn't fit him. Sure, while rescuing me, he'd treated me like a task, but he'd been concerned and trying to be a gentleman. Even beyond his sarcasm, there was definite kindness and charm.

Maybe he was only nice to me because he found me attractive? Maybe he was a total asshole to everyone in town? I hadn't met anyone else, come to think of it, just that cashier, Azalea.

I doubted it, though. He wasn't cranky or guarded, maybe a bit . . . intense. Passionate, deep, thoughtful, but yeah, intense.

Even when he was smiling and relaxed, there was an undercurrent of passion. Everything he did had a reason, or at least it felt that way.

Finishing up my sandwich, I tidied up from my impromptu nap. Pulling on my sweater along with my boots and winter coat, I exited through the French doors and went down the steps before I trudged my way toward the barn on the north side of the cabin. Harley had cleared a path and the snow was already up past my knees.

I knocked and let myself in. I had no clue what he did in here. The garage attached to the mudroom housed his truck and other mechanic stuff. Walking into the barn, I could see it was a mash-up of a woodworking shop and a man cave. It was tidy, but not as tidy as his home. Random posters pertaining to the national parks, sports teams, and, I was guessing, outdoorsy brands hung on the walls along with a poster for the movie *Top Gun*. It could be worse. There could be questionable flags in here or something. Fucking yikes.

The shop was toasty with a wood-burning stove that blazed in the corner. Long tables and shelves lined the walls, stacked with various cans of paint, lacquer, and old pickle jars filled with screws. I had to walk around a pile of sawdust on the floor and weave around table saws and other machinery I didn't recognize.

He had mounted a flatscreen TV on the wall, and overhead lights filled up the ceiling. I was sure both the TV and lights would be on if he'd had power, but the shop remained shrouded in limited light cast from several lanterns he had strategically positioned. Harley was listening to a podcast, something about a Bears Ears National Monument, whatever that was. I bashfully walked in, not knowing if it was rude.

Harley looked up with a smile, his eyes flickering at the sight of me. He appeared to be glazing an Adirondack chair he'd made. The way his fingers gripped the brush made the veins on top of his hands stand out. "Hey, girl." His sexy voice mixed with the podcast. Approaching him, I took a deep breath, ripping my eyes away as he set the project down, paused the podcast, and washed his hands at a sink.

"I take it you found my note," he said as I walked closer to him. I felt flustered seeing how handsome he looked in his heavy Carhartt jacket and beanie, and how his boots made him even taller. Turning around, he looked me up and down with a smug expression.

"I did. This place is . . . something." I glanced around at all the man shit I knew nothing about.

"I'll take that as a compliment."

"What's a Hoyt?" I asked, gesturing to a canvas flag on the wall behind him.

He looked over his shoulder and back at me with an amused smile. "It's an archery brand. They make compound hunting bows."

I let out a small breath, feeling slightly intimidated. "Okay, Robin Hood. Is there a dead animal in there?" I pointed at the freezer chest behind him.

His cocky grin flashed white against his dark beard. "Several." He pulled me into a hug, the smell of his beard oil overtaking the lacquer and sawdust for a moment. He loosened the embrace to make eye contact with me. He was so broad and tall that when he was this close to me, he blocked out everything around us from my sight, almost making our own little world, like what had happened in the shower. I fucking loved it.

Looking up into his eyes, I felt a deep roll of giddiness and attraction. "I like how you look like a lumberjack in flannel," I said, reaching for his collar peeking out from his coat.

He chuckled and kissed me. "I mean, I chop down trees, so you're not wrong."

"Do you ever feel bad, killing a tree, taking it away from the forest?" I asked, peering up at him while resting my hands on his chest. His arms rested on my lower back, holding me close.

"No. Some are already dead, but you can't tell by looking on the outside because the decay is in the center of the tree. They get overly dry, which makes them flammable. That's what makes wildfires extra bad. Felling trees that have invasive threats helps stop the spread."

"What sort of threats?" I asked.

"Up here in Maine, we have beech leaf disease, which causes stripes on the leaves that kills them and effects the canopy structure. Then there's my mortal enemy, hemlock woolly adelgid." He said it like a curse word or the name of his sworn nemesis. It made me chuckle.

"Is that a bug?"

"Yep, it's an aphid that covers twigs and makes the pine needles look coated with tiny cotton balls. Once they spread, it's hard to get them under control because they cause so much needle loss in the pine trees. Damn bastards. So no, to answer your question, I don't feel bad because so much of my job is making sure the forest is healthy, and part of that is culling it."

"That makes sense." I nodded, thinking about how intelligent he was. I gestured to the chair he had on the table. "Then you make whatever you need?"

"Yeah, woodworking helps me stay sane when the weather is like this." He stepped out of our embrace and picked up a bottle of beer from his shop table and offered it to me. I took a sip. It was cool and crisp running down my throat. I handed it back to him with a thankful nod, and he brought the bottle to his lips for a drink. Seeing his lips pressed to the bottle sent a bolt of hunger down to my core.

Those lips were all over me not so long ago, and I craved for them to explore my body once more. They were so kissable and a dark shade of pink, darker than mine. I didn't want the main thing we bonded over to be sex, but I hoped to do it again with him tonight. Something about being wrapped up in him made me feel alive.

I swallowed hard to stop thinking about all my naughty fantasies and brought my attention back to Harley. He was talking about different variations of wood, stains, and what kind of table saws he liked. He gestured to the bottle he was using, something about walnut oil and how it helped the wood remain nice. I mostly nodded in enthusiasm, loving hearing him talk about something he enjoyed.

"I think you mentioned it already, but did you made all the furniture in your house?"

"Hmm, a lot, yeah." His eyes darted around as he thought about which pieces he'd made.

"Like your mantle? It looked like it had a story."

My question triggered a happy memory, causing a smile to break across his face, crinkling lines around his eyes. It almost knocked the wind out of me with how handsome he looked. "That piece was from a tree that was hit by lightning. It looked so cool, I decided I wanted to incorporate it into my home. I love storms." His gaze drifted down to my lips, as if he were thinking about the storm that was keeping me here.

"It looked like the same wood you used for your coffee table, right?" My attempt to wrangle him away from a horny stupor was hard since I wanted to be there, too.

His brow crumpled as he took in my question. "Yeah, I liked how you could see exactly where the bolt struck the wood, how it made that unique design. Wow." He shook his head side to side a little. "You're very observant. It's a little disarming. I mean, in a good way, but yeah." He searched my face, not used to having someone taking notes. I bit my lower lip and shrugged a little. I didn't want him to think I was watching him like a hawk, even though I was.

"You know what else I made?" His voice was now lower. He stepped closer to me and slowly wrapped me in his arms again.

"What?"

"My bed." He leaned in for another kiss and pressed me against his body, dragging me to him. The kiss was slow and full of need. Our heads tilted to deepen it as I felt myself dissolve into him. I could feel my whole body react to being this close. My nipples hardened and a tingle shot down between my legs. I sighed into his mouth when he reached down and grabbed my ass, squeezing it to quell his passion.

He broke the kiss and looked down at me. "Hey, I have a question about something I noticed earlier. Are you a gambling woman?"

I giggled and pecked his lips playfully. "Yes, but I think you already know that. What do you have in mind?"

"A friendly bet, a wager of sorts." He unzipped my coat, pushing it off with a smile before dropping it on the table behind me. He then took off my sweater, kissing my neck in the process, only to reveal the concert T-shirt I wore underneath. "So, you're a Jimi Hendrix fan?" He raised his eyebrows with the question, looking devilish.

"Mm-hmm, that I am."

His gaze lowered as he watched his fingers trace the graphic on my T-shirt, making my nipples pebble and visibly poke the fabric. I had to fight from fluttering my eyes in pleasure. "If I guess your favorite Hendrix song"—his eyes shot up to mine, simmering with a rogue look—"then I get to make you come as much as I want tonight."

A flutter erupted in my pussy, and I swallowed quickly to hide my shock.

"And what if you guess wrong and I win? Then I get to torture you by touching myself while you watch across the room?" He tilted his head, amused by my candor. "Oh, and you'll have to tell me your trail name."

His eyes widened for a second before he sized me up. "Damn cold, woman. Deal."

I kissed his Adam's apple, sealing the bet. "Deal."

He walked around me in a slow circle, surely trying to intimidate me, considering. His hands trailed around my body as his low voice came out. "Mmm, 'Purple Haze' is too common, especially for someone as unique as you." His hand brushed across my mound, making its way to my hip. He leaned into me from the side. "'Wild Thing' is too obvious, too easy," he said before grabbing a handful of my ass, causing me to bite back a smirk.

He walked behind me, touching my lower back in silence. My entire body buzzed in anticipation before I watched him walk back to the front of me, where he passed his hands up my curves only to pull me to his chest. He stared down at my lips and said, "My final answer is 'Voodoo Child.'" He paused for dramatic effect, tilting his head while adding the last part of the song title. "'Slight Return.'"

I fought a smile, reaching up to touch his neck. His confidence was so fucking sexy, and mixed with his gorgeous eyes and smile, I felt downright lightheaded.

"I'm right, huh?"

I nodded. "Is that your favorite, too?" I brushed my lips against his. He nodded and kissed me. I unzipped his coat to get closer to him. My hands reached inside to feel his hard torso and the distinct warmth of a man. He pushed me up against the workbench before sliding his hands behind my thighs and hoisting me up before I could even think. I let out a surprised squeal, which he found funny by the feeling of his smile on my lips.

He ran his large hands up my knees, parting my legs dominantly to stand between them. His hands skimmed my inner thighs, his thumbs brushing against my core over my leggings, making us both breathe heavily into our kiss. From there, his hands grasped my hips and brought me even closer to him. Loving the feeling of being manhandled, I wrapped my legs behind him, pulling him close in our frenzy.

While still kissing me, he reached an icy hand under my shirt, touching my breast that jiggled freely without a bra. The contact immediately caused a surge of need to form between my legs, pooling with heat. Feeling it, he hummed into the kiss. I pushed off his coat before his kisses covered my mouth once more, holding the back of my neck with one hand as he continued kneading my breast. He whispered into my skin devilishly, "I just want to make you come. It turns me on so much. The noises you make echo in my mind."

"I know the feeling," I said in a throaty tone.

"Oh, yeah?" His sexy voice challenging me made my pussy throb even more.

Brushing my hands under his shirt, I greedily pulled him even closer to me, grabbing his ass. "I want you inside me again. You fill me up and touch me like no one ever has."

"Kaylee," he breathed on my lips before searing me with a hungry kiss. I brushed the front of his clothing, reaching for his cock, causing him to let out a filthy, strangled noise. He reached down to take off my boots, shucking them quickly. He slowly pushed me back on the table, where I braced myself on my elbows as his hand boldly trailed a path down my body, pulling my leggings and underwear off together before I could even help.

He spread my knees slightly, looking at my center before leaning forward to kiss my mouth feverishly. "You're so damn pretty. All over," he said against the kiss, bringing a hand up between my legs to cup my pussy. I giggled against his lips, feeling warm and drunk with his praise. He lunged to his left side to grab a stool to sit down in front of me. His large hands grabbed my calves and placed them on his shoulders.

"Jesus Christ," I said, realizing he wasn't fucking around.

He looked up at me, kissing my inner thighs to gauge if I was okay. I nodded for him to continue, sucking in a breath while he pressed his hot mouth against my center. My body tensed, and I felt simultaneously turned on but self-conscious I was on the table with everything on full display. Harley trailed a palm over my torso, encouraging me to lie back. He murmured against me, "You deserve this. Let me make you feel good, baby."

Behind my head, my coat served as a slight pillow, making me comfortable against the hard table. I closed my eyes, letting the pleasure wash over me, fully feeling all the things he was doing to me and how much I trusted him. He continued his onslaught, catching onto what I liked but keeping me guessing at the same time. I tugged off his hat so I could rake my hands through his hair.

I clutched his forearm that braced my lower stomach. Almost pushing his head away from me in overwhelm caused him to growl, continuing to ravage me.

In the commotion, a lantern knocked over on its side. My eyes damn near rolled in the back of my head when I realized our shadows were cast on the wall in the dimly lit woodshop. The figure of Harley eating me out made me moan. Seeing the shadow of my legs over his shoulders and his head moving slightly between my thighs made me shudder at how dirty it looked.

"Baby, look," I said, gesturing to the wall.

He pulled from me to look and let out a low, strangled grunt, realizing our shadows filled up his shop before he looked at me and nipped my thigh. "Don't stop watching us," he commanded as I gripped the edge of the table to hold something. Soon after, a thrilling surge ran through my body as an orgasm crashed over me.

Barely able to speak, I muttered, "Harley, I don't know how you're so good at that."

"Your body was made to feel this good." A smug smile tugged at his lips while he pulled up from my center, unzipping his pants. He rolled a condom on while I positioned myself at the edge of the table so we could be chest to chest. He swiped my drenched pussy with the tip of his thick cock. We both watched hungrily as he pressed into me without pretense.

He kissed me feverishly, low groans escaping his throat in a way I loved. I pulled back and moved against him, granting him a chance to look at our shadows. The low light of the lanterns in the dark shop made him look wolfishly handsome. His angular jaw was on full display while he turned his head with a hungry stare before looking back at me, torn.

I wrapped a leg around him, loving how he couldn't stop watching us. Bracing back on one arm and holding his shoulder with the other, I lifted myself slightly to grind against his dick while he clutched my hips. A few strokes in, I felt a jolting prick in my ass cheek. I yelped and pulled away from him. Harley's eyes grew enormous in shock as he tried to figure out what had happened while I rolled off the table.

"I got a splinter in my ass!" I let out a self-deprecating laugh, holding my cheek where it creased into my leg, trying to run away from Harley. He let out an amused chuckle, swiftly sitting down on the stool while he manhandled me across his lap. Once I was ass up, I giggled even more.

"Probably not the kind of wood you wanted in you." I fought back more laughter and swatted his leg playfully. "I see it! What a fucking prick!" He plucked it out, brushing my cheek to soothe the sting.

I let out a snicker and stood up, only to glance down at his still erect dick. "You're right, that wasn't the wood I had in mind." I watched him haze over, ripping back into his lust. He covered the table's edge with his coat and set me back on the ledge. Both of our faces broke in a smile before kissing, returning to what we'd started.

Afterwards, he handed me my leggings with a smirk. "What?" I said, bashfully putting them on.

"Girl, you know how to have fun. Nothing gets in your way, and I love it."

"Why thank you!"

"Sorry about the splinter, though." He held open my coat, helping me put it on like an absolute gentleman, as if he weren't just respectfully disrespectful. He pulled me close and hugged me, rubbing his hands over my body to warm me up even though I was barely cold with the wood-burning stove heating the shop. I wiggled in his arms, loving how small he made me feel.

"Long John," he murmured into my hair.

I pulled away from the hug to look up at him in confusion. "Huh?"

"Long John was my trail name."

I looked down at his groin, causing him to laugh. "My stream was the longest."

"Wait . . . what? Huh?"

"It was a pissing match with all the guys on the edge of a cliff. Mine was the longest." He bit back a smile.

"Ew!" I swatted at him and stepped out of the hug in playful disgust. "Harley Kouris, that is just gross! You should be ashamed. Men!" I scoffed while rolling my eyes.

"Men are disgusting, sweetheart. Never forget that. But don't ask questions you don't want answers to." He wiggled his eyebrows, making me push his shoulder again to fight my amusement.

He walked over to the wood-burning stove and messed with it to stoke the flames. Watching him from across the shop, I got a sickening feeling in my stomach and a prickle ran up my neck. The edges of my vision tunneled in panic while I felt the hair on my arms stand up.

"Wait, come here. I don't have a good feeling about something," I said, looking around the shop, trying to figure out what my intuition was telling me. Harley could tell by my tone I was serious. He rushed to me and clutched me in his arms, looking around the shop with me in concern.

A powerful gust of wind whipped through, causing the walls to shudder, and with it the beams of the barn rattled slightly. Before I could register what was happening, a small metal boat that was hanging from the rafters of the shop dangled down on one side, swinging like a pendulum, only to crash to the floor right where Harley had been standing prior.

He looked at me and back to the boat. Walking closer to the scene, he peered up at the barn ceiling and then bent down to look at the ties and bungees on the boat, like he was inspecting a crime scene. I sat there watching him while my stomach heaved in distress. My jaw clenched and my knees locked, as if my body was subconsciously bracing myself for a verbal battle.

When people, mostly men, saw my intuition in action, it freaked them out. There wasn't anything supernatural about it. I just considered myself someone who really leaned into gut feelings. But when people saw what they didn't understand, sometimes they cast you away, deemed you as too untamed, too close to the wild currents of life they didn't ever want to touch.

He shot a glance back at me in horror. "Jeezus Christ! If I were alone, that would have knocked me out! I could have frozen to death passed out on the floor alone or something." He continued to stare up at the rafters, deciphering how the boat had fallen. Luckily, nothing else up there looked as dangerous.

"Thank you for listening to me. Some people don't."

"Holy shit!" He looked back at me with raised eyebrows. "Wow! I mean, the tarot convinced me, but you really are psychic." He walked back to me, his face searching mine, deep in thought. "How often does that happen?"

"I learned to listen to my hunches or else it just puts me in worse situations." I could feel my brow crease, nervous he would think I was a freak.

Harley held my face, still searching my eyes for something before he brushed the pad of his thumb against the pinched spot between my eyebrows then gently kissing the same spot. "Don't worry, I believe you. I think it's special. Thank you for watching out for me." He brought me into a quick kiss. When he pulled away, he could tell I had frozen over, speechless. I had never had this type of reaction.

"You okay?" he asked, concern edging his features. His large hands still held my face tenderly.

"Yeah." I nodded, unable to say much more. He kissed me again, in his own way to soothe me, and mumbled, "I guess that rune thing you carved into the candle worked."

I broke the kiss, feeling lightheaded and needing time alone to process. "I'm going to let you finish up here. Can I make you dinner?" My tone was overly casual to cushion the anxiety running through my body.

"Dinner would be great. Do you know how to work a propane oven?"

I bobbed my head confidently. He squinted at the wall clock. "How about we plan on like 6:30? I left a lantern on the kitchen island if you need it."

I stood on my tippy toes and planted a quick peck on his cheek before heading back to the house, stubbornly refusing Harley's escort. The gusts of wind rushed past my body, making the icy sting hit my legs through my leggings. The distance between the barn and cabin was short, but the small walk was difficult with how much snow swirled past me. I could feel Harley's eyes on me the entire time, until I opened the French doors on his porch.

I freshened up and shimmied on the satiny bra and panties I'd gotten at the market. *Just in case*, the whorish voice in my head purred again, making me smile to myself. I was ready to drive Harley insane tonight. Putting on dry leggings and a burgundy sweater, I felt better, warming up quickly.

Bringing out the big guns tonight, I was making Harley my chicken parmesan. I wasn't super into cooking, but this was one dish that was always a crowd pleaser. I was going to do a side of angel hair pasta, plus steamed zucchini and butternut squash. It was a process to make, and I was grateful for the distraction.

We needed to eat like adults. Like civilized adults. Before we totally fucked. Boundaries.

Remembering Maisie's suggestion to stay hydrated, I got a glass of water. Mid-chug, I realized there was nothing to be nervous about. We'd already had sex. He'd seen everything and heard me cry out like a sex-crazed fiend. Why was I so nervous?

Oh, I knew why . . . . It was because on some level, Harley intimidated me.

He did what he said he was going to do, which was a rarity among people, especially men.

He had this way about him that made me feel devoured and seen, in the most intense and vulnerable way. A slight rush coursed through my body as I remembered the first big O he'd given me when he'd gone down on me. The way he'd slowly, expertly coaxed the orgasm out of me while making me feel positively worshipped. The gradual unfolding of it had made the orgasm that much more intense.

Harley fucked like it was his favorite thing in the world, like it was his damn birthright. Frankly, it was. While most men were inflexible in bed, bound by their own muscles or toxic masculinity, Harley was the opposite. He was fully present, immersed, generous, and unbothered by the pressure to get off. He treated it like pleasure was the goal, not an orgasm.

It was like he was there with me, and only me, just in the moment. Not putting on an act or preoccupied with some bizarre order of things.

He moved his body like he knew exactly what to do with it. He had a way of just moving his hips, thrusting it without smothering me with his massive chest. It was impressive. I wasn't a blushing virgin, but I'd never had a lover like Harley. The consensus of all the women I'd talked to was even with clear communication, most guys were self-indulgent or obviously porn obsessed. It was fucking awful. But not Harley. What we did together felt like something beyond the trappings of modern times, like an instinctual bliss we could tap into together.

I took another big gulp of water, trying to focus my mind away from Harley and his warm mouth on me, all over me. Good fucking hell! I needed music. I retrieved my phone and shuffled my playlist and began my creation. As I got completely swept away, time went on, and I jumped when he came in the cabin. He took off his boots, beanie, and coat in the mudroom and made his way over to the kitchen.

"Damn, woman, it smells good in here," he said while keeping his distance. He had snow in his beard, and I could see sawdust on the sleeves of his flannel and some on his pants.

"You, my dear, get to experience my chicken parmesan tonight," I said in a flirty tone over my shoulder. "It'll be ready in about 15 minutes."

"Perfect, I'm going to hop in the shower quick." I watched his cute butt while he walked toward his room. He was so distinctly masculine while his legs took long strides with each step and his hips shifted like he was hauling around a big 'ol dick. I mean, he was. I giggled to myself at the thought. It was, dare I say, a swagger. Even his walk was hot. I wiggled my body and shook my head to clear the yearning forming within me. It didn't work.

I wanted to make tonight special. Last night was amazing, but it was a haze of unbridled lust. Tonight, I wanted a bit more romance. Between the living room and the kitchen was a long, dark wooden table. By the looks of it, Harley had made it himself. Considering my options, I resolutely decided we were going to eat there instead of at the kitchen island. I turned off the music before setting the table and fetching the wine. Now that dinner was almost ready, I felt newly accomplished and calmer.

Harley exited his room smelling divine. He had on dark pants and a black sweater. Even in something so simple, he was hot as sin. I could see his muscles ever so slightly underneath, which made me gawk for a moment.

"Thanks for cooking dinner," he proclaimed, approaching the table. His mood was calm, as if he were probably unsure of mine with how I'd left the shop. I wasn't used to people rolling with my hunches.

"I figured we could eat here and enjoy the view of the blizzard." I hoped I wasn't making too big of a deal about this, but a little voice in my head reminded me it was because I was crazy about him already. Hell, I was even cooking for him, giving into the primal instinct to feed and fuck him.

"Yeah, but something is missing. Here, have a seat." He pulled out a chair at the table for me. "Close your eyes, promise not to peek."

I did what he'd said. Moments later, the timer I'd set on my phone went off for the food, which made me giggle more. I could hear Harley move about the house, and various noises filled the air. A scraping noise followed by a pop came from the far end of the room. The faint smell of smoke tickled my nose, and I nervously smiled into my hands where I had my face resting in my palms. I heard glass grazing the wooden table in front of me.

"Okay, open your eyes." Harley's low voice sounded like velvet in the darkness surrounding me.

One of the beeswax candles we'd used yesterday was on the table between us. The other two were lit on the mantle, above the existing fire. He'd turned off the lantern in the kitchen as well. I smiled at him, pleased with how romantic he'd tried to make it in here.

"To set the mood?" I tilted my head coyly.

He smiled and stepped closer to me, lifting my chin for a kiss. The scent of Harley made me dizzy. The timer on my phone beeped again, and I broke our kiss with a huff. "Have a seat. I'll be right back." Returning with a plate in each hand, I sat down to join him.

"This looks delicious. I cook but"—he stabbed a piece of steamed squash with his fork and held it up to inspect it—"you somehow make everything taste better. Wait, is this part of your magic? Making amazing food?"

"You could say that. Everything tastes better with a witch."

He raised his eyebrows roguishly. "I'd agree with that."

I fought blushing while I held my wineglass, watching him dig in. I had so many questions for him. I picked the first one that came to mind. "You mentioned your family has lived here for a while and you inherited this land?"

He nodded, swallowing before he continued, "Yep, like a typical white guy in America, living on stolen land. Right? The guilt is real. I was lucky the lake hadn't dried up yet. Who knows what will happen at this rate with climate change evolving. I figured I might as well enjoy a lakeside property while I can."

"I agree completely," I said, cutting into my chicken, hoping he'd expand on that.

"Sorry, I shouldn't talk about imperialism and climate crisis over dinner. It's not exactly comforting." I chuckled while he wiped his mouth politely on a napkin and continued. "But yeah, I inherited the land, like some lucky asshole. Only to build the cabin myself, like some stubborn asshole." I giggled at his self-deprecation. "I wanted a dock for my boat, you know, the one that almost just killed me. And I didn't want neighbors close by because I deal with stupid people at work all the time. But saying that out loud makes me realize I sound grumpy." He squinted self-consciously, considering what he'd admitted.

"If it's any consolation, I don't think you're the grumpy-hermit type."

"No?" he asked hopefully, cutting into his chicken.

"A hot hermit, sure, but not grumpy. Plus, there's a hermit tarot card. You would have gotten that if it were true." I twirled a noodle and speared a chunk of chicken. "Do you fish a lot?"

"I do now. Some old guy died and left me the boat in his will."

"Oh? Why did he pick you? Were you fishing buddies?" I prodded curiously.

"Yeah, I guess you could say that." I stared at him, sensing there was more to the story. Harley caught my gaze and batted with his fork, downplaying the truth. "I kept him and his wife in wood all winter. Apparently, that was something he felt he needed to thank me for."

"Aw, that's cute actually."

He scoffed. "I planned on having a dock eventually, but when I plotted the land, I tried to use as many responsibly sourced materials as possible and made sure I laid it out in a way that made sense. Like keeping the bedroom on the north side so it was dimmer and cooler, allowing the sun to cast on rooms where I could use warmth and light, like my study and the kitchen."

Considering everything he was saying, I realized how strategic he was.

"Like an Earthship?" I asked with a small smile.

He grinned back, nodding with recognition lighting his eyes. "Are you talking about those solar shelters they have in the desert made of random stuff like clay, recycled tires, and glass bottles? They look kind of like Hobbit holes?"

"Yeah, I lived in one in New Mexico one winter with my dad. He was into permaculture for a hot minute. Nothing says you're a well-adjusted citizen like growing peppers on your roof."

"You've had such a badass life, Kaylee." He looked down at his plate while his utensils moved, shaking his head with a grin. "You're beautiful and well-rounded. It's unfair."

His praise made my chest tight. "Really?" I breathed out bashfully.

"Yeah, I mean, what woman knows about passive solar methods and looks like . . ." He gestured to me with his hand, searching for words. "Fucking gorgeous."

I smiled and took a sip of wine. "Thank you. I could say the same about you. I've never met a guy who knows what comfrey root is good for and can go down on a girl like you. Most men think labia minora is a Def Leppard cover band."

He damn near choked on his wine, trying not to laugh. "Don't say that, babe. It'll give me an ego complex."

"If it makes you feel any better, the Earthship experience quickly ended. A flash flood happened and the hay bales in the walls got soggy. It was a hot mess." I looked around the cabin. "You went with the solid choice of actual walls and not having your kitchen be part of your bedroom."

He chuckled. "I tried to keep it how I liked but built it out bigger than necessary in case I needed to grow into it or change my design plans." His eyes shifted to me for a moment then back to his food.

In that split moment, with that one glance, I could read what he wasn't saying. Harley meant to say something like, *I built it bigger than I needed in case someone else lives here with me someday.* He wanted to grow into it with a spouse, maybe even a family. He let that detail slip.

With one glance, we both knew . . . I knew.

The vision from earlier spurred into my head again, the sight of his handsome profile looking out at the lake while I walked toward him to sit down. My heart hurt for a moment, the sting of loss of something that could never be. I was a passing fling for him, a damsel in distress, nothing more.

I took a sip of wine to wash all of that down. I had this moment, and I needed to enjoy it, even if I was only staying until the storm passed and my car was fixed. The way Harley made me feel and how much I already cared for him meant our time together was important, perhaps a much-needed respite for both of our spirits. I couldn't have him forever, but I could at least have him tonight, and that needed to be enough. Taking another sip of wine, I pushed myself to continue past my selfish longing.

"That makes sense. Okay, follow-up question. Do you have a TV in here?" I tilted my head and smiled, happily diverting the topic away from Harley's future wife. Lucky bitch.

"I do! I hate when people make a gorgeous fireplace and ruin it by putting a TV over it. The fire is the showstopper, not CNN."

"You know what? I like that! And I agree."

"I'm glad you get it. Like, what a fucking shame!" he said enthusiastically. "That wooden built-in over in the corner opens to a TV. Sometimes I sit in here like a lard ass and binge-watch bizarre shit on the Discovery Channel. One weekend, I watched hours of this show called *River Monsters*. Please don't judge me."

I giggled at his confession, and we talked more about what TV shows we liked, how we both loved *Game of Thrones* and couldn't wait to see how it all ended and our mutual love for *Outlander*. It horrified him I'd never seen *Indiana Jones*. I felt the same way about him never watching *Grey's Anatomy*. Impressively, he was a fan of *Buffy the Vampire Slayer*, which gave him major brownie points. Apparently, he had a thing for blondes. A flutter went through my chest when he admitted that.

The small voice chimed in my head again. *He obviously thinks you're pretty. He was balls deep in you last night, this morning, and a few hours ago.* I pushed that thought out of my head with another long sip of wine.

I mused, "It's funny because on the surface, it would seem we have nothing in common. I hug trees, you chop them down. I cry when I see roadkill, you hunt. Things like that. But we're both introverts, and we love nature." I held up a finger with each point I was making. "We both want to do sketchy things in the forest."

"Just a casual fuckfest under the full moon," he injected.

I nodded. "Exactly, and we're both hyper-independent. And our families are unhinged."

"It's true. All of it." He bit into his chicken playfully. "Okay, here are some rapid-fire questions. Are you ready?"

Butterflies filled my stomach. I felt so excited and flattered because it had been so long since a man had shown an innocent, lighthearted interest in me. Someone who was talking to me for the sake of conversation and nothing more.

I nodded resolutely. "I'm ready."

"Best album of all time?" he said in a rush.

"Easy, *Rumours* by Fleetwood Mac. Literal perfection. You?"

"I agree. Stevie is a badass. Um . . . I'd say *Rumours, Dark Side of the Moon,* or *Back in Black*—"

"Pick one!" I interrupted in a fake frenzy, giggling.

"*Back in Black*, final answer."

"Craziest place you've had sex?" I asked.

He fought back a smile, looking bashful. I rarely saw him like this, on the verge of blushing. It was so endearing. "You tell me first," he finally said.

"I almost did it in a hot-air balloon in New Mexico because I was dating a guy who had one and it was just us up there. I chickened out because I had this fear I would somehow get tossed out, only to fall to my death."

Harley's face crumpled into laughter. "Can you imagine the people on the ground? Just watching you fall, bare ass out?"

"Right?! I regret not doing it because now I can't brag about it. The craziest place for me would have to be on a balcony during Mardi Gras."

His eyebrows shot up while he bit his lower lip. "Damn, girl."

"Now spill."

His face pulled into a grin. "In a slot canyon in the desert or on a ski lift would probably be mine."

"No! A ski lift?!"

He shrugged. "I'm outside a lot."

My jaw hung while I stared, immediately imagining myself in the two examples with him. "Sure, you treat me like I'm a loose cannon, but you have a wild streak in you." I saw him in a fresh light, which thrilled me. "Okay, what character from *The Office* do you think you're most like?" I asked.

"I love this question. Simple answer. If Dwight hate-fucked Jim, it would turn out like me."

I cackled in agreement. "Tell me more."

"I'm like Dwight because I'm unironically prepared for the apocalypse, loyal to a fault, and I have a crazy ass family. But I'm like Jim because pretty girls distract me"—he gestured to me, making my stomach drop—"I love a good prank, and I get myself into bizarre situations. You?"

"Honestly, people think I'm a Kelly, but I'm more like the lovechild of Creed and Pam. I'm caring like Pam, but a little unpredictable like Creed. Artsy, but a little out of place." He chuckled at that in agreement.

"Okay, are you a pickle girl?" Taken aback, I could only imagine my face morphed into something resembling confusion. "What? Pickle girls are hot—you're hot. Hot girls love pickles. Not like dicks, but actual pickles. Are you a pickle girl?" He smiled while rattling all these assumptions off, realizing his train of thought was messy.

I laughed, hanging my head in shame that he was onto me. "I am! I'm even brave enough to get the ones from gas stations."

"I knew it! Okay, so, what do you think is your deepest fear?" he asked, leaning in conspiratorially.

"Wow, you're not messing around. I'd say being tortured. You?"

"Oh, that's easy," he said in good humor, batting at the air dismissively with his fork. "Being tortured by Kevin Bacon."

I giggled again, remembering his Wi-Fi password. "Fair enough! What did he do to deserve your wrath, though?"

"Just his face. It's so punchable."

"What's your zodiac sign?" I asked.

"Oh, no!" he moaned out, rolling his eyes and raking a hand through his hair.

"You're not one of those dudes who makes fun of women who are into astrology, are you?" I liked astrology and found it useful. Maisie and I had deep-dived into it together in high school. She was a fiery Aries.

"No, no, it's not like that, I promise. I dated enough girls in Oregon to catch onto some stuff with astrology." He raised his eyebrows and pointed at me. "That shit is real. I can tell when Mercury is in retrograde. Ask any ranger, the full moon is like a fever dream with people doing wild stuff and the animals going berserk. I don't enjoy telling people my sign because it's polarizing." He squinted and clenched his teeth, squirming to avoid answering.

"I'm a Cancer," I offered. "I mean, nothing is worse than saying *I'm a Cancer*. It sounds horrible. And having a crab or the symbol 69 represent you is rough." I let out an amused snicker at my misfortune.

His eyes flickered to my lips for a moment then back up to meet mine. "I think 69 and you could work well together."

I smacked his arm, laughing. "You perv!"

"Mm-hmm, exactly." He took a sip of wine, completely unperturbed, slowly and sensually while his whiskey-colored eyes held mine.

Sex. Piercing eyes.

"Oh fuck! You're a Scorpio, aren't you?!" I yelled out in sudden recognition, my eyes wide with shock.

He chuckled, happy with himself. "Yep! Indeed, I am." He nodded, thinking before putting his wineglass down.

"That's hot," I said, staring at him while it all clicked into place. His need for control, his solitary ways. His intensity and desire to protect me. The loyalty and attentiveness. The way he railed me. How nervous he made me because I felt so completely seen, unlike ever before. Yep, that was all Scorpio. I'd now slept with an infamous Scorpio. My mind drifted to last night, this morning, and the woodshop. My body hummed with an urgent need for more.

I cleared my throat, noticing I was sitting pin straight from the shock. I relaxed my body and rested my chin on my fist, leaning on the table. He pushed his plate farther away from himself. He'd completely cleaned it, which was a good sign.

Harley had a glow on his face from the candle between us. His beard darkened the lower half, his cheekbones cutting upwards as if to frame his warm eyes. The flames cast light and shadows on the columns of his neck, showing off his virility.

A gust of wind came down the fireplace, almost dimming the fire out. I looked around, noting how everything else in the cabin had darkened. "When I'm here tomorrow alone while you're at work, do I just need to throw logs on the fire?" I looked past him toward the fireplace again, assessing the wood cradled off in the room's corner.

He reached his hand across the table and touched mine. "Baby, I'm not leaving you alone. Don't worry, I already took the day off."

"What? Why? You promised I wouldn't interfere with your ranger shit."

His grasp tightened on my hand comfortingly, his long index finger lazily stroking up my wrist. "You're not. I promise. There isn't much to do anyhow, and I'm supposed to protect the forest from harm, which is basically keeping you from driving through it," he teased while I huffed, pulling my hand away. He continued kindly, "And it's my responsibility to make sure visitors are safe, which is what I'm doing right now. In a very roundabout way." He smiled naughtily, causing me to put my hand back on his.

He picked up his wineglass in a salute. "To fire and calm in the storm." His eyes simmered with things unsaid while we clinked glasses in a toast.

Trying to gain a traction of control, I asked him a deep question. It felt even more appropriate in the shadows. "Okay, Mr. Scorpio, tell me why your last relationship ended. I know that's taboo, but Scorpio folks don't stray away from taboo topics."

I knew how forbidden this must be, but I didn't care. He pushed his sleeves up, revealing sinuous muscles and veins on his forearms. He put his elbows on the table, deep in thought.

"Well, let's see. My last serious relationship was back in graduate school. Three years ago, I had a girlfriend. We didn't live together, but we spent a lot of time together. We were very much involved. Anyway, one night, she started talking about our future and it wigged me out."

I tried to keep my demeanor nonchalant and nodded slowly to urge him to continue.

"I wasn't afraid of commitment, never have been. The problem was, she wanted vastly different things than I did. Without talking to me about what I wanted, she created this picture-perfect future that I had no say in. It was a big turnoff." He rubbed his hands together as if to punctuate his thought. Then he brought one hand to his napkin to play with its edges while he considered his words. "I guess it made me feel like a jerk for ending things, but it wasn't fair to string her along. I respect the women I date. Even if it doesn't work out for us together, I would never want to drag something out or waste someone's time if we want different things."

My voice was small and confused. "What things did she imagine?"

"She wanted a very social life with a full calendar. Suburbia. White picket fence." His eyelashes fluttered up, and then his eyes met mine with an even look. "She also wanted children."

His voice was intense, guarded. My entire thought process imploded in on itself like a collapsing galaxy. Bits of stardust and space matter debris floated around in my head, almost giving me tunnel vision, like a black hole. Was this why he didn't date? He didn't want kids. My stomach rolled in shock and all my blood felt like it was jolting in my body for a second. I had to play this off cool. I willed myself not to squirm or break eye contact. With an overly casual voice, I asked, "Oh, so you don't want kids?"

He looked extra brooding, surrounded by his dark hair, beard, and sweater, lit only by the candle and the storm. It was as if he were completely in the shadows except for his hypnotic eyes. Still staring at me, he slowly shook his head from side to side. A touch of something crept into the corner of his eyes. I couldn't peg it, but it looked a little sad or discouraged.

He went on, "I don't want children. It's a deal breaker for most women."

I shrugged, holding my wine closer to my face, getting caught up in my own thoughts. "You're not alone. I don't want them either. I mean, I have one of those birth control bars implanted in my arm for the same reason. Five years of peace of mind is priceless." Taking a sip, I looked away from him, trying not to lose my shit while I realized I'd said that out loud. Putting my glass on the table, I dared a glance back up at him.

Harley's eyes bored into me. I could feel behind his eyes was a tumultuous storm thrashing about. Considering me for a few heartbeats, he finally murmured in a husky voice, "Good."

Sweet mother goddess! My heart fluttered and then dropped into my pussy, only to throb wildly while low in my belly heaved in a whorish way, hungry for him. Holy shit! The way he'd said that had been primal and intense, an approval of sorts. I replayed the vision in my head of his sexy lips mouthing *good*.

"Oh, by the way, The Empress card you got in your reading can sometimes indicate a pregnancy, but rest assured, I knew that wasn't going to happen." I held up the arm with the birth control implant which made him smile.

"What about you?" he asked.

"What about me?"

"Why did your last relationship end?" he prompted, arching an eyebrow.

"Oh, I, um, well, it's a funny story. Terrible really. I, um, found my ex cheating on me."

"Oh." He turned his head, wincing, taking in the information.

"Like, in the act."

He winced again in the other direction.

"I knew the girl, too. It was awful."

"Gah! Wow! What an asshole. Cheating is bad enough, but to not appreciate a woman like you?" Harley's eyes scanned my face empathetically. "What a dumb fuck." His voice was cutting at the end in disgust.

"Yeah, pretty rough." Remembering the moment, I took a deep breath. "I've never had a shortage of guys who want to date me. Guys like the blonde hair and the positive attitude." I rolled my eyes. "The problem is they don't want to date me for long."

Harley scowled in clear disgust. "Why?"

"I don't know. I guess I'm just weird. They find my different slant on life intriguing for a bit, but then it gets inconvenient when I'm too opinionated or headstrong. Even though I try really hard to help the people around me and I'm always friendly, people treat me like this wild child. Then they're always hesitant to introduce me to people in their lives."

I took a sip of wine angrily then continued, "Like, I had one guy bring me home to his mom. She couldn't use her arm because of a tennis injury. He leaves the room and comes back and I'm massaging his mother . . . which apparently isn't something I should do?"

Harley puffed out an amused chuckle.

"Where is the logic? He could kiss me, but heaven forbid I touch the woman who brought him into this world? Bitch, please! She was in pain, and I knew I could help her with a massage. It worked, and she thanked me and called me a miracle worker because she could move her arm by the end of the night. She still puts an angel emoji on all my social media posts."

I smiled, thinking of her, and then realized Harley was smiling and looking at me.

"What?" I asked.

"Sounds like you need a guy with an actual backbone and a functioning level of empathy." He scoffed and continued leaning forward more. "Kaylee, you need to know that what you bring to the table is really something. You wear your heart on your sleeve and you want the best for people. The lack of filter is refreshing."

"Well . . . I mean . . ."

"You're not weird. You're unique. Any man would see that if they were on your level. Instead, they're threatened by it."

My entire body buzzed with his praise. I felt a sad smile pull at my lips, threatening to spread them. Sensing I didn't quite know how to accept his praise, he went on, "Whoever made you feel like you're too much needs to go find less. Have you heard that saying?"

"I have. You're not wrong. I mean, I can't dull myself down. I refuse to. And it's not like I'm a menace or a creep. I'm a very curious person who reads a lot, so I know a bit about everything. Also, my dad was a biker and my mom was a hippie. I mean, with the childhood I had, it's no wonder I'm a little . . . I don't know . . . kooky?"

"Unique," he stated.

"Unique," I echoed.

"One of a kind. Truly. I talk to so many people during the busy season up here, and no one has ever been as bright or funny as you."

"Wait, do you do this often? Date girls who are just visiting Maine? No judgement, just curious." I gestured between us, secretly ready to be offended.

"God, no! My grumpy ass?" He shook his head. "I've dated tourists in town, but you're the only woman who has stayed here with me." His confession made me feel special, like I was privileged to have this intimate access to him. Butterflies swirled in my stomach, only to scatter to my heart while some horny ones fluttered to my pussy, clearly with minds of their own.

Before I could pry anymore, a powerful gust of wind howled around the cabin, causing the flames in the fireplace to dim from where it plunged down the flue.

Chapter Eighteen

Harley followed the sound and caught the sight of it. "Sorry, I gotta . . ." He stood from his seat and booked it over to the fireplace, kneeling before it to nurse it back to full strength.

I picked up the dishes and cleaned up dinner, unsure of what to do with myself. I walked the candle that was on the table to Harley's nightstand so the light would be in there. Soon after, I found myself drawn to the flames and Harley's crouched body. He murmured under his breath, almost talking to the fire while he put different sizes of wood on the coals, coaxing it back to life. I sat on the rug crossed-legged, watching him.

The sound of pelting jolted me from my calm, causing me to look around for clues. Harley stared at the fire, unable to take his eyes away from it, only to murmur, "Relax, babe, it's the storm getting icy. You can hear it on the metal roof." Looking at the windows, I could see the dark night, and sure enough, I could spot sleet falling outside the cabin. The wind gusted around us, the mix of rain and hail hitting the roof in a soothing sound along with the pattering against the windows.

With the fire roaring, Harley moved back by me, away from the flames. The layered rug and furs cushioned us, creating a cozy spot between the coffee table and fireplace. He leaned his back against the coffee table and pulled me to his chest, where I sat between his legs and leaned my back against him. His low voice murmured, "I got you," before he kissed my temple.

"Sorry, I'm jumpy." I took a deep breath, watching the flames and breathing in the woodsy smell of his beard oil I could only imagine was a mix of cypress and cedar. He dragged his beard against my neck, causing just under my skin to heat in need. His lips kissed at my neck, and his velvety voice filled me once more, this time in a language I didn't understand. His tone was sexy, but when speaking Greek, his cadence went up and down hypnotically, spinning me deeper and deeper into his audible trap.

"Do you speak in Greek to all the girls? Is this your trade secret?" I fought a smile.

"No, I'm just too polite to say it in English. Maybe I should if it'll make you blush even more." I felt the flush rise from my ear onto my cheek, surely a traitorous shade of pink. I jutted him with my shoulder playfully. He moved some wisps of hair off my neck, exposing it even more while he continued. The words came out steady, quicker than his English but in an even lower timbre. It sounded ancient and forbidden and, most importantly, just for me.

I smiled at whatever he said, loving the way he said it. A wave of desire poured over me, starting at my neck and coursing down to between my legs. I clenched my thighs together in response, hoping he didn't notice. Harley nuzzled my neck and murmured something else in Greek that sounded like a question. I bit my lip and nodded, fighting the urge to wiggle against him. He dragged his nose up the side of my neck, breathing me in and nuzzling my hair.

"What did you say?" I asked.

"That's for me to know and you to find out." He moved to the other side of my head as the soft weight of my breasts gently rested on top of his forearms. He continued, "But I will say, I miss the taste of you already."

My pussy clenched at his admission. I hitched a breath, my chest pulling his arms to rise with my inhale. His declaration echoed in my brain, sending a shiver throughout my body. I wanted him filling me up again. I wanted him to transform that shiver into ecstasy.

"I like the feeling of your mouth on me and you all over me," I murmured into the night.

"Mmm, like this?" Harley's hand drifted confidently to my center. I nodded, pressing my legs open from where his long legs framed them, bent with feet flat on the rug. Feeling the solid muscle and immovable strength of him pushed my desire even higher.

He rubbed me over my leggings, unknowingly gliding against the satin I wore for him underneath. Feeling the shape of me, he moaned into my ear, kissing my neck to spend lustful energy. He swiftly lunged, ripping throw pillows and blankets off his couch. He cast them around us on the thick rug, creating a cozy, sensual space next to the roaring fire.

I looked at him demurely over my shoulder. I kissed him deeply, turning my head so his tongue could brush against mine. Behind my closed eyes, I could see the warm colors of the fire and the faint green of Harley's aura. He held my face and kissed me deeply, his hand possessively holding my neck while the other still grazed between my legs. Feeling how wet I was already getting, he pulled me to the floor.

Beneath me, he dragged me close to his body so I could feel his hard cock pressed between us, making me yearn for it more. His hands went to my ass, grabbing hungrily, only to pull me closer, smashing me against his hard chest. He groaned at the feeling of our bodies pressing together. Breaking the kiss, he pawed at my waist and lower back. "We should—" he said, but I couldn't fight kissing him, interrupting him completely. He pulled away. "All night."

"Mmm, take our time," I agreed in a breathy way, nodding and kissing him, darting my tongue against his and slowly sucking his bottom lip for a moment to hear his groan against my mouth. I kissed him again, this time nibbling his bottom lip, which caused him to get even harder from what I could feel.

Harley slowly stopped kissing me and maneuvered me to straddle him. I sat up and braced myself on his chest with my hands resting on his pecs while he held my hips. This close to the fire, his eyes scorched golden with the flames mixed in with the cognac color of his irises. I could feel him taking me in visually while simultaneously trying to calm himself down. His eyes drifted to the top of my head.

"Will you let your hair down for me, sweetheart?"

Without question, I plucked the hair tie from my top knot, tossing it on the coffee table while I shook my head, making my long waves fall around me, wild from being coiffed up all day, making me feel like some sexy lioness.

Lying on his back, he reached up between us, purposefully grazing one of my breasts with the back of his hand. He delicately grabbed a tendril of my hair and twirled it around his fingers. "Has anyone ever told you that your hair smells like heaven?" His voice was husky. The fire cracked and sputtered at our sides, adding to the tension. I shook my head, unable to answer with something witty. "Well, it does. And I love the way it feels against my chest when you lie on it." He grabbed the tendril higher up and let it skim through his palm.

"Good, because I love lying on your chest, in your arms. How your beard feels against my inner thighs." I bit my lip and looked down at my hair between us. He dropped the strand back down to my chest with measured slowness, driving me crazy. I leaned down to kiss him, my hair curtaining us and darkening our kiss from the fire. Harley reached for the hem of my sweater to pull it off me with the same measured, languid motion.

His eyes grew lustful as he took in the sight of my boobs pushed up in my red satin bra. I could see him biting the inside of his cheek, making a dimple appear. I felt a pulse from where his dick pressed into me. His hands roamed up my sides and reached for my breasts, skimming both slowly, feeling the soft satin under his palms. He gazed at me for a few heartbeats, clearly not expecting this. "Oh, baby . . ." his deep voice murmured in pure awe. His hands roamed to the tops of my breasts, where they spilled out of the cups, tracing reverently with his fingertips before kneading each one in a hand hungrily. I hummed, loving what he was doing to me.

He rolled me on my back while hovering over me, continuing to kiss down my neck and cleavage, slowly blowing warm air on the ticklish skin. I let out a throaty giggle, trying not to squirm. He peeled my leggings off me. I lifted my butt to help him, bending my legs, trying to be as graceful as possible. Newly freed, I put my arms above my head, jutting out my hips to one side to accentuate my curves. I arched my back to heave my chest up and gave him *come fuck me eyes* to drive him wild. He shook his head, knowing I was teasing him.

Harley kneeled and leaned closer to me, steadying himself with one hand while the other one moved up sensually to the right side of my throat. His muscular forearm rested between my soft breasts, trapping the fabric of my bra even closer against them. He whispered in my ear, "Baby, you look so damn good. Did you do this just for me?"

I nodded, trying to fight back a smile. "Just for you."

He gently kissed and nibbled my ear and the soft flesh below, making me moan. His head moved down my throat and onto my breast, kissing and nuzzling in my cleavage while he reached to undo my bra. His beard tickled my skin. It was a delicious distinction between that and his warm, soft lips. Pulling the bra from my breasts, he kissed the mounds that were now revealed. Too quickly, he leaned back up on his knees and looked at the crimson satin bra in his hand once more. Beside himself, he shook his head with a playful smile before he slowly tossed it on the couch.

"Turn around for me," he said, jutting up his chin with a dominant edge, his playful smile turning amused and hungry. Still between his kneeling legs, I twisted my body and propped myself up on my elbows so he could see my backside. I smiled to myself while I tilted my pelvis, making my bum stick up a bit from where I lay beneath him. The underwear was satin in the front and moved to lace on the sides and over to the back. The cut was cheeky, leaving most of my bum exposed, but not a full-on thong. His groan showed he liked what he saw. "Mmm, I like this." His fingers traced the border of lace on my exposed cheeks. He leaned down, pinning me with the weight of his chest on my back. One hand steadied him and the other ran up my leg to grab a cheek approvingly. His large middle finger traced my pussy lips from behind. I opened my mouth at the sensation of it.

"So soft," he murmured into my ear from behind before nuzzling my neck to kiss me. I giggled then gasped, realizing how good it felt. I tilted my hips so he could gain even more access. His finger continued to glide against the satin, making me squirm, eventually drenching the fabric. Feeling what he could do to me, he hummed and gently nipped and kissed at the hem of lace, and with his teeth, he dragged it down. A giggle fled my throat, mixing with his throaty chuckle. He continued to take off my panties as I rolled back over.

"I enjoy surprising you." I smiled at him, pulling him closer to me.

He shook his head with a smile. "You did. You look like a damn dream." He ran his hands over my naked body, a ravenous look edging his face. I pushed off his sweater. The indents of his muscles sculpted against his body made me even more hungry for him. His tan skin lit by fire was my new favorite sight. I playfully pushed him on his back, kissing down his chest, across his pecs, and to his torso. Looking up at him, I slowly unbuttoned his pants and pushed them down to his knees. He shimmied and kicked them off the rest of the way, grabbing some condoms out of his pocket before we did the same motion again for his boxer briefs. His eyes flickered smugly while I watched his dick emerge from the waistline of his underwear. It was thick and still intimidating.

I deliberately grazed my nails down the outside edges of his chest, down low on his abdomen, over his hip bones, and onto his muscular thighs. In the firelight, I could see a large scar running down the outside of most of his right leg that I hadn't noticed last night. His eyes fluttered shut as he shuddered at the sensation. Gazing at him still, I feathered a teasing touch up his inner thighs. I gently grabbed him and cradled him for a moment with one hand while I stroked his length in my other, causing his chest to move with newly ragged breath.

I enjoyed knowing that with only a light touch, I could bring a man this powerful to his limit. That my feminine magic could make him surrender to the unmatched softness and sweetness of being loved by a woman. Seeing his mouth open with a silent groan felt like a victory I didn't know I needed.

I traced my thumb across the head of his dick. Seeing how much he was enjoying this, I slowly lowered my head and licked the underside of it, running the tip of my tongue from the base to the head before swirling around it. He tasted salty and warm. With a moan, he bit his lower lip, staring at me with eyelids heavy with passion, struggling in his haze.

"Tell me how good this feels," I whispered against his dick, looking at him. All he could do was nod and touch my hair. Dipping my head down, taking his shaft into my mouth, I began to further derail him, seizing him completely again and again. I felt the tension in his body rise, his sounds becoming more untamed. I pulled away to lick the underside of his head where it met the shaft while still stroking him. Harley held his breath, and after a few heartbeats, he let out a gasp and put his hand under my chin to raise me up to him.

"You're too good at that," he whispered. His thumb rubbed against my bottom lip while trying to calm down. I caught it with a playful bite, causing him to pull me up to him, crushing me with an intense kiss. His mouth was feverish on mine, unyielding and barely allowing me to catch a breath.

His heavy cock shifted against me, making me crave him. He kissed me deeply, slowly grinding his dick against my mound. My body rolled against him in pure need. "I like touching you, seeing you by the firelight," he said while pushing hair off my shoulder before kissing it. "This feels like our own little world."

"Mmm, I agree," I said.

We pressed against each other, melting into one another while the fire crackled and morphed, burning into the night. Past the sound of our pleasured moans and kisses, I could hear the muffled tinks of the ice hitting the metal roof and the side of the cabin. A steady reminder of the storm that had put me in this situation.

The feeling of our naked bodies pressed together caused our kisses to become more frenzied, and we undulated on his fur rug with the fire roaring beside us while the storm crashed on. The frenzy built both outside and inside. One of my hands traveled down to his shaft, and I glided my grip up and down it. Moments later, he broke our kiss and groaned. "Babe, you can't keep touching me like this."

I kissed him back playfully. "Why is that?"

"I'm not done making you feel good. I won the bet, remember?" His kisses ran over my shoulders and cleavage. I opened my mouth to protest, and he kissed me before I could, turning me over only to push me on my back, flat against the rug. Running his hands up both of my arms, he placed them over my head, his palms gliding over the delicate parts of the backs. "Stay like this for me." His voice was gravelly and delectable. Warmth pooled under my skin, erupting with his command. It was irresistible. I'd never been into letting a man tell me what to do, but in this moment, Harley could tell me anything and I'd comply.

His hands roamed down from my arms and drifted behind my back, where he gently lifted me, making me arch my breasts up. His mouth wandered over my left breast, languidly licking around the nipple before sucking it into his mouth, nibbling it then licking away the sting.

I let out a moan and squeezed my inner thighs together. Sensing my need, he trailed a knowing hand down. With light fingertips, he teased the area in gentle circles. I opened my legs, beckoning him in farther. He ran his row of fingers down to trace my slit softly.

He glanced up at me darkly, looking like fucking sin. Moving to the other breast, he changed his pattern, flicking his tongue against the peak of my nipple. His mouth felt silky and warm against me. He continued, making me squirm and clench my inner thighs again, trapping his wrist between them. Pulling away from my chest, he leaned to the side of me and slowly slid his fingers to open my pussy. I whimpered, resting my head on the pillow.

He was eager to keep me guessing all that he could do with his hands. He pressed two fingers, one on either side of my sensitive bundle of nerves, and slowly rubbed up and down and in tantalizing circles before slowly dipping a finger into me, only to bring the moisture back up to my clit.

Harley knew what he was doing. I was drenched at his touch, noticing he smiled smugly at his ability to make me clench and buck under his hand. His eyes flashed to mine and smoldered as he enjoyed his power over me. The side of my body closest to the fireplace was warm and buzzed with awareness. The fire crackled and flashed flames of bright gold to dark amber. Hearing the roaring fire with the storm outside and Harley's ragged breath put me into a deeper frenzy. It felt ancient, primal.

I clung to his shoulder and pawed at his chest in fear I'd drift away in my stupor. The fire was so warm, being this close to it made my senses even more heightened. I could feel its dry heat on the most sensitive parts of me, making everything more vivid and undeniable. I felt crazed with need. "H-Harley, I want you." My voice didn't even sound like me to my ears. It was unrestrained and throaty.

He leaned down to kiss me, his erection pressing against my side. Between lingering kisses, he whispered, "I'm going to make you come first. It's what I want."

I opened my mouth to argue, causing him to take his hand away from me, making his point. He continued to kiss all over my body while his wet hand marked my skin wherever he touched, buying time or outright ignoring me. Stubborn ass. I raked my hands through his hair and over his strong, muscled shoulders, feeling like I was going feral. I needed him.

"Please," I whispered. He got to his knees and trailed kisses down my torso, nipping the soft flesh of my tummy and kissing my thighs. Looking up at me intensely from where he knelt, he slowly opened my legs back open.

"Don't rush me," he said darkly with an edge of dominance. His tone made me clench in pure desire. He noticed, cocking an eyebrow, looking at my dripping pussy and back up to taunt me before lowering his face to separate me with a kiss. I trembled and grabbed the fur rug beneath me, trying to find anything to anchor me to this moment.

I wasn't sure if it was the wine, the buildup of the day, or the heat from the fire, but every sense in my body peaked. The world around me became vivid and suspended in a moment of time. I was hyperaware of the crackle of the fire, the feeling of his short beard against my delicate skin, and the storm now thrashing. Something instinctual and unnamable brought me back to the moment, only in time for me to catch Harley's hungry eyes locked in on mine, still smoldering while he engulfed me. The glow of the fire lit up his muscular body and his large hands clutched the tops of my legs. Seeing him made my insides clench tighter with pleasure, making me flood even more against his mouth and beard.

Clearly loving that, Harley let out a gruff noise as he grabbed a pillow and swiftly put it under my bum, giving him easier access to devour me. Recognizing what he was doing, I slacked my mouth in realization.

"Baby!" I cried out.

"Mmm," he rumbled, returning to his spot. His hands gently moved to my inner thighs, skimming them open before grabbing my hips to tilt me against him with a slight hum. It was lustful and bold. I felt myself getting choked up with silent cries trying to leave my throat.

His mouth settled back over me, nuzzling me as he moaned out. "You taste so good. It drives me wild." My back arched when I felt his voice vibrating against my core. Not even giving me time to adjust back down from the sensation, he ran his tongue against me with small half-licks. I gasped, overwhelmed, causing him to find one of my hands and lace our fingers together. He continued with more pressure.

Panting and feeling everything in my body build, I ran a hand through Harley's dark hair and to his muscular traps and shoulders, almost pushing him away from me because his teasing was too much. He remained unfazed and continued his onslaught, feathering gently around me in half-strokes with his tongue.

"Mmm, I like that." I clutched his hand harder, grinding against his face, loving every moment of what he was doing. He let go of my hand and slid his palm under my ass, as if to hold me where he wanted me against his face. With his other hand palm up, he slowly slid one finger into me, causing me to whimper for another. Making me wait a couple thrusts, he added the second, pushing both of his fingers to the front of my body in a pressure so maddeningly euphoric, it made my vision go spotty.

With perfect motion, he stroked the inside of me while he continued to lick, making me clench around his fingers in my building orgasm. My cries echoed in the large room, but I didn't care. We were alone at this moment and in the secluded privacy of the cabin. That was all that mattered. I bucked against his hand while he went on, not stopping or changing his pace or pressure. My orgasm spun tight as I felt the tug of pleasure about to take me. "Mmm, I can tell you like this."

With eyes closed, I breathed out a desperate, "Yeah," only to feel him stop with his tongue and move away from my center with gentle kisses. Still keeping his fingers in me, he kissed my hips, my lower stomach, trailing kisses over my ribs and back up to my boobs.

I chanced a look at him in confusion, only to see a roguish look on his face. "I said don't rush me."

I covered my eyes in overwhelm, knowing this was so hot but so frustrating. I couldn't tell if I wanted to cry, beg him for more, or straight up jump his ass. Harley made his way to one of my breasts, moving a tendril of hair away and licking my nipple to get it hard again, still pressing his fingers inside me. He moved up to the side of my neck. The faintest waft of my arousal flooded my senses, making me hornier from knowing he had the most private parts of me on him.

"Are you ready for more?" he asked.

"Yes," I whispered while lowering my hand to rest on his. He held his breath, searching my face while our hands explored together. He swallowed hard, the ridge of his Adam's apple bobbing. I kissed it and bucked myself against his hand, causing his two fingers to dip into me even further. He moaned out something low in Greek and bit his lip. "You're fucking sexy, Harley." I kissed his neck up to the edge of his jaw, pulling him closer to me. "You're in control."

He smirked. "I don't know about that." He slid down my body, and I skimmed my hands over his back while he moved, appreciating the sight of his muscles shifting. Continuing his onslaught, he slid his tongue up and down my slit. "Mmm, you're so wet for me," he said before kissing my pussy sloppily. I gasped and grabbed the fur rug again while he ran circles around my clit with his tongue, awaking the rush of orgasm that had barely ceased.

He still had two fingers in me, never ceasing his tantalizing pressure. Shifting his head from side to side, he then tilted it to slide his tongue diagonally against my clit, then in circles. I began grinding against his face, unable to help myself. "Yeah, like that." I arched my back, feeling him tilt me even closer to his face as his nose ridge against my pussy. I ran my fingers through his hair, trying not to suffocate him in my thighs. Short panting built in my chest as I got closer and closer. My orgasm burst all around us with one giant euphoric throb. Soon after, several smaller throbs trailed it. I couldn't even breathe because it was so powerful and consuming. Harley put his hand against me, feeling the pulsing and allowing it to travel through me. The flat pressure of his hand on me increased the sensation.

I closed my eyes, completely engulfed and shuddering. After several breaths, he placed gentle kisses on my legs with wet lips. Slinking toward me, wiping his face on his forearm, he crawled up my body and kissed me deeply. Still trembling with my orgasm, I reached for his dick and stroked him, hearing his groans escape his mouth. He reached for the condom packet, ripped it open, and rolled it onto his shaft. I watched impatiently, thinking about what was soon to come. The small trailing beats of my orgasm still quietly crashed on inside me. My legs trembled, and a hush of tingles ran over my skin.

Still surrounded by the blankets and furs, it felt like a cocoon made for us to enjoy each other. The sight of Harley hovering over me in his masculine strength and confidence made me feel even sexier. I was fucking a man. A red-blooded man who loved tasting me and had a way of filling me up that was so dizzying, I simply wanted more of it.

The firelight cast shadows on his muscles and lit his complexion up. His forearms and biceps had veins bulging at certain spots, followed by portions of firm muscles wrapped around his arms. When he steadied himself over me, the veins were more visible, and something primal in me fluttered at the sight. Tracing his chest lightly, finally able to touch and have better access to his body now, I grazed his flesh with my nails, making him shudder in response. "Mmm, I want you all over me tonight," I said with admiration. A small smile tugged at our mouths in unison before a deep kiss.

Harley touched my face, looking into my eyes. His fingers brushed the hot flush that had crawled up my neck and onto my cheek. "I like this," he said, touching it. The feeling between us was deep and intense. We were both being pushed to the edge in pure passion, and we had enough mutual respect that we wanted it to be savored. His eyes darkened, and he moved his hand to my breast, then to the space between us.

"This is all I've been thinking about all day, tonight . . . with you," he admitted.

"Me too. All day," I breathed into the space between us. He let out a groan, like what I'd said was all he needed to hear. And with that, Harley settled over me, sinking his thick dick into me. I gasped, taking it all in. He kissed my neck and plunged into me again, letting my throbbing pussy from my previous orgasm lead him in. I spread my legs wider, allowing him to go even deeper.

Harley shook his head from side to side, nuzzling into my neck, trying to gain composure. "I love being inside you, here with you." It was almost like he was admitting it to himself, realizing something I couldn't pinpoint.

Between thrusts, I nodded. "You were made for me. We fit so well together."

He melted into a passionate kiss against my mouth, our lips gliding across one another, opening into French kisses that were exhilarating and made me even wetter. The taste and the feel of him all around me were the only things I needed. His thick mass separating me, his hard chest pressed against my soft breasts, and his mouth covering mine. It didn't feel like fucking. It was something more.

The passion and chemistry were undeniable, but beyond that, having sex with Harley felt like a surrender of sorts. There was no ego or shame, only the inevitable bliss of what happened when we were together. It was an instinct, a ritual we knew was integral to coming back to ourselves while finding each other. Something we created together that was just for us.

I loved feeling his touch on my breasts, the small of my back, the nape of my neck, the sensitive skin behind my knees while they bent up around him. His large hands brushed every spot in a hush of tenderness and amazement. I felt cherished. But along with that sweetness, there was an undeniable undercurrent of desire and complete carnal need.

I brought my hands up his chest, over his shoulders. I could see him watching my breasts jiggle with our movement, his gaze traveling down to my center, seeing us move together. His eyes clouded over in deep desire, and he set his jaw as he lifted me a little higher, bringing my center even closer to him. After a few strokes, his ragged breathing made his abs move gloriously.

I encircled my legs behind him and rolled my hips, watching him close his eyes in the sensation. "Do you like that?" I asked, running my hands down his chest and over to clutch his ass. Unable to respond, he nodded and rutted even deeper into me. My core squeezed tighter against his dick as my orgasm built. Each thrust pushed against me, right where I needed to feel him.

Feeling my response, Harley let go of my hips and braced himself on either side of me. His muscular arms felt like a delicious trap, the smell of manly musk filling the air. He undid me with shallow bucks, hooking his pelvis upward, causing his dick to hit a spot inside me and drag against my clit in such a way that I went speechless. My mind blanked in the sheer intensity of how absolutely intoxicating it all felt.

The energy of both of us on the brink of orgasm made the warm air around us feel like raw static. It was wild and untamed. My pussy got wetter and wetter, throbbing and fluttering, while Harley gave me the pleasure only he could give. My sensual cries mixed with his low groans. Outside, the storm crashed on into the night, much like the storm of ecstasy that raged on in our bodies.

Harley's eyes were closed in a trance of his own orgasm building. Bringing my hands to his face, I stroked the side of his beard, silently willing him to look at me. As if sensing my wish, his eyes opened and locked in with mine. We stared in a deep knowing that what was happening was raw and real, potent and powerful.

My mouth opened as it hitched with my orgasm. Unlike my previous one, it was a series of powerful waves. We both smiled right before it crashed, feeling it and letting my desire flood us even more before Harley pulsed with his own. He let out a deep groan and ducked his head.

From there, he fell apart, breaking and erupting into me and all around me. His gravelly groans filled my ear as his enormous frame slumped down on mine. His mouth planted mindless kisses on my skin before he rolled off to the side, where he lay on his back. A slick of sweat lined his body, making it shine in the firelight as his brawny chest lifted and fell with his breathing. His hand closest to me rested on my torso like all he could manage was barely touching me, but he didn't want to disconnect.

My body hummed and flushed with the passion and the fire. The crux between my legs was damp and sated, used in the best way as the pulsing continued. I gathered some deep breaths and waited for the trembling in my legs to subside. Minutes stretched on, and the flames continued to roar.

When I knew I could move again, I got up on wobbly legs, making Harley let out a low chuckle at my obvious need to recoup. I cleaned up in the bathroom and returned to our spot by the fire. Harley did the same in the second bathroom and promptly came back to me. His head on one pillow, he settled in the spot farther away from the fire than me and pulled me to his chest with a manly grunt, still unable to speak. The fire warmed my naked back, but a slight chill ran down my body. Harley lifted a blanket, tucking it around us protectively.

He put his hand under my chin to pull my face up from his chest to look at him. His eyes roamed over my face, taking in something. I let him look at me in silence, keeping my gaze steady and adoring, relaying I was completely vulnerable and present with him. I wanted desperately to know what he was thinking. My hand rested on his chest, and I could feel his heart still pounding. He brushed a piece of hair away from my face gently. A lump of emotion formed in my throat, and I could not speak. I felt whatever it was he was getting at. What had happened between us was . . . unspeakable, indescribable, completely new to both of us.

I leaned up and kissed him as an answer to his silent gaze. It was a slow, scorching kiss that conveyed a sense of intensity to match his observation. And with that, I settled back down onto his chest while he held me, the fire still crackling and the storm now morphing back into silent snow.

Together, we lay there like lovers, limbs entwined, bodies pressed, hands caressing each other tenderly. The candles on the mantle cast circular glows on the ceiling, their own flames dancing in opposition to the fire. The rug beneath us was soft, and the cozy blankets mixed with the heat of our bodies lulled us off into a silent trance.

It was, dare I say, bliss.

Chapter Nineteen

Harley

Kaylee lay on my chest, surrounded by furs and flames like some Barbarian queen. Long lashes cast down on her cheeks from where she watched her hand trace my torso. Her curves pressed into my bare skin along with her silky hair flowing over my arms where I held her. I wanted to soak this feeling of contentment into my bones. I wanted to remember this night I spent with the flames and her affection.

We'd been lying like this for what felt like hours, not wanting to fall asleep and end the night but needing time to recoup. Our breathing was now deep and silent, synched together. The fire crackled as a warm presence and the storm was in full force, its gusty winds howling around my land in intervals.

"Harley?" her soft voice whispered into my pec, finally breaking the silence.

"Yes, babe?" I kissed the top of her head.

"Do you ever get lonely? Living out here all alone?"

I kissed her head again, stalling. That question might have been innocent, but it hit me like a punch in the gut. I let out a deep sigh, feeling called out. "Yeah, I guess you could say that."

"Then why do you?"

"Do what?"

"Why do you live so far out here by yourself?" She looked up at me, the fire making her eyes look extra doe-like, causing me to feel even more helpless faced with her beauty and question.

"I'm a ranger. It's a loner job unless people need help. I spend my days deep in the woods. And I inherited the land."

Hadn't we gone over this?

She rolled her eyes playfully. "I know that, but what's the real reason?"

"That is the real reason."

"I don't buy it." She kissed my chest to pepper on affection alongside her questioning. And dammit, it worked; I couldn't feel fully offended. Fucking sorceress. My hand collected the long hair that trailed down her back, forming it in a swath as I stroked it, running the strands through my fingers. Touching her mane made me feel secretly possessive of her. I liked it. She had the softest hair of any woman I'd ever been physical with. Lit by only firelight, it looked like liquid gold.

"Just because you chose a rugged life doesn't mean you need to be devoid of all company."

"Well then, what's your theory?" I shot back.

"That you're punishing yourself in some sort of way."

"Like you're one to talk!" I playfully imitated her voice while saying her unofficial title. "Miss I Hate Boston but I Will Continue to Live There for No Fucking Reason." She erupted in giggles, burying her face into my chest bashfully. I continued in my Kaylee voice, "And I will help my Ambien-drugged grandma, my chaotic bestie, and my biker dad, but heaven forbid someone helps me! Especially if my wild ass gets stuck in a blizzard! It's not like I drove past warning signs for 200 miles or anything!"

Her giggles morphed into cackles, her fingers jabbing me in the sides playfully. Dropping the Kaylee voice, I proclaimed, "Oh, wrong move, missy! I don't fight fair!" I rolled us, pinning her to the rug to snuffle kisses into the side of her neck that wasn't bruised. She wiggled and continued to laugh, squirming to get away from how my beard tickled her.

"Harley! Stop! I'm ticklish!" she pleaded, pushing against my shoulders. I leaned up, hovering over her, yet our bodies pressed together from the ribs down. She poked me in the side again with an evil smirk.

"Oh, you fight dirty!" I bent down again, returning to my crazed kisses. She wiggled lower and hoisted her hip up against me, almost turning me over, but not really. I let her think she did so she could flip me over flat on my back to get on top.

Little did she know that was exactly where I wanted her.

Her breasts jiggled underneath her long hair while she settled over top me. Her hands moved to my armpits and along my sides, trying to find ticklish spots. "You won't find anything! I'm not ticklish!" I batted away her hands, our laughter echoing in the cabin.

"Dammit!" She huffed and slowly sat all the way down on me in defeat, her warm center nestling somewhere between my belly button and the base of my cock.

My traitorous cock . . . the same one that was now hardening with the sensation of her on top me. The same traitorous cock that made my hands drift up to her perfect tits to sweep away the strands of hair that covered them. Her nipples peeked through her golden hair as I moved my hands over her shoulders and down her arms. Goose bumps covered her chest, hardening her nipples and causing her to tremble. I squeezed and kneaded the sensitive softness of them hungrily. Kaylee's hands covered mine, moving along with them. With each grasp, she would roll her hips against me in unison, causing both of our gazes to turn heavy-lidded with lust.

Within seconds, our playful wrestling had morphed back into a horny haze. Kaylee leaned forward past my head, all but dragging her chest against my face to reach the stash of condoms I'd pulled from the front pocket of my pants. On her drag back, I nipped her breast and kissed her moving body until her soft lips melted into mine.

"No power with the storm," she whispered between kisses.

"I'll keep you warm," I said, making her smile and drop the condom next to us while we continued to kiss. I held her, loving every inch of her naked body pressed against me and how her smooth legs intertwined with mine underneath the blankets. Enjoying how her body was slightly warmer with the fire roaring beside us and how its sputters, cracks, and pops underscored the sounds we caused each other to make.

Hugging her to me, I ran my hands down her back, loving how it flared to her sexy hips and soft butt. I squeezed it to push her against me even closer, hoping she could feel what she was already doing to me. With her body flat against me, she felt accommodating, smooth, and supple.

Her hands touched my neck and raked up through my hair. She broke the kiss to look at me from where she rested her chin between my pecs, her gaze unabashedly fixed on mine. Where she held my face, she ran a thumb over the line of my beard and then gently over my eyebrow that had a faint scar. "You're so handsome it hurts," she said, sounding slightly sad, almost like it knocked the wind out of her.

I tilted my head so I could kiss her palm. "Don't say that, baby. I never want to hurt you." Her face looked wistful, causing me to pull her back to me for a kiss. "You're breathtaking. I'm so lucky." I kissed her some more, loving how she was softening under my affection, becoming pliant with my praise, so I continued telling her everything I was thinking. "You're addicting. I love how you kiss me." I kissed her again, stroking her jaw sweetly. "Everything about what we do together just feels so right. I could stay here forever with you. It's like no one else exists right now."

"I agree," she breathed on my lips before kissing me again. I could feel a level of emotion filling her because it was filling me too. "Everything just feels right with you," she said between kisses, echoing back my sentiment. "Everything."

I rolled her gently over and began kissing down her neck, along her shoulders, and down her sternum. Her legs splayed underneath me, beckoning me to nestle between them. Feeling her heat press low against my groin created a spark of some primal initiation back into our lust. Her nails grazed my back while I brought my mouth to her breasts. She sucked in a breath in anticipation, letting it out the moment my tongue teased her nipples with a swirl, causing them to become rosy and rigid. I licked each bud once again, covering them with my mouth, feeling her nipples harden, her chest trembling under my beard.

My cock stiffened at her reaction, its heavy length bulging between us like some silent invitation. Pulling my groin away from her, I braced myself on my forearms on either side of her body, letting my kisses move down her sternum, hearing the small, needy cries escape the back of her throat. "Baby," she begged while I continued to drag my mouth down her body, the short hairs of my beard skimming her skin trailed by soft kisses. Her panting brought her chest to meet my lips as I hovered over her, each breath returning her flesh to my mouth. She wiggled in sheer need, causing her curves to ricochet between my arms where I surrounded her.

"More," she breathed.

I looked up to see the light from the flames shining in her eyes, reflecting their beauty. Time ceased to exist. I kissed low on her ribs. "I wish you could see yourself right now. You look like a goddess."

"That's because I am," she said as a wild glimmer flashed through her eyes, and I felt her maneuver herself on top of me. I lay beneath her, newly stunned she could get even sexier. Her mouth covered mine in a searing kiss while she intentionally ran her body against mine before she settled over my dick, gliding herself up and down it while she reached for the condom, hardly breaking the kiss while sliding it on.

She muttered against my lips, "I need you filling me up, worshipping me."

All the blood had rushed to my dick, so I couldn't even talk. I just nodded and ran my hands hungrily down her chest, holding my cock to help her shimmy against my head. Her hips wiggled softly while she adjusted to the length of me. My cock pushed against her soft warmth, and I instantly felt her scorching heat all around me. She opened for me, clenching just for me, causing me to fight every shred of patience not to go crazy.

Locking into the moment, I held my hands up and laced hers with mine, helping her steady herself while she slowly began to grind on my dick. The flames lit her up, causing her hair to shimmer as it fell all around her, making her truly look like a goddess. She bit her lower lip, taking me in deeper and deeper. With each stroke, she sunk herself against me, letting me all but bottom out inside her, causing me to strangle a growl and clutch her hips harder. The sounds of her pleasured cries and the roar of the fire filled up my head while the storm and ecstasy crashed down all around us.

Afterwards, we lay in front of the fire, holding each other, dozing off and on. Without power, we were depending on it to keep us warm throughout the night. I'd find Kaylee shivering when the fire died down, only to prompt me to put another log on it to keep her warm. I held her there, wrapped up in my warmth along with the blankets and furs.

Deep into the night, she stirred, waking me. We were spooning, and she had assumed her rightful position of the little spoon in front of me. I instinctively held one of her breasts where my arm weaved in front to hold her, as if to claim her. When she realized I was holding her, she wiggled her butt against my groin, starting a tortuously tender, languid cuddlefuck.

Waking up after that, I had no sense of time or space. Had it been hours or the entire night?

Kaylee had some hold on me. Four nights and almost five measly days was all it had taken for me to fall for this girl, this fleeting free spirit. A part of me knew I was being an absolute fool. I shouldn't be falling for the first woman who came to town, made me laugh a lot, fed me bomb ass Italian food, and fucked my brains out, but oh boy, here I was! Catching feelings.

I'd promised myself I'd never fall for another woman who was visiting Maine. I'd broken that promise with Kaylee here.

Her bare shoulder was poking out from the blanket as I looked down at where she slept. I kissed it gently and rested on my side, staring at the fire and contemplating how everything had brought us to this moment.

After being outside this morning, I'd come in and noticed her sexy yoga fuckery. It had been astounding to see her upside down, pressed against my wall, spread-eagle with her tits almost in her own face. I'd had to go move some trees that had fallen in the storm and were blocking the road. Touching wood that wasn't mine had apparently been the answer.

Hours later, I'd come in and seen her sleeping on the couch, her beautiful face relaxed and my book spread open on her chest. It had started a downward spiral of me imagining her here all the time. Seeing her doing something as mundane as reading, making coffee, or doing yoga shouldn't put a haze in my head and a sting in my chest, but it had. Kaylee living out her life in my cabin was making me think of so many things I knew I shouldn't. I'd had to go out to my shop to get my mind off things even more than before.

She'd visited my woodshop and saved me from my boat clobbering me to death from where it had fallen from the rafters because of the wind shaking the barn. I'd known I should have strapped it down with another bungee, dammit! If I'd been alone in this storm, if she'd never crashed into my life, that incident could have killed me. I could have frozen to death if it had knocked me out. I could have burned myself on the wood-burning stove trying to dodge it, or so many other things could have gone wrong.

Seeing Kaylee's face cloud into deep worry while genuine panic bolted in her eyes like lightning had made me uneasy. It had been the purely instinctual side of her I didn't think many people saw. Premonition had flashed through her while she'd looked around, sensing her surroundings before I could reach her. I'd known she was intuitive from how eerily accurate the tarot reading had been, but seeing her impulses, her magic play out differently had made me feel privileged I could fall under her layer of protection. I didn't entirely understand this witchy side of her, but I knew one thing, I respected it.

Along with apparently being psychic as fuck, she was also intoxicating as sin. Seeing her take in all the details of my shop had made me adore her even more. Instead of being put off by my guy stuff, she'd seemed genuinely intrigued. That had made me feel better. Seeing Jimi Hendrix spread across her chest as she'd panted while I'd touched her certainly hadn't sucked either. "Voodoo Child" had rung in my head the entire time I'd tasted her, until she'd pointed out our shadows on the wall of my shop, then all hell had broken loose inside me.

Seeing something so filthy and damn near depraved was going to live rent free in my brain for the foreseeable future. Fucking hell!

Wood. Think of wood that's not your own, I chided myself while staring at the flames in the fireplace in front of me devour the maple log.

This afternoon, I'd finished the Adirondack chair I'd been working on. In a couple of days, I could finish it. I'd had a plan to make a small table for the dock, but now I had new ideas in my head. There was a window in my study that had a slight alcove. I'd imagined putting a window seat there someday, but now I wanted to do it because I could see Kaylee sitting there, the window flooding her with sunlight while her delicate hands held a book.

I wondered what she'd look like in a little sundress, imagining her smooth legs bare and crossed. I wanted to see her licking an ice cream cone and putting her hair up when the summer days got humid. It felt forbidden, but I caught myself often picturing her out in nature with me, exploring the land I loved so much. I wanted to show her all my favorite places where I'd spent moments wishing there were someone beside me. Countless nights alone staring up at the sky, endless sunrises spent lonely, wishing I could talk to someone about the beauty around me.

I reminded myself to get a grip. There was no way someone like Kaylee would ever want to live here with my ass. She wandered from place to place, apparently doing good deeds but also not committing to one person aside from her family and Maisie. Why would she ever want to stay here? Why would she commit to me?

I wasn't ready to come to terms with the gravity of my desire to have her. It was visceral and irrefutable. I wanted her by my side. When she wasn't, I worried about her or, worse, craved her.

The last time I'd felt anything remotely similar had been in grad school, when I'd dated Abby. She was such a stark contrast to Kaylee—both were beautiful in their own way, of course. Abby had been a social butterfly who'd fluttered from party to party and talked about our relationship with everyone. She'd told her friends our inside jokes and all about our sex life. Every date, we'd had to snap a selfie to prove it happened. It had felt like there was no privacy, something I'd deeply wanted.

The final straw had been when she'd casually mentioned the names of our future children. It hadn't been the names per se, but that she'd wanted children to begin with. That was a deal breaker for me. Sure, I didn't mind talking to kids about why we didn't litter and the importance of staying on trails in the park, but to have some of my own was the last thing I wanted. Ever.

She'd thought we were going to graduate and launch into marriage and children right away. We'd broken up that night after I'd explained how I felt and how weird it was she was planning our future without ever asking what I wanted. I hadn't wanted to be a dickbag and ghost her, so I'd told her it was over. I'd been the bad guy, which was fine by me if it meant she could move on and have the family she wanted.

I'd come back home to Maine, university degrees in hand, and had built a life for myself here by nabbing my dream job and building my cabin. My family had given me shit for being single and dumping Abby, but I wasn't a total loner. I went to bars, concerts, and sports games when I could, but admittedly, I thought I was self-isolating. I felt like damaged goods, and I also had a situation with my brother that got messy and made me avoid town.

Until now, I'd been keeping my head down and trying to survive. Living remotely on your own wasn't easy, but I liked the challenge. I also liked being a ranger. Now I realized, even with my years of loneliness here in Maine, it had been the right decision to not be with Abby. Even if it hadn't been for the kids being the tipping point, I could see now how poorly of a fit she'd been for me. She was a super-extroverted person who wanted to live a loud, busy, public life. I preferred situations that were calmer. Most of the time, I enjoyed quiet. I liked to go at my own pace, taking in life, like long walks in the spring, a slow paddle in my boat in the summer, hunting in the autumn, and the frozen stillness of winter.

I had control here in my cabin, in my job, and in my woods. Now Kaylee was here, and she was the only thing I couldn't control. And I couldn't control the way I felt about her.

She looked like a seductress in red satin, writhing by the glow of the firelight on my fur rug. Her hair all around her like a halo and her perfect tits pushed up. The roundness threatened to spill over the cup with just the faintest wiggle. I'd almost gnawed my arm off trying not to have her the first moment I'd seen her there.

She tasted so feminine, and the sensation of her quivering under my touch made me feel like a man. I loved feeling her squeeze around me and breathe heavier and how her panting made her breasts move tantalizingly up and down. The way she touched me, her soft mouth around my cock, like she knew exactly what she was doing. I enjoyed watching her beautiful face change as pleasure washed over her, her perfect mouth opening a little to let out moans only for me.

It was heaven for me to make her feel that good, to distract her so delectably while the storm crashed. That shit had felt different. Having sex with her last night had been explosive, but tonight had been a slow burn, something deeper and more meaningful than anything I'd felt with someone else.

I mean, I was a guy, so the thoughts running through my mind during sex were scarce, but whatever had happened made me ache, made it feel like I'd had too many emotions rising in my body that I didn't know how to unpack. With each thrust, I'd felt like we'd been exchanging energy. With each kiss, I'd felt we were relaying things unsaid and emotions too deep to admit. The way she'd open and met me with my movements had felt like a beautiful blend of flesh and need.

How could I keep her by my side? How could I ask this woman to stay? Was I ready for that, or was my dick doing all the thinking?

Here I was, sexed up with a gorgeous woman in my arms. Having our naked bodies strewn together mixed with the fire and fur made me feel happy on a primal level, like I was a provider. This was shelter in the storm. It was bliss. Feeling drunk and buzzing with sensations, I watched the candles flicker on the ceiling. Trying to gather my thoughts, warmed from the fire and her body, I drifted off into a deep sleep.

I woke a few hours later to find the fire slowly dwindling down. I blinked awake with her still beside me. She faced the fire and burrowed deep in the blankets for warmth in the fetal position, so only her back touched the side of my body. She woke around the same time as I did with a little sigh. I nuzzled her neck, breathing in the sweetness of her. Realizing where she was and who she was with, she wiggled her back even closer to me.

"Mmm, hi, baby," she said sleepily.

I could feel her smooth skin against me as I kissed the top of her head. "Are you still tired?" I whispered.

She nodded and wriggled deeper under the blankets.

"Okay, let's get up and get in bed."

"Your bed?"

"Yes," I answered, smiling at her slight stupor. Looking over her shoulder, I could tell she still had her eyes closed.

"Are you sure? I can sleep out here," she offered in a small, drowsy voice.

"No, babe. You belong in the bed with me." Did she not get how special she was to me? That I wanted her near me? I got to my knees and stood up with a miserable groan, feeling my right knee pop in a very unsexy way. It was so cold, I felt like my dick was going to disappear into me. She remained where she was, slowly falling back to sleep.

I walked to the kitchen and grabbed a glass of water, chugging it and filling it up again. After all that sex, I felt like a dry husk of a human. I got a glass for Kaylee and got the bedroom ready by closing the shutters, and turning on my gas fireplace (a much less needy version of the one in the living room) before turning down the covers on my bed.

Walking back out, I bent down to swoop her up, but she stirred awake and blinked at me in groggy confusion. She was like a naked, little fairy surrounded by all the blankets and pillows, her long hair covering parts of her body as she sat up. I fought back a smile at how cute she was when she was sleepy.

"Come on, sweetheart, before you get cold." I reached to pick her up again, and she grunted at me to stop. How could she be so cute and defiant at the same time? Cringing and groaning, she held my hand and hoisted herself up. Even in my sleepy haze, I enjoyed watching her naked butt move side to side while she walked into my room ahead of me.

"Drink this." I handed her some water.

"Ah, water." She drank it in an uncoordinated manner, still half asleep.

A trickle of water dripped from the cup and down between her breasts. I curled my finger to catch it, and she hummed at my touch.

"Mmm, I, like, really, really adore you," she said in a sleepy Southern drawl. "You're so cute, mmm, and warm, with a big 'ol dick," she added, eyes closed, crawling into my bed naked. I chuckled because she was basically acting drunk. Had the wine gotten to her and I hadn't noticed?

"Are you drunk?" I asked.

"Drunk on your dick!" she slurred indignantly before turning over and promptly falling back to sleep.

God, I adored this woman.

Chapter Twenty

Harley

I had lots of weird dreams. I dreamt of a fox chasing Kaylee throughout a forest, her bare feet mucked up with black mud. Her usual blonde hair was now an ashy shade, almost white instead of its golden hue. The pale dress she wore appeared tattered and too thin for what appeared to be the chilly spring weather around her. She was running and looking back, screaming at the sight of the fox right on her trail. A gray wolf emerged from the trees, only to sneer and leap, catching the fox's neck with a gruesome chomp, splattering blood on the forest floor in a semicircle and up the back of Kaylee's pale hair and dress.

Her screams echoed up into the trees in the dream, reverberating in my mind while I shot awake. My heartbeat rang in my ears, almost sounding like the wings of an eagle flapping. My stomach lurched on instinct. Something wasn't right.

I sensed her next to me. Blinking away the sleepiness from my mind, I noticed a blue glow coming from her phone on the dresser. It must've buzzed and woken me up.

I took several deep breaths, calming myself down from the nightmare, reminding myself it was only a dream. The logical part of my mind chimed in that although we had two species of foxes in Maine, they weren't a threat. The phone blinked and buzzed again, lighting up the wall and ceiling above it. I scowled over at it with annoyance, but before I could even get properly frustrated, it buzzed again.

Jeezus! I slowly got out of bed to turn it off, so it wouldn't wake Kaylee. Walking over, I gently picked up her phone in its sleek case and it buzzed again. This felt like an invasion of privacy. Like, sure, my lips might have been on both sets of hers before, but I didn't know if she was okay with me touching her phone.

I stood there like a creeper, buck naked and holding her phone to my chest so it didn't light up the entire room in its blazing glory. The last thing I needed was her to wake up only to see me naked, clutching her phone like Gollum, about to murmur *my precious* into the dark room. I scuttled to the bathroom, continuing to look at the phone to make sure it wasn't her mom or something. I mean, it was past 2 a.m. on a weeknight. Whoever was messaging her now needed attention.

But it was worse than I'd thought. So, so much worse. On the alerts, I saw several messages from a contact titled **Tyler Beige Sweater** with a sleepy emoji next to it. Huh?

A preview of a picture came up, and I swiped the phone on reflex to see it. Fuck!

Before I could un-see it, I saw it all.

It was a photo taken in a room with red lighting and a distinct shot of some guy penetrating a woman while she squatted over his lap. Both adults were staring at the camera with their tongues out. Subtle.

Instantly regretting my actions, I flinched at the photo and the situation with an audible, "Guhhh!"

I had no right to check her phone, even if it was buzzing on the dresser like some haunted vibrator. I'd already done the deed, so I committed. Setting my jaw, I clicked on the notification and saw a backlog of messages that had trickled in throughout the day from this Tyler guy.

Tyler: You're such an uptight priss. I thought hippie chicks were supposed to put out? Free love and all that shit.
Tyler: Like seriously, what grown-up doesn't fuck after the third date?
Tyler: You embarrassed Rosie and now she won't talk to me. Thanks loads, you fucking bitch.
Tyler: Bitch.
Tyler: What? Are you too good to talk to me?
Tyler: You're wrong. I am an alpha. And I get all the pussy I want, when I want. That's why I didn't fuck you. I could have. Remember New Year's Eve? You wore that black dress like a little whore. I know you fucking wanted this dick. Fucking slut.
Tyler: Why aren't you answering me?
Tyler: Why aren't you answering your work phone?
Tyler: Why aren't you at work?
Tyler: Why aren't you home?
Tyler: Babe, please come to the door.
Tyler: Why aren't you home? You should be off work by now. I just want to talk.

Hours had passed, then the photo had come through. Maybe I was imagining things, but it looked like they were in a club.

Tyler: Hey, blondie, tell your alpha to chop this wood, biiiiitch.

I laughed uncomfortably at the last text. How freaking random and out of left field was this douche? I scrolled up to the messages from Kaylee asking him to leave her alone a couple days ago and put the phone on the counter to splash water on my face. Who the hell was this guy? Who talked to a woman like that and then sent a nasty picture? Sure, a dick pic was basically mainstream, a habit hanging on from the invention of cell phones, one we should retire. At best, it was unoriginal. At worse, it was a permanent record of Tyler's bald package that looked like a ferret going through chemo.

I looked back at the picture, noticing my dick was bigger and I knew how to manscape. Pursing my lips, I felt the mannish instinct to compare dicks overtake me. Kaylee had dodged a fucking bullet with this guy. I fleetingly imagined grabbing my junk, showing enough of the trunk to make a point, and sending a video saying something like, *Don't worry, brother. She's with me now.* I refrained, knowing that wouldn't be mature or helpful.

I silenced the conversation and locked the phone. Turning off the light and returning to the bedroom, I placed it on the dresser where it belonged. Sliding in next to Kaylee was reward enough. Maybe she wouldn't be with me indefinitely, but I had her now.

I woke up to the smell of bacon and a slight beat of rock music coming from the kitchen. Stretching awake, I opened the shutters in my bedroom to reveal the blizzard still wrecking the world outside. The snow was falling in huge flakes without a stitch of sun in sight. The washed-out light flooded the room, making everything feel gray, muted, and moody.

I freshened up and put on some gray sweats and a white, long-sleeved shirt, exiting my room. The cabin was toasty with a newly stoked fire thanks to Kaylee. I could feel my eyes widen behind her back when I found her in the kitchen.

Fucking shit!

She was standing with her back to me at the stove, her long hair swaying with her movements. She was wearing a T-shirt and wiggling her hips, dancing to the music playing from her phone. I recognized the song as "Suzie Q" by Creedence Clearwater Revival, which made my heart burst because she had excellent taste.

I stood there, gawking, watching her hips shimmy side to side perfectly to the beat, the fabric of the navy shirt revealing bits of her legs with each movement. My eyes trailed down and noticed she was wearing gray knit socks that went over her knees, so only a bit of her soft thigh showed between those and the baggy shirt. My mind glitched, and I didn't have a single brain cell for a moment.

Feeling my gaze, she put the bacon on a plate and turned around with a sexy smile. She kept dancing, moving closer to me with confidence. I noticed the shirt she was wearing had Acadia National Park scrawled over the swell of her breasts. A rush of longing pooled in my chest when I realized she had a piece of my life displayed across her gorgeous tits.

"Good morning!" she purred, bringing me to her to dance playfully.

"Good morning indeed, you look fucking sexy." I brought her close and grabbed her hips to move with her. She giggled and looked me up and down.

"Harley! You dance?" she said in amusement, her face lighting up.

"It's more like enthusiastic swaying."

"I'll take it!" She beamed. I held her hand and twirled her. She kept dancing and giggling, shimmying her body up and down against me, erasing any thoughts in my brain with each drag. I wrapped my arms around her and moved with her, twirling her around and then dipping her as the song finished.

"CCR, twerking, and bacon? You're really trying to distract me, aren't you?" I said teasingly, making her shove my chest before I pulled her up to lock into a kiss.

"Okay, dance party aside. How do you like your eggs?" She turned down the music and gestured to the stove with a spatula and a sassy pop of her hip.

"Scrambled?" I suggested while sliding onto a stool at the kitchen island.

"Sure thing. How did you sleep? We got so much snow, this is ridiculous!"

"I had a weird dream. Actually, it was more of a nightmare." Noticing my reflection as I looked down at my coffee, I realized I looked haunted. I didn't like that. Comparing myself to the glow of Kaylee, I felt almost guilty for having the nightmare. She was happy, making her lover breakfast, and here I was ruining the moment.

"Nightmare? Oh no! Can I ask about what?" Her voiced pitched higher, making her sound even more gentle and caring.

"It was about you. You were running in a forest and this creepy fox was chasing you." My voice sounded detached, guarded. She looked up from where she scrambled the eggs on the stove.

"Me?"

"Yeah."

Kaylee's lips set in a firm line as she concentrated on scrambling the eggs but also filtering the information I'd given her. A slight wrinkle formed between her brows and her lips pursed even more. I was ruining the mood. She'd gotten up to make me breakfast, and here I was, wanting her to psychoanalyze me. All of this felt like a letdown from what a good night we'd had. I wasn't used to waking up to people. I wasn't used to people caring about me on such an intimate level.

She finally asked quietly, "What do you think that means?" She put the final touches on the food, dishing up the scrambled eggs, bacon, and fruit. She even put ketchup over my eggs in a tight zigzag, exactly the way I liked it, without even asking. She just knew.

"I don't want you to think you have to decode my dream or analyze me or anything. I'm sorry, I shouldn't have brought it up. It's just—" She stood across the kitchen island from me and cocked her head in concern. "Who's Tyler?" I blurted out. Her eyes widened momentarily in shock.

I continued, "I woke up from the nightmare and saw your phone was lighting up the room and buzzing a lot. I-I picked it up to turn it off so it wouldn't wake you, but I saw some creepy texts from a guy listed as Tyler Beige Sweater."

For the first time since I'd met her, her eyes glowered and pierced through me like daggers. The pale color that looked gray and luminescent now froze over for a moment before she squinted at me in discernment. I felt the frost already filling up the space between us. "You, you looked at my phone?" Her tone was instantly a frigid mess of accusatory and offended, like this stamped a permanent change in our relationship. *Not that we have one,* I reminded myself.

"I mean, yeah, but not in that way. Just to shut it off, and I saw a creepy photo pop up." I gestured at her phone on the counter like an idiot. She shifted her eyes from me to it and back to me. Another moment passed, and her mouth drooped, and her shoulders slumped. I gestured to the phone again. "Look at the messages, please."

She came to sit by me and cautiously picked it up, swiping the screen several times with her thumb while she sipped her coffee. I saw the red haze of the photo from last night, and her eyes crinkled in disgust. "Ew," she said under her breath. She scrolled up to read all the hateful messages, her face crumpling even more. I could see her nibbling inside her lower lip in unease.

"I'm sorry, Kaylee. I didn't mean to be nosy. You're right, I totally looked. It kept buzzing and that"—I gestured to the image—"was hard to miss. I promise I'm not in the habit of looking at phones. I don't even check mine most days." She shot me an icy look and then stared at the texts longer, noticeably hurt by Tyler and not satisfied with what I'd said. "I shouldn't have tapped the alert to see the gross photo. It wasn't cool of me. I'm sorry."

Finally, her eyes drifted up to mine. It hurt me to see how defeated and guarded she looked. "I appreciate you owning up to it and apologizing. I'm usually an open book with things like that, so it feels intrusive since we just met and you're totally in control up here. One shred of privacy would be nice."

"What do you mean, I'm in control?"

She shrugged.

I persisted. "What do you mean?"

"I feel like the ball is in your court. This is your place . . . your space." She ran a hand through her hair anxiously. "I don't even know who the guy is looking at my car. You're totally in control. Look, I know I'm just some tourist warming your bed, but this guy texting me, calling me a whore, is my real life."

"You think that? You think I consider you just someone warming my bed?" I could hear the hurt in my voice. I was blindsided. My vision tunneled a bit. Hadn't we talked about how different this felt last night? In the middle of everything?

"I mean, maybe, I'm not sure," she said blankly, shrugging again.

"Why is he even texting you like that?"

"Some guys are assholes. When a girl doesn't sleep with them, it automatically turns her into a slut. I don't get the man-logic there, but it's a reality for us women. He works in the same building as I do. To be honest, I wish I had never given him my number."

"The logic there stuns me too."

"Hey, you're not much better, being nosy, even if you saw a bizarre photo." She threw her hair over her shoulder with a sassy huff.

"You're right. I wanted to make sure it wasn't someone trying to reach you with an emergency or something. And the phone just kept buzzing and buzzing. It doesn't matter. I messed up and hurt you and I'm sorry."

"Thank you for apologizing. I get why you did what you did." She rubbed my leg reassuringly before she snickered, breaking the tension. "And what is with his weird dick? It looks like a damn croissant." Her face twisted in disgust before she giggled some more.

"Chop this wood, biiiiitch!" I said mockingly before we both laughed at how stupid he was. "Wait, why do you have him listed as a beige sweater? Was he wearing one when you met him or something?"

"Oh no, he's just really bland and basic, but always hanging around. I didn't want to pick him, he never made me feel special, but he was just always . . . there. Like a beige sweater."

I nervously chuckled, my eyes growing wide, feeling anxious about her ruthlessness. "Damn, woman. I wonder what I am to you."

She studied me, her eyes softening. "Oh, I respect you too much to compare you to clothing, but if I had to?" She ran her hand up my shoulder, squeezing the muscle before grabbing the beard hair on my chin sweetly. "I'd say you would be flannel: warm, complex, loveable, timeless."

Hearing her muse, I felt my lips pull into a small smile. Before I could ask her more about this Tyler guy, her phone rang. Kaylee's eyes grew large in recognition, and she mouthed, "Sorry," before answering it.

"Hey, Mama. What's up?" Her voice changed to a slight Southern accent. I could hear her mom on the other end with how close we were sitting next to each other.

"Hey, sweetie, I just ran into Maisie. She mentioned you're up in Maine riding a Harley. Now, what in the hell is going on?!"

Kaylee spit out some of her coffee in pure shock before her head rolled back in a loud cackle. She held her phone away from her face while her laughter continued to rip through her throat. "Mom!" She threw her head back again in more roaring laughter, unable to talk.

"What? When did you get a motorcycle? God, you're just like your father!"

"Mom, H-Harley is a man," she choked out.

"You're riding . . . a Harley . . . . Oh my!" Her mom's voice got breathy when the information registered in her brain, making Kaylee press her lips together to hold in her laughter.

"Good for you!" her mom said playfully. "How did you meet him?"

Kaylee side-eyed me and cleared her throat, realizing I was eavesdropping on her conversation.

"Well, I kind of wrecked my car, but don't freak out! I'm totally fine!"

"Kaylee Litha Waters! You wild child! Dammit, why didn't you tell me? When did this happen?"

"Saturday night. I went for a drive and ended up in Maine. I almost hit a moose and lost control of the Coop. It totally mangled it."

Her mother gasped and murmured something I didn't catch.

"Harley is a ranger, so he found me. The wreck stranded me in some forest. There was a huge snowstorm and no lodging, so he saved my ass. I'm actually still snowed in, so I'm staying here with him until I can leave."

The mention of her leaving so nonchalantly put a sting in my chest, but seeing her talk to someone familiar was endearing. She was vibrant and warmhearted, downright captivating with how charming she was.

"Oh, how romantic! Is he a gentleman?"

I got up to give her privacy, but Kaylee mouthed, "Sorry," again. I pressed a kiss on her forehead to let her know it was totally okay.

"Yes, of course. He's great." She paused listening to another question before answering, "Very handsome."

I walked into my study to check my work email, only to realize I still didn't have power. I'd have to run my generator soon to make sure the meat in my freezer didn't spoil. Staring out the window at my land, I fought the urge to go outside, not wanting to leave Kaylee inside again. She had positively taken up all my attention and energy. She was consuming me and my time in the best way. I knew I should be out clearing snow or at least checking on my land, but I was sick of being responsible and practical. All I wanted was to stay with Kaylee, all wrapped up in her, until the storm cleared. We deserved that much.

Her light footsteps filled the hall, causing me to turn my office chair more to see her. She smiled at me bashfully in the doorway. The bright light of the snowy day made her look extra feminine.

"Sorry about that," she said.

"No problem."

"I had to deal with some real-life stuff, you know? Without the Wi-Fi, it took forever to send emails."

"I get it."

"So, you took the day off?" she asked.

"I don't want you to feel like a burden or anything," I said, rolling my eyes in good humor, "but I took some time off this week. It's the slow season, plus I found some other things I'd rather do with my time." I purposefully took in the sight of her. She stepped closer to me, standing in between my legs from where I sat on my office chair. My hands held her waist on instinct while I looked up at her. "You have my full attention."

"Oh, is that so?" she countered playfully. Her eyes looked hungry. I'd never seen them quite this way. All I could do was nod, unexpectedly turned on. "So, we're all snowed in. Whatever shall we do?"

I began kissing her, unable to help myself. Before we could get too carried away, I felt her smile against my lips. "Harley, I have an idea," she said, putting her coffee mug on the coaster beside her on my desk. She ran her hands up my chest, onto my pecs, and around my shoulders. Her soft hands all over my body felt so good. With so many years of being touch starved, it felt intoxicating to have even the lightest touch from her. She locked eyes with me and pushed me back in the seat more.

Holy fuck.

She leaned down and kissed me, placing a knee on the chair between my legs, right at my groin where I sat. Her kisses were quick and playful, then smoldering more into deep and consuming. Her tongue moved against mine, with hungry noises filling up my mouth. I could do this for ages. Being near her felt like a drug. One of her hands moved down my torso and gently brushed my dick, and she squeezed and familiarized herself with it. Under her touch, I quickly got hard. She trailed kisses down my neck and picked up the hem of my shirt to lay kisses on my abdomen. Before I knew it, she was kneeling on the floor and settling down between my legs.

Was she doing what I thought she was?

She looked up at me through long lashes, and in complete confidence, she pulled down my pants and underwear to my thighs to reveal my rigid cock jutting up at her. She looked at it and then back up to me with a satisfied smirk before she dipped her head to kiss both of my hip bones, as if she were locking in some sexual ritual while skimming her nails on my thighs. I gulped as her hands surrounded my dick and began pumping my shaft. Her pink tongue darted against her lips to wet them. The sight of it made my stomach drop in anticipation.

"Just sit back," she said with a glint in her eyes, pushing at my chest and trailing her delicate hand back down to my dick.

While maintaining eye contact, she licked the tip of my cock before swirling her tongue around it. She ran the tip of her tongue along the underside of my shaft from base to tip. Her wet lips and mouth instantly sent shivers down my body. Like other parts of her, her mouth felt so warm and soft.

She covered the head of my cock with a sloppy kiss before taking it into her mouth with one plunge. "Yeah, just like that," I breathed, watching her. All I could do was look at her, completely entranced at how lucky I was to have this gorgeous woman on her knees. From where she knelt, I could see her soft thighs spilling over her thigh-highs. My eyes bounced between her mouth that was around my cock and her soft thighs pressing into my legs. Her hair tickled my thighs and torso. I gathered it lightly, holding it to one side by her shoulder, completely at her mercy.

She continued to pump and suck in perfect motion, using both her hands, her warm tongue testing, her cheeks hallowing with suction. Her voice came out husky. "I'm so lucky to have you here with me. I like having your big cock in my mouth," she whispered, gliding her lips up the side of my dick with a loaded look. I could only rub my thumb over her jaw and suck in more air through my nose for a fighting chance of a full breath. "I want you like this more often," she said, feathering her tongue over my head while running her hand up my length, causing me to groan.

She continued her onslaught, making the filthiest noises as the rings on her fingers ridged against my cock in a way I'd never felt. Her eyes never left mine, except to flutter closed when she took me to the back of her throat.

"Fuck," I hissed.

Pulling away from me, she sat up, only to grab her mug on the desk to take a sip while staring at me with knowing eyes. Her face broke into an impish smile before she ducked her head back down. I felt her now hotter mouth on my dick. The sensation of it made me heave in shock. It was mind-numbingly warm and even softer than before, making me hold my breath. The scorching trap of her mouth on me was consuming, relentless. She was completely derailing me, making me lose my mind.

What kind of move was this? I couldn't take it much longer. I let out a breath. "Babe, I'm going to," I warned her.

"Do it," she murmured against my cock.

She continued her slow torture, and before I could stop myself, I felt a warm pulse. The distinct feeling of pressure escaping while the tug of finishing filled my body. I burst into groans that echoed in my head. Looking down at Kaylee, I noticed my cum dripping out of the corners of her mouth and down her hand. She stood, staring at me naughtily while she licked the outside of her pinky before turning to leave.

Fucking hell!

I didn't know my name. I didn't know what the hell she'd done to my cock with her hot mouth, but it was the best thing I'd ever felt in my 31 years of life. Slumping in the chair, I hung my arms heavily while I regained something resembling sentience, after feeling like I'd just gotten my soul sucked from my body.

Kaylee left me there while she washed her hands. I heard her footsteps returning, which snapped me out of my delirium, causing me to pull up my pants and exit the study to find her in the hallway. She snickered, looking smug, happy she had some hold over me.

"Fucking hell, woman!" I playfully chased after her, hooking my arm around her waist to spin around and run with her like a football before putting her down so I could kiss her. As I walked her backwards to the bedroom, we both laughed between kisses, knowing what was about to go down. "Where did you learn that?" I asked between breaths, wondering why I'd never thought about the warm liquid trick before. She giggled and shook her head, refusing to tell me.

I pulled her onto the bed with me, our bodies moving together instinctively. With the shutters now open, I was so grateful to see her in all her beauty in the cool light of the storm. Heavy snowfall muted the day of sound and color, creating a unique type of calm. We lay together on our sides, pressed chest to chest. A smile lit up her face while she rubbed my beard and ran a hand through my hair.

"You're so handsome, Harley. You have such pretty eyes. They look kind." Her delicate finger traced my cheekbone and my lips. "And I love your smile."

Hearing her say that made me feel even luckier.

"Are you blushing?" she teased.

I fought back an embarrassed smile. Her kindness was disarming. "No, it's just not something I'm used to hearing. I'm usually around asshole rangers and . . . Dane."

She snickered at my hesitation over my best friend. I began tracing her pretty face. "You're so gorgeous. I mean, look at you. You're the type of beautiful that's dangerous. Like a goddess they'd make sculptures or paintings of." She rolled her eyes bashfully.

I continued, brushing her jaw with my thumb while I held her pretty face. "No, I'm serious. You're beautiful. And these eyes," I stuttered staring. "These eyes are never the same shade when I look at them. Sometimes blue, sometimes gray. I like how they keep me guessing, just like you."

Those eyes flooded with emotion, searching mine earnestly.

"I love the shape of your lips, and this part right here." My thumb grazed the slight vertical indent between her top lip and nose. She kissed my fingertip lightly with a coy smile.

I wanted to memorize every detail of her face, so when she was gone, I could still remember her. Sadness filled my chest, and I brushed the length of her perfect nose before moving to the smooth forehead above her pale eyebrows. She hitched her leg over mine, bringing herself closer to me. I ran a hand down her body and onto her leg. My longing became overturned by my instinctual need for her.

I smiled and looked down at the T-shirt she was wearing, slowly tracing the letters on the front, skimming one of her nipples. A small hum of pleasure escaped the back of her throat, and the nipple grew hard beneath the fabric. My speech was slow, entranced. "And these are driving me absolutely crazy." I skimmed the edge of her thigh-high socks, noticing how they dug into her flesh ever so slightly, making her luscious thigh spill out over the hem.

"Oh, yeah? You like them?" We both looked down at where her leg rested on my thigh. I dipped a finger into the hem, feeling the soft skin underneath the material.

"Mm-hmm, I like this part right here." I moved my fingers to the soft part of her thigh. "This exposed part." She sucked in a breath, and I covered her sigh with my mouth. She moaned into me, rolling her body against mine. I liked that she enjoyed me touching her. I roamed my hand up higher on her thigh, over to her butt, only to realize that was all she was wearing.

I broke the kiss. "Oh, you're only wearing a T-shirt?"

"Mm-hmm." She nodded and batted her eyelashes. I groaned, feeling blood pool back into my dick already. Realizing she'd been running around in a T-shirt and socks made my mind scramble. I fought for the proper response to a gorgeous girl going commando in my home the second morning in a row.

"Babe, I need you to sit on my face."

She chuckled softly, assuming I was joking.

"Oh yeah, that needs to happen. I need you to please sit on my face." I rolled onto my back with a smile, grabbing her hips to bring her up to me.

With another laugh, she shyly protested, "What if I crush you? Or suffocate you?"

"Then I die doing something I love." I pushed her closer to my neck before she could protest or feign modesty. I held her thighs with my hands and forearms, gently pushing her onto my face with her knees on either side of my head. She gasped at the sensation, steadying herself on my wooden headboard that she faced. I'd known that headboard would come in handy. "Good thing I built my furniture to be fuckproof," I added.

Her mouth formed little cries of pleasure while I gently kissed her open, nuzzling her sweetness and exposing her core to me. Pushing her closer to my face with my hands, I buried myself deeper against her. My lips and tongue explored her center. Her weight slowly settled more onto me while her indulgence unfolded. She slowly began grinding on my mouth, discovering how good it felt. My hands drifted to her lower back, as I felt her undulate on my face.

It was so fucking sexy. I could feel her soak my beard, and her soft thighs on either side of my face made me want to smother in her sensual, feminine flesh. With each thrust, her thighs muffled out my hearing so I couldn't catch all her desperate noises above me. I reached a hand under her shirt and ran it up her torso, making my way to one of her breasts. The tissue of her nipple was soft and ached to be teased. I rubbed, rolled, and pinched it until she moaned even louder.

"Baby, I can't. It's too—" Cutting her off, I moved to the other breast and continued to make each bud of flesh tighten with my touch. She let out an unbridled cry as she rolled herself against my face, helping me fuck her with my tongue. Thrust after thrust, I continued patiently devouring her, letting her fuck my face for as long as she needed to.

"Oh my god," she purred out, hovering over me. I moved into horizontal licks, shaking my head from side to side before diagonal half licks, feeling her throb against me.

"Harley," she moaned out. "I can't."

But then she did. She quivered and pulsed on top of me, rubbing her juicy pussy on my face. It was absolute heaven. It was my new favorite thing. I wanted her to sit on my face every damn day.

Bracing herself against the headboard, she let out a self-conscious laugh followed by a breathy moan. I guessed this was her first time sitting on a man's face. What a damn shame. It made me want to have her even more.

Kaylee lifted off me just enough to make eye contact, only to whimper hungrily, truly dick hungry. "More, baby, I need more." I felt my dick get even harder at her throaty plea. She tore my pants off while I took off my shirt, rubbing my face dry with it.

Pushing the T-shirt off her, I leaned up to all but motorboat her. I didn't fucking care! I'd wanted to do it since the first time I'd seen her naked. She had perfect tits. I nuzzled them and licked both nipples, feeling her get wetter against where her pussy pressed into my body.

Each time with Kaylee was different, and right now, this felt like a no frills fuck. We just needed to feel each other. I got a condom out of my bedside table and put it on my dick while Kaylee hungrily touched my body, her breasts pushing together with her arm movements making every thought drain out of my brain.

Capitals.

States.

Fuck.

Maine . . . Augusta

Oregon . . . Portland . . . Wait . . . Salem . . . Holy fuck, that felt good. Pulling my attention back, I witnessed Kaylee hungrily staring at my dick while stroking it.

"Get on it," I said with a smirk, causing her to fight a smile while she bit her lower lip before sinking down on my cock with her throbbing pussy. I pulled her to me with a hungry kiss before murmuring, "Good girl." That made her gasp in my mouth as she clenched immediately around me.

Unable to control myself, feeling overly fucked, I felt the tensing in my body like I was going to come already. I'd gotten riled up eating her out, and this was happening too soon. I enjoyed savoring my time with her, but this felt fevered and carnal. She smiled at the response. "Do you trust me?" Her lashes fluttered while she looked down at me.

"Yes," I said. Because what the hell else did you say when a woman was naked on top of you? Fuck, I'd be up for damn near anything naked with her.

A devious smile spread across Kaylee's face while she lifted one of her legs and gracefully twirled around to sit herself across my groin, facing the other way in reverse cowgirl position in one swift motion. The immediate view of her perfect ass made me spank a cheek hungrily, only to rub away the sting. "Fucking hell!" I bit out while she slid back down on my cock and gently touched my nuts.

I threw my head back in, gripping her hips. "What in the flexible fairy fuckery was that?" I groaned in anguish, completely at her mercy. Kaylee's back shook with laughter before she shot a devious look at me from over her left shoulder. She moved her hips in a tilting circle while sliding up and down my cock, grinding against me in the perfect torture.

The sight of her backlit by the blizzard enshrouding us was hypnotic, her curves shadowed against the falling snow in the window just beyond her, its silvery light making her look radiant. Her hair almost touched her ass with how she arched her back. I splayed my hands over her soft hips, liking how my fingers indented on her skin there and how her thighs jiggled with every thrust. She was all woman. All mine.

"Wait, slow down," I whispered, trying to hold her hips still. "Touch yourself," I demanded. I tightened my jaw, trying to get ahold of myself.

She shook her head with a playful laugh. "You're so bossy. I think I'm calling the shots." She squeezed my dick with her most intimate muscles. I felt my mouth open at how good she felt gripping me, moving on top of me in this sensual torment.

How was I going to forget this?

I started moving against her, hitting the spot on her body only I could. I listened for her breath to hitch to tell me I was doing it right. After a couple of strokes, she drenched my dick even more. "You're gonna come on my cock," I commanded, kneading the softness of her hips and ass.

"Yeah," she said in breathy desperation, apparently liking that and admitting that she was getting close.

"You're completely filled with me, with what I do to you."

"Yeah," she agreed once more between filthy, little noises.

Oh, fucking hell, this unlocked something in me. This was dangerous. Her pussy clasped my cock so tight, her orgasm tipping hard and fast. She throbbed around me, making me burst. Pulse after pulse, I emptied into her. It felt feverish and almost too much to keep up with. I watched Kaylee all but tilt off me, slumping to my side while we stared at the beams on my ceiling, trying to recover.

After a while, I took care of the condom and cleaned her up with a rag then held her, pulling her top leg across my body so I could trace the skin on her thigh with my fingertips. In the light of day, I could see faint lines across the sides of her hip, spreading to her cute butt cheek. They were even paler than the alabaster of her skin.

Noticing my gaze, she asked in a small voice, "Are you checking out my stretch marks?"

I nodded my head contemplatively, unable to take my eyes off them. "They're beautiful. They made you into the woman you are." I traced them reverently, thinking about how soft and voluptuous she was beside me. "They're your lightning bolts." I ducked my head to nip her hip with a kiss. Feeling I should show her mine, I held up my arm that wasn't cradling her to show the faint lines on my biceps by my armpit. "I have them too." She kissed my arm in the same fashion.

I found the small scar from her birth control implant on the inside of her upper left arm and feathered a reverent kissed there too, knowing that getting it must've hurt. She fought a small smile and then glanced at my hand. "What's this from?" She picked up my hand and rubbed her thumb across the scar forking out between my pinky and ring finger.

"Oh, that? That happens when you try to stop a throwing knife with your hand when you're a drunk teenager."

She scanned my body for more. "What about your leg?"

Ugh. I knew that was coming. I took a deep breath to gather my thoughts. How much did I want to tell her? Moreso, would it freak her out? "When I was 13, I had a serious accident camping with my brother and dad. I grew up about thirty minutes north of here, so we camped a lot growing up. Well, being the little shit I was, I wandered off from camp. My dumbass was off trail and trying to scale a mountain and the ground fell out beneath me, causing me to slide down in a deep ravine. My fall knocked large rocks loose, and they ended up falling with me, pinning me there."

Kaylee's eyes widened. "Seriously?"

"Yeah, I was stuck there for a while. As it got darker, I remember being scared shitless a bear would come by and eat me, or worse, I'd slowly die there pinned to the earth. For hours, I stared up at the tree canopy and hoped someone would find me. I yelled, but the ditch was so deep, I got the feeling no one could hear me."

Kaylee shifted her weight beside me, propping herself up on an elbow.

"When they found me, it was horrific. My right leg had shattered bones and torn ligaments. The scar is from the incident and some surgeries. I had to learn how to use my leg again and spent that entire summer rehabbing it."

"That's so scary!" Kaylee's jaw dropped slightly as her hand roved over my leg.

"I was lucky that's all that happened." I lifted my leg to inspect the grizzled scar that ran down the outside of my right thigh and knee, curving under my kneecap only to fork down my shin. It was lighter now that it had been nearly 20 years, but the raised edges still provided proof.

Kaylee's eyes drifted to the scar and back up to me. "I am so glad you were okay."

"Thank you. It's humbling to be in a situation like that. I always wanted to be a ranger, but after the accident, there was no doubt in my mind. I wanted to prevent it from happening to others or to at least help find people in nasty situations."

She nodded in understanding, putting her hand on my chest.

"I don't think you understand how many dead bodies I've seen. Rescuing you was disorienting because you were so alive." I brushed her face, remembering when I'd first seen her. "You were so achingly alive, it nearly took my breath away. I'm not used to finding people okay, let alone so bright and bold."

Her face tugged with a worried expression. She rubbed the pad of her thumb up my cheekbone while holding my face. "Harley, I'm so sorry. I didn't even think about that. You've probably seen so much."

I leaned into her hand, slowly blinking away the memories of the victims I'd found over the years that strobed through my mind. Their lifeless eyes staring up at me, the pools of blood beneath them sinking into the soil. How distinctly heavy a waterlogged body was to pull from icy lakes or rapids. Animal attacks, suicides, burn victims, people who fell and their body contorted in gruesome ways. I'd seen so many people stony and cold, even ones I'd known personally. I closed my eyes and took a deep breath, trying to allow myself this shred of peace in this moment of solace here with Kaylee.

"So, that's why you are so prepared, huh? It's beyond a habit. It's part of you because you got a second chance?"

"I guess you could say that." My stomach sank in a distinct burning sensation from feeling vulnerable and reliving past trauma. I wasn't sure if it was just the flashbacks or the realization that Kaylee was seeing right through me.

"And seeing people who didn't make it, that puts another layer of grief and guilt on it," she said, unknowingly twisting the metaphorical knife in me.

"Yeah," I breathed out, trying to collect myself. "I-I've studied first aid and survivalist techniques ever since. I get it, I was a little dumbass who put myself in that situation, but spending hours wondering if you're going to die a slow, painful death is fucking traumatizing."

"Absolutely." She patted my chest reassuringly in agreement. "It's understandable a situation like that would make you want to be prepared in the future. I'm so impressed you didn't let it slow you down. I mean, hiking the Appalachian Trail and all the other stuff you've done. It's impressive." Before I could respond, she kissed me sweetly. "Saturday, you told me you know what it's like to be stranded. Was this accident what you meant?" she asked.

"Yeah, part of it. I've been in some tough situations. I didn't want you to be stranded because I know how bad things can get."

She stared at me, her soft breasts smooshed against my ribs and spilling over. Her gentle hand ran up the side of my face and over the scar that veined through my eyebrow in the faintest way, as she no doubt wondered where I'd gotten that one, too.

"That's from that night," I said, nodding, offering information in a moment of vulnerability. "And this." I turned my arm so she could see the gnarly scar on my right elbow as well.

She gently leaned over and kissed it. While doing that, I saw her neck injury and moved her hair off her shoulder and gently kissed the bruise that was still there. It had changed from reddish purple to now a dark blue. It made my stomach lurch seeing the violent color against her porcelain skin. I was grateful her hair was covering it most of the time because it was so upsetting to look at.

"I don't like the thought of you being hurt," I said, gazing at her.

"I don't like the idea of you being hurt either," she said before kissing me sweetly once more.

Chapter Twenty-One

Harley and I had fucked too much. Not figuratively, but literally. I was sore. I stood in the shower alone, slumped over to touch my toes to stretch my back and hips. The warm water rushed over my skin, calming me down enough for the aftermath of our trysts to expose a physical exhaustion that hit me in waves. I washed my hair, enjoying the feeling of the water flowing over my face as I willed it to cleanse my energy. I loved Harley's company, but I was glad to have a moment of respite to recoup. Being within feet of him made me feel hyperaware of his allure. Here in the steam, I could think and gather myself.

What was I doing here? Was I naïve enough to think I was waiting for my Mini Cooper to be fixed and I'd drive off with Harley in the rearview mirror? Bitch, please! A level of panic rose in my chest, and my heart raced. How was I going to get myself out of this one?

Some aspect of me, perhaps it was my intuition, knew my time spent with this amazing man had permanently changed me as a woman. Our kisses, his touch, and his hazel eyes on me had carved out a distinct pathway in my heart that I hadn't known was possible. I felt seen, cherished even.

Last night had changed something within me. Seeing him hungry in the flames had opened a part of my heart even I hadn't been aware of. Everything about Harley made me feel simultaneously nervous and giddy, yet also calm and safe.

For the first time in my life, I wanted to stay instead of run.

I swallowed hard and put my hand over my heart that was beating wildly in my chest with that realization. What was happening to me? I was Kaylee Waters, a certified wild child. I didn't stay for men. No one had ever given me a reason to. Their inability to appreciate or understand me caused me to run, to escape before they could hurt me. You didn't get hurt if you left first. So that was what I did . . . I ran.

But I couldn't now.

The thought of it put an even worse feeling in my heart. The idea of never seeing Harley again felt tragic, cruel, and downright fucked up. I couldn't fathom running from a man who appreciated and tried to understand me. Not just that, he also made me feel sane, like my quirks were perks, not hassles.

Harley made me laugh, and his sense of humor was perfect. I loved talking to him. His perspective and life experiences fascinated me. He was thoughtful, open-minded, selfless, all while being serious but lighthearted when it mattered. He had a vibe that made him feel a bit out of place in space and time, but in a good way. Unmarred by the decaying societal standards of men, Harley was in a league of his own.

His protective nature made me feel calm, so much so I sensed sleeping next to him was healing. We could lie together just to feel close and relaxed, cared for without attempting to get to a specific point in physicality like sex. Yet when we had sex, it felt like something we were supposed to do together. The way he could tell what I needed made me question if I was the psychic one in the situation. Most impressive were his eyes. They remained kind, mischievous even. As if to relay, *yeah, we're really fucking doing this, aren't we?* It made everything feel like some secret only we were in on. I loved it.

How was I supposed to say goodbye? How could I leave all this?

I put my forehead on the shower wall after turning off the water. The cool tile brought me back down to a calmer perspective. I needed to think about this logically.

What if he wanted me to leave? Perhaps I was already overstaying my welcome and I didn't know it because I kept feeding and fucking him. A shrill squeak escaped my mouth when I realized that was a possibility.

What if I only liked this place because it was a wonderful escape from work and a sad, empty apartment? Sure, being snowed in was fun, but for how long? I toweled off and put lotion on my body, thinking of all the ways I could see this wrong.

My life in Boston was depressing, but I should at least be craving my bed and I wasn't. Last night, I'd kept waking up to him and the fire, feeling cozy and cared for. The entire night had made me feel like a warm puddle of a woman, completely blissful and surrendered. I wanted more of that, and I couldn't think of a better way to spend long winter nights than together. This morning, I'd wanted to keep dancing to rock music with him while I'd made breakfast. I loved the way he'd actually boogied with me and had known the song.

I should be eager to go back to the city that had small perks like coffee and Wi-Fi, but I imagined myself here instead. Almost hourly, I'd catch myself in a new daydream of what life could be like with Harley. I wanted to watch a solstice sunset with him. I bet he looked handsome swimming in the lake with his broad shoulders moving with each stroke. My mind concocted all these things I wanted to see him doing, like cheering alongside him at a baseball game, seeing what he looked like when he was sick, and how his beard would gray with age.

I blinked hard in disgust, thinking of someone else seeing all those things instead of me. Deep confliction rattled in my brain between knowing Harley was sincerely into me, but also a mountain man with a life packed with his own interests and career.

A prickle in my mind reminded me he'd fleetingly mentioned he'd built his cabin bigger than he'd needed last night at dinner. That was . . . something to consider. His confessions in front of the fire also meant something to me. His low, deep voice revealed unexpected insight as he'd proclaimed, *You're addicting. I love how you kiss me. Everything about what we do together just feels so right. I could stay here forever with you. It's like no one else exists right now.*

I swallowed hard, trying to push out memories of how glorious and sensual last night had been. Another prickle reminded me that Harley didn't know how recently the Tyler situation had gone down. What if I only liked Harley because Tyler had been a complete jackass? It was then I realized I only ever thought of Tyler when he texted me. Saying goodbye to him had hurt my ego, but that was about it.

Harley had showed over breakfast he had feelings for me, or else he wouldn't have been concerned with another guy texting me. Hell, he'd been concerned enough to look at my phone when Tyler had sent a horrific selfie of himself impaling a bottle service girl at a VIP room in a club. My mouth twisted in disgust at the memory.

I needed to position myself to find out more answers. I needed to know how I felt about Harley with my clothes on before I took the risk of not running from this. We needed to keep our hands off each other so I could see him accurately.

Running a plan through my head, I exited the bathroom to see Harley still on the bed with his eyes covered by his forearm, blocking the bright, snowy daylight, half asleep. It was nice to see him unaware of my gaze. I noticed for the first time how beautiful his long, tan legs looked sprawled out on the bed. His ragged scar twisted down his leg and over his knee before his leg gave way to his large foot. His face was soft with relaxation, making him look younger and more innocent. My chest tightened as I thought of how much I already cared for him.

Feeling my stare, he stirred sleepily, wincing at the bright light of the snowy day when he opened his eyes. Without a word, he got up and went to the bathroom. I heard the shower turn on and sighed in relief. I had a few more moments to collect myself.

I put on the purple leggings and the black sweater I'd worn the night of my wreck, my unofficial Pine Bluff uniform. Too tired to mess with makeup, I let out a miserable sigh, not knowing what to do with myself. I pulled out my phone, only to see an email from my boss.

Kaylee,
Any updates? We have a client meeting on Friday. Will you be back?
Thx,
T

I rolled my eyes. I fucking hated it when people spelled "thanks" with an x, and it was even worse when they used their initials to sign off on an email. It was Wednesday morning. I told her I'd be out the entire week and she was already hounding me. As a salaried employee with more than enough time off to cover my absence, I was a little miffed. I hit reply and composed an overly formal email because I was a professional, dammit. A professional with a dick appointment lasting a week, apparently.

Hi, Tamara,
I'm still managing this personal emergency out of state. Regretfully, I don't have an exact timeline, but I expect my absence will extend into early next week. Please push

the client meeting to next week. I will update you as soon as I have more details.
Thank you,
Kaylee

I hit send with a scowl and waited for my spotty service to respond without the help of Wi-Fi. She didn't need to know that by handling this personal emergency, I meant handling Harley's perfect dick, but hey, a girl had needs. Ugh, but reality was creeping in. Eventually, I would have to face life again. Shit, shit, shit! I needed answers!

I clicked on my messages from Maisie. She'd sent a dorky selfie with some butt plugs beside her, along with a text.

Maisie: Inventory is such a pain in the ass!

I snickered at the photo then snapped a selfie with my tongue sticking out, showing the messy bed behind me. Along with it, I sent a teasing text.

Me: Sorry, I can't come to the phone right now. I'm too busy sitting on a lumberjack's face.

She instantly wrote back.

Maisie: The best seat in the house.

I snorted a little at her joke.

Me: Lots to update you on, but basically, I'm doing well. My mom called and asked why I'm riding a Harley though.

Maisie: Oops! I forgot to mention to her it was a metaphor. Honest mistake!

Me: Maisie Quinn, you will pay for this! The man damn near had an aneurysm when she asked that.

Maisie: Vroom, vroom.

I put down my phone snickering, tidying up the bed, figuring it was the polite thing to do. Picking up his pillow I hummed in enjoyment. It smelled like Harley and the cabin, all clean and woodsy. I held it close to my chest, not sure what to do with it. Harley appeared from the bathroom, causing me to put it casually back as I sat on the edge of the bed, waiting for him. He walked toward me, holding a towel around his waist. He caressed my face pensively. "You're so beautiful, even without makeup on."

My chest got tight, and I felt like a jerk because I knew I was about to ruin the moment. I forced a small smile and placed both my hands on either side of his torso, steadying myself and keeping him distanced from me. His skin was still damp, and I could feel his solid obliques under my palms. I took a deep gulp, trying not to get distracted by his body.

"Do you know how long the storm's going to last?" I hadn't checked my weather app for a bit.

"Um, today should be the last bad day of it, and it's expected to ease up by tonight." Harley's eyebrows pinched together with concern. Talking about the storm stopping, along with my stay, put him in a weird spot, too. Seeing it play out in his body language was oddly reassuring.

"I have an idea. I hope you're open to it." My voice was quiet.

"Sure, what is it?" I could see his demeanor change, getting more nervous while he read my tone and body language. He clutched the towel tighter, shifting his weight from foot to foot. I felt small and stupid sitting beside him, but something reminded me it wasn't unreasonable to pump the brakes with him physically. This was not an outlandish request.

"I think we should hold off on anything physical for a bit," I said, staring at my hands on his torso before chancing a glance up at him.

His head cocked to the side in confusion. "Oh?" is all he muttered, his brow gathering. "I mean, of course, whatever you're comfortable with," he added, blinking in uncertainty.

I nodded up at him. He raked his hands through his hair and squeezed the back of his neck. I couldn't tell if this was a motion of self-soothing or pure frustration. He stepped backwards, granting space away from my touch, and my hands felt heavier now where I rested them in my lap. He bit out a frustrated grunt, considering something in his head. Squeezing the back of his neck again, he shook his head in disgust, only to roam to his walk-in closet.

"That's all you're going to say to me?" Before I could stop myself, I huffed at his retreating figure. I had a slight temper, I knew it, but I could control it with people I didn't know super well. I guessed I knew Harley better than I thought.

He turned around, halfway through the doorframe of the closet. He flung his hand out, gesturing up and down at me, clearly beside himself. "Jesus Christ, Kaylee! What the hell do you expect me to say to that?" It was the first time I'd heard his voice above the rich rumble of his conversational tone. Hearing it now on the verge of a yell made it sound even deeper and more powerful. It was a little scary but a little hot. What the fuck was wrong with me?

I took a deep, ragged breath and moved the ring on my pointer finger around with my thumb. I could hear him bustling around, getting dressed. He came out in thick thermal pants that clung to his shapely legs, showing off his cute ass. He finished buttoning a heavy red-and-black flannel shirt, not making eye contact with me. "I respect your choice. I just don't get it." His voice lowered at the end, sounding almost ashamed or sad. He walked out of the bedroom with long strides. I got up and watched him make his way through the mudroom.

"It's not anything you did," I added pathetically.

He stepped into tan, heavy-duty Carhartt overalls, snapping the straps over his wide chest with ease before stepping into his boots.

"Nothing I did?" he asked, fastening his boots. "What the fuck have I been doing besides you?" His tone was terse, barely controlled. He stood up and stared me up and down, challenging me before yanking his beanie on his head. I stood there speechless with my mouth gaped like a dead fish. He rolled his eyes in annoyance at my silence before reaching right by my face to grab his coat on the way out.

There it was. He was a runner, too.

I walked mindlessly back to the bedroom, only to fall on the bed, tears threatening to sting my eyes. My wet hair was annoying, and the air in the room was unexpectedly too hot.

I knew this was too good to be true. I fucking knew it! The emotions moved up my chest, only to get stuck in my throat. I didn't want to cry, but I felt like this was an impossible situation. I'd just been cheated on and had flung myself into this relationship, if you could even call it that. Here I was, getting dicked down on this weird version of a vacation. And worse, I was already falling in love.

I was whole on my own, but Harley would have been a lovely addition to my life, a welcomed companion. I didn't know if that was what he wanted. I shifted to my side and curled up, crying in a fetal position. A flush of embarrassment surged through me while my face pinched into an ugly sob. I shuddered and was wracked with the tears and gasps. The bedding dampened under my face from all my tears and wet hair.

I needed a good cry. It was cathartic to let it course through my body.

I cried because I didn't know what to do in this situation or how to move on and what path to take.

I cried because I was falling for Harley, but I was unsure how he felt about me and how willing he was to welcome me into his world beyond my brief stay here during the storm.

I cried because Tyler had hurt me and because I hated where my path post-graduation had taken me. What I was doing in Boston was bullshit, and I'd lived out everyone else's needs, not my own. I missed my parents and Maisie so much that my heart ached most nights when I got back to my empty, stale apartment.

Regardless of what happened with Harley, I knew I needed to wrap up my life in Boston. Being this close to nature clarified for me that city life wasn't something I enjoyed. My energy up here felt calmer and clearer. It felt good, and I dreaded going back to my high-rise apartment in the city, surrounded by strangers and bright lights.

I needed to face why I was still living in Boston. Basically, I was being a stubborn ass. My mom had been supportive of me going to college. My dad couldn't get behind learning for the sake of learning and because of the risk involved in opening businesses. His incredulity had stopped me from opening my own, so I'd used Maisie's dream of Pretty Kitty as a shield. While they loved and supported me, when I'd graduated college, there had been a tone of expectation to see what I'd do with my fancy-schmancy degree.

I'd wanted to prove to myself and others that I could make it in a big city all on my own, that I could burn through my student loans and pay them off in a few short years. Letting it drag on longer than needed, I was damn near torturing myself. If I took anything away from this situation, it was that I needed to find ease and stop being so hard on myself. And to hell with what people thought of me!

I got up, newly determined, and blew my nose, retrieved another cup of coffee, and curled up on the couch. I opened my phone to see an email from Tamara. Fuck.

Kaylee,
I need you in the office by Monday morning. You being away has made me realize what an asset you are to the team and our clients. If you're unable to come back by Monday, let me know and I will overnight you a laptop so you can begin working and holding remote interviews. I hope everything is fine.
Thx,
T

Shit, shit, shit! I had to get out of here! I rolled my eyes and dropped my phone, plopping it on the couch beside me. A second wave of worry filled my body. I didn't like that I was fighting with Harley, and now I was worried about work and real life crashing back into my mind. Thinking about my situation, I took matters into my own hands. I picked my phone back up, and with a quick Google search, I found Dane's number.

After several rings, a gruff voice picked up. "Dane's Auto."

"Hi, Dane. This is Kaylee. You have my Mini Cooper, I believe?" The line was silent for a moment. "It's blue. I hit a tree over the weekend."

He chuckled, humored by something. "Oh, hi, moose killer. What can I help you with?"

I scoffed at the apparent nickname. "I didn't kill the moose! If anything, I'm the victim!"

"What would the nickname be? Moose survivor? Doesn't have the same ring to it, does it?"

"Hey now, we haven't even met! You can't taunt me for my moose mishap." I smiled into the phone. I could see why Harley liked this guy. He was a funny smartass already.

"Where are my manners? I'm sorry. How can I help you today?"

"I was wondering if you've had time to look at the damage?"

"Yeah, so, um, well, do you want the good news or the bad news first?"

"Um, I guess the bad?" I held my breath.

"So the car is totaled. You busted it up real good. The good news is you can now get a reliable car."

My jaw dropped in pure shock and offense. "Excuse me?" I squeaked into the phone.

"Yeah, you bent the frame, busted the—"

"How long have you known it was totaled?"

A slight pause punched the conversation. "Not long . . ."

I could tell he was lying. Had Harley kept this from me? Also, why did every man in this town disapprove of my car?! I wrapped up the situation and agreed to visit Dane's shop once I could make it there in the storm. I still needed to get a few things from the car, and I wanted to say a proper goodbye. Hanging up, I felt defeated and even more pissed at Harley.

I opened the door to the garage from the mudroom but didn't see him there. Deciding to find him outside, I put on my boots and coat and headed out. I discovered him off to the side of his shop, clearing snow with a small orange tractor. He shut it off and hopped off it, walking toward me. He glowered when he realized I was fuming.

"I just got off the phone with your buddy Dane. We need to talk." My voice was curt, and I knew it set my face in a scowl.

Harley stared at me for a few moments. With no pretense, he grimaced and shook his head. "Kaylee, since the moment I met you, I've been trying to protect you."

"Protecting someone isn't the same as keeping someone completely in the fucking dark!" I yelled. Around us was so quiet with the falling snow that my voice felt extra loud. Snowflakes fell in steady streams, creating a running barrier between us. The flakes were already collecting on my lashes and the wisps of my hair escaping my wet bun.

"Please, let me get you inside. You shouldn't be out in this cold weather with wet hair." He walked toward me, almost grabbing my elbow to lead me. I stepped back from him. "No! I'm not some porcelain doll, Harley! Fucking talk to me right now!"

"I didn't want you to worry about your car while you were stuck in the storm!" He raised his voice while looking down at me in exasperation. "You couldn't drive out of here anyways! With the storm, road closures, no rental cars nearby . . ."

"How long have you known?"

He moved his beanie on his head, uncomfortably looking away from me.

"How. Long. Have. You. Known?"

"We knew Sunday morning." He pursed his lips in shame.

"Sunday?! You knew Sunday?" I screeched.

"I wanted more time with you, dammit!" Harley barked out, now yelling too. "Jeezus, it doesn't make a difference! You already had a claim with your insurance, and you couldn't leave because of the storm. I didn't want you to worry about it until we could get you on the road again. I figured we'd deal with it when we could. It was as simple as that."

I could feel a pit forming in my stomach, and the taste of copper flooded in my mouth, something that only happened when I was furious. "I deserved to know! It's been three whole days of limbo!"

"You never fucking asked!" he countered, throwing his arms out.

"I was a bit preoccupied with your dick!"

We stared at each other, seething.

Lowering his voice, he filled the silence. "You're right. You're right, I should have said something sooner. I can see why that would make you mad. I wanted to know you were safe." He took a deep, miserable breath. "I just needed more time . . . with you." He gestured to me with his gloved hand.

I knew on some level it must hurt his ego to admit that he wanted more time with me. That he was being vulnerable in the moment.

"Well, how about what the fuck I wanted?" I grimaced and slumped my arms in defeat, exhausted by the situation. I turned around and waded back into the cabin and shook the snow from my boots and leggings before entering.

I was so fucking over this situation! I was over the back and forth. One moment I felt like I was where I needed to be, and the next I was so unsure of myself. Even worse, I wasn't in the comfort of my own space, not that my apartment was some glorious fortress.

Harley came in right after me and stared at me in silence. I kept eye contact with him to assert dominance. He broke first and walked into the mudroom to put his jacket and things away. I followed him. "You know, since I've met you, you haven't thought once about what I want! Or what I feel is best for me!"

After tugging his coat on the hook, he turned on his heel, towering over me. His height and mass, which had once felt gloriously masculine, now felt threatening. I pushed at his chest to create space between us in the mudroom. He grabbed my hands delicately, calmer than me. "Kaylee, you got yourself into a mess and I pulled you out of it, quite literally. The least you could do is to be grateful and not demonize me." He squeezed my hands affectionately and dropped them, only to reach for a pair of boots from a shelf behind me before walking away unbothered.

I followed him into his spare room, fuming. "Sure, you pulled me out of the wreck, but I like to think I pulled you out of something too," I spat out indignantly, tears welling up in my eyes.

He picked up what looked like a metal chain, placing it around one boot. I stared at his process in confusion before realizing it was some snow spike, cleat contraption for his boots.

"Yeah, you pulled me out of a slump. And you saved me from that damn boat. Having you around has been great, but I don't like how you're painting me into this controlling asshat. I didn't tell you about your car because it would have stressed you out and there was nothing you could do about it until we can get you out of this place safely." His eyes shifted to mine, and he continued in a more hushed tone. "Baby, I planned on driving you back to Boston myself when the snow cleared."

Something about his open commitment to me, his thoughtfulness, and, dammit, those piercing eyes made a flutter rise in my chest. *Damn you, body! Don't betray me now with your whorish needs!*

"I honestly didn't think it was a big deal. I see now it was. But I think maybe you're a little . . ." He looked up at the ceiling, weighing his words before looking back at me. ". . . on edge. You're hyperaware of this whole situation because you feel out of control. Now that we've been intimate, and your mom knows, and my friend knows, and even the damn tarot knows, you're having a hard time accepting we have something here."

He dropped the boots on a table, making me jump. He stepped closer to me once more, his voice low and hungry. "And I think you're trying to turn this into a fight because you like what we have and it scares you." His eyes fluttered to my lips.

I stepped back, pushing at his hard chest, glowering at him. "Give me space, dammit!" He set his jaw and stood up even straighter, crossing his arms over his broad chest. "And stop standing there looking like a goddamn Brawny paper towel ad!" I gestured in disgust at how handsome he looked when he was angry.

"That's pretty rich coming from a girl who walked around commando in my cabin for days," he bit back dryly.

I continued, pointing at him. "You should have told me about my car days ago. Even if we have something here, I feel out of control and I'm defensive. You don't get to decide what I worry about. It was a fuckup."

He nodded. "It was a fuckup. I fucked up, and I'm sorry."

"And I don't like how you ran away when I told you I didn't want to have sex anymore."

"I mean, can you blame me? You came bursting into my life unexpectedly. Like some bizarre, burning comet with a crippling coffee addiction and crystals coming out of your tits." His large hand gestured to my chest in bewilderment.

He went on, "I rolled with it, only to find out I love being around you, and we end up having the most *ridiculously* mind-blowing sex for days. *Then you sucked out my soul* with your morning coffee like some succubus." He scoffed and pointed towards his bedroom. "You asked me about scars from my past so I bitched to you about my leg, and then immediately after I gushed my sob story to you, you casually ask to stop having addictive sex while being sheltered in a cabin together! I mean, it's a freaking fantasy wrapped in a nightmare, Kaylee! Can you blame me?!"

His mouth twitched in discomfort. "You're sending mixed messages and I have a vulnerability hangover. I respect your decision, but damn, woman, it stung. It made me feel like I . . . like I did something wrong. Did I?"

"No!" I took a deep breath, collecting myself. "We can't keep our hands off each other. And we need to!"

His eyes squinted. "Why is that? Do you not like the way I—"

"No, I do." I stepped closer to him and ran my hands up his chest and held the straps of the coveralls. "I'm crazy about you. You already mean so much to me, but I don't want this to be only sex. I get it. We don't have a lot of time left and I don't want to cheapen it."

We both grimaced at each other, discomfort pluming between us with the realization of our limited timeline. His gaze went to my neck fleetingly and cast down to the floor uncomfortably.

"Harley, I'm fine. You didn't hurt me."

The house clunked with the power coming back on; the fridge hummed loudly. It had been so warm with the fireplaces, I hadn't even noticed aside from the lack of Wi-Fi and lighting.

Harley looked around at the lights coming back on in his cabin and nodded in agreement. "I don't want you to feel like it's just sex to me." He gazed at me, unsaid emotions teeming under the surface of his demeanor. We stared at each other for a few heartbeats as we both mentally mulled over the details.

I looked down at his boots, wondering what the hell his plan was. "Well, now that we're celibate, what should we do?" I asked.

He cringed at the word celibate. I felt lame saying it—we weren't priests. He pulled my hands off his chest, leaning forward as his mannish voice broke the air, hard and biting. "Why would you want to explore things with me? I thought I was just some alpha lumberjack with a cabin you're fucking until you can drive your car?"

I reared my head back. Was this how he felt?

"Why would you say that?"

"I saw your texts to Tyler. You were bragging about being with some guy who built his own cabin. I mean, for a woman who insists on not being treated like a piece of ass, you sure treat others like something you're using." He leaned forward even more with a disgusted hush. "What's worse is you act innocent the whole time."

I backed up a few steps, completely offended. "You don't know jack shit."

Anger dashed behind his eyes, followed by pain. "You made me feel used."

"I'm done with this conversation."

"Fine. I'm going back outside. I have things, responsibilities, I shouldn't ignore. I'll be back in a couple of hours." Harley picked up his boots and looked down at me with a pained expression, not loving how things were going between us. "Don't leave this cabin," was all he bit out while he walked past me and out the mudroom door.

And there I found myself alone in Harley's cabin for the second time today, tears filling my eyes.

Chapter Twenty-Two

Harley

The deck was freezing from where I stood at my grill. It had snowed all day, and now with it being after dusk, the freeze was creeping in, cementing in the moisture and making it feel even more brisk. I turned over the elk meat. Remembering the hunting trip I'd gotten it from made me miss my friends and the wild woods out west.

Something about hunting was so primal. The preparation of tracking the markings and paths the animals left. Tracking the moon and seasons for ideal conditions. The chase and the sound of my compound bow ticking while I pulled back, aiming for the target. Taking the life of a creature wasn't some sport for me. It was my way of living synched up with the land and perhaps even honoring some ancestral knowledge.

Being cooped up indoors or stuck in a certain spot for too long made me antsy. Even in college, I'd worked as a tour guide and junior ranger to avoid a desk job. I'd spent time in places like Yellowstone, Zion, and Yosemite. I'd even worked as a white-water river rafting guide for a couple of summers. It had been hilarious to watch tourists bounce in terror while coursing a rapid only to pitch them out safely. It had made me happy knowing I'd played a part in their adventures.

Along with feeling cooped up from the storm, things with Kaylee were getting complicated. She'd gotten pissed I hadn't told her about her car right away. She'd also proclaimed she wanted celibacy to boot. Wonderful. Now I must fight every urge in my body that wanted to throw her over my shoulder and make her mine again. I absolutely respected her wishes. It just hurt my pride to hear her want to pause sex after I'd been super vulnerable, telling her everything about my accident. Finding out she'd called Dane behind my back to arrange a way out of town had been the last blow I felt I could take.

So here we were, prudish with bruised egos, snowed in together. Perhaps I should break out Scrabble?

I'd come home to her scrubbing my already clean kitchen sink. She'd been scowling at it in pure rage. Apparently, she cleaned when she was upset. To pass the time, I'd distracted her with the first *Indiana Jones* movie. She'd fallen asleep twenty minutes into it and woken up the last fifteen, only to pretend like she'd watched the whole movie. It had been adorable and frustrating—a common theme with Kaylee.

From where I stood, I kept catching myself glancing at her inside the cabin. The injury on her neck turned even darker as the hours went by, making the bruise sweep indigo. People didn't realize bruises always got darker before they got lighter. I'd offer her more meds or another ice pack, but she was so stubborn, I knew she'd refuse any help.

I also thought we'd fucked the energy out of her because she was uncharacteristically still and calm. Most of the time, she danced around playfully, or at least smiled when she caught me looking at her. This afternoon, she'd curled up with a blanket and assumed the fetal position on the oversized chair.

Something was off. I pulled out my phone to text Dane.

Me: Hey, fucknuts, you blew my cover.

Dane: Sorry, man. Moose killer called me and could smell my bullshit. How deep in the doghouse are you?

Me: Not bad, but not great. On a scale from 1 to 10, 10 being having to butt fuck Kevin Bacon after going to Taco Bell, I'm at a solid 7.

Dane: Don't overthink this. Enjoy yourself. She had a sexy voice. Does she have a sister?

Me: Back off. She's an only child.

Dane: Yikes. Good luck with that.

    I chuckled and checked the rest of my texts. One was a link to an old skit from SNL that was on YouTube. Terry had texted it to me like it was brand new. I rolled my eyes and sent him a laughing emoji. The other was a family group text with everyone showing pictures of how much snow they had outside their places. I snapped a dorky selfie, holding up a chunk of elk steak with tongs with my snowy land behind me to placate them.

    When I walked into the cabin, the energy between us felt weird. I wanted her by my side, even if we weren't physical, but I'd completely pissed her off earlier. I fleetingly wondered where she'd put her boob knife.

    I got her attention and nodded for her to join me at the kitchen island. I pushed a plate with an elk burger and sweet potato fries toward her. She picked it up without words and squinted at the meat in confusion. The moment when she'd called Sherry at the police station flooded back into my brain and made my chest hurt. How had that been Saturday? Here we were on Wednesday with a completely different story. When we'd first met, she'd been so energetic and quick-witted. Now she was exhausted and sad. She bit into the burger and nodded like it tasted fine enough, politely adding, "Thank you for making me elk. I get why you like it."

    The rest of the night comprised of watching *Grey's Anatomy*, which was basically torture for me, but I did it anyway. What was even more torturous was Kaylee on the oversized chair away from me on the couch, wanting her own space. The night stretched on in silence and sadness until she stood up, her curvy body still wrapped in a blanket like a cape.

"I'm tired and I'd like to go to bed."

I nodded. "Okay. Can . . . Would it be okay if I came to tuck you in?" God, I was so screwed. I had it so bad.

She nodded, refusing to make eye contact. I could sense on some level she needed to be held. Some storm was brewing inside her, and I couldn't figure it out, but I knew I could at least be there to comfort her. I slid into the bed next to her, scooping her body close to mine. Her back and shoulders felt extra small against my chest with how she hunched.

"Kaylee, baby, what's bothering you?" I murmured into her ear after several minutes of holding her.

Her body instantly flinched with silent crying. Her frame shuddered and hitched with her sobs. I held her closer, hoping the pressure of my body soothed her. Feeling her upset made me heartsick.

"Life is just h-hard." Her sobs hitched her breath. She held her face in her hands, weeping a few more moments until sleep stole her.

Even with everything we'd been through, I'd never seen her cry, and it was harrowing. The night stretched on, and I lay there beside her sleeping frame. I had so many questions that were still left unanswered. It felt like Kaylee had a way about her that made her appear open and forward, but there were still so many mysteries.

What brought her to Maine? Where was she heading in life? Had she ever been in love? How did she feel about me?

I woke her early in the morning so I could take her up on the bluff by my cabin for the sunrise. I thought perhaps the view would be a distraction and boost her mood. She was sleepy and mostly silent the whole way up the mountain. She'd never ridden a snowmobile and looked adorable in the helmet

I gave her. I only had one, but she was precious cargo, not me, so she wore it.

Her hair was in a low, thick braid that peeked out underneath the helmet in a way I didn't expect to be endearing. I gave her gloves that dwarfed her hands as she hugged my chest tightly from where she sat behind me.

At the top of the bluff, I parked the snowmobile where a patch of the forest cleared for a view of the same lake that was visible from my cabin. From this vantage point, the sunrise was stunning year-round.

"This is beautiful, Harley," she said, looking around at my special spot. As if reading my mind, she asked, "Is this your favorite place?"

"Yes, and it's also where my favorite tree is in the area. Can you guess which one?" I grabbed her hand and walked her farther into the clearing.

Her eyes looked calmly around and locked with the exact tree. She walked right up to it and glanced at me expectantly. "This one? I don't know why, but it looks like something you'd feel an affinity for."

I nodded, unable to fight my smile. She let out a soft squeal and hugged the tree, unable to wrap her arms fully around the white pine with mature bark. Seeing her made my heart feel heavy, while a lump of emotion filled my throat.

"Tree hugger," I teased, watching her sigh, only to tilt her head to look up at it.

"It feels good. It's a happy tree. You picked a good one." She winked at me, still holding the tree. "What? Why are you looking at me like that?"

I held out my hand for her to take. "Nothing, it's just you're really cute."

We sat on the snowmobile side by side, using a tree stump as an impromptu coffee table. I pulled a thermos of hot coffee from inside my coat and poured some into the lid to share with Kaylee. I'd even added cinnamon and sugar when I'd made it so she could tolerate it. The sky was a pale purple, and our breath made white clouds with each exhale. The forest was quiet, aside from the chatter of the male birds.

"Do you hear that? That per-chick-oh-ree?" I imitated the birdsong with practiced sounds. She nodded with a small smile. "That's an American goldfinch. And that cheet cheet noise is a house finch. They're all over up here."

Kaylee stilled for a moment to hear what I was explaining. The birdsong rang out again and her smile deepened. "Tell me more."

We both paused, shallowly breathing in order to hear the various bird calls. "Ah, okay, do you hear that?" I pointed in the general direction from where the call was coming.

"Those high-pitched sounds almost like metal clinking?" she whispered. We paused, listening a few moments more before making eye contact and nodding to each other in agreement.

"Yep, that's a brown creeper. They're hard to spot because they blend in with the tree trunks so well."

"What a creeper," Kaylee dryly replied. "Now that I think about it, I guess all the bears are sleeping in caves right now, right?" She looked around where we were sitting, visibly nervous.

"Yes, we're safe. Besides, most predators hunt at night." I shrugged, trying not to scare her.

"That's why the moose was on the road, wasn't it?"

"Yep, and he was foraging before the storm. Animals are such intuitive creatures. We don't give them enough credit."

"Have you had issues with bears or other wild animals since you've lived here?" she asked, scooting closer to me for warmth. I put my arm around her and brought her even closer to me.

"Yeah, it's a real pain in the ass because sometimes I'll come home to raccoons or deer camped out on my porch. Bears, not so much. I don't keep out food or my garbage cans, so they mostly leave me alone. You know what scares me most about being out here?"

"What?"

"People. Tourists." I chuckled. "People do some wild stuff on vacation. I've had to rescue toddlers alone on kayaks and break up drunken bachelor parties with illegal fireworks. You don't even want to know how many people I've caught feeding birthday cake and hot dogs to wildlife."

"Do you, like, write tickets and stuff?"

"Nah, I decided a long time ago I went into forestry because I wanted to protect the land and be a bridge for people to understand and appreciate it. I don't want to police it. I'm not some forest fed."

She chuckled. "Is that what you call rangers who are power hungry?"

"Exactly. I try to give warnings and educate. Unless someone brings in a metric ton of illegal fireworks, then I have to say something." I smiled at her, tucking her even closer to me.

"I want to see what this place looks like at the height of summer." She looked around wistfully.

"You could," I blurted out. I couldn't help but stare at her intensely, visualizing it myself. I instantly saw Kaylee surrounded by summer sunlight and wildflowers, like the solstice witch I knew she was. A fierce longing built up in my chest.

"You have a whole life up here. I can't interfere with that." The first shreds of dawn lit up her beautiful face. Today she wore some mascara, making her eyelashes flutter with every blink. Her cheeks and nose were a rosy pink.

"Who said you'd be interfering? You're a welcome distraction."

She looked down at her lap, moving her hands in the gloves she'd borrowed. "I worry that's all I am." A sad smile spread across her face as she looked back up at me. "A distraction. I've been that so many times with other men. Just a passing, kooky, witchy, hippie chick who they fetishize will put out or awaken something in them. Like I don't have my own life or purpose." Her expression pinched in disgust at her own words.

I grabbed her face and kissed her boldly before I could even think. The sunrise lit up my eyelids in a buttery hue while I closed my eyes. She sighed into my mouth and encircled her arms around me. I broke the kiss.

"Kaylee, you're not a distraction or some diversion. You could never be just a distraction if you're my priority." I tucked a piece of hair that had escaped her braid behind her ear. Her face looked sad and overwhelmed for a moment. "You're so kind and intelligent. I would be so lucky to have you in my life beyond the storm."

"You honestly feel that way? About me?" Her eyes searched my face while she tried to steady her breath, as if my words had knocked it out of her.

I nodded, unable to stop myself from touching her beautiful face. Perhaps to keep it warm, but mostly for my own selfish longing. "Since the moment I met you, I knew I wanted you by my side. I love being around you, and now your happiness and safety are the only things I really care about. Not sure how that happened so quickly, but it did. I'm crazy about you."

She held my hand that was holding her face, eyes searching mine. "I'm crazy about you too." She seared me with another kiss. "Touch me," she pleaded, breaking our kisses. I shook my head, leaning in for another kiss.

"I'm done with celibacy. It was stupid. I miss you. I want you."

Hearing that, I pushed her back on the snowmobile, the black leather seat acting like a cushion. Trapping the fabric in my teeth, I yanked my gloves off and tossed them beside us before bending down to kiss her more. Unzipping her coat, I pawed at her hips and looked at the pale-blue flannel shirt she had on. Since I'd met her, she'd worn sweaters that were easy to take off, but now with the button-up shirt, I felt my frustration rise. I needed her. I needed to see and touch her naked flesh.

Unbuttoning the bottom buttons of the flannel with my icy fingers, I grunted in frustration when I saw a lavender thermal underneath. Sure, the one time she was *actually* responsible and layering for warmth was when I wanted her naked. Clenching my jaw in minor frustration, I frantically unbuttoned the flannel. Kaylee threw her head back in a giggle at my trial. Opening her flannel, I saw her nipples instantly harden under the thermal she wore beneath it. The hard buds poking out into the waffle weave made me instantly crazed.

I pushed up the fabric hastily and smiled, dragging my beard against her sensitive skin as I brought my mouth to her breast. She moaned, bending her legs at the knees, trapping me between them from where I knelt. The dawn shined a pale light on her skin while the forest came alive all around us with sun-filled, twinkling snow.

"Harley, it's so cold," she breathed out, clutching my shoulders.

"I know. I'm getting you hot." She sighed at my bold response. I watched as her nipples hardened with the frosty morning air. I covered one with the warmth of my mouth, only to feel it soften with the reprieve from the icy air. Kaylee rolled under me, small cries escaping her with the winter air on her chest. I pulled back, letting her nipple escape, only to watch it harden again.

Whimpering, she wiggled beneath me. I continued my torture on her other breast, covering the one I'd already tasted with my hand. An idea floated into my mind. Pulling up from her, I exposed her breasts to the winter air once more, both tightening instantly. I took a sip of the hot coffee while slyly making eye contact with Kaylee. She bit her bottom lip in anticipation while I swallowed and dipped my head back to her. With a moan, she held my head to her, arching her back to me. My warm lips covered her sensitive flesh, my hot tongue swirled her nipple.

"How do you like that?" I asked, nuzzling into her soft breast.

She nodded, letting out a little, desperate cry. My hand traveled down her body and dipped into her pants, where I held her possessively. The immediate heat of her core on my skin made my vision hazy. Without pausing, I ran my middle finger down the seam of her pussy, feeling how wet she was with the parting sensation.

"Harley . . . baby . . ." Her breath hitched as I spread her with my hand. We both moaned into each other's mouths, and without waiting, I continued my onslaught, rubbing her clit with my middle and ring finger on either side of it, feeling her coat my fingers instantly with her desire. Her body spun tight, already being pushed into deep yearning.

"Take me, right here," she murmured into my neck, her teeth rattling with a shiver. I pulled my hand from her and ran my middle finger horizontally between our lips while we kissed, making her taste what I'd done to her. She let out a breathy, filthy moan, making my restraint even harder. I kissed her sternum in withdrawal, nuzzling her ribs before pulling down her thermal.

"You'll get too cold."

"N-no . . . no . . . I won't," she said through chattering teeth. I chuckled and pulled her up. A violent shiver shook her body without her ability to control it. She glowered, realizing she couldn't hide how cold she was. What the hell was I doing? I knew damn well I couldn't be out in this cold of weather with my pants down around my ankles. Fuck no! Frostbite was real.

"I'm sorry, sweetheart. I shouldn't have riled you up. When we get back, I'll make up for it," I promised. She wiggled her eyebrows at that idea and assumed her position behind me on the snowmobile.

"I'm going to make you regret that," she said flirtatiously, only to lean in and whisper, "I guess once a Boy Scout, always a Boy Scout. Who's the prude now?"

I fought a laugh, turning the snowmobile back on, no longer feeling exiled.

Chapter Twenty-Three

Kaylee

    Clutching Harley on the back of the snowmobile was one of the most exhilarating things I'd done in quite some time. His broad shoulders made it so I could barely see where we were going as the world surged past in colors of alpine white, wintergreen, and oak brown. Birds chattered, and the air felt extra crisp in the aftermath of the blizzard. Most of all, it was nice to be wrapped around Harley, holding him tight.

    After the beautiful sunrise, he took me on a trail that looped around the lake and to the other side of the forest. He checked on caches of firewood he'd scattered in little huts, ensuring they were still dry. He maintained them for people in his community sprinkled throughout the area, so if they needed firewood, they could easily access it.

    He explained to keep all the firewood in one place was risky because it could burn up all at once. Not only would that result in a large fire, but it would ruin chances of survival because there wouldn't be any wood left to keep you warm. I realized so much of Harley's life was strategic, but even more so how charitable he was with his efforts and resources. His actions helped protect and provide for people living nearby. The notion of it made my heart ache.

We made our way down a hill and took a road that forked to the right. Riding along, I saw several entrances for other cabins, all with signs with unique names like *Second Chance, Betty's Fault,* and *Cabin Nabbin'*. I chuckled, remembering Harley's said something like *Fuck Off.* I gripped him closer, smitten at the thought of him.

A sensation prickled along my neck, and I turned around to see a vehicle trailing us about a half a mile back on the remote country road. The late-morning sun cast shadows from the trees, obscuring my sight. With the helmet I wore, it was hard to make out, but it looked like a small SUV. I turned back around and gripped Harley tighter. Unable to fight the creepy sensation, I turned around again, only to see the SUV approaching hot on our trail. The closer it got, the more familiar it looked.

When I squinted, a silver Audi SUV slithered into my vision with Tyler at the wheel, speeding up with an intense stare.

All my blood froze in my body and a panicked shriek echoed in my helmet. I whipped back around and pointed in the side mirror at Harley, who had already noticed the SUV. As we stared at each other in the side mirror, Harley gave me a resolute nod, urging me to hold on tighter.

He weaved through the snowy roads at a faster pace than what was probably safe, turning on paths confidently, losing Tyler for moments before he'd pop back up in the side mirror. I could feel a mannish grunt escape Harley's chest from where I pressed into his back. Shaking his head, he entered his own private drive, gunning the snowmobile to propel us quickly down the tree-lined road. Moments later, Tyler followed, revving his Audi and pushing it as fast as it could go in the deep snow.

I bit back a screech and glared at him, even though he couldn't see me through the helmet. He probably only knew it was me because of my blonde braid. I held up a hand and swatted him away before flipping him the bird through my lumpy glove. He revved even closer, his wheels spinning out.

Harley throttled the snowmobile at breakneck speed, careening us toward the cabin. He drifted the snowmobile, causing the machine to sputter sideways while it stopped with a dramatic whoosh of snow. We got off together, and I ripped off my helmet while he walked in front of me with arms outstretched.

"Harley, get him the fuck out of here. I know this guy, and I don't trust him." I tucked the thermos under my arm.

"Get inside the cabin." He took off his gloves and handed me his keys without looking.

Tyler parked his car while staring at me. Loud music rang and came to a halt when he slammed the door, turning to skulk toward us. A black knit hat covered his sandy hair, making him appear even meaner. Instead of his usual suit, he wore jeans, a white hoodie, and a black coat. Even with the casual attire, he looked out of place, too polished for such a rugged setting.

Harley stepped forward, claiming his turf. He was of larger build and maybe only a few inches taller than Tyler. Where Harley was mass and brawn, Tyler was all lean muscle. Despite that, both men were taller than the average guy, and watching them prowl toward each other already looked dangerous. I instantly panicked, feeling the macho energy saturating the area with tension.

"Hey, man, this is private property. Get the fuck out." Harley jutted his jaw toward the road.

"Fuck off, I'm here to get my girl," Tyler said with a snobbish look. He peered past Harley to lock eyes with me. "Kay, get in the car. You're coming with me. We need to talk."

"She's with me, and she doesn't want to talk. Now get the fuck out." I'd never heard Harley's voice sound so biting.

I stepped out from behind Harley, handing him the keys back with a pleading look. I continued walking closer to Tyler so he could see how serious I was. "Tyler, you need to go. Now." I forced my voice to sound detached and logical.

"Like hell I do! It was all a misunderstanding!" Tyler bit out. "You embarrassed me at the coffee shop." His gaze drifted to the bruise that was peeking out from under my coat. "Shit, did he do that to you?"

"No! I got in a car wreck running from the shitshow I caught you in!"

"Why Maine?" he asked in disgust. I could hear the snow crunching with Harley slowly stepping closer.

"I went for a drive. That's all you need to know. Harley saved me, protected me." My stomach dropped when I realized I'd never told him where I was. "How the fuck did you even know I was here?" Terror built in my chest as I tried to piece together how everything was colliding so quickly.

Tyler's face contorted in a wicked grin. "Oh, baby girl, you're such a dumb blonde. You posted a picture of a stupid pizza box from a place in town. It took me a quick Google search to find this hellhole. I went for a drive to find you. I stopped at the market in town and showed them your pretty photo. The cashier said you were with a park ranger."

He cocked a snotty look at Harley behind me, curling his lip in disgust. "I visited the ranger station, only to have an old guy tell me where to find this ranger douche. This Har-Ley." He said his name in mockery of my feminine voice and slight accent. I felt Harley press into my back, putting me in the middle of this dreaded man sandwich. I stretched out my arms, holding him back to hear more details, even though I could feel his rage permeating the space behind me.

"Tyler, this is stalking. It's creepy. You fucked things up and your ass needs to go home."

"I figured you had a side piece. Why else would you lead me on like this? I wanted to see for myself, and I was right. You know, I was only tolerating your ass because I made a bet with the guys in my office that I couldn't bag the weird hot chick across the hallway at work. You owe me a chance. Just come back to Boston with me."

"Like fuck she is!" Harley barked. Both men quickly stepped closer to one another, trapping me. Harley slid me to the side to get me out of the way, causing Tyler to grab me, only to yank my braid violently, whipping my head back until I saw all white. Tyler's thick fingers nestled in the nape of my neck, tearing down on my hair, made me whimper in pure shock and stinging pain.

Harley hooked Tyler with a hard punch, the sound of a revolting pop filling the air. I felt blood land on me while I regained vision, only to feel Harley all but drag me back to the cabin, walking so quickly I could barely keep up.

"Get in the cabin, please. For the love of God, listen to me this one time!" Harley pleaded with his arms around me. He looked over his shoulder to change his course while watching Tyler recover from the punch to dig around in the back of the Audi. Muttering under his breath, Harley opened the back door of his truck and got out a shotgun.

"Get in the goddamn cabin!" he barked back at me, but I couldn't. I stood there frozen in horror, wondering if I was about to watch a murder.

Tyler closed the hatch of his SUV, revealing an L-shaped tire iron in his hand. The metal of the shotgun glinted in the sunlight as Harley maneuvered it with long-practiced skill. His boots crunched the snow where he ate up the space confidently, ambushing Tyler, herding him away from me.

His voice roared, "GET. THE FUCK. OFF MY PROPERTY!" Punctuating the request, he pumped the rifle, loading it with a loud metallic chink that echoed in the surrounding air. Birds scattered from the trees in an eerie departure.

Tyler looked at Harley with a menacing chuckle as he lunged toward him, swinging the tire iron. Harley held the long rifle with both hands and jutted it outwards, blocking the tire iron and smashing Tyler's hand in between both metal weapons. A loud, airy crunch popped as his fingers broke.

Tyler hissed and dropped the metal rod, only to throw a punch at Harley with his other hand. Hitting with a left hook, he bashed Harley's temple, causing him to let out a pained bark. Harley stepped to the side in recovery, only to swerve, avoiding another punch from Tyler. He swung the gun, twisting it to smash Tyler's jaw by his ear with the butt end. The sickening crack of bone escaped the direct blow. Tyler groaned, and Harley let out a guttural grunt before socking him with his bare fist in pure rage.

"DON'T YOU EVER TOUCH HER AGAIN!" Harley yelled down at Tyler, his powerful voice booming in the brisk air, the echo ringing into the silent winter day.

Tyler clutched his disfigured jaw and bent down farther, trying to get the iron. Harley shook his head, putting the safety on his gun. Holding the shotgun in one hand, he lunged to grip Tyler's throat only to push him against the Audi, making his head bob on impact. Blood streamed from his nose and mouth, running over Harley's tan hand like rivers of vile crimson.

Tyler spat it in Harley's face, causing it to splatter in a semicircle around them with a gruesome sprinkle. Seeing red, Harley turned and spit out his own wad of blood, wiping his face against his shoulder, only to let out a growl. He clutched Tyler's neck tighter in the webbing of his hand, his bloody fingers against the unhinged jaw that jutted out sickeningly. Tyler gasped for air, bubbles of blood forming in his nose and mouth. His hands viciously clawed at Harley while his body slackened in the relentless grip.

"Stop! Stop it!" I shrieked, shattering their haze, trying to keep them both from killing each other. Both men breathed heavily, grunting back and forth. "Harley, you're going to fucking kill him!" I pleaded, picking up the tire iron and chucking it toward the lake.

I could already tell Tyler's jaw was hanging from his face in a contorted, gruesome way, likely dislocated along with his broken nose and fingers. Any more head injuries and he wouldn't be able to drive away, which was all I wanted at this point.

Harley growled, perhaps at me or in frustration. "Get in your stupid fucking car and never come back!" He shoved Tyler against the vehicle, rocking it with pure force. Tyler slumped, losing strength, his white hoodie soaked red from the blood. He clutched Harley's hand and with one defiant spit, he splattered more blood on us, adding to the red arc in the snow. Harley turned his head, mostly unperturbed, and spat out even more blood, only to look back at Tyler.

"Do you understand me? You fucking cum stain of a human? You are to never think of Kaylee again. Never come to this town again. You hear me?"

Tyler glowered at him and tried to step loose of the grip. Harley shoved against him once more, straightening him from where he pressed him to the car at his neck. Harley leaned in, his forearm pressed against Tyler's chest, their noses almost touching. In the most murderous tone, Harley's deep voice filled the air between them. "I am not someone you want to fuck with. I can hunt you down and no one would ever find you in these woods. In *my* woods. Do you understand?"

Tyler closed his eyes and breathed deeply in surrender, finally nodding his head. Now free from Harley's grip, Tyler opened his door to get in as I walked closer, pushing Harley aside with a glare, signaling I needed the last word.

"Tyler, I don't know what creepy bet you had going, but you are to never fuck with me again. Leave Rosie alone too. I know curses that will make your dick rot off and your teeth fall out. I know several biker gangs that would gladly take that tire iron and shove it up your ass so far you choke on it. I might not brawl it out, but it would be wise to forget me. Never fuck with me again. Do you hear me?"

He nodded, standing by his door. Turning to get in, he hiked up a leg and muttered, "Witch bitch," under his breath. Before I could think, all the years of softball kicked in and I swung the Stanley thermos, clobbering his dick with a distinct bong. He bent over, wincing in agony. I heard Harley let out a chuckle.

"Fucking asshat," I muttered, unable to look at him anymore in pure disgust on so many levels. I felt bad seeing him injured. Seeing anyone that hurt made me upset, but I needed distance, so I turned my back on him, trusting Harley to watch him as I walked away.

Closer to the cabin, I turned to look over my shoulder to see Harley holding his gun, aiming it at the ground out of a habit of safety. Tyler looked at me and Harley, purely fuming as he wiped his face against his coat sleeve while slamming his door. The same shitty music blared as he ripped a U-turn around where Harley stood. He drove down the road as fast as his tires would take him. Harley watched, staring dominantly while gripping his gun.

Once Tyler was out of sight, he swallowed then turned to look at me. The man I saw differed from what I'd seen for five days. Now covered in blood, he stood there, clearly devastated.

Chapter Twenty-Four

Kaylee

Harley looked himself up and down, realizing the bloodbath that had occurred and that he was clutching a weapon in my presence. From where I stood, I could see blood on his hands, across his neck and face, and splatters on his coat.

He walked toward me with a furrowed brow. "Kaylee, I am so sorry he grabbed you like that—"

"No! I'm sorry he came at you. Are you okay?"

Harley shot a troubled look toward his road, grabbing my hand to lead me into his cabin. The situation quickly turned instinctual.

I wanted to wash the blood off him.

I wanted to wash the situation off him.

In the mudroom, Harley put his shotgun on top of his dryer while I unzipped his coat and quickly unbuttoned his flannel and pushed the thermal off his chest. He stared down, focusing on his breathing and trying to read me. He undid his pants and stepped out of his boots hastily while I undressed myself.

Moving to the shower, I turned the water on a little hotter than normal and fetched a washcloth. I caught a glance at myself in the mirror, seeing splatter against my neck and jaw.

The blood of two men clashed together on the canvas of my skin, along with the sickening bruise of how I'd gotten here. I battled sudden dizziness and tried my best to refocus on Harley.

Following him into the shower, I watched his wide shoulders slump as he adjusted to the heat of the water and safety of his home. He stood in silence with his eyes closed, trying to calm down. I wet the washcloth and began wiping blood off him, causing him to suck in an unsteady breath. The unanswerable question of it was from Tyler or Harley made my stomach heave. Luckily, it wasn't too gory, more heartbreaking than anything. I wrung out the washcloth, realizing my actions had led to this traumatization of Harley.

He opened his eyes and took the washcloth from me, wetting it while cradling my head to clean up the carnage against my skin. His large palm held the back of my head, gently rubbing where Tyler had hurt me while he swept away the blood. His face looked haunted as he stared down at me, his forehead and eyes wrinkling with concern. When he was done, he brought me in for a long hug.

He washed his face, hair, and beard vigorously. Bubbles erupted while he scoured away what I imagined were visuals of beating Tyler to a bloody pulp. I helped wash his body, slowly skimming his tan skin with loving kindness. In my own way, I was trying to love up on him, filling him back up with the usual goodness he innately possessed.

This man had protected me.

This man had risked his life for my safety.

I gently kissed his back while I washed it, caressing his butt before walking my way to his front. Picking up his large hand, I saw where his knuckle had split from punching Tyler. I gently kissed it from where I stood. Harley's eyes fluttered open. He let out a pained breath. I shook my head as if to relay that he shouldn't be ashamed.

Without words, he picked me up and pressed me against the wall of the shower. I wrapped my legs around him and brought him closer to me. I began kissing him, unable to stop. He melted into me under the steam and heat of the shower, and my breasts pushed into his rock-hard chest, gliding and deliciously slippery.

The raw rage of him fighting Tyler for me sparked a primal urge to want him even more. This man had guarded me since the moment we'd met. He had now put himself in physical harm to protect me.

Harley had earned my trust indefinitely. Since the moment we'd touched, all I'd wanted to do was love him back. Now that everything had deepened, I craved to love him in every way I could. Having the same reaction, I felt Harley's dick press against me in an invitation. Accepting with pure need, I slid down on him while he pressed me harder against the cool shower wall.

Gasping at how good it felt, I opened my eyes to look at him. We nodded in agreement while he continued to sink into me raw, clutching my hips with a clenched jaw. I kissed his neck from where I clung to his broad shoulders and lifted my hips, taking him in all the way to the hilt. We both groaned in ecstasy at the bare sensation of it. He shook his head and bit out a strained breath. Holding me in place, he pumped into me, his chest muscles rippling while the force of his hips and ass flexed with each thrust. The flashes of what I could see made me even more starved for his body and strength.

The feeling of his bare cock was irresistible. It was the first time I'd experienced anything like this. The immediacy of our need filled the space between us where the words never came. I lifted my arms above my head on the wall to lean back, causing my tits to bounce with each thrust. Harley's hungry gaze roamed up to my body, darkening with desire.

"You feel so good," I whispered, moving my hips against him.

Harley shook his head and said in a murmur of disbelief, "You have no fucking clue."

Our eyes met in a mutual plea, both of us stunned. I turned off the water in a swift motion before he whisked me out of the shower and over to the vanity. The steam fogged the large circular mirror, creating a mist around us, shrouding us further in a haze that smelled like his woodsy body wash.

We slid against each other in perfect motion, our skin gliding, my softness mixing with his hardness. He sat me down while continuing to kiss me deeply. His hands roamed my body hungrily, starting with my breasts before squeezing my ass with both hands. The frenzy caused me to turn around and bend over the vanity. The cool granite against the warmth of my skin gave me goose bumps while I pressed the front of my body against its surface. The sound of a deep, primal hum came from behind me while I rubbed side to side against his groin. He plucked the hair tie from my braid. His fingers lightly zigzagged to free the wild tresses, spreading them over my back.

"Mmm, mine," his velvety voice growled. He gently grabbed the swath of my hair possessively and twisted it overhand and around his wrist while he held the head of himself against my pussy. With one confident plunge, he filled me back up from behind.

His actions made me greedy and unashamed. Nothing had ever felt so raw and instinctual. I inched back, wanting to take in as much of his length as I could, feeling him hit deeper inside me than ever before. Letting go of my hair, he moved his massive hand under me, spreading his fingers dominantly on my lower abdomen to tilt me up even farther on his cock, forcing me on my tiptoes.

I gasped at the new angle, making him sensuously hum in approval. The realization of him picking me up only to hungrily angle me on his dick made me feel depraved. The sheer boldness caused my pussy to clench in response. He held me there, slowly pushing deeper inside me, letting me adjust to his size. "Baby, it's so—"

"I know you can take it all for me," he whispered huskily. I opened my mouth in a silent moan at his response, rolling against him on sheer instinct. "You're doing so well," he murmured while smoothly rocking into me. His praise made my mind sputter, turning my body even more pliant.

His hand pressed my lower abdomen again. "Feel me here?" His silky voice filled the air along with the mist. I whimpered at the sensation of the pressure on both sides hitting just right. Swept up in how deep it all felt, I came hard and fast after a few strokes. My entire body shuddered because the sensation was so intense, I almost couldn't remain standing. With each thrust, my breathy cries filled the foggy mirror in front of us, its surface turning almost opaque. A devious thought filled my mind, and with one wicked swipe of my hand, I cleared a space in front of it, revealing the sight of us.

Seeing us in the reflection, Harley let out a beastly noise through gritted teeth. "Fucking hell, that's hot," he bit out, staring from where he continued to plunge into me. I watched myself smirk, only to stand up slightly, arching my back to keep our connection while bracing myself against the counter with flat hands. My new stance revealed the front of my slicked-up body.

Watching Harley's eyes drink me in through the gap in the mirror, I grabbed one of his hands and sucked his finger, watching his mouth slacken before I brought it to one of my breasts. He groaned while nuzzling my neck and rubbing my nipple, trapping it between his fingertips. He slowed his onslaught, holding his breath and moans back, trying not to come.

"I want to love you right, not here," his throaty voice muttered before he kissed my ear. *Love me?* Before I could get too hung up on the semantics, he pulled me to his bedroom. Kissing me sweetly, he slumped down, taking me with him while dampening the bedding with our skin still dewy from the shower.

"I want you, all of you," I said against his lips, touching his damp hair and neck. He looked at me tenderly, pushing the hair that clung to my cheek behind my ear. The animalistic urge to fuck had now morphed into a more intense worship of each other. His calloused hands traced down my body, and he pressed himself to my core once more. I nodded, encouraging him. We gazed at each other while he entered me again, this time feeling more significant, knowing that whatever barriers between us, both physical and emotional, were now stripped.

I kissed his bearded jaw sweetly, moving to his cheek and lips. The padding of his thumb ran across my lips, gently over my bruised neck. His hand lovingly held the back of my knee, drawing my core even closer to him, and with it our rhythm began once more, our eye contact only breaking for kisses.

"Harley," was all I could whisper in amazement at how potent the moment felt as we moved together. Feeling him this way was sending me over the edge. Seeing him with all his strength crashing into me made me feel like I was a part of something bigger. Something cosmic or divine, bittersweet and hopeless. I was heartsick because what we had was so damn good, but I knew it couldn't last.

I loved this man.

I loved him fiercely, desperately so.

But Harley had created a life for himself, up here in this forest of solitude. Even if he thought he wanted my company, I knew the reality was he'd soon tire of me. He had feelings for me now, but they wouldn't last past the storm.

Our bodies entwined, our breaths matched, and I watched as his pupils dilated.

"Do you feel it?" Harley's gaze searched my face intensely as he touched my cheek. I knew he wasn't talking about feeling something physical. I nodded, overwhelmed, feeling so torn between loving him and letting him live a life alone, unsure which would make him happier.

"Me too." Harley leaned down and kissed me passionately, trying to convey what he was feeling toward me. And with that, both of us exploded in release and restraint.

Chapter Twenty-Five

Harley

I kissed Kaylee's neck, collapsing on her damp, warm body. Her legs shook on either side of me. Her chest heaved while she fought to catch her breath, causing her breasts to smash against me lusciously. We pressed together, our entire bodies in contact that could only happen with intense intimacy. It felt distinctive and dangerously addictive. I was still deep inside her, filling her up completely. I kissed below her ear, trying to catch my breath. Her fingers lovingly skimmed my back while her soft mouth planted kisses on my shoulders. I didn't want to retreat from her. Having her so fully was euphoric.

She hummed at the feeling of how I felt inside her. I trailed kisses down her neck and chest before slowly pulling from her. She hummed again, closing her eyes, love drunk. I rolled onto my back, pulling her to my chest. I grabbed her leg and lifted it over me, already feeling her drip on my thigh. Some caveman part of my brain liked that my woman had remnants of me in her. I flung my head back, completely spent.

Exhaustion hit me in waves, crashing against my body for different reasons: from making love to her like a man possessed, the bloody brawl, and the roller coaster of emotions Kaylee had pulled from me. All of it from being so in love with this woman who'd crashed into my life like a storm.

I closed my eyes as memories rotated in my head like a carousel of extremes with flashes of desire and trauma. First, I saw Kaylee leaning back on the snowmobile, the light of dawn brightening her beauty while birdsong rang in my head. It morphed into watching Tyler brutally grip her hair, yanking her head back. I should have just punched him the second I'd seen him. The next memory was seeing Kaylee's face freeze in horror while I got my Remington 870 12-gauge from the gun rack in the back of my truck.

The next memory was watching Tyler spit blood in my face, causing me to see red both literally and metaphorically. My body still held on to the acrid smell while feeling my knuckles crack against him—and how the bloody semicircle had splattered on the snow, like what I'd seen in my dream. Kaylee's frightened face came next, looking at me after the fight, covered in the blood of another man. And finally, the intense need that washed over me when she took me within her. The scalding heat of what it felt like to be loved by her.

All of it was too much emotion, too much blood and flesh and instinctual desires. All of it felt like my fault, and on some level, I blamed myself for letting Tyler get that close to her. Too close.

My dad had taught me how to fight, and I'd had my fair share of scuffles growing up. What people didn't realize was even if you knew how to fight, it still hurt like hell. My temple ached from where he got in one good hit, and my hand hurt from punching his stupid face. I looked down at where I held Kaylee's ribs and saw the glistening wound rip across my knuckle, a glossy pink of flesh swelling already. I swallowed hard, getting nauseous.

"Babe, who did I just beat up for you?" I let out a dark chuckle at how ridiculous that sentence was.

Kaylee stilled in my embrace, holding her breath. Her voice finally came out small. "That was Tyler."

Hmm, so I'd been right. That guy in the photo had been texting and harassing my girl. Everything had happened so fast, I hadn't even caught a name. I barely even understood the story. Something about a bet with his coworkers. My mind had gone blank with rage the second he'd touched Kaylee.

"What was he doing here? I tried to give you time to understand what he was saying to you, but then, you know . . ."

"Honestly, I'm not sure. I don't know why he thought coming up here would work. What a sociopath. He scares me, always has. I couldn't put my finger on exactly why, but now I feel validated. I'm sorry you got hurt protecting me, though." She looked up at me with concern.

Not wanting to ruin the moment, I held her close, breathing her in.

"You'll always be safe with me. Always."

"I know that, without a doubt. Thank you for protecting me." She squeezed me for a moment. Her nails skimmed comfortingly along my chest, down to my hip and thigh, only to trail back up again. It was simultaneously soothing and sexy, like her.

"It feels so good to be this close to you," I said abruptly, changing the subject, following the rotation of thoughts in my head.

"I'm yours," she said simply.

I grabbed the soft flesh of her hip. "Mmm, this is mine?" I asked, playfully jiggling her sexy curves. She nodded, looking up at me. I dove and stole a quick kiss. My hand grabbed her butt. "And this?" She giggled, nodding. My hand roamed up to her breast. She nodded before I could even ask. I laid my hand flat on her chest, overtop where her heart was beating quickly.

"Yes," she whispered without hesitation before she leaned in to passionately kiss me. Her affirmation rang in my mind, filling me up with hope.

My stomach growled loudly, the fucking traitor. Kaylee laughed and left to clean up.

"What can I cook for you, my dear?" she asked. I watched her walk past the bed wearing a flannel of mine she'd snagged from the closet. The navy and green made her gray eyes appear even darker. Her pretty face looked serene while she buttoned up the shirt. My chest tightened as I watched her do something so mundane, like walking to the dresser to put on underwear and whip her hair up in a wild, messy bun on top of her head, parts of it damp from our escapades in the shower.

"Something, anything," I said groggily.

"I have an idea. It will either be glorious or gross. With the day we're having, let's go for it." She walked out with a playful giggle. I stayed in bed, trying to regain my energy. The exhaustion from fighting and fucking had sapped my willingness to move.

Half an hour later, I met Kaylee in the kitchen after pulling myself together. A bizarre mix of smells filled the air that I couldn't put my finger on, but my stomach grumbled once more in hunger. Kaylee turned around, scooting a plate toward me.

"I present to you"—she paused dramatically—"elk tacos!"

I smiled at her cuteness, my mouth already watering. "I mean, pretty weird, but worth a shot."

She pushed a bottle of beer across the table. "I guess you don't find value in guacamole. I couldn't find any avocados, which is a shame because I make a mean guac. The secret is nutritional yeast, chia seeds, and lemon pepper." She nodded, pleased with herself. "But I hope it's good. If not, we can do grilled cheese sandwiches."

I bit into the taco and moaned. It was so damn good! Why hadn't I thought of this? I looked at her, eyes wide in amazement.

"Pretty good, eh?" She delicately bit into hers.

We sat eating in companionable silence. After wolfing down two tacos, I slumped in my chair in heaven. "Kaylee, babe, this is amazing!"

She fought her smile and inspected her taco. "I mean, I grew up mostly vegetarian, so I'm still new at cooking meat, but I think I nailed it."

"You were a vegetarian?" I asked between bites, unable to slow myself down from snarfing the tacos. I brought the crisp beer to my lips, washing it down in perfection.

Something about a fistfight, a fuck, and a beer made you feel extra alive.

"My mom is kind of a hippie who had to grow up. So is my dad, but he likes meat. When we'd ask him what he wanted for dinner, he'd say *something that had a mother.*"

I tried not to choke on my food from laughter. "That's so fucked up!"

"Right? Like, geez, just fucking say you want steak, a burger, or eggs! Anyway, yeah, it was an interesting way to grow up. I always felt torn between two worlds."

"Do you still feel that way?" I lifted another taco to my face. She looked down at her last one and slid her plate across to me. I picked it up to put it on mine without question.

"Absolutely, I'm not made for the corporate world, but I've flung myself into it to pay off my school loans. It's hard because I love knowing I'm hiring people who save lives. But I hate sitting in meetings wearing stifling clothes, talking to boring people while I drink shitty coffee."

I nodded. "I get it. You want to help people but not be part of the grind."

"Exactly! I want to open my own businesses or make a living by cobbling all my passions together. I would love to help give people jobs that might not get hired otherwise. I've seen how competitive the workforce is, and I think it's toxic as fuck. And I love my pottery and reading tarot."

I nodded, remembering the tarot reading she'd given me. The Lovers card being turned over by her in shock felt like a distant memory at this point. I was already so deep into loving her.

"Speaking of being torn between two things. I want you to tell me about this Tyler guy. It's the elephant in the room."

"Well, you met him. What a gentleman, huh? What would you like to know?"

"Between you bragging about me to him and him sending you the gross photo, I can only imagine he'd your ex. Tell me what's going on there."

"That's hard to answer. I don't know how to unpack it." She stood and huffed in frustration while she cleaned up our dishes in silence, collecting herself.

I got up and retrieved an ice pack from the freezer for my head. Holding the pack and my beer, I looked at her with a nod toward the couches. I was physically exhausted, but I felt even more lethargic with this heavy conversation. I walked to the couch and slumped down. Kaylee sat on the oversized chair diagonally from me. She folded her legs nervously and looked at me, setting herself up for a tough answer.

I cleared my throat, leaning into the ice pack from where I braced my arm on the side of the sofa. "Look, I normally would say you don't owe me any details of your past. But now that I've literally assaulted a man for you, I feel I need some answers—"

"I found him cheating on me. That's why I drove away from Boston and ended up here. Tyler cheated on me, and I ran. I bolted in pure shame and disgust. I ran and my escape led me to you." Her tone was frantic and deeply shaken.

I took a deep breath and tipped the bottle of beer to my lips. After a sip, I wiped my mouth, considering her words.

A sudden sting filled my body. It traveled from deep in my belly up to my heart, constricting my chest in a way that made me audibly hiss, wincing in pain and repulsion. "That makes it even worse."

I looked at Kaylee, and her face crumpled in disgust. She pulled a blanket over her bare legs, fiddling with the edge. I stared at the floor, trying to piece together the part of the story

I knew. Righteous anger flooded my body, trailed by hurt. She'd run from him to me? For fuck's sake! The betrayal boiled up in me quickly, replacing the sting with an ache.

"How am I supposed to move on from this? From you keeping this from me? You're acting holier than thou about your car, but you kept a whole ass relationship from me? The very thing that put you here. How am I supposed to feel about that?"

"I don't know . . ." Her nose crinkled as she realized she'd been holding a double standard.

"So, there was no gap? None at all? Between him and I?"

She slumped against the arm of the chair. Her pretty face morphed into a painful sneer as she shook her head, fighting tears. "No, no gap. None at all."

"Well, isn't that fucking great! I feel so damn special now," I snapped. I rolled my eyes in exasperation and tipped my bottle back. "You ran from him and right into my arms kind of thing, huh?" I scoffed while she turned her head away from me in a grimace.

Her voice trembled as she fought a sob. "It's not like that!" She turned her head back to me, her stormy eyes sparkling in the dim cabin with unshed tears. "I had a whole life before this. I still have a life that I'm completely ignoring to spend time with you! I didn't know I was going to stay here. I just ran. It's what I do."

"Why did you stay with me?" I retorted. "Why did you prance in here like nothing was wrong?"

"Harley, I don't know. I don't fucking know! How could I have planned any of this?" She pulled a throw pillow onto her lap and held it miserably. She took a deep breath, her tone getting more intense. "I watched my grandma die a slow, drawn-out death. Shortly after, I had to help my friend flee an abusive asshole, only to leave that shitshow to help my dad recover from a motorcycle accident." She sucked in a deep breath in exasperation. "Only to launch into a job I hate, in a city I *loathe*. I thought maybe, just maybe, the freaking universe was giving me a pass! A fucking sliver of happiness because lord knows I haven't felt that in years!"

I rolled my eyes like a total asshat. "I'm so glad I could be your good time. Some story to tell your friends."

"It's not like that," she said, pursing her lips.

"I thought you said I was the only person . . . the only man you've been with in a while." I felt the flinch in my own facial muscles. It pained me to consider any possibility of her recently fucking the douchebag I'd just broke my hand punching.

"I told you I hadn't been with anyone in a while because that's true. I didn't trust Tyler, and that's why we never got physical. The vibes were off. I can't explain it! The most he got was maybe a handful of my tits over my dress on New Year's Eve."

I cringed, thinking of him touching her. Saliva pooled in my mouth with anger.

Her voice trembled with emotion while she leaned forward in her seat, her pleading eyes teary, "I promise. I've never felt for someone the way I feel for you. I've never . . ."

"Kaylee, we just had . . . raw sex. I've never done that."

She dabbed at the tears threatening to spill over. "Me either."

"You're the only person I've done that with," I said with clarification, so she knew the gravity of the situation.

"You're the only person I've experienced that with, too." She exhaled, not in anger, but in defeat.

A mix of confused emotions flooded my body. I hated seeing her cry, but I was so damn angry she'd kept this from me. I finished my beer, scowling at it while I put it on the table in deep annoyance. I stared up at the high-pitched ceiling, putting my free arm behind my head on the couch, trying not to feel the pain in my hand and temple. And now the even deeper ache in my chest.

"Tell me everything that led up to when you met me." My voice was terse and commanding. I couldn't help it. I continued scowling at the ceiling, ready for the onslaught of information.

"I moved to Boston last July. I work in one of those horrid high-rise buildings, you know, for a staffing agency. Across the hall from my work suite is a law firm where Tyler is a junior associate—"

"He's a fucking lawyer?" I interrupted.

"Yep."

"That tracks," I spat out and then chuckled at the irony.

She continued, "We ran into each other in the elevator from time to time. After months of small talk, he asked me out, and I said yes."

I listened intently, but I could feel my entire face contort in disgust at hearing the details. I moved the ice pack from the side of my face to my knuckle.

"He isn't my type. I don't like suits or snotty, rich guys. I'm too down to earth for that shit. He looked like he could own a yacht or something. I don't know." She shrugged. "We casually dated since this past autumn. It wasn't like I saw him every day. We both worked a lot, and frankly, I didn't enjoy having him over at my place. I didn't trust him, and it kept me from getting super serious with him."

"I don't want to call you out on your bullshit, Kaylee, but if it wasn't serious, why did you react the way you did? It had to be serious enough for you to fly off the handle when you found him with another woman. It had to be serious if his psycho ass drove up here to find you."

"I guess it was more serious than I wanted to admit, but it wasn't serious in the typical way."

I chanced a look at her, noticing her eyes squinted as if she were deep in thought. "What does that even mean?" I asked.

"I was serious with the potential of what things could be with him. I fell for the idea of him, not for what he *actually* brought to the table. I guess I fell for potential, not reality. Tyler was always up for my kooky adventures, but it was only a surface-level connection. I wanted it to work out because for the first time, I almost felt accepted by a guy, especially someone so different from me. I think that's why I tolerated him."

She flung the pillow off her lap in frustration. "I'm not used to guys thinking my titty crystals and boob knives are endearing. I'm not used to guys asking me about my lucky yak tooth necklace or letting me read their tarot. Not every guy is like you, Harley."

A pang in my heart erupted for her.

"Looking back, I believe I just needed a clear sign to proceed or give up. Everything felt so murky with him, and now I know why. It's weird. He wasn't outright rude to me, but I never felt cherished." I noticed her eyes staring at me for a moment before she nervously fixed the collar of the shirt she was wearing.

I nodded rather miserably, glowering back at the ceiling.

"I mean, yes, of course I'd like to find a guy who makes me feel secure and loved, but sometimes you have to date around and even date the wrong person to find out what you want. You never know what might be right in front of you one day—"

"Sweetheart," I interrupted her tangent in a pained tone, my patience dangling by a thread. "What happened with Tyler?"

"He kept telling me I was the only girl he was seeing. He even brought me to this fancy New Year's Eve party with all his friends. We got a little drunk and went back to his place. We made out, but he wouldn't wear a condom, so I left. I couldn't shake the feeling that he was up to something, so I dodged him earlier this month when he wanted to take me on a trip to the Bahamas or some shit. Anyway, I went to my favorite coffee shop Saturday and walked in the bathroom to find him fucking my favorite barista against the wall."

I turned my head in shock at how outrageous this was. She'd had to see it? All of it?

"You saw them fucking in the coffee shop? Like, the whole thing . . . this past Saturday?"

She bobbed her head, looking like a scared, little animal. "Yes. All of it."

"That motherfucker," I drawled.

"What's worse is I made a big scene about catching them and ran out dramatically. I mean, I hope I didn't get Rosie fired. She didn't know we were dating."

"To fuck you over is one thing, but to fuck over your coffee is just rude. Even I know that."

She stared at me innocently, causing my body to hum with love for her and hatred of the situation.

"Go on."

"I got in my car and headed north just by chance. I mean, I stopped for coffee and saw the moon and it just felt right. I kept going once I got on the interstate with no strategic plan. I am kind of a wild child with adventures. That's one thing I inherited from my dad. But that damn moose and the wreck, then the storm." She looked at me, her eyes pleading for me to see how everything had spiraled out. "I didn't want you to think I was some crazy chick running from a psycho ex. Turns out, I am."

"You're not crazy."

Her luminous eyes filled with longing. "Thank you for saying that." She gulped, gathering herself. "Then, in some twist of fate, I found you and you made me feel safe and so damn cherished. I know I deserve to feel that way, but it was a lot to take in. You're a rarity too, you know. You do exactly what you say you're going to do, and that kind of integrity is intoxicating."

Warmth pooled around my ears, down my neck, and over to my chest. Everything felt alive and tingling with awareness. I'd never felt my body react like that from someone's words, but I knew it was a rush of happiness. Bone-deep joy.

"I love your sense of humor, and you're an amazing kisser," she said, looking flustered for a second while she ran a hand up her neck to soothe herself. "It felt wrong to bring it up. I didn't think I'd be here, and I didn't think I'd feel this deeply for you."

That made the tingling in my chest stronger, and with it my stomach knotted in sadness for her. My whole body had a slight buzz, feeling her emotions and understanding her newfound story.

"I fucked it all up and I'm sorry. I could've at least told you I was fresh off a breakup after the night we . . ." She gestured to in front of the fireplace. The intimate night we'd spent in front of it was when I'd realized I had serious feelings for her.

I looked at the rug and back at her. "Kaylee, that's when I fell for you. Hard."

She nodded earnestly. "Same. That night changed everything for me. It changed me as a person and how I feel about you."

A twinge of hope and longing filled me. A longing for more time with her, for more nights like that. As soon as the hope came, so did guarded disbelief, much like a yapping dog biting my ankles out of habit.

"Is that because I'm lodging you? Or is that your mysterious tarot cards talking?"

She cringed. "Please don't say that."

"Why? Because it's true?" A voice in the back of my head told me to stop being a suspicious prick.

"No, because it invalidates how I feel about you." She got up and walked over to the couch I was sitting on, needing to close the space between us. The scent of her wafted toward me. I silently hated it because it registered in my brain as something I liked and craved. She picked up the ice pack and held it to the side of my face, her eyes boring into mine to relay her message. "I need you to know I'm here because I want to be. That I would adore you with or without the storm and tarot cards. Sure, the tarot spelled out what I was thinking, but I had feelings for you before that."

I looked at her, urging her to continue. My gaze searched her face for understanding. No line, tug, or flinch to be found, only the gray eyes I loved. She went on. "And I think it's telling how easily I stayed with you and how quickly we got physical. How I feel about you is drastically different, and deeper, than how I've felt about anyone else before you. I'm so used to running, but you've made me want to stay and feel something. To witness it unfold."

Hearing her want to stay in some capacity made me dizzy. I gazed at her a moment longer, taking in what she was saying.

I swallowed hard. "You're right. And that I let you into my world says something, too." She nodded as I put my arm lazily around her on the back of the couch. My voice sounded sad, even to my own ears, "I knew the second I met you that our time together would not be simple or fleeting." My free hand cupped her beautiful face. "But you're making me second-guess everything."

"I didn't tell you about Tyler mostly because I forgot about it in all the commotion. I wasn't trying to be deceitful."

"I get it." I blinked somberly.

"But do you?" She squinted.

"Yeah, I do."

"I couldn't just say, *hey, I found my boyfriend balls deep in a girl who makes a killer latte and now I'm here*. It's embarrassing. I didn't want you to treat me differently. It bruised my ego, along with my stupid neck. Regardless, I hope you know how differently I feel about you. How differently I feel about us."

Us.

Her cute voice saying *us* felt like a threshold we hadn't yet stumbled over. I liked the sound of it. It planted some seed deep in my chest I wanted to tend to.

"Why was he still texting you?"

"I'm not sure. I wish I'd just blocked him. Maybe some part of me wished he'd apologize."

"Guys like Tyler don't apologize," I said flatly, hoping she cemented that into her brain.

"You're right." She looked down at her lap sadly.

I stroked her cheek. "But you're valid to want an apology. You're a kind soul, and you expect the same goodness from others."

She nodded and continued, "I thought he'd get the hint if I told him I was with someone else. Mentioning you was easy because I was happy I had someone who could appreciate me, a damn good man. Plus, I knew it would piss him off and I'm petty." She chuckled to herself, making me fight a smile.

Her face quickly morphed into a sad expression while she stared at my ice pack. "I mean, I know I'm enough. It's okay to be on my own, but it's hard to be in a new city without knowing people. I feel like I need to prove to my parents, and if I can use my degree and thrive on my own, the craziness of college and Florida would be worth something."

"That makes sense."

"But I'm missing human connection in Boston, something I've found so easily elsewhere. I had more friends in the middle of the desert than I do there." She dropped the ice pack, holding it for me to grab. She looked out the window for a moment, lost in her own thoughts.

"Tell me what you're thinking," I prodded more.

"I'm exhausted. Weary. Like that soul-deep kind of tired. Have you felt that before?"

I nodded, remembering times I had to grind through school for years on end. "Usually that's a sign of lack of balance. What is out of balance in your life? Just too much work?"

She looked out the window a few moments longer, then a sad, considering hum vibrated her body before she looked back at me. "I love that insight you just gave me, thank you. Hmm, balance. I guess I would say everything is out of balance in my life right now."

I put my hand on the inside of her thigh, holding her leg intimately. "I could kind of sense that. That's why I really wanted to protect you and give you some happiness while you're here. Maybe I'm not intuitive like you, but I could just sense you needed healing."

"Thank you," she whispered, looking at my lips and then back up to my eyes. "Thank you for understanding me. I feel misunderstood in most aspects of my life. Maybe I didn't want you to think I was some weirdo. It's funny though." She let out a sad laugh. "I came here and crashed your party with all my weirdness, and I didn't want to scare you away."

"Kaylee, you're not weird at all. I love how unique you are." My chest stung when I thought of all the people who'd put those horrible thoughts in her mind. "I wish you'd told me. Finding out you're being cheated on by walking in on it and then getting into a wreck is a lot to deal with. You've had so much thrown at you and you managed it in silence. Now you've had some crazy ex track you down. I mean, that shit is hard! You're tough." Seeing her side of it made me angry for her. She had endured so much in silence, like a fucking warrior. She was a strong woman.

"Thank you for hearing me out. I guess we both kept information from each other for the sake of not ruining things," she said.

"We both kept things from each other because we didn't want to mess this up." I gestured between us, hinting at our relationship and further clarifying what was going on.

"Right, because it wasn't something we saw coming."

I cupped her face again, needing to hold her beauty in my hand, needing to feel the woman I'd fallen for. I kissed her, unable to help myself. She put her hand on where I held her face, and I winced at the pain in my knuckle. The wound was open and swelling fast. My head rang, and my muscles felt sore from the adrenaline crash. Coming into the house after the incident, I'd been riding a high. Now that the sex and violence were over, the physical reality of what I'd put my body through settled in, but it had been worth it.

To stand up to a man who'd hurt Kaylee.

To have Kaylee, all of her, the way I'd wanted since the night I'd met her.

Now we hung in a limbo state. The storm had passed, and she was never getting her car back. We were now blindly avoiding the inevitable: her leaving.

Chapter Twenty-Six

Harley

The ice pack on my knuckle was a half-assed attempt to nurse the wound. Removing it, I realized I needed stitches. I could probably do them myself if I could use my right hand, but since I'd used that hand to slug, I was in quite the predicament.

I didn't want to drag Kaylee into town with me because it would fuel rumors. Even more dangerous, my sister Chessie was a nurse at the small medical clinic. I didn't know her exact schedule, but I didn't want to risk her and Kaylee colliding. Yet I feared if the skin tore any further, it would damage the ligament. I looked over at Kaylee to see her scowling at her phone. Maybe this was my loophole to go alone?

"Hey, everything alright?" I nodded toward the phone in her hands.

"Ugh, yeah. My boss, Tamara, is up my ass. Some of my emails didn't go through when the power was out, so there were some communication issues. I mean, I get it. I didn't plan to be away for a week, but c'mon, let a girl live a little." She scowled at her screen, not even looking up.

"Well, while you handle that, I'm going to go into town and get my hand looked at."

Her head whipped to look at me. "Oh? Okay, I can probably be ready in a couple of minutes."

She stood up, freeing her bare legs from the furry blanket she'd cocooned herself in. I touched her bare thigh from where I sat, loving her exposed skin. "No, stay here. Deal with that." I looked pointedly at her phone once more.

"But what if you're dizzy? Or you get tired? Honey, it's the least I can do." She touched my hair and beard in a nurturing way, concern painting her face. I knew I had to bring out the big guns for this one. She was unrelentingly loyal, which I adored.

"Babe, my ego can't handle much more today. Having you hold my hand while the other one gets stitches . . ." She got the hint and shrugged, sitting back down.

"Will you at least bring me back a decent cup of coffee? I can't keep drinking your black trucker brew."

I smiled. "Sorry, no coffee shops in town. Just some sketchy sludge from a local diner."

She clutched her phone to her chest in horror. "Not even a Dunkin'?"

"Nope, I'm sorry."

"Ugh, that should be illegal," she whispered, mostly to herself.

Walking into the clinic, I saw the top of my sister's head bobbing in front of the reception computer while she typed like a maniac. Her eyes widened at the realization of me visiting.

"Hey, man, what the hell?" She shot to her feet to look me up and down in worry. Even though she was my little sister, she was still quite tall. Like my brother Carson and I, she was all long limbs and olive complected. Her hair was curlier than mine, and she wore it in a giant pile on the top of her head.

Her tattoos peeked out from her dark purple scrubs, showing portrayals of mostly flowers. I remembered her asking me what flowers were native to Maine and Greece so she could incorporate them into the designs. She went with dianthus flowers because they were part of the tale of the goddess Artemis gouging out a man's eyes in anger, which honestly tracked knowing Chessie.

"Hey." I lifted my wounded hand.

"Oh, shit!" She grabbed a clipboard and beckoned me into one of the two exam rooms. Pine Bluff was big enough to have a clinic, but not big enough to have hordes of patients. They saw lots of poison oak, sunburns, and sprained ankles from drunken bonfires. They sent more complicated stuff, like births and surgery, to the hospital four towns over.

Chessie shut the door and led me to sit down in a chair along the wall of the exam room. She put her hands on her hips and conspiratorially whisper-yelled, "Harley, what the actual fuck?!"

"My hand accidentally smashed into a bastard's mouth. Happens to the best of us, Ches." I shrugged, hoping she'd chalk it up to a bar fight.

"You've never been one to fight people, except Carson. You usually just brood and stare at them until they go away."

I shrugged again and yanked off my beanie in quiet shame. My temple and forehead had swollen with a shiner.

"Oof, wow. Okay. Let me get supplies." She pointed at me while walking out the door. "And you're going to tell me what happened."

Five minutes went by, and I got the sneaking suspicion shit was about to hit the fan. My phone was rarely by me, and it never had the ringer on. I groaned and checked it, seeing I had a missed call from my mom. I opened our texts to tell her I'd call her back in a minute, only to have my sister barge in on a video chat with her.

"Jeezus, Chessie, isn't that a HIPAA violation?!"

"Oh, shut it! Here." She handed me her phone and washed her hands to put on gloves. I held it in my left hand, feeling trapped. I looked at my mom's kind expression and took a deep sigh.

"Hey."

"Harley, are you okay? Tell me everything, dear." My mom's no-nonsense tone filled the call. She squinted to see my injuries, her wild hair framing her face in copper and gray waves and curls, her shaggy bangs giving way to funky glasses with thick, dark-purple frames.

"Mom, it's nothing. Men fight. It's a perfectly normal response in nature—"

"Harley Demetrios Kouris, stop your biology babble and tell me what the hell is going on! I shoveled myself out of the house today to visit the market. While I was there, I ran into Ginger, my nail lady. She was telling me all about how some pretty girl crashed her car this weekend and several people saw you helping her into your truck by the market. I thought to myself, that doesn't sound like Harley. I don't think he has a girlfriend right now, but I ran into Karen, and she said some guy came into the ranger station to talk to Terry. He was looking for a young woman who people saw with a ranger who saved her from a wreck."

I huffed and rolled my eyes in frustration. Of course, it'd been Terry who'd blown my cover. Fucking Terry!

Chessie put a rolling tray under my hand and began the stitches. "Hagrid was on Conifer Road. She almost hit him and wrecked her car trying to avoid him." I flinched at the first hook of flesh. "She crashed Saturday night," I said through gritted teeth.

"And?" Chessie and my mom both prompted in unison.

"She didn't have anywhere to stay. You both know there's shit lodging around here with Eugenia gone. She was exhausted, and the storm was rolling in, so I let her stay with me."

Both of their jaws dropped in unison at the scandalous news. The moment made me think of a phrase Kaylee had said right after her wreck, something like wanting the earth to open up to swallow someone whole. I completely understood the feeling now.

"Harley! That was such a gentlemanly thing for you to do!" My mom beamed, putting her hand to her chest.

"So damn cute!" Chessie added warmly.

"Is she still with you?" my mom asked.

"Yeah, Dane sent pictures and a video of the damage to her car to the insurance adjuster, so it's about wrapped up."

"Is there a romantic connection, Harley?" My mom's therapist lingo made me cringe internally.

"Yes." My tone was as flat as Nebraska.

"Oh my goodness! Why isn't she with you? I want to meet her!" Chessie gushed.

"Um, this is the exact reason. You guys are embarrassing. I'm a grown man and you're all up in my business."

Chessie stitched a little rougher than what was probably necessary, making me hiss in pain and give her a dirty look.

My mom teased, "Oh, sweetie, you've always been so private. Let us have our fun! Is she nice? Is she a kind person?"

"Very kind. Smart. Stubborn as all hell . . ." I caught myself smiling like an idiot.

"Is she pretty? What's her vibe?" Chessie asked.

"Oh yeah, she's gorgeous. Probably out of my league if I'm being honest. She's a bit of a free spirit, kind of . . . I don't know . . ."

"Bohemian?" my mom offered, wiggling in her seat and clasping her hands together under her chin.

"Sure, I guess," I answered in bewilderment. "She's witchy. Like, she has tarot cards and talks about the moon all the time. She was upset it was snowing so much because she wanted to frolic in the forest," I added, unsure if it helped.

My mom and sister squealed in unison once more. "Oh man, you've got it bad!" Chessie said, smiling down at my hand.

"So how did you get hurt?" my mom asked.

"She had a creep follow her up here. The guy who talked to Terry, apparently. He's basically a stalker. I told him to get off my private property, but he refused to leave, so I hit him."

Ches and my mom gasped in shock. I turned the phone so Chessie could make eye contact with my mom then twisted it back to face me.

"What?" I asked, confused.

"Harley, we don't hit people in this family."

"He yanked her hair like a psycho and was threatening to take her. He had this creepy bet with his coworkers that he could bang her. It was revolting. I had to do something."

"Ooooh," they said, nodding in understanding.

I added, "But hey, she held her own. She got a nut shot in."

My mom cleared her throat uncomfortably. "It's horrible he hurt her. I'm so sorry you both had that happen to you. I'd love to hear this entire story. When will we be meeting this . . ."

"Kaylee," I offered with a reluctant smile.

"This Kaylee. When will we have the pleasure of meeting her?"

"Um, probably never. She'll be gone by the weekend at the latest. She has a demanding job back in Boston." My tone was overly simple and way too detached. I felt like I was hovering over my body while I divulged this information. None of the events that had happened today made much sense to me.

Life since Saturday had felt like some alternate reality. Gorgeous women didn't crash their cars in front of me. Funny, witty, pretty, single women didn't hang out in the forest or Pine Bluff. Conversations didn't easily stretch on for hours, sex didn't feel that tantalizing right off the bat, and no one could make elk tacos taste decent. Kaylee felt almost like a figment of my imagination. If it wasn't for the physical remnants of her, like my busted knuckle fighting her stalker and her scratches on my back from our long nights together, I might consider myself imagining everything.

My sister's voice broke through my anxious train of thought. "You should fight for her. I mean, more than you already have. She's obviously special to you if you're willing to beat a guy up, and she must be easy to be around if you've been with her for days." She snipped the last of the stitches and cleaned up her workspace.

My mom enthusiastically nodded at what she could hear Chessie saying, adding, "Your sister is right, and you've already experienced a shared hardship. That's bound to bring people closer. If you can get through a wreck, a blizzard, and a stalker, that says something. Have you been intimate with her?" she asked, squinting and fixing her glasses.

"Mom," I chided her, my eyes wide with embarrassment. I didn't like it when she tried to therapize me. I especially didn't want to talk about blowing Kaylee's back out with my mother.

"What? Sex is a normal part of every romantic relationship."

"I'm not gonna talk about railing some girl in front of you and my damn sister!" I raked my freshly stitched hand through my hair. Chessie grabbed it instantly, clucking at me, and continued dressing the wound.

"Okay, I'll take that as a yes. Does this mean you put that sex swing I gave you to good use?"

I plopped the phone on my lap with a groan. I covered my face with my free hand, hiding my pure mortification. My mom's voice flitted up from my lap. "What? You have some solid support beams in that cabin, dear. You could totally go for it. Is she limber?"

Chessie took off her gloves while cackling. I handed the phone back to her in frustration.

"Mom, I'll make sure he's okay. I think we've traumatized him enough for one day. Okay?"

She ended the call and looked at me from where she swiveled on her stool. Even though she was younger than me, she felt much wiser. She was an old soul and saw right through my bullshit. Even though I was the middle child, she'd acted like a buffer between my family and me for most of my life. They were always up in my business, wanting to know every detail.

"Harley, you look like shit."

"Thanks," I said wryly while she looked over the injury on my forehead.

"But beyond the injuries, I can tell there's something different about you. You're more patient or something. I don't know. Maybe even happier. I think this Kaylee is good for you."

"I don't disagree with you."

"Well then, what gives?"

"We just met. I think I'm just some hookup for her. Years from now, I'm sure she'll tell everyone about some ranger who saved her in a storm. I'll be just an outlandish story for her."

Her head tilted in curiosity. "Is that what this is for you? Just a story?"

"No, not at all."

"Okay, then stop acting like it."

My stomach sank, and my blood felt icy with shock. She was onto something.

Chessie continued, "I mean, she dropped everything and trusted you enough to stay at your cabin. As a woman, that says something. You're assuming she wants different things than you do, so maybe find out exactly what she's feeling."

I nodded, taking in the advice.

"Don't be so quick to write her off," she added.

I stood up with Chessie and brought her in for a bear hug.

"Thanks for stitching up my hand. Even if you ratted me out to Mom."

I grabbed a bottle of coffee creamer at the market for Kaylee and took the long way home, enjoying how beautiful the land looked after the heavy snowfall. I took a loop through the part of the forest that I found to be tranquil with how the river flowed through it. Parking my truck, I got out to stand by the river's edge. Large rocks in the stream looked like marshmallows rounded with snow. The water was a gentle flow of black and brown, carving through the fluffy white of snow with trees shrouding its course, protecting its simple beauty.

I stood still, willing myself to ignore the cold and focus on the gurgle of the stream. The brisk air filled my lungs, and I could feel the weak winter sun cast on the side of my face from where it sat. I took deep breaths, rejuvenating my senses while coming back to my center.

I felt so swept up in Kaylee. She was infiltrating every aspect of my life. I yearned for her, but I wanted to have a few moments alone to sort out my thoughts and feelings. Being near Kaylee instigated a buzz in my mind and body that made me feel like I couldn't think clearly. All I could do was fall deeper. That was a theme with Kaylee and me. We never intended things to get deeper, but one move, one confession, or a meaningful look would plummet us further into the depths of each other. Intertwining our minds and stories together. Our lives now permanently coalesced.

I stood by the river and tried to assess the situation, considering how it was changing me physically, emotionally, and mentally.

Physically, she was taking up space in my life by staying with me. I loved the reality of her presence. She was simply fun to be around. Everything felt right when she was near. I'd had chemistry with other women before, but something about Kaylee felt exceptional. Now that I'd tasted her on my lips, reveled in the way she felt against me, and knew intimately what it was like to be with her, I yearned for more. I felt selfish for her, wanting more, needing more.

She was taking up my emotional space by awakening something in me I wasn't ready to admit. I was living a guarded life, going too long without love, needlessly punishing myself by living under the shrewd assumption that my lifestyle and past prevented me from being someone's partner. That not wanting children tarnished my character as a man. That I was fatally flawed because I'd seen such horrific things as a ranger that caused me to put a guard up.

Kaylee reminded me of all the myriad of ways to live life, that someone's *hell no* is another person's *hell yes*. That what I'd endured as a ranger had joyous endings, not always tragedy.

She was taking up my mental space because all I could do was think about her. I went to bed thinking of her and woke up the same way. Usually a man of few words, I couldn't stop talking to her. She fascinated the shit out of me, and not because she had teeth on her necklace or rocks in her bra, but because she was smart, resilient, irreverent, and fucking hilarious. Even worse, I found myself constantly worried about her health and safety, all while fighting off the intrusive musings of what life would be like with her next to me.

I was a man consumed by new love and deep lust. I knew it. Outside of our situation, I wanted to know how I felt about Kaylee. I flipped through scenarios in my head.

Did I trust her? Yes.

Did I want to get to know her even more? Yes.

Would mundane things with her make life tolerable? Like going to the DMV or arguing over paint samples? I chuckled at the thought of it and realized I wanted that so badly, so yes.

Would I want to go on vacations with her? Hold her hair back while she puked? Watch horribly written medical dramas while she put her cold feet on me? Yes.

Would I want to unwind from a long day with her? My chest burned with longing. Yes.

Regardless of what this wild woman decided, would I think of Kaylee for the rest of my days? Absolutely.

I opened my eyes to look down at the river. A pale rock morphed under the slight wave of the water. I squinted, looking at it further. Getting down on one knee while taking off my coat, I rolled up my sleeve and dipped my unwounded hand in the water to grab it. It stung from the cold water, causing me to hiss. I flipped the large palm stone over in my hand, smiling like a fool. The water had smoothed the pale gray stone, morphing it into the shape of a crescent moon.

A perfect moon, for my perfect moonchild.

I put it in my jacket pocket, shaking my head. Oh, I had it bad.

When I came home, I couldn't wait to hug and kiss Kaylee once more. It was a welcome distraction from the pain. She squealed at the sight of the coffee creamer and jumped up and down before launching at me with a hug. She wasn't at all suspicious about why I'd gone into town alone. Instead, she was completely in the moment with me for the first time in days. She was usually so worried or fretting; it was nice to see her finally in the present. A warm hush of pride filled me at seeing her look so calm. It was nice knowing I'd brought her back to a place of peace. The slight shadows under her eyes had disappeared with her days of deep sleep next to me. I was sure the orgasms had helped too. Whatever was going on with her work had been settled by the time I got back, and now we had each other's full attention.

"Hey, let me show you something outside," I said.

"Let me put pants on!" She got up and ran adorably into the bedroom, only to emerge still wearing my flannel and a pair of leggings. Her hair was down now, in slight curls from being in a bun and the steamy shower earlier.

"Why are you smiling at me like that?" I couldn't help but notice how her cute voice rang through my mind.

"Nothing. It's just . . . you look extra gorgeous today."

She smiled and stepped into the boots I'd left by the door, shuffling behind me to the section of the wraparound porch that ran outside the living room. Her arms instantly folded across her chest with the chill.

"Come here," I said mischievously, holding her close by wrapping my arms and Carhartt coat around her. She wiggled against me and fought back shivers. Feeling her close to me made the pain of the day seem justified. I didn't mind busting up my hand and head to protect her. She was worth it.

"Hey look!" She raised her jaw out toward the sky where a half-lit moon hung.

"Yep, waxing gibbous," I whispered into her hair.

"I'm impressed you know that!" I could hear the smile in her voice. We watched some clouds drift over the moon, blocking it out before its lunar light escaped triumphantly again.

"What do you believe in, Harley? What's your take on life?" she asked pensively.

"Hmm, let me think." More clouds flitted across the moon in a procession of gray tufts. I continued, "I believe that nature is the greatest teacher and kindness pays off. How someone conducts themselves in the world says more about them than any of their riches. And losing your curiosity is the quickest way to waste your life."

She nodded and leaned back against my pec. "I love that."

"What do you believe in, Kaylee?" I mirrored her question, nuzzling into her hair.

"Mmm," she said, considering. "I believe in good men and the rhythm of the moon. That most people are just scared, and that an orgasm and a cup of coffee can cure just about anything."

I chuckled and kissed the top of her head. "I couldn't agree more."

We stood watching the moon until the bitter cold seeped into our bodies. I reached into my pocket and pulled out the smooth river stone I'd found earlier.

"I want you to have this, to remember your time here in Pine Bluff." I held the crescent-shaped stone in my outstretched hand so she could see the shape of it against the sky. She gasped and stilled in silence for a moment before turning around as much as she could while still in my coat. The moonlight glinted in her stormy eyes while she stared up at me, speechless.

"Harley! That is so thoughtful!" She turned her head back to gaze at it before adding, "And perfect, just like you." She held the stone, looking at it carefully in the starlight. I held her close, kissing her hair, taking in the moment that felt overwhelming and fateful.

"I figured you should have a Harley-rock for your bra."

We both chuckled and stared up at the moon. I could feel her heart beating faster against me, her body melting into mine for warmth. I wanted to savor her here with me, under the beautiful moon. As if reading my mind, Kaylee took a deep sigh.

"I wish I could bottle up this moment. Being here with you," she said.

"You could," I murmured into her ear before kissing it. My voice came out too husky, too intense.

She turned all the way around to look at me, the heat of her body leaving my coat. Now shivering, her body shuddered against her will. "H-Harley, I wish I could. M-m-more th-th-than—" She took a deep, gathering breath. "More than anything."

Her beautiful face looked forlorn. I couldn't tell if she was fighting back just the cold or tears as well. I kissed her forehead and opened the door back into the cabin, ushering her in as her teeth chattered.

My injuries overtook me, much to my annoyance. My energy had waned while my head pounded like a monkey had busted it open like a coconut with a hammer. Unable to broach our plans out of pure exhaustion, I changed into comfy clothes, ate an epic grilled cheese sandwich made by Kaylee, and cuddled her while watching shitty reality TV the rest of the night.

Around midnight, she all but dragged me into bed. I'd fallen in and out of sleep for hours on the couch. Instead of holding Kaylee, I let my guard down and let her hold me. My head nestled in her soft boobs. It felt like heaven. It didn't help that while watching TV, Kaylee had slowly dragged her nails all over my back and through my hair, putting me in a relaxed haze. Her touch alone could heal me better than any medicine could.

Sliding into bed with her, my heart twinged at the tenderness of what we had together. We lay on our sides, facing each other while Kaylee caressed my beard and hair, rubbing my shoulder, soothing me in her feminine way. The moon cast silvery light through the window, illuminating her beautiful face next to me in the bed.

"I love you." The words escaped me before I could overthink anything.

A small smile spread across Kaylee's face. Her eyes washed over me in their stormy depths.

"I love you." She breathed on my lips before putting hers on mine.

Chapter Twenty-Seven

Kaylee

Harley's eyes fluttered as he fought to stay awake. We were lying chest to chest on his bed as the moonlight filled the room with a cool glow. His features looked devastatingly handsome this close with his face softened with sleepiness.

The slight swelling on the side of his face by his temple reminded me of his injury. An empathetic wave of discomfort rolled through my body. It made me realize why he'd been so hesitant to touch me our first couple of days together. I stroked his jaw, feeling the bristle of the beard I loved, and rubbed his shoulder to relax him even more. He needed rest. He'd been on alert to keep us safe since the moment he'd rescued me. The least I could do now was soothe him.

His eyes opened and searched mine while his hand cupped my face, his thumb stroking my cheek before stilling. His eyes hopelessly oozed with emotion, searching mine.

"I love you." His voice escaped his mouth in a low tone of conviction.

"I love you," I responded immediately, without even having to think about it.

After brushing my lips against his, I kissed him deeply, sweetly, trying to fight the shock of his confession. I had to hold back from crying or giggling, unsure which my body wanted to do more to offset the sheer intensity of my love for him.

Sensing how truly exhausted he was, I slowed my kisses and pulled back to say it to him again.

"I love you too, Harley. You'll always be a part of me."

"I'm so happy someone like you exists," he all but slurred out. I rubbed his shoulder, trailing down his arm, causing his hand to drop from my face as sleep overtook him. I continued touching him, encouraging him to fall into a deep sleep while I watched his face lighten, his breath deepen. Seeing him let his guard down put an ache in my heart because I cared for him so profoundly, not just as a lover, but simply as a human.

It was an honor to love Harley in all his depths. That I disarmed this intimidating man and that he let me see this special, hidden side of him made me feel privileged, like we were in on some secret no one knew about. Being around him was simultaneously arousing and calming, a potent mix I was quickly becoming addicted to. He knew when to be soft, and he knew when to be strong. He knew when to let me be free, and he knew when to be steady to inspire me to ground down. I needed that so badly. I'd just never known it.

The unanswered question on if Harley wanted company past the storm was still unclear. In the calm, moonlit room, I stared at him while searching through my memories. I recalled how he'd promised I wasn't a distraction but a priority with the sunrise today. How he'd come back from town with my favorite coffee creamer he'd somehow just known about, along with a crescent-shaped river rock he'd found for me.

Butterflies swirled in my stomach at the recollection of how sweetly he'd given me the stone under the moonlight tonight. I'd told him I wished I could bottle up the moment and be here with him. All he'd said was I could. What did that mean?

Did he mean just staying a day longer? Visiting? Spending the weekend together and then never seeing each other again because he just wasn't ready yet? Had I broken down Harley's walls and warmed up his heart for someone else in the future? My heart sank at the thought of it, and a tinge of jealousy crept into my body. It wasn't a sensation I was used to. My intuition told me the fresh bite of possessiveness was also an indicator of how intensely I felt for him.

I was unsure how things with us would end up, but regardless, I wanted Harley happy and well loved. I knew deep down I would think of him every day for the rest of my life. With this awareness, I'd also come to terms with how I needed to show up more in my own life.

Harley made me want more for myself. He showed me I could ask for things in life, like protection in a storm, and that I didn't always have to be the one rescuing others. When I'd realized this after our night in front of the fire, I'd since tried to use my time at the cabin to sort out what I wanted my life to look like. It hadn't been fruitful because all I wanted was to be here with Harley. I wanted to create a life for myself here in Maine.

It also didn't help that Tamara was hounding me to tell her where I was so she could ship a laptop to me. I understood my time away from work had been unexpected, but something about the lack of boundaries and concern was off-putting. I'd proven time and time again that I was more than willing to stay late, work through lunch, meet quotas, and exceed expectations. Her pushiness was a hint of the parasitic nature my future clearly held at Tate Staffing.

The storm cleared, and tomorrow we planned on visiting Dane to wrap up the shitshow. It felt like Harley and I were in between stages of our relationship. Openly caring for each other but unsure of what the future held. Uncertainty was layered between our foundation of loyalty and our undiscovered fate.

Could I really return to my sad existence in Boston now that I'd had a taste of life here? I couldn't imagine Harley driving me home this weekend and just hugging me at my doorstep.

Had our time together changed his mind? I wondered if he was ready for a relationship beyond the storm. Was I just a flowerchild fling who danced with him in his cabin to rock music and made fun of his mountain man tendencies?

Could I be happy having a long-distance relationship or an occasional hookup when I wanted a vacation? I felt my nose shrivel in disgust just thinking about it. Even worse, thinking of Harley alone or with another woman in the meantime.

I gently raked my hand through his hair, watching his handsome face twitch with a dream. I looked over my shoulder at the river stone I'd placed on the dresser near my things. A surge of emotion filled my throat as I realized how hopelessly I loved Harley.

He was mine. But was I his?

Chapter Twenty-Eight

Harley's truck tires crunched over the packed snow while we pulled into the back lot of Dane's shop. My Mini Cooper was there, and I got out to inspect the mangled bumper. I cringed looking at the damage I didn't realize had happened Saturday.

"Kaylee, this is Dane." Harley's voice sliced through my horror.

I turned to see a cute guy standing next to Harley. His face was attractive—piercing green eyes were between stubble and a thick knit cap. He wore navy Carhartt coveralls covered in grease that were rolled up to his elbows which revealed sleeves of tattoos on both arms along with thick muscles from wrenching. His eyebrow cocked as he looked at me. He sent Harley a quick nod of approval I didn't think I was supposed to catch.

"Hey, moose killer." He outstretched his blackened hand for me to shake before realizing it was dirty. We playfully fist-bumped instead.

"Nice to meet you, Dane."

"Sorry about your car." He handed me the keys.

"I guess it was just time. Thanks for taking care of it."

He nodded and shoved his hands in his pockets.

I retrieved my things from the glove compartment and trunk while the men talked. Piling everything into my duffle bag, I hoisted it up into Harley's truck. It felt like the end of an era. The Coop had been my car throughout college down in Florida. I'd driven it all the way from Florida to Texas, then from Texas to Maryland. I skimmed the roof of the Mini with my hand, sad to see it go.

"Hey, babe, Dane needs help with something. Are you cool to wait a sec?"

Staring at my hand on my car, I felt annoyed at the chipped nail polish. I was pretty low maintenance. Hell, I could stay in a cabin for days with cheap shampoo and limited clothing. But my nails had bugged me since yesterday. Thank gods I'd put new eye contacts in before the wreck on Saturday.

"This is pretty random, but is there a nail salon nearby?"

Dane chuckled. "Yeah, just three shops over." He pointed in the general direction.

Walking into the salon, a ding alerted my arrival. Five women swiveled their heads to look at me. One lady was perming an older woman's hair as she slumped over in the chair, half asleep with a gossip magazine on her lap. Another lady was hunched over a table, doing nails for a young woman with gorgeous curly hair. The fifth woman was lounging on the couch with her phone. She was matronly with a heavy chest that made her look almost like a mother hen about to topple over. She stood up and met me at the front counter.

"Hey, how are you?" I grinned, grateful to be around women for the first time in almost a week.

"Hi, dear. I'm good. What can I help you with?"

"I don't have an appointment, sorry, but I was hoping I could get a fill?" I held out my hands to show her what she'd be working with.

"Beautiful set, honey. You have good taste. Take a seat." She pointed to the chair by the woman with curly hair. "Can I get you a Diet Coke?" she asked over her shoulder.

"Sure, that'd be great." I couldn't help but smile at her warmth and the promise of caffeine. I was a girl's girl and being around women made me feel better. Also, something about this lady made me miss my mom. I shot a side glance at the woman sitting next to me. We made fleeting eye contact with small smiles.

"Ginger, I need those two fingers short," the curly haired woman explained to the lady doing her nails.

Ginger stared at the woman's hands for a few moments. "These two fingers?" She pointed at the woman's pointer and middle finger on her right hand with the nail file she was holding.

"Yep, those stay short and the others I want oval." Her tone was simplistic, like she was trying to be polite with the woman misunderstanding.

"Oh, you must need them short for work, huh?" Ginger responded.

I snickered, realizing what was going on. The curly-haired lady probably had a girlfriend and needed her nails short in order to do certain . . . things. I tried to hold my giggles, but the curly-haired lady looked over at me in recognition.

"Yep, I need them short for work." She bit her lip, her shoulders shuddering with silent laughter. I chuckled even more at her response, causing her to giggle even more. Ginger looked from me to her and back to me, trying to figure out why we were laughing.

"I'm Frankie, by the way," she said, diverting the situation.

"I'm Kaylee." I smiled between Frankie and Ginger. My nail lady returned with a Diet Coke for both of us and introduced herself as Barbara.

"What brings you to Pine Bluff?" Barbara asked, holding up a swatch of gel colors to pick from. I picked a plum, knowing jewel tones looked best against my pale skin.

"Oh, I'm just passing through." I smiled and shrugged.
"Where are you from?"
"Texas, but I live in Boston now, unfortunately. What about you?"

Barbara filed away the oxblood gel that was already on my nails. From what I gathered, all the women were born and raised in Maine. Barbara and Ginger, who'd been friends for decades, kept trying to remember details about a guy Ginger had dated who was from Amarillo. They'd taken a road trip to Texas one summer to watch him in a rodeo. Their memories were spotty, so recalling the details led to more side tangents. I spent most of the hour smiling politely while they tried to cobble the story together. All the while, I kept catching Frankie sneaking glances at me.

As I was finishing up, Frankie caught me at the register. "Hey, if you have time, do you maybe want to grab a bite to eat? Tilly's Tavern is just down the road. They make a killer veggie burger. My girlfriend, Meg, is a vegan. We finally talked them into carrying it, so I feel obligated to continue ordering it." She smiled good-naturedly while hoisting her purse over her shoulder.

An excited feeling rushed through my body. Yes! My resounding answer was yes. I missed girl talk and vegetarian cuisine! "Absolutely! I need to check in on some things at Dane's Auto first. Want to come with?"

"Sure!"

I pushed the door open politely, letting Frankie walk through first. With a yelp, she almost slipped on the icy sidewalk. I grabbed her arm, locking it with mine so she wouldn't fall and bust her ass. We giggled at the squeal she let out and continued walking arm in arm for stability.

"I'm so clumsy. Meg always makes fun of me. She calls me Flailing Frankie. It's so embarrassing!"

"No, it's endearing!" I insisted, patting her hand where she clutched my arm.

"What about you? Do you have a significant other?"

"Um, no, not officially. I mean, I wish I did, but it's complicated. So complicated I don't even know how to explain it."

Approaching Dane's, I saw Harley walking around the shop from the back lot. His stride was confident. For a split second, I got giddy looking at him. He was so handsome it hurt. His muscles were now covered in a heavy winter coat, along with a hat that concealed his bruised forehead. His long arms and large hands swung as he walked.

"Harley!" I raised my voice so he could hear me.

He looked our way, his eyes growing wide. He stopped mid-stride, only to shove his hands in his pockets while waiting for us to cross the street. Getting closer with each step, I could see his face had gone placid, his eyes darting between Frankie and me. He sucked in a breath and swallowed hard.

"Hey, Harley, this is—"

"My sister," he interrupted, ducking his head in scorn, shooting daggers at Frankie.

I looked at Frankie, who had a rueful smile. Had she known the whole time?

"Oh," I said, dumbfounded.

"I wondered if you were the mystery woman Harley had holed up in his cabin." She squeezed my arm, letting it go, only to step forward to slug Harley playfully.

"I thought you said her name was Chessie, like short for Francesca?" My voice hitched playfully to hide my confusion.

She swatted the air dismissively with a shrug. "Ah, yeah, my brothers call me that, but I go by Frankie everywhere else."

Holy shit! I'd been sitting next to Harley's sister the entire time? The whole fucking time?! My stomach sank and my brain went haywire. Instinctually, this situation didn't feel good. I felt duped. I wished I'd known so we could have gossiped! Now that they stood by each other, I could see the family resemblance with their heights and flawless olive complexions.

Harley uncomfortably looked between us. Frankie added, "I was going to take her over to Tilly's for lunch. Want to join us? I'm sure she's sick of your bachelor cuisine."

Harley cleared his throat. "I actually made plans for us so . . ."

"Makes sense, perhaps another time." Frankie shrugged. "It was lovely meeting you." She scooped me up into a warm hug.

"It was so nice meeting you! And I love the way your nails turned out, by the way. The lilac looks perfect with your skin tone." I gestured to her hands. She smiled at me and then smirked at Harley before leaving.

Harley put his arm around my shoulders, leading me back to his truck. In the hour it had taken to get my nails done, someone had already come and taken my Mini Cooper. Seeing the empty spot made me feel queasy. The large tire tracks from the tow truck dug into the snow-packed ground, exposing the blacktop underneath. Thick clouds blanketed the sky, snuffing out the early afternoon sunlight, making everything feel colder than it probably was.

"What are we doing? Where are we going?" I asked anxiously.

"I figured we'd go back to my place." He shrugged, looking around. "I slept in so late this morning. It feels like we just started our day."

"Oh, but I want food. Can we at least get some in town?"

"Yeah, how about Yeti's again? I could swing by and pick up another pizza." He walked me to the passenger side of the truck and opened my door to usher me in.

"Like, to take it back to the cabin?"

"Well, yeah." He pulled his phone out, as if to order on an app or something. My stomach sank a little more.

"Why can't we go inside somewhere? I've barely left your cabin."

Harley looked around, darting his eyes to the street and the back of Dane's shop. Why was he acting so sketchy? Were we in danger?

"Harley, why can't we go out into the world together? If I didn't know any better, I'd think you don't want to be seen with me." Right when I said that, it clicked in my brain. That was it. He didn't want to be seen with me. My blood froze in my body, my back went stiff straight, and I could feel my pulse throbbing in my head. "Oh my god! That's it, isn't it? You don't want to be seen with me?"

Harley's handsome face turned stoic. "It's not like that."

He tried to hold my hands, but I shoved them in my coat before he could. "Then what is it like?"

He held open the truck door wide, gesturing for me to get in. "Kaylee, just get in the truck. Let's talk about this calmly."

"Like hell! Tell me what the fuck is going on? Do you have a wife and kids or something?"

"No! God, no."

"Are you some womanizer? Am I the flavor of the week?"

"No. You know that's not true. I'm not trying to hide you. I don't—"

"Want to be seen with me?" I pulled my hands from my pockets and crossed my arms defensively. I took a deep breath and willed myself to recall the past several days.

Okay, I'd met him Saturday in the wreck. He hadn't let me talk to the police officer or the tow guy.

He hadn't gone into Pine Mart with me.

He'd gone to see Dane about my car, alone.

He'd gotten the pizza for us, alone.

He'd checked in with work the next day, alone.

He'd plowed the streets after the storm, alone.

He'd gone into town yesterday to get his hand stitched, alone.

We could easily hang out in town today with the storm cleared, but no, he wanted to go back to his cabin, to be alone.

Holy fucking shit! My body went tingly with pure panic. He was hiding me from everyone! The man had hidden me from the entire town! He'd seen me talk to my mom and Maisie on the phone. I hadn't heard him talk to anyone, aside from a short call from his dad in Greek and his mom in passing. The memory of him mentioning he only used Greek to talk openly without people knowing what he was saying pinged in my head. My stomach churned into a grizzled knot of nerves.

The only person he'd introduced me to was Dane. Harley had looked at me like I'd just kicked a kitten when I'd been with Frankie, Chessie, whatever the fuck I should call her!

He was keeping me a secret . . . his dirty little secret.

Rifling through this information, I could hear my breathing intensify. It came out in small puffs with the cold air. The constriction of betrayal filled my chest and made my voice quiver. I looked him in the eyes, searching for what shreds of truth I could see in them. "Y-you kept me a secret, didn't you?"

"Not like that. I promise. The people in this town are nosy, and I knew you were going through a lot."

"You didn't want people in your town to know that you were with me? Wh-why? Am I the weird girl who wrecked her car and kept your bed warm in the blizzard? Is that it? Am I just someone no one can know about?"

"Kaylee, babe, you don't get it. You don't have a small hometown like this."

I scoffed at his saccharine mansplaining. "Don't *babe* me. I'm not your babe. Hell, you can't even be seen with me! What the actual fuck, Harley?!" I spat, swinging the truck door shut to help punctuate my statement.

"You lied to me! You kept me stowed away in your cabin, away from the town. Let's not forget you failed to mention for days my car was a total loss. For days! And you kept me here, with you, so what? S-so you could toy with me?" I hissed in disgust.

Harley shook his head, trying to get closer to me. I held my hands up and shoved against his chest. "Give me space."

"I'm sorry," he said, taking a step back and putting his hands in his pockets.

"What the hell was your plan? Why are you so ashamed to be seen with me?" Emotions welled up in my throat, clogging it with shame. Why was every man ashamed to be with me?!

"I'm not. Please, take a deep breath."

I opened the back door on the passenger side of his truck to retrieve my duffle filled with the random things that were in my car. With a swift sling, I hoisted it over my shoulder and across my chest, cutting into my underboob uncomfortably.

"If you're so ashamed of being seen with me, fine. You don't get to be around me at all. I'm not some secret project, you fucking prick," I spat out in disgust.

"Wow!" he said, blinking quickly.

"You need to leave me the fuck alone!" I pointed in the general direction of his cabin.

"Kaylee, no. Please, take a deep breath. You're spiraling."

"Don't tell me to breathe! I can't breathe when you've hurt me this way! The audacity!" I huffed and fucked with the strap of my duffle.

"I'm not like Tyler. You know I'm not like that. You know that!" He set his jaw in anger and continued, "I get that people have treated you like shit in the past, but that's not what is going on here. I just didn't want to parade you around town if I have no clue what your plan is."

"Right, because I'm some loose cannon, some wild child." I rolled my eyes. "You were okay with not having a plan the whole week. You really liked the free-spirited thing when I was hiding away in your cabin, but now that you're not in control, it's an issue."

I hit a nerve, causing him to stare at me while he took some deep breaths to calm down. His hazel eyes pierced mine, blinking slowly with inner turmoil. After a few moments, his deep voice came out in a pleading murmur. "Please, let me at least get you a way home." He shifted his beanie anxiously on his head, his face twitching uncomfortably.

"No, I can do that myself. Leave. Now." Each word barely hissed out, leaving my mouth like a dark threat. "I never want to see you again. I thought you were different. That's what hurts the most." My lips went numb with how they pursed around my clipped words.

He stepped closer to me. "Babe, please, dating in a small town is tricky. Fuck, we aren't even dating, are we? You don't understand what happened last time I—"

I dropped my voice into a rage-whisper. "Go away or I will scream. Then your precious fucking town will think you're hurting a woman. I'm sure you'd hate for that to happen, since you care more about what they think than the woman you claimed to love." I looked up at him, knowing that was a low blow, even if his betrayal had triggered me.

My vision blurred out and I could only notice the dark color of his beard, the gray overcast sky above him, the movement of him walking around the truck and climbing in. He churned the loud engine on, rolling down the passenger side window. "Kaylee, please. Let me drive you. I won't say a word."

I turned my head to shoot daggers at him from where I stood alongside the truck, adjusting the strap across my chest once more to balance the weight of the duffle.

"I wish someone else had saved me that day, Harley. Anyone else. All you did was hurt me and fuck with me when I was already down. What a gentleman." I let out a sad sigh to stop a sob, feeling my face pull in the threat of a cry.

"Just get in—"

"Go," was all I could bite out.

"What if this is it? The last time we see each other?"

A sad, small, manic chuckle left my chest. "Good," I blurted out his favorite mantra. Using it on him this way felt especially cruel, but I didn't care. My vision got blurry again and my heartbeat rang in my ears. I heard the window roll up, but

Harley's truck didn't move to pull away. Instead, it rumbled as it idled in the parking lot like some persistently loyal beast.

Sitting in your truck wasn't illegal, but Harley's defiance made me even more angry. I stood in Dane's lot for several moments, staring blankly up at the sky, gathering my will to move. I was horrified. How had I gotten here? I didn't have time to think about it. My overriding emotion was wrath.

Layers upon layers of feeling out of step, out of place, welled up inside me. The boys in Texas and Florida had thought I was fucking weird. They'd never taken me seriously. Tyler had felt the same way and even taken it a step further to bet on me like some weird racehorse who was too stubborn to be broken but too desirable not to try out. I was even more hurt that Harley, the man who'd just proclaimed his love for me, had intentionally hid me from his town and the people in his life.

Sure, we'd spent most of our time together in the cabin because of the storm, but it was clear he'd purposefully maneuvered situations to avoid being seen with me. Even if I was just a stranded tourist, would it really be all that bad to hang out with me in Pine Bluff before I left?

Letting it all sink in, I could taste the copper in my mouth from the adrenaline. Squaring my chest, I made my way around the side of Dane's shop, opening the front door with one swift motion and barging in dramatically with a loud sigh. Dane rolled out from under a car, his face twisting in confusion when Harley didn't come in after me. His eyes shifted from me to the front door, then back to me.

He picked up a rag, wiping his hands while making his way to the small front desk by the entrance. I hiked up the strap of the duffle bag, hating how it was cutting into my shoulder while I waited for him to meet me there. Various awards and certificates in picture frames hung on the wall behind the counter. I could see my reflection on the glass surfaces. My eyes were wild, wide, and crazed. I looked murderous, truly unhinged.

"I need a car," I proclaimed.

"Um, we had yours towed." He gestured to his back lot with the rag.

"Any car. I need a car. I need to get out of this frozen hellhole."

"Kaylee, I don't rent cars. I fix them." He shifted his eyes to Main Street and back to me, still trying to figure out what had happened.

Stuck between a rock and a hard place, my dad's infamous words floated through my head: *if it has a transmission or testicles, it's bound to give you problems.*

Thinking of my father and his antics, I unzipped my apocalyptic-ready, pirate pack in a resigned sigh. I grabbed the large bottle of Jameson whiskey and clunked it on the countertop between us. It was the good shit, the 18-year-old limited reserve kind. Dane looked at it in bewilderment before I asserted dominance and slid it across the counter.

"I need a car. Now."

"Your car was totaled. I don't have another Mini sitting around here."

I looked back down into my duffle bag and saw the pale green stack of cash, almost the same shade as Dane's eyes. I grabbed it and slowly slapped it on the counter next to the whiskey. "You're trying to tell me you don't have some old beater out back? I just need to make it to Boston. That's it. There is five hundred cash. I also have a card if you need more."

He stood there shaking his head, taken aback.

My voice was biting, lower than normal. "Dane, I grew up around mechanics. I know you have something back there that runs enough to get me where I'm going. Your friend fucked me over, and you didn't tell me my car was totaled for days. Cover your own ass and get me out of here."

He shifted his weight from foot to foot with discomfort. As I stared at him, I could see my nostrils flaring in the reflections behind him.

"Fine. I have a 1993 Corsica. If you break down, I can't help you."

"Get the keys. Let's go." My jaw clenched so tight, I felt my ears ache.

He shook his head and made his way to the key cabinet. "You're really fired up about all this, aren't you?" he asked.

"Yeah, call me crazy, but being stuck in a town with everyone fucking lying to you grates on your nerves."

He handed me an old-school car key and looked me up and down. "There's more to the story. You should hear Harley out. The car is out back. It's mostly white. You'll see it."

"Thanks." I grabbed the key, exiting the door, feeling like a damn pack mule with my purse and duffle. I turned around right before leaving. "You're a fucking Leo, aren't you?" I spat.

He reared back. "Um, yeah. That's creepy. How did you know?"

I rolled my eyes in disgust and left before I could even entertain him with an answer.

Harley's truck was still rumbling when I walked past. I avoided making eye contact with him, but I could feel his gaze burning into me the entire time. It was preposterous to think that smolder had kept me giddy all week. Now it felt intrusive.

The door croaked as I got into the pale car, and the dark maroon cushions smelled like a mix of old cigarette smoke and mothballs, along with the faint stank of something like a cat with bladder issues. I held back a gag while I turned the engine over with the key. I cranked the heat as high as it would go, hoping it would blow out the smell, but instead it reeked like an ancient hair dryer about to explode. A high-pitched whining escaped the car and ceased once I began driving. As I turned right out of the lot, my eyes flashed in the rearview mirror to see Harley staring at me in his truck. His face pinched with deep concern. I swallowed the bile that rose in my throat and turned right on Main Street, away from Harley and the fleeting sanctuary I'd found within him.

I felt like Cruella de Ville as I tore my way through town. Taking the roads heading south, I escaped Pine Bluff into the outskirts filled with forests and winding roads. A prickle ran up the back of my neck and something caught my eye on the right side of the road. Slowing down, I glimpsed at what appeared to be the same moose, Hagrid, with the red Christmas tree ornament dangling from his antler, slowly chomping near the side of the road.

A hysterical shriek escaped my throat, ripping through me in unbridled rage. I flipped off the moose and bellowed, "Dammit! You fucking cocksucking whore ass bitch! This is all your damn fault! You hump backed forest whore!"

The screaming morphed into tears as I clutched the wheel, the moose in my rearview mirror now while sobs wracked through my body all the way back to Boston.

Chapter Twenty-Nine

Harley

Coming home to my cabin felt like a prison sentence. I was so alone. Where had things gone wrong? My phone buzzed, and I pulled it out of my pocket to see it was Dane. I rolled my eyes and retrieved a beer from my fridge.

"Hey."

"Your girl paid me off in whiskey and cash for a car."

"I saw her leave in it, but I didn't know what the fuck had happened."

"Yeah, she came flying in my shop like a bat outta hell and demanded I sell her a car. She pulled out some Jameson and cold hard cash from her duffle, cursing like a pirate until I sold her that dumpy ass Corsica we found that raccoon family nested in."

"Fuck," I said under my breath, slapping the counter. I'd hated watching her leave me. Seeing her eyes flash in the rearview mirror tormented me, but I could tell my presence had been giving her a full-on panic attack.

"I wanted you to know she was on her way home in a mostly safe vehicle."

"Thanks for helping her. She ran into my sister at the nail salon, and they came back all buddy-buddy and ran into me."

"No shit!"

"They were walking together, arm in arm, planning on grabbing lunch at Tilly's. I almost shit myself. I don't think she realized it was my sister until they saw me. She put two and two together and figured out I was keeping her away from this nosy ass town."

"Oh, so your sister kind of blew your cover?"

"Unintentionally, yeah. Now Kaylee thinks I was ashamed of her or something. I'm not ready to date in town, what with everything that happened with Whitney and Carson."

The line went silent.

"Dane?"

"Har, get over yourself."

"It's not that simple."

"I don't know who keeps whiskey and cash on hand, besides the Irish mob, but she was special. You acted different around her. I could tell. You even called her *babe*."

I let out a pained sigh. Dane yammered on, "Besides, what happened between you, Carson, and Whitney was the mindfuck of a lifetime. It can't get much worse. I mean, to have your brother secretly fuck the first girl you date when you're back home from college. Yikes."

"It wasn't just that and you know it," I bit out sourly.

"Look! All I'm saying is it can't get much worse."

"I need to go. I haven't been alone for almost a week."

"Fine. Fair enough. Let's grab a beer sometime, when you're ready."

"Okay, sounds good."

"Oh, and is she a psychic or something? She knew I was a Leo."

"Something like that, yeah. She's just . . . unique." The thought of Kaylee giving Dane a piece of her mind made my heart hurt. I already missed her feisty spirit.

"Remember that. Remember that this woman stayed with you for days, and you let her into your home without hesitation, and that you felt whatever you two had going on was worth protecting," Dane said resolutely.

"Okay."

"Okay, love ya, man." Dane hung up abruptly.

I scowled and opened the fridge for something to eat. Elk meat and taco fixings stared back at me on the middle shelf. I scowled once more and shut the door with a haunted blink. I reached for an orange on the counter and slowly peeled it, thinking of the past couple of days and how everything had exploded. Anger, sadness, and regret surged through my body, overwhelming me. Now that I was alone, I could sit with my thoughts.

I loved her.

I loved her deeply, intensely, and without bounds.

Why the hell was I so protective? Was it because it scared me the town would see us and pry? Or did I subconsciously find myself unworthy because things with Abby had ended so quickly? Because of how tragically Whitney had left my life, our time together cut short?

I got up to shower. I needed steam and solitude. Plus, crying in the shower made me feel less pathetic. Walking into my room, I saw the bed and felt the first sting in my heart. Walking to the side she'd been occupying, I grabbed the pillow and brought it to my face, sniffing it deeply. The clean smell of Kaylee's hair filled my senses.

Putting it down, I turned and opened the dresser drawer she'd put her clothes in. In slight horror, I stared at where the clothing still appeared, neatly folded in stacks. She wasn't supposed to leave today. We only went into town to complete her car situation. She hadn't even packed up her things from my cabin. I ran my hand over one of her sweaters. A hiss of pain escaped my mouth, and I shut the drawer slowly, trying to blink away the tears forming on the edges of my eyes.

Walking into the shower, I cranked on the hot water and went into the steam, feeling it damn near burn the bruise on my forehead from Tyler. Water trailed from my hair over my eyes. I blinked to clear it, only to see Kaylee's pink, frilly loofah hanging on a knob. The sight of it hurt me more than it should. I yanked it off, chucking it from the shower into the trash bin across the room. With it, an angry, sobbing cry rolled through my chest, echoing in the cabin that now felt heartbreakingly empty.

The night stretched on, slowly and silently.

I realized I didn't even have Kaylee's number. We'd never left each other's sides long enough to need it. Something about that made me even sadder. I'd have no way of getting ahold of her. Our time together had felt monumental, permanently etching memories and feelings into me like someone carving their initials on an oak tree. Something in fleeting history that would show for ages to come.

Now here I sat alone, the only reminders of her being sweaters in my dresser. It felt cheapened and wrong.

I sat in front of my fireplace, the flames roaring differently now. I stared at their tangles and dances of auburn, red, and green. Completely lost in thought and memory, I tried to piece together my feelings and why I'd done what I had. How could I change this? Was this how it was supposed to end?

I opened a book on my coffee table to read, only to find a note I'd left Kaylee tucked into its pages like a bookmark. It was how I'd told her I was in the woodshop the day we'd lost power. Right before we'd spent the night falling in love. Staring at the benign piece of paper, I felt flattered she'd appreciated the note enough to save it. I grimaced at the painful realization while closing the book.

As I lifted the covers to get into my bed, the smell of us violently wafted at me. The scent of her mixed with me, blending into something that was distinctly *us*, felt like a punch in the gut. I slumped in and stretched my arm across her side of the bed, running it under the pillow. Something small and hard rolled under my palm. I picked it up only to realize it was one of her crystals.

Feeling like an absolute fool for having a rock push me to tears, I put it back where I'd found it. It was too painful, too much to process.

That night, I didn't have any dreams of wolves, foxes, or Kaylee running.

I felt no warmth beside me, no energetic pulse of a woman who awakened so much within me.

Just bleak, hollow nothingness.

Driving into work the next day, I was grateful I had to return. It was Saturday morning, and even in the slow season, I was sure I could find something that needed to be done. I was almost positive Terry had left tasks unfinished in my absence. Driving into the sunrise, I saw a glint of gold out of the corner of my eye. Looking around the cab of my truck to find it, I realized it was tangled in my beard. I grasped my chin hair, trying to tug whatever it was, only to realize it was a long Kaylee hair.

Pulling it from my beard where it had coiled, I let out a sad laugh. She was nowhere and everywhere. She was even in my damn beard. Pulling the long hair out, extending my arm almost completely, I freed myself from her mark. Holding it outward, I watched as the sun glinted on the strand, shimmering gold like the edge of a Bible. With a sigh, I flung it off in the air of my truck, emotion clogging up my throat.

What lovesick idiot swooned over finding someone else's hair in his beard for fuck's sake?

I looked at myself in the rearview mirror. My eyes were haunted, even to me. I needed to shave, and the bruise on my forehead was now obvious. I pushed my beanie down farther, hoping to hide it from the other rangers.

Sadness shrouded the days following her departure. Everyone in town had found out about the mystery woman who'd crashed her car and stayed with me during the storm. They'd also heard snippets like I'd brawled with her stalker, and several people had spotted our fight at Dane's. People had also put two and two together and noticed the Corsica in his back lot was gone.

My mom brought me dinner one night at the cabin. She even made galaktoboureko, my favorite Greek dessert. She rambled in her therapist lingo about attachment styles as I ate in silence, unable to talk. Dane and Noah both tried to get me to go out for a beer, but I left the texts unanswered.

Three days after Kaylee left, but who was counting, I drove to my family's hardware store, letting myself in the back door. My brother's neurotic husky, Kiszka, greeted me. I crouched down and played with him for a moment, letting the simple love from him put a much-needed smile on my face. Kiszka followed me with his ears perked while I weaved through stacks of empty boxes to find Carson in the office. His stupid face scowled at me, and he looked me up and down before rolling his eyes.

"What do you want?" he snapped.

"Shut up. I'm here for a project, asshat. I need your help."

Chapter Thirty

Kaylee

I pulled into Boston metro on Friday evening. The Corsica puttered pathetically as a white cloud of exhaust followed the car like a noxious ghost. I drove into the parking garage of my apartment building with a heavy sigh. A sinking feeling of being sucked back into life here swamped me. Even though Pine Bluff was only hours away, my departure from it made me feel like a stranger in a strange land.

Opening the door to my high-rise apartment, I looked around at the foreign place I called my own. My houseplants had limped over without my watering and care. A basket of fruit rotted on my counter, and I had some takeout in my fridge that needed thrown away. Everything else was fine. My presence was barely needed. The realization made me feel even more insignificant.

I peeled off my clothes in a huff to shower. A loud plop brought my eyes down, where I saw the pale river rock shaped like a crescent moon spinning on the floor. Harley had given it to me the night he'd told me he loved me. When was that? Last night? How had that only been last night?

A gasp left my throat. I'd had tucked it in my bra the whole day. I bent over to pick it up, inspecting its soft surface. Harley's face lit by snowfall and moonlight flashed through my mind, making my stomach drop. I kissed the stone, my tears wetting it before I placed it on my bedside table next to my favorite crystals and went right to the shower to cry.

Looking at my naked body in the mirror, I could see not only my bruised neck, but now a sickening constellation of fingerprint bruises on my arm. They were from when Tyler ripped me closer to him before jerking my braid. Both marks were physical manifestations of all the ways he'd hurt me in the past week. Staring at them, I thought of all the ways Harley had loved my body in place of Tyler's brutality. The thought of Harley's hands skimming my body caused sobs to roll out slowly, only for me to slip into a hysterical, ugly cry.

It felt like I hadn't even taken a shower alone in a week. Stepping into the water, I realized I had too much time to think and feel everything. I took several deep breaths to steady myself. "Kaylee, you're a strong, independent woman. You don't need the love and approval of a man." A sob squeaked out of my mouth. "Or some Scorpio to dick you down *real* good."

I laughed and cried in tandem, covering my mouth to muffle the sobs that took prominence. Taking an even deeper breath, I allowed myself to truly feel everything. I shuddered at the intensity mixed with the heat. My neck and shoulder muscles ached. The bruise still healing on my neck stung with the temperature and pressure of the water.

I braced myself against the shower wall, letting the cries move through my body. Harley's handsome face flashed through my mind once more. The memory of loving him in front of the fireplace, with the furs and flames. I opened my mouth to gasp for air and more memories flooded my brain. His kind face the night I wrecked, the feeling of his beard against my smooth skin, the way his lips curled in a smile.

I squinted my eyes closed, willing to forget him, but more memories shuffled by, like Harley imitating birdsong at dawn, his rough hands splayed on my thighs, The Lovers card being turned over, and how peaceful he looked while sleeping.

I felt dizzy and realized I was too hot. Turning off the water, I hummed to distract myself from all the memories filling up my mind.

The sound of Harley speaking Greek rang in my head, the feeling of his body rumbling in a laugh when he held me. How his brow pinched together when he was concentrating. The way his face lit up when he talked about backpacking or when a deer ran by his cabin. How he held me in silent support when I cried, not repulsed. The way he danced with me and kissed my crystals reverently. The way he was gentle with me, even when we were fighting. How the flames lit his eyes when he made love to me as the storm crashed all around us.

Bile violently rose in my throat, causing me to run to the toilet to hurl. I was still sopping wet from the shower, clutching the toilet while shuddering. More tears filled my eyes in distress as more puke escaped me, beyond my control. I cleaned up, dried off, and flopped on my bed wrapped in a towel. I stared at the city lights until the sobs stopped and sleep took me.

I woke up the next day, realizing it was Saturday, an entire week after the crash. I wasn't ready to go back to normal. For most of the morning, I was in my bed staring at the ceiling. I couldn't eat, listen to music, or even look at myself in the mirror. Everything reminded me of Harley and my heartbreak.

I moved from my bed to the couch and stared at the brick wall of my loft for probably a good hour, clutching a rose quartz and chrysocolla crystal to soothe my heart. Hoping it would distract my mind, I fetched the book I was reading from my purse. I opened it only to find Harley's note staring back at me. My fingers traced his silly Wi-Fi password and how he'd written *Good morning, beautiful.* I closed the book and flopped it on my coffee table, haunted.

I went to leave my apartment for some coffee, only to realize I still had the Corsica as a vehicle. I was sure my insurance policy still covered a rental car after my wreck, but I didn't want to mess with the process. I was ready to push past the whole ordeal and needed something concrete to call my own. I'd always wanted a Jeep, and with my time in Pine Bluff, I'd realized I wanted more adventures. A Jeep would encourage me to get out of the city. I Googled the nearest dealership and made my way there.

Hours later, I left their lot with a burgundy, beefy Jeep Wrangler with a black hard top. It was used, but new to me. I even got them to give me a few hundred dollars for the Corsica that I'd traded in. It felt like the first step to my new take on life. I was more in control, even if I was heartbroken.

I called Maisie later that day to unpack the entire Pine Bluff incident in extreme detail. We examined every angle down to the minutia. What Tyler had done horrified her, and she vowed to use her sleuthing skills to send an anonymous tip to authorities about his conduct. I could tell Maisie thought my reaction to Harley keeping me a secret was harsh. She even called me out as a hypocrite because I hadn't told him about Tyler. But she was supportive and comforting, as always. Toward the end of our call, we had a plan on how I should move forward, which gave me some shred of hope.

The weeks following Pine Bluff were a foggy funk of the most wicked emotional hangover I'd ever experienced. Like the bruise on my neck that I expertly covered, day by day the hurt was being erased, but I couldn't truly forget it.

Every morning and night, memories of Harley flooded my mind upon waking and sleeping. I thought of him at 3 p.m. in a boring work meeting and at 3 a.m. when I sobbed in my empty bed. His hazel eyes even haunted my dreams. Every so often, I'd feel his energy with me so intensely, I could have sworn he was right behind me. I wondered if in these moments, he was thinking about me and I could sense it.

As silly as it might seem, when I'd feel him close like this, I would send good energy back to him, blessing him or hoping he could feel my love. Even if he hurt me, I never wished him harm.

I chalked it up to the wrong place, wrong time, and wrong girl. I seemed to be the wrong girl for everyone.

I even discovered my favorite incense reminded me of him, with its earthy notes with a hint of spicy musk. When I lit the stick to meditate, the sensory overload caused me to clutch my altar while loud sobs burst through my throat, erupting from somewhere deep inside me. Watching the smoke escape in tendrils, I willed my heartache to escape with it, knowing damn well it was no use.

I pulled up to Rise-N-Grind on a Friday afternoon, two weeks after coming back to Boston. I eyed the vase of yellow roses I'd expertly cushioned in a box on the passenger seat of my new Jeep. With a deep sigh, I picked up the vase I'd made for Rosie. It had glazed swirls of warm saffron, rust, and burnt umber over the surface. I wanted it to look earthy yet fiery, like her. On the bottom of the vase, I'd carved **the only prick you should tolerate is a thorn from a rose** along with my signature and date.

I spotted Rosie instantly when I entered the coffee shop. Her eyes grew large in shock while she watched me nod for her to come sit by me. I'd purposefully gone in the middle of my workday, hoping early afternoon was a slower time to ensure we could talk. Sliding the vase across the table, I cleared my throat.

"Rosie, please consider this a peace offering. I'm very sorry if I embarrassed you or jeopardized your job with my reaction." I had rehearsed that for days.

Her voice finally creaked. "No, I'm sorry. I didn't know . . ." She shook her head with scared eyes. "I didn't know about you. He told me I was the only girl he was seeing. I thought we'd locked the door."

I let out a deep sigh. "He told me I was the only girl he was seeing, too. We were both being played. If you don't mind me asking, how long have you been seeing him?"

"We met at a barbeque over the summer. I mean, he took me home to meet his family over Thanksgiving and Christmas. It was serious, or so I thought. What about you?"

Betrayal hedged my mind. I felt resentful and foolish.

"I work in the same building as him. I mean, he's the one who suggested Rise-N-Grind to me." We both scowled, thinking about how he'd suggested his girlfriend's coffee shop to the new girl he was cheating on her with. I continued, "We went on our first date shortly after Samhain. I mean, Halloween." I was unsure if she knew about sabbats, even though I had a sneaking suspicion she was witchy too.

Her face morphed into a sallow expression, almost like she was about to puke.

I shifted in my chair uncomfortably. "Yeah, come to think of it, it was after Samhain because he asked me what I was doing for Halloween, and I simply texted back witchcraft. You know . . . to be cheeky and test the waters. He didn't text me back for like two days."

Rosie shook her head, annoyed by Tyler. "What a fucking asshole. He never supported my craft, either. One time I told him I couldn't hang out because it was a full moon. He asked if I could just do my full moon ritual the next week." She looked at me in exaggerated horror, blinking slowly. "And I had to explain to a grown ass man that the full moon doesn't last a week."

"Wow."

"I mean, something clearly detached that motherfucker from the natural cycles of life. It made him selfish. That's part of his issue." She tossed her long red hair over her shoulder.

"I had a nagging feeling I couldn't trust him fully," I admitted. "He was flirty in texts, but I never felt like I had his full attention. I thought it was because he was super busy with work. Ugh, gods, I'm so stupid!" I held my forehead in my hand in pure misery.

Rosie reached across the table and rubbed my arm. "No, you're not. He's stupid. He had two incredible women and fucked it up." We both nodded. "If you don't mind me asking, did you . . . you know, hook up?"

"No, I just didn't feel safe with him. It never got to that part."

"I guess that's the silver lining here. It's so hard because I feel like he was a different person with me. He was so charming and attentive. He texted me every morning and night, sent me flowers, took me on vacations. I had suspicions, but mostly I felt blindsided."

"Well, I also came here to warn you." I leaned forward and covered her hands with mine in solidarity. "Rosie, he's dangerous. After I saw you two banging, I ran out of here and drove to get my mind off things. Long story short, I crashed my car in a little town in Maine, where this hot lumberjack saved my ass."

"Girl!" Rosie's eyes widened in intrigue while my giggles filled the air.

Sobering, I went on, "Tyler found me and tried to abduct me. He hunted me down and taunted me with gross pictures of him screwing a girl at a club. He yanked me by my hair, and the guy I was with beat his ass. But before that, he was talking about how some guys at his law firm had a running bet that he couldn't bag me. Like, what the actual fuck?!"

Rosie gasped. "No!"

"Yes! Please tell me you're not seeing him?"

"No, it ended the moment you found us. I knew something was off, even though he swore up and down you were a jealous ex. Fucking hell, I'm so done with men!"

"Good, that's good to hear. I wish we didn't have to bond over this, but do you forgive me for acting like a drama queen?"

"Of course, totally forgiven. You reacted the same way I would." A smile spread across her face, lighting up her green eyes. "Friends?"

"Friends." I nodded and got up to hug her tightly.

"Now, let me make you a coffee. I've concocted this drink I think you'll love." She pulled me to the counter with a lighthearted giggle. It was the first thing that had made me smile since Pine Bluff.

Back at my office, I rolled my eyes in annoyance while my phone chirped. It was Friday, and I was so fucking done with work. I answered the call with forced kindness. Aiden's voice filled the line in a perky tone. "Hey, Kaylee, your guest is here for the 4 o'clock interview."

I glanced at my schedule in confusion. The time slot was blank. I seldom held interviews on Friday afternoons. Everyone wanted to start their weekends, not their job hunt. Had I forgotten to schedule something in my heartbroken delirium?

"Oh, okay, I'll be a sec. Will you please put them in the small conference room?"

Aiden warmly replied, "Sure thing."

I finished the email I was working on and took the last sip of the cookie-dough-flavored iced coffee Rosie had made me. It was dangerously good. I popped a mint in my mouth and grabbed my trusty clipboard with my interview questions, along with my favorite pen. Exiting my office, I made my way down the hallway to the conference room. From the frosted window, I could see the broad shoulders of a man sitting at the table.

I shut the door. "Good afternoon! My name is Kay—"

The man turned around in his chair and stood up to greet me, instantly towering over me. All my blood instantly froze over. A chill went up my spine while my stomach plummeted in a sickening heave. All the air knocked out of my lungs, only to feel like sand had replaced it, making my entire chest heavy. My jaw locked up in pure shock, keeping me from speaking.

Staring back at me were all-too-familiar eyes. His velvety voice rolled out, saturated in an apologetic tone. "Kaylee. I needed to see you."

My jaw finally slacked, causing my lips to spread open in shock. I drew in a ragged breath, disbelief still thrashing my mind and body. "Harley, w-what are you doing here?"

Why had he done this? Why had he appeared here now? To stir up hurt and yearning within me seemed cruel.

"I needed to talk to you. This was the only way I could get a half hour with you. I'm sorry if this feels intrusive." He pursed his lips. His eyes squinted with remorse as he searched my face.

He had shaved his beard clean off, revealing a chiseled jaw and smooth skin. The sight of him clean-shaven sent a twinge of sympathy throughout my chest. I knew it shouldn't, but it hurt seeing him like this, so unlike his authentic self. He looked heartbreakingly handsome, slick in a dark suit, but I could tell by his movements it felt foreign to him. His calloused hands showed evidence that he didn't live his life in an office. His hair had grown out, revealing perfectly tousled curls I wanted to run my fingers through. A faint gray shadow hung under his eyes, showing exhaustion. He looked simultaneously suave but tortured.

"I-I don't know what you want me to say." Shock still coursed through my body. I'd gone weeks thinking I'd never see him again, but the remembrance of him echoed in my mind daily. Now face-to-face, I was awestruck, partly scared he'd hurt me more yet smitten at the sight of him. His presence changed everything for me.

"Just give me 30 minutes, please." He gestured toward the table while pulling out the chair for me, ever the gentleman. Eyeballing him, I took my seat at the end, breathing out a cautious sigh. He sat down diagonally from me. Only a foot away, close enough I could touch his chest if I wanted. I gulped down the urge.

He looked me boldly in the eyes. "You've haunted me. I'm here to do whatever it takes to get you back."

His frankness sent a thrill through my body, awakening hope within me. I crossed my arms over my chest before realizing the gesture was inadvertently covering my heart. "You made it pretty apparent you didn't want me in your life."

Ignoring my jab, he continued, "I'll get a job in Boston. I have EMT training. I'm sure you could stick me somewhere. Or I can find a job on my own. Whatever, that's beside the point. I-I messed up, and I want to show you I'm serious about this." His brow furrowed. "I'm serious about us."

"But your job and your cabin are in Maine."

He leaned forward. "Yes, but my heart is with you. I can land a new job. I can sell my cabin." His eyes scorched into mine, oozing with earnest conviction. I felt a surge of emotion, as if his words were awakening something in me that was coming to life. "I can't find another you."

My voice came out shaky. "Why did you hide me from everyone? I mean, I didn't expect any grand gesture or introductions. We'd just met, but I look back on the week and I see all the ways you kept me a secret." His frown deepened because he knew I was onto something. "Like getting the pizza to-go and sending me to the market alone. You went to get stitches alone. I know I was an impromptu visitor, but you made me feel like a damn leper. Are you ashamed of me or something?"

"No, I'm not. Not at all. I didn't want anyone to mess up what we had. It's a small town and people talk. You heard what Sherry said when you called the police department the first night. You didn't know, but the whole week I had to dodge questions from nosy people in town. Their meddling would have put more stress on you, and I didn't want you to feel pressured by them or to get the impression that I was some creep trying to convince you to stay with him."

"You're not a creep. I never felt like you were. That's why it's confusing that you kept things from me."

"We were already in a tricky situation. I didn't want to add stress."

I stared at him, my sadness morphing into anger, knowing he'd kept details from me. I picked up my clipboard and held it against my chest like a shield. He slumped slightly in his chair in defeat. "Listen, I'm going to lay it all out here for you, so you know everything. And I mean everything."

This piqued my interest, so I nodded for him to continue.

"As a ranger who helps with search and rescue efforts, I've seen some shit, some seriously traumatizing shit. I can handle most of it, but one victim haunts me. What I saw that day made me freeze, kept me stuck, like in some holding pattern that wouldn't let me move forward with my life."

He stared past me while he sucked in a shaky breath. "I told you about the last serious relationship I had in grad school with a woman in Oregon, Abby. The one who wanted suburbia?"

"Yeah."

"Well, she wasn't the last girl I dated altogether. I dated a woman the summer I moved back to Maine." He swallowed hard, saying her name. "Whitney. She was a seasonal employee, visiting from out of state. It wasn't serious, but I had feelings for her. She passed away, and I . . . found her."

My jaw dropped at the scandalous news. My brain tried to keep up.

"It was a freak accident where she was with a friend and lost her footing." His breath hitched thick with emotions. "She fell rock climbing. I-I had to find her. I held her body, but there wasn't any breath or a pulse." He blinked quickly. "She was so stiff. She felt w-wrong. Her eyes and face," he hissed and closed his eyes, trying not to cry.

"Harley—"

"What's worse is when she died, I found out Carson was dating her too."

"Carson? Your brother?"

Harley's jaw set, and his knee jiggled under the table in discomfort. His eyes could not meet mine. "I wanted to kill him. I lost Whitney, and I was unknowingly in a love triangle with my brother, who I already had a strained relationship with."

"I am so sorry."

"But Carson didn't have to find her dead body. He didn't have to carry her back to civilization. He didn't have to call her family and tell them what happened, I did. It was all on me." He swallowed hard again. "It was all on me."

I reached across and held his hands, holding the moment for him and his story, fighting the zing I felt touching him.

"No one knew Carson was dating her, either. He swore up and down he didn't know she was seeing me. I don't know if Whitney realized we were brothers. I mean, we look alike, but I don't know how she couldn't figure it out. But who fucking knows?" He shook his head in disgust. "It was fucking nightmarish. I tried to mourn her in silence, but the other rangers could tell finding her had affected me differently and they figured it out."

He sat up and crossed his arms over his chest and took a deep breath.

"Word got out. The whole town buzzed about it for months. The Kouris brothers and the rock climber girl from out of town. Like there wasn't anything else on TV that could beat the soap opera we gave the town. I was at Tilly's Tavern with Dane one night and Carson came in and tackled me off the bar stool. It took like six men to pull us apart. Carson basically went mute to dodge questions at the hardware store, and I avoided people all together. I didn't want their pity or judgment. Most of all, I didn't want to talk about how I had to find my dead girlfriend on a rescue mission."

He let out a sad laugh. "I don't think anyone knew what to do. Her life being lost was already tragic, but, I mean, what do you say when two guys lose a woman? Two brothers. It's haunting." His mouth curled in disgust at the recollection.

"It is," I agreed.

His brow creased deeply, and his mouth moved uncomfortably, almost like he was chewing his words. "So, there you go. That's why I didn't want the town to know we were snowed in together. I was fucking traumatized to begin with, and I didn't think it was their business that I was with a woman or seeing someone again. Or whatever you'd consider us. They treated the whole thing with Whitney and Carson like a debacle and it made it worse. It has nothing to do with you, Kaylee. I'd be lucky to be seen with you, and I'm sorry my actions showed otherwise. I'm so sorry I hurt you. It was my own stupid shit."

"Harley, that's a lot to live with."

"Yeah, but I hope it at least helps you see why I didn't want to be so public. Why I was so taken aback when I found you and why I wanted to protect us."

"Is this why you feel you don't deserve companionship? Why you hide out?"

"I felt like what I want in life isn't what most people want. I was sad and I guess a little insecure when I had to end things with Abby over not wanting kids. Finding out Carson was dating the same woman I was right after was like a final blow. I was damaged. To make it even harder, my job is demanding and how I live can be isolating."

"That's not true."

"I'm glad you think that because meeting you pushed me to realize what I've needed all along. What I want in life."

"And what's that?"

His eyes pierced into mine, and he answered immediately. "A quiet life with a lover. With you, Kaylee." I sucked in a breath, hoping he didn't notice. He swallowed hard, his Adam's apple gliding up and down the thick columns of his neck on full display. "I want you by my side, doing whatever you want, for the foreseeable future."

My heart beat a little faster at hearing his statement. "How can I trust you won't keep things from me?"

"I'm working on being more vulnerable, like coming here and telling you the last thing I kept from you. I've also started mending things with my brother, which I think will help. Whitney died almost three years ago, and I worked with a therapist for the PTSD that happened working as a ranger. I'm not perfect, as you can tell. I didn't have time to adjust to things with you since it was all so sudden."

He stared off at the table in front of him as he tilted his head in consideration. "I feel like in a different situation, I could have handled this better."

"I'm proud of you for talking to someone about what you've endured. I think that's important," I said. Mental health was already a touchy subject, and mental health among men even more so. I was proud of Harley for facing his struggles.

I glanced at the wall and noticed the time. I was so done with this place. "Listen, I want to keep talking, but not here, not like this. Want to see my place?"

His eyes softened as he nodded. I could have sworn the faintest tug at the corner of his lips looked like he was fighting a smile. Standing up, he reached into his suit jacket to pull out a single white rose he had tucked into his waistband. He held it out to me silently, in a chivalrous way. His eyes were full of intensity and things unsaid.

"Thank you. I usually get resumes in this room, not roses." I fought back a stupid grin while taking the rose, feeling the warmth of his hand brushing against mine in a way that was all too familiar, yet almost forgotten. Now standing in front of him, I could tell we were both fighting the urge to hug, to step closer to each other. Even one inch would be too much, too tempting.

"Wait, how did you even find me?"

He looked coy for a moment, buttoning up his jacket and straightening his tie. "Well, I never got your number, but I remembered you said you worked at Tate Staffing, so I Googled it. I called and spoke to that nice guy at the front desk and innocently confirmed an interview."

"Bold," I said, considering what he'd done. It was flattering how intently he listened to me. I'd only mentioned the name of the staffing agency once in passing. Tilting my clipboard, I wrote my cell number, address, and gate code on a piece of paper.

"Here's my number. It feels a little weird giving it to you, considering what we've been through. Talk about bass ackwards." I let out a nervous giggle, handing it to him. He folded the paper and put it in his chest pocket without looking, his eyes fixed on mine instead.

"Meet me at the elevators?"

I nodded, feeling stunned. Clutching the clipboard to my chest, I did my best to hide the rose. Looking over my shoulder while grabbing the doorknob, I instructed him, "Act like this was a real interview."

I could feel his gaze on me while we exited the room. Walking him back to the front desk with a formal goodbye felt like some weird inside joke. We stood there shaking hands like business professionals, as if I hadn't been sitting on his damn face and moaning his name two weeks ago. Harley thanked Aiden and held open the door for another guest, once again ever the gentleman. Aiden's eyes darted from Harley's retreating figure back to me with a knowing smile.

After grabbing things at my desk and saying goodbye to Aiden, I met Harley by the elevators. His eyes widened when he saw me carry a box filled with mostly plants. A nervous chuckle drifted from his mouth.

"I needed to take this plant home," I offered as Harley took the box from me without me even asking. We chuckled nervously waiting for the elevator, realizing this was unfamiliar terrain for us.

A door behind us swung open, causing us to turn around to see Tyler exiting his work suite. His face was puffy with swelling and badly bruised. He squinted, discerning if it was Harley or not without the beard. I sneered at him, willing him to fuck with us again. In a pathetically panicked scuttle, he walked backwards into his office and tried to play it cool.

Harley and I looked at each other over the monstera plant sticking up out of the box, eyes wide in bewilderment.

"Chop this wood, biiiiitch," Harley whispered-yelled, causing our cackles to echo in the tall ceiling of the silent lobby.

Chapter Thirty-One

Kaylee had looked like a bohemian in the boardroom when she'd swished into the cold, sterile space with her dress billowing and her high-heeled boots announcing her strut. The dress had floated above her knees before thick tights went down to cool-looking boots that showed off her sexy calves. She'd worn her lucky necklace. Hearing it jingle slightly had made me happy. She'd looked too soft, magical, downright witchy to be in such a drab place.

Seeing her realize it was me waiting for her had been one of the most memorable moments of my life. It was like seeing the summer sun again after a long winter. Her eyes widened with a daring concoction of need and disbelief.

She'd been open to talking and had even granted me the privilege of seeing her place. Exiting the elevator in the parking garage, I held her box with a plant in it and let her lead me to her car. She approached a burgundy Jeep, almost the same shade of nail polish she'd worn during the time she'd spent with me. It was then I realized she'd moved on in ways I wasn't ready to comprehend.

I teased, "A Jeep? Really?"

"Damn straight," Kaylee said, nodding and pulling out her keys from her hippie sack of a purse.

"Woman! As if you needed anymore power to do damage with! This thing could be deadly with you behind the wheel!"

She tossed her hair with a sassy look. "Well, consider yourself warned."

My guts twisted in knots as I followed her to her apartment in my truck. Was she taking me back to her place so she could brush me off in private? Or worse, was she seeing me as an ex she had to placate? Another side of me was downright excited to at least have her in my line of vision.

When I entered her apartment, the intoxicating smell of her hit me like a freight train. She opened the door with a nervous laugh and stepped aside so I could take it all in. It was like she'd described, a clash of worlds. The space was a luxurious loft that was overly modern and in direct opposition to her belongings that were a mix of earthy and sensual.

She had art on the walls, macrame hangings, a cool, embroidered tapestry that looked like something from her time in India, and large potted plants by the floor-to-ceiling windows. I made my way to her kitchen and lost my shit at a picture of Jesus cradling a baby T-Rex on her fridge. Hearing my laughter echo in her space, I chanced a look at her to see why she wasn't laughing along with me. Instead, she looked at me then back at the picture with a knowing smile.

Turning around, I saw an infamous boob vase on her kitchen island, making me chuckle again. The vase was smooth, expertly constructed with a white glaze. After a few moments, I cocked my head and realized they looked a little too familiar.

"Did you? Did you cast your own chest to make this one?" I asked, unsure of how to word it delicately.

Kaylee's head bobbed with a grin. "I sure did."

"I knew those looked familiar. I could spot them anywhere." Dashing a devious look at her, I kept walking to explore more. She cleared her throat behind me.

"Can I get you some chai tea?" she asked.

"Yes, please. May I?" I pointed to her room, wanting permission to head in. She nodded, filling up a kettle with water. Seeing her room put a smile on my face. It was just so Kaylee, every little thing an extension of her. It felt calm and cozy. It was clean and perfectly decorated, with no clutter in sight. Her bed looked soft with a frilly white comforter, colorful blankets, and enough throw pillows to shield a small army.

The sight of the river stone on the bedside table stirred excitement in my body and made me gulp. She'd kept it close. Good.

She had a white dresser that was distressed to look rustic when it wasn't old. I noticed several display stands of her cool jewelry, a small sword, a vase that held some unique feathers, and a giant crystal ball that almost looked like the bottom of a pool with its Caribbean blue and white veining.

Above the dresser hung several frames with photos. One was of Kaylee as a toddler with, I was assuming, her dad holding her on a motorcycle with big, cheesy grins. Seeing her as a little, white-haired fairy put a smile on my face. There were some photos of a teenage Kaylee in a softball uniform jokingly smacking another girl's butt with the bat. The next photo was of her hugging a woman with hot-pink hair in front of a beach sunset. I wondered if it was Maisie.

There was a photo of her in a graduation robe with her tongue out flanked by her parents, and then another with her dressed up as a busty pirate with a group of friends at the Renaissance festival she'd talked about. Seeing her body in a corset made me drag in a deep breath. I turned and walked back into her living room, sitting on a cool purple couch that felt like some type of velvet.

Kaylee handed me a mug with a vulva on the side of it. I stared at it, unable to hide my shock. "Yep, that's all me too," she said, chuckling. I blinked hard and drank the glorious tea she'd made me, unable to say anything remotely polite.

"You chill there. I'm going to change out of my work clothes."

I couldn't help but watch her retreating figure, how her hips whooshed her dress from side to side with each step. How her hair was curled and coiffed in a way I'd never seen it, half up and half down.

I looked around the rest of her living space. It was a mash-up of cool trinkets from all over the world paired with humble coziness, exactly how I'd pictured it. Even in the icy darkness of the Boston winter night, her space felt warm and colorful.

A large paper lantern covered in ornate filigree in the shape of a seven-pointed star hung from the rafters. Big, round cushions to sit on along with a vibrant rug covered the floor beside the couch. Her coffee table had a stack of books that I instantly got lost in. She had some respected classics, like Shakespeare, Byron, and Whitman. I recognized some author names, like Gaiman, Butcher, but some names were brand new to me, like Cunningham and Eliade. I saw a piece of paper sticking out of one and wondered if it was the other note I'd written her. A smug hope brimmed in my chest.

Next to the books was the largest pinecone I'd ever seen, along with a giant piece of amethyst geode. In a corner against a brick wall, I spotted what I could only assume was an altar. It looked like her witchy stuff: crystal balls and towers, melted candles, little jars, wooden boxes, pictures of goddesses and the moon, and some herbs hanging from the wall. I could have sworn she even had a small cauldron, but I couldn't be certain from where I was sitting. In the other corner was her infamous pottery wheel and shelves with various supplies.

Her TV was outdated and flanked by large Himalayan salt lamps that glowed an amber hue. A yoga mat, didgeridoo, and another sword leaned between the TV console and a ladder bookshelf. Before I could snoop any further, Kaylee walked back out wearing an even more flowy black dress that covered her legs but showed off her cleavage.

I couldn't even savor the sight of her because she was clutching a penis vase in her hand. I had to fight back an audible yelp at the sight of it. She positioned it in front of me on the coffee table, surely to taunt me, and slid the white rose into it with a mischievous smile. I stared at the wang vase, realizing its girth, length, and shade of tan were all too familiar. I looked back at her in shock, only to catch a smirk on her face before she sat down on the other side of the couch.

SHE MADE MY DICK INTO A VASE?

I gestured to the vase, speechless. "Did you—"

"I know a work of art when I sit on it, I mean, see it."

I stared at her, still speechless.

"So, tell me why you're here. Why did you drive to Boston instead of calling me at work or something?"

I welcomed the change in subject and went with it. She was closed off. I could tell by her tone and body language. She crossed her legs under herself like some yogini and held a pillow over her lap. Taking note, I purposefully tried to remain open and facing her.

"I told you, you've haunted me, and I'm here to do whatever it takes to get you back. I wanted to show you I'm serious about this, about us, so I wanted to do this in person."

"Get me back? What does that look like in your mind?" she asked, tilting her head.

"I don't know what that would look like exactly. I mentioned I would move down here to be with you, and I would. If you don't want that, we could figure out something else. I don't like the idea of long distance, but I'm sure we could make it work. I want you to have a say in this as much as I do. If it were up to me, I'd throw you over my shoulder like some caveman and drive you back to Maine tonight." I let out a miserable sigh. "You're the best damn thing that's ever crashed into Pine Bluff. You're the best thing that has ever happened to me."

"But that's just it, Harley. I don't want to be happening to you. What about what's happening to me? I have my own life. I'm not some accessory to add to yours."

"I see your point, but I don't want you to get caught up in the semantics. It's a defense mechanism and not super helpful. I see right through it. Since I met you, you've complained about your job and this place." I gestured to her apartment and the city lights past the window. "So don't act like you're happy here, and don't act like what we had wasn't something real."

She stared at me and sucked in a shaky breath.

I went on, "Jeezus, don't you believe in fate or whatever? Don't you think maybe the universe made you drive toward me and crash right in front of me because my hermit ass wouldn't find you unless you barreled through my woods? And that your wild ass wouldn't stay still long enough to let me love you unless we ended up snowed in together?" I chuckled at how ridiculous this all was. "I'm not witchy or spiritual like you, but even I can see this wasn't some accident," I added defensively.

I reached forward and grabbed her hand. "We were never an accident or a mistake. We have something so magical. Now let's fight for it."

"No, you're right. I've thought that too. I can't figure out why we were—"

"Stormbound," I answered. "We were stormbound."

Chapter Thirty-Two

Kaylee

I stared at him, feeling his energy. I'd missed it. Seeing him in my apartment was surreal. His broad chest filled up my sofa, and his beautiful green aura was so vibrant it made me awestruck. He looked incredibly handsome, yet uncomfortable. He took off his suit jacket and rolled up his dress shirt sleeves, revealing corded forearm muscles. His legs looked even longer on my dinky, little couch.

I bit my lower lip. "Stormbound. Right. That's what we were."

"We were also good together. So damn good." His face twitched at the memory. "God, I miss you. I miss you so much it makes me sick."

"I feel the same way. I could barely eat the first week back here. That I care this much about you after only six days together is scary. I realize it wasn't a typical week. I feel like what we went through was a pressure cooker of sorts."

I needed to meet him halfway. He'd driven down here and made this grand gesture. I wanted to close the distance between us. I scooted closer on the couch, holding both of his hands so we were facing each other. His large hands in mine felt warm and rough. I missed them all over my body. I appreciated all the ways they'd loved me.

He looked down at our hands and took a deep breath. When he glanced up at me, his eyes were full of sincerity. "Kaylee, this scares me, too. Don't you think it's scary to love someone who's so quick to leave?"

He had a good point. I'd run away from Tyler and now him.

"I'm sorry for running away from you when I found out you were keeping things between us private. Finding out you were inadvertently keeping me a secret hit the biggest nerve."

"I am so sorry," he said slowly, slightly squeezing my hands. Feeling him, hearing his words and cadence, seeing his face, it all made me soften. I couldn't help it. I loved this man.

"I'm sure not telling you about Tyler also hit a nerve, given your past in a love triangle." I wanted to give credit and compassion where it was due.

He grasped my hands tighter. "Thank you. I trust you won't run. I trust that what we have is worth taking a risk on. You took a chance staying with me, and I took a chance letting you in. Not only into my home or bed, but into my heart. And that's not nothing. That means something to me."

"If there is anything I've realized, it's that I'm sick of running. I only leave because I think it's what people want," I confessed.

"I want you to stay. I want to always make you feel safe, so you never feel you need to run." His hand reached up and touched a tendril of my curled hair. "I love how different you are. I'm going to always want your presence around me."

"Well, I want you to take up space and love me where it doesn't make you feel you're giving up too much. In whatever way feels best. How can I be sure you're ready for a relationship?"

With conviction, he stated, "I am."

"How can I be sure I won't scare you away with my shenanigans?"

"Clearly, I'm not someone who's easy to scare. Consider everything I've seen in my life, everything I've pushed through. I'm loyal to you, Kaylee."

"How can I be sure you don't like me because I was simply alive when you found me?" He flinched at that. I knew on some level, it was immature, or maybe bluntly insensitive, but I needed to know.

"Whitney passed three years ago. I've had time to sort out what I need to. I think I was keeping myself from fully stepping back out into life. You've inspired me to do that. I want to love you openly. Boldly." He took a deep breath. "I made mistakes. I can't take them back and I fully own up to them. What I did was wrong and hurtful."

I nodded in agreement. "You know, I wasn't ready for any of this either, falling for you." My voice trembled, filled with pain and sadness. I could feel the tears filling up the bottom of my lids, threatening to spill over. Now that he was here, I needed him to hear me out and see the ways he'd hurt me.

"I know I hurt you." He brushed away a tear that ran down my cheek. "Things with you felt so right. I didn't want to share it with the world yet. I was trying to get used to it myself. It all felt so . . ." He stared off for a couple moments, trying to find the right word. ". . . big. Everything felt so big between us. I was being an idiot to hide you away, but I promise it wasn't because I was ashamed. I was an overwhelmed dumbass."

He shook his head at the memory. "And I hope you can see that I wasn't trying to mislead you. I was trying to protect you and surround you with a couple of days of calm and safety. Even if that didn't work, I promise that was my reasoning. I did all that and I still don't have you."

He looked miserable. That pulled at my heart, causing me to want to own up to my wrongdoings as well. "I forgive you. I wish you hadn't assumed all these things. You need to have faith in people who care about you, like the people in your town, your family, and even me."

The intensity of what I was saying bubbled up in my throat, filling it with emotion. "If you would have asked me to stay, I would have. When you gave me the river stone under the moon, I was serious about wanting to stay with you." I bored my eyes into him, hoping he felt the intensity of my words. "I would have stayed."

He frowned. "But how could I have been sure you weren't staying to avoid Tyler?"

I shook my head wearily. "I would have stayed for you and only you. Your heart knows that."

"I get he hurt you. I sometimes can't help but wonder if you met me outside of this situation, if you'd still feel the same way is all." Harley tilted his head in sorrow, a frown pulling at the corner of his mouth.

"Harley, you are perfect, so heartbreakingly perfect. I would have loved you in any situation we met in." I could feel my lips trembling and pulling across my face in a miserable way. Admitting it all was so harrowing. It hurt to love him so much and not be with him.

New tears stung my eyes and freely gushed over the edges of my eyelids more rapidly. I pulled a hand away from his to dab at them, and Harley got up to sit right next to me. His arm encircled my shoulders, pulling me to his side. He brushed the faintest kiss on my forehead and whispered, "I trust you weren't using me to get back at Tyler. Do you trust I wasn't ashamed of us?"

Without thinking, I nodded. "Yes, yes, I trust you." The tears poured, and ragged breaths morphed into those embarrassing hiccups you got when you were crying so hard you could barely breathe. I was grateful we hadn't had this conversation at my office. It felt liberating to let it all out. I'd held so much in, I needed to rid myself of the burden. Harley had made the bold move of coming down here to show me how much he cared. I felt justified in showing him how much this touched me, how heartbroken I was.

"Look at me, crying like a total Cancerian because your secretive Scorpio ass got us into this mess." I laughed at the absurdity.

Harley chuckled. "You're not wrong." He rubbed my back and gently swiped away tears from my face. "I'm sorry," he whispered.

"I'm sorry," I replied.

My body shuddered with the aftermath of my sobs. Harley lunged to get a tissue from the box on the table and handed me one while gently touching my hair. His deep voice pleaded, "We took a risk staying together during the storm. Can we take another risk and try again?"

With complete confidence and relief, I nodded. "Yes, I'd like that." I believed and trusted him. Since I'd left Maine, I'd wanted this, or some version of this. I almost couldn't believe it was unfolding this way. Two weeks apart had felt like a prison sentence.

Harley leaned in and brought me to his chest in a hug. The feeling of his energy flooded my senses. I gripped his neck tighter and held him, peace settling into my body with him now close to me. He leaned back on the couch and just held me for a few moments while my body settled down from crying. The warmth of his chest burned through the thin dress shirt. His large hands held my body and stroked my hair, calming me in a way only he could.

I appreciated that he was giving me time to process everything, his patience was a gift to someone like me, a loose cannon.

He pulled away and kissed me. A faint brushing of our lips felt tender and sacred. It filled me up with so much love. Harley kept his face close to mine when the kiss ended. His hands gently skimmed my lips and face. His gaze felt intense but loving, steeped with yearning. "Please come live with me in the cabin. I know you don't need me to, but I want to take care of you. I want to share a life with you, and I can tell you're not happy here. Let me get you out of here, Kaylee."

I searched his hazel depths, trying not to burst into tears again.

His deep voice continued, "I love you and I need you close."

"I love you, too. And all I want is to be close to you."

His eyes softened as he pulled me in for another kiss, this time hungrier. I pulled away. "I want you so damn bad," I whispered before kissing him. Feeling him pull me even closer to him with his large hands on my body. I stopped our kiss once more. "I daydreamed of living with you in the cabin since the night in front of the fire," I stated, nodding happily. We smiled at each other, completely swept away in the sea of potential and a fresh start. I touched his bare face for the first time. His beard was already growing back with a five o'clock shadow that was sexy.

"The cabin begs for you to live in it. You filled it up in such a beautiful way. The second you left, it felt empty. I built it for you, I just didn't know it. You must believe on some level I wanted you before I ever met you. That part of what I could do to be ready for you was to have a place to make our own. A place I've never shared with anyone else."

His notion filled my chest with so much warmth, it radiated all over my body and made my mind flicker with too many blissful thoughts. I tried to pace myself from just tackling him and squealing with joy.

"You want me to come live with you? After only spending a short amount of time with you?" I braced my hands on his chest, nervously fiddling with the button while his hands held my back.

He playfully scoffed. "Kaylee, babe, don't act like this is the craziest thing you've done." We both smiled. "I think you've wanted a home base for a while. I can sense it. You kept saying you were homesick. What if the cabin is your new home? You've already found it."

I smiled, feeling butterflies and even more warmth filling me up at his request. I was the free spirit, not him. This was a simple decision for me, but how he felt so sure of things made me all giddy inside.

He went on, "You would have your own life in Pine Bluff. I mean, the town could use your spirit." A wry smile spread across his handsome face. Seeing him smile without a beard was like seeing it for the first time all over again. It was heart-stopping and distracting. "Plus, I know you. You've already thought of at least three businesses the town needs."

I let out a small, self-deprecating laugh. "You're right. Y'all could use some coffee, that's what I think. I don't want to admit it, but I thought about opening a coffee shop there." I fought back a smile.

"See! We need you." He put his hand under my chin to ensure I looked at him. "I need you. I want you. And I love you. Please, let's build a life together." His eyes held mine. Their depths looked honeyed in the soft lighting of my apartment. I was breathing heavily, wanting to kiss him again. His kisses tasted like the chai tea I'd just made him, all spicy and deliciously addicting. I swallowed hard to fight my lust.

"I love you, too." I nodded, "Yes. My answer is yes. My crazy ass will come with you." I smiled to hide my fluster.

He pulled me in for another hug, his stubble brushing the side of my face. "When is your lease up here?" he asked, forcing me to fight back a smile over his shoulder where I embraced him. I pulled back and looked at him bashfully.

"Well . . . um, when I got back from Maine, I decided I didn't want to be in Boston anymore. I put my two weeks in at work and planned to move back to Austin. I was going to work with Maisie and stay with her until I found my sense of direction. My lease is up in a few weeks, but today was my last day at work. I'm supposed to pack up this weekend and I already have a U-Haul reserved. Rosie, the barista, even offered to come help me move some furniture into it."

"Woman! Way to bury the damn lead!" He laughed and kissed me again, then pulled back to hold my face, searching my eyes in awe. "Talk about good timing."

"Good timing for sure. If you would have requested an interview on Monday, I wouldn't have been there." I couldn't stop smiling. "Oh, and this!" I grabbed his hand and walked him over to my altar, loving how he looked at it with adoration and curiosity, not disgust. I turned a long, cylindrical vase around. It was earthenware with gray and brown swirls. The front of it had the depiction of The Lovers tarot card in a raised brown square. His face crinkled into a huge grin as he looked at it, his fingers tracing the design adoringly.

"I planned on driving up to Pine Bluff on Monday, your day off. I just wanted to see you again, to say sorry for accusing you of not being a gentleman. You saved me in the wreck, and I just needed—"

"You saved me too, you know. The boat and in so many other ways."

With my elbow, I jutted him to break his worry. "I know, babe. I saved you for sure, in my own way. Your life would be so boring without me."

"You were going to come see me?" He looked at me, innocence lighting his face, making him look younger.

"Yes, you haunted me too. I realized I ran from the wrong person. From *my* person." He stared at me in wonder before brushing a tender kiss on my lips.

He picked up the vase. "I love the colors you used." He traced the pattern of grays and browns with his thumb.

"Thank you. I picked the colors of our eyes. Something uniquely us. I missed seeing yours." I looked up at him, falling into their hazel depths. He put the vase down gently and drew me in for a kiss before he pulled away, remembering something.

"Oh, and this happened." He pulled out his phone and showed me a picture of an empty room. I blinked up at him in confusion.

"This is the spare room in the cabin. I cleaned it out so you could make it yours, however you see fit."

"Harley, I-I don't need—"

He leaned down, sneaking a quick peck on my lips. "You deserve space in our cabin." The sound of *our cabin* made my chest tight.

He swiped his phone to another picture. It was the sign over his cabin entrance. Instead of saying *Fuck Off* in Greek, it now said *Stormbound* in English.

"Harley—"

"Woman, stop being so damn stubborn and let me love you."

I sighed, "Okay," into his mouth as he walked us backwards to the couch. He held me tighter, his hands greedily feeling my waist. I pushed my chest against his as his hands grabbed my ass, bringing me on his lap. I pulled up my long dress, freeing my legs to straddle him. My center pressed into his groin eagerly. He broke the kiss and ran his hands up my neck.

"I've missed you so much, Kaylee. I'm glad your neck is all healed." He kissed me, running his hands up and down my neck, grateful the bruise had disappeared.

I closed my eyes and swayed in pleasure at how good it felt to have him freely touching my neck and collarbone, running up both sides with his hands, making warmth pool between us. His fingers touched the chain of my necklace, causing me to open my eyes and look down.

"This is a pretty pendant. What is it?" he asked.

"It's a rose quartz. It helps heal a broken heart. I've been wearing it since I left Maine."

Harley kissed the stone and then me feverishly, holding me close. "You deserve to be chased. You deserve someone to put you first for once."

Between kisses, I said, "Thank you for chasing me, for finding me." My eyes searched his face, helping my mind adjust to this reality. He was back for good, in my arms, in my life. He'd come back for me.

He clutched me to his chest as he kissed me, pushing my hips against his groin. I let out a little, breathy cry into his mouth against my will. "I want you," I whispered. He kissed me more intensely.

"Me too," he said against my lips before he kissed down my neck and then nuzzled my cleavage. "I missed you. I missed your warmth." His hands grazed my breasts, his eyes flicking up to mine in a moment of devilish realization. He smirked, dipping his hand into my cleavage only to pull out a polished stone from my bra. He held it between us, almost like a trophy, while I giggled.

"Aquamarine. Great for communication," I said.

He kissed my sternum, fighting laughter while his hand dipped into the other side, pulling out two crystals this time. "This one is labrador something." He looked at me with uncertainty.

"Yep, labradorite. Great for bringing your innate wisdom to your words. And the other one is sodalite, very calming and helps you avoid conflict."

"God, you're adorable," he said lovingly, kissing my collarbone before setting the stones on the coffee table. Shifting my leg straddling him, he shoved his hand in his pocket. He revealed the green aventurine crystal I'd had in my bra the first two days I'd spent with him. I hadn't even realized I'd lost it!

"I found this in the bed the night you left. It about gutted me. Regardless of how today went, I wanted you to have it." I kissed his hand holding the stone in response, fiercely trying to convey how much I loved him before placing it with the other crystals.

"Speaking of mystical stuff, Harley, did you realize you had a prophetic dream about Tyler? He was the fox chasing me."

His face twisted in unease. "Yeah, I realized that too."

"Do you usually have dreams like that? Dreams that have more or less come true?"

"Yeah, it's happened a few times. But nothing that specific." He looked down at my body hungrily and held my hips. He stared at where we pressed together while pulling me closer to him. "Having a witch in my bed certainly awakened some intuition. I like it."

His velvety voice saying that with so much open hunger flooded me with need. I opened my mouth, speechless before he grazed his lips against mine, thrusting his groin against me, his hands never leaving my hips. I raked my hands through his curls, loving how soft they felt. My entire body responded to his, craving him so desperately.

My voice came out breathy. "Baby, I've missed you so much. I've been so heartbroken. My entire body aches for you to touch me all over."

"Show me, I'll make it better," was all he whispered against my jaw. He ran his hands up and down my body, causing a wave of desire to roll through me. Feeling his muscles under his dress shirt made my center throb as he held me, walking us into my bedroom. He gently lowered me to the bed, sweeping the throw pillows off with a confused chuckle, only to cover me with his body. Both of us moved in perfect motion together, as if we had never been apart.

The room was dark with the lights off, lit by only the city. Harley sat up and started unbuttoning his shirt while I undid his pants. I traced his bare chest and looked up at him. Shrugging out of his dress clothes, he leaned back down to me. His eyes dashed to the crescent moon river stone mere inches from our heads.

"I love you, Kaylee."
"I love you, Harley."

Chapter Thirty-Three

Harley

Coming home to Kaylee everyday felt like a dream. She healed parts of me I didn't know hurt. I liked to think I had the same effect on her. We both agreed that we slept better next to one another, and we could sense each other across the valley. I could be deep in the wilderness at work, having a rough day, and she'd text me, sensing I was upset. I'd never had that kind of connection with anyone.

I enjoyed keeping her safe, and I liked how she kept me on my toes. The cabin felt homeier with her feminine presence. She put flower crowns on some of the taxidermy animals and did witchy stuff like dancing naked under the full moon (which I enjoyed watching) and hoarded jars and candles (which I didn't fully understand but supported). I found crystals tucked in random places like her bra, under our bed, and in the shower. I'd carved out a spot in our headboard to affix the moon-shaped river stone I'd found the day I'd professed my love to her. Having it above the bed reminded us of what we shared each time we made love.

Sure, it wasn't all peaches and rainbows. She was getting better at not running, and I was getting better at not walling up. After moving her into our cabin, I took her on a date in town, showing her I meant what I'd said. Everyone in town loved her because what was not to love about Kaylee. She quickly found her place in Pine Bluff, opening her own shop. She named it Silver Springs Coffee & Crystals. Silver Springs was a nod to a Fleetwood Mac song about a scorned woman. Considering she opened it with Rosie, the barista from Boston, it was fitting.

It turned out scorned women made damn good coffee because they'd been busy with locals and tourists ever since it opened. They even named their black coffee God's Favorite, an inside joke between Kaylee and me. I never imagined I could love a wild woman who had a business named after a Fleetwood Mac song or that she'd sell her penis pottery at the farmers' market. My mom already had quite the collection, and Dane had a boob mug holding his pens at work.

We flew down to Texas in the springtime so I could meet her mom and Maisie. They apparently liked me a lot because her mom insisted on reading my palm the second I sat down and Maisie refused to call me anything other than lumber daddy. Kaylee's dad rode his bike, which, mind you, wasn't a Harley, up here and I took him fishing. It won him over, and we had some important conversations.

My family welcomed Kaylee with open arms because they noticed how much happier I was with her around, especially Frankie. But even Carson, who I was slowly warming up to in new chapter of my life. The projects I'd completed updating the cabin for Kaylee's arrival had helped provide some middle ground for us.

I'd built her a studio for her pottery on the northwest quadrant of the land once the snow had melted. She called it her Witch Bitch Barn. We even made a sign for it. I'd also built out the alcove in the study, making it into a window seat for her to sit and read. I'd surprised her with it the day she'd come to live with me. She'd squealed and promptly sat down on it, only to spread her legs to show me she wasn't wearing anything underneath her flowy dress.

Ah yes, the sex. That hadn't tapered either. We'd christened every room in the cabin. Not to mention against my favorite tree, and then again on the forest floor under the full moon. My favorite place by far was still in front of the fireplace, where I'd fallen in love with her.

We got two dogs together. A German Shepard that helped me at work and a Golden Retriever she took to her shop. We named them after what had brought us together, Storm and Moose. It felt good to have so much love and companionship around. I'd spent too many years without it, too many years without Kaylee.

The summer stretched on in a happy lull of warmth. We'd often spend evenings on the lake when we weren't working. I'd catch her staring at me, saying the water reflected on my face just like she'd imagined. It was now early September and I couldn't believe it was only this past January we'd been stormbound together. It felt like such a turning point in my life, like a part of me hadn't been fully living until I'd met her.

She'd changed me, much like a storm. Clearing away all the debris and nourishing growth, shocking me into seeing the world around me differently while inspiring me to be vulnerable enough to witness something incredible unfold. She was my favorite storm, my favorite turn of fate.

Chapter Thirty-Four

"Harley! My love!" I walked around the cabin trying to find him, my airy sundress trailing behind me in the breeze of my stride. I rounded the corner only to see him sitting on a rocking chair on the porch. The stars dappled the sky behind his handsome profile as he turned to look at me.

My heart skipped a beat, and my breath hitched. I'd seen this before as a vision when I'd first met him. The stirring of longing I'd felt so strongly that day felt like a clipped memory. Now deep contentment warmed its place.

He stood and took my hand. "Happy full moon, lover." His voice was a low timbre against the sounds of the late summer night. The entire world around us was a calm, dreamy indigo. As we walked down toward the dock hand in hand, I could see the moon gleaming on the lake, reflecting in silvery ripples. I craned my neck back to stare at the moon, completely transfixed by her ethereal light.

Harley's hand moved in mine, and I pulled my eyes from the sky to him, only to find him on bended knee, the moon reflecting in his warm eyes.

"Kaylee, you mean the world to me. I'm so glad you crashed into my life. Will you marry me?"

My breath sucked in my chest against my will, my body shuddering with shock. How had I not seen this coming?!

"Yes, absolutely." I felt like my chest was going to burst with emotion.

Harley slid a delicate banded ring on my finger. The cushion-cut diamond twinkled under the light of the moon. "Oh my gods! Harley!" I whispered in awe, looking at the stone and then back to him, feeling how pivotal this moment was.

"I figured you had other stones, but not a diamond."

I held his head between my hands, crouching to kiss him from where he stayed on bended knee. "You're not going to believe me, but I swear back in January, when we were stormbound, I had a vision of you on the porch just now."

He kissed me again, pulling me down onto his lap at the end of the dock. "I believe you." His face brightened into the smile I adored. "Tell me more."

"It was one of the first nights we spent together. I was looking out the French doors and I saw you rocking on the porch, the full moon behind you and everything. I remember being heartsick for a moment, wishing I could live out that moment with you. But I knew I couldn't because I wouldn't be around in the summer."

His arms wrapped around me tightly. "Good thing we didn't get in our own way for too long."

I nodded and kissed him deeply. My hands traveled to the beard I loved and over his muscled shoulders. Harley's kisses moved to my neck where he murmured, "Did you have a vision of this?" His strong frame rolled me on my back, his brawny body covering me sensuously, his knees dashing side to side to open my legs wider.

I let out a fleeting giggle and undid his pants. He grabbed the edge of my sundress and lifted it playfully. "Ah, no undies, 'atta girl." He smirked before leaning down to kiss me. From there, in the moonlight, we made love slowly and tenderly.

Sprinkles of rain fell on our bodies, first gradually then in a steady flow.

Harley's lips moved with his uncontained laughter, trying not to break our kiss. Finally, in an absolute downpour, I found myself on top of him, my lover, my now fiancé. The rain caused my white dress to cling to me. Harley's hungry eyes took in the sight of me, causing him to chuckle as I tilted my head toward the sky and outstretched my arms, letting the rain wash over me.

"What is with you and storms, my love?" he exclaimed, moving my hair away from where it clung to my chest and face.

I shrugged, leaning down to kiss him. "What can I say? They bring me good things."

Thank you for reading *Stormbound!* I hope you enjoyed Kaylee and Harley's story as much as I did! If you would like to stay updated on future Pine Bluff shenanigans, freebies, and sneak peeks, please join my mailing list at **MaggieMaren.com**.

Reviews are immensely helpful to me as a new author, please consider sharing your support by rating this novel on Amazon and Goodreads, so other readers can find this story.

Much love and many blessings!
-Maggie Maren

Extend Your Stay in Pine Bluff

What happens when a coffee shop run by scorned women moves in across from your hardware store? Carson Kouris, the resident grump of Pine Bluff, is about to find out.

Find out in Rosie and Carson's story, ***Feverburn***.

Listen to the Stormbound playlist.

Also by Maggie Maren

Pine Bluff Series:

Stormbound
Feverburn
Hellbent

Yule with the Wild God

About the Author

Maggie Maren is a lifelong weirdo and misunderstood mystic. Combining her deep love for nature and romance, she enjoys playing mountain man matchmaker. Her stories transport readers to cozy cabins and the great outdoors, where kooky characters find love.

While earning her English literature degree, she worked as a bookseller, because clearly temperance isn't her strong suit. Her curious ways have led her to some interesting forays as a librarian, professional tarot reader, crystal merchant, and some dark ages in corporate America.

She spends her time tucked away in the wild woods of Maine, with her own mountain man. If she isn't writing or reading, she is either dancing, sipping iced coffee, yipping at the moon, adventuring, or ugly crying over a majestic sunset. She loves to hear from her readers, preferably in the form of a haiku, but hey, no pressure.

To stay connected, visit her at MaggieMaren.com

Printed in Dunstable, United Kingdom